A MODERN PIRATE ROMANTASY

VINCENT & SIVAN

BOOK 1
RUM-SOAKED AWAKENINGS

CALI KITSU

Winnipeg, Canada

Copyright © 2025 by Cali Kitsu
Cover design copyright © 2025 by Story Perfect Books
Cover and interior illustrations copyright © 2025 by Anna Kumo

This is a work of fiction. Names, characters, business, places, events, and incidents are either products of the author's imagination or used in a fictitious manner. Any resemblances to actual persons, living or dead, or actual events is purely coincidental.

Editor: Craig Gibb
Proofreader: Margaret Larson

Published April 2025 by Deep Hearts YA, an imprint of Story Perfect Books.

Deep Hearts YA
PO Box 51053 Tyndall Park
Winnipeg, Manitoba R2X 3B0
Canada

Visit deepheartsya.com for more great reads.

Note from the Author

Vincent & Sivan is an explicit, best-friends-to-lovers, dual gay awakening, adult MM romance novel.

Thank you so much for picking up the story of Vincent and Sivan. I wanted to write a modern-ish version of piracy that had aspects of current times, but still kept some of the older traditions. My pirates use swords and pistols, because, well, swords are just cool, and what's a pirate book without swords? But cannons…there are no cannons. When this book starts, the pirates are in a time of peace, thanks to a mutiny over twenty years ago, but peace will always be threatened by those who are unhappy…

Table of Contents

Chapter 1: Captain and Crew	1
Chapter 2: The Taste of Him	23
Chapter 3: The Beginning of the End	44
Chapter 4: Get Out of My Bed	68
Chapter 5: Flamingoes, Pigeons, and Ship Trash	88
Chapter 6: We're Pirates, Vincent	106
Chapter 7: Blue Looks Good On You	145
Chapter 8: The Messenger and the Crescent Moons	160
Chapter 9: Throwing the Trash Out	169
Chapter 10: He Called Me Baby and I Liked It	196
Chapter 11: Did You Notice Something?	212
Chapter 12: Fuck Me Now. Kiss Me Later.	226
Chapter 13: Cameras, Monkeys, and Sneaky Pirates	237
Chapter 14: Wholeheartedly and Undeniably	254
Chapter 15: So Many Gay Pirates	278
Chapter 16: Quisling's Quarters	292
Chapter 17: Your Dimples Are Gonna Ruin Me	305
Chapter 18: He's Not Wearing His Coat	315
Chapter 19: Captains and Sons	325

A MODERN PIRATE ROMANTASY

VINCENT & SIVAN

BOOK 1
RUM-SOAKED AWAKENINGS

CHAPTER 1
CAPTAIN AND CREW

Standing on the bow of my father's ship, I can finally see the Port of Darshley in the distance; after four days of travel, it's a welcome sight. I run my hand through my hair, it really needs to be brushed. The winds were brutal this trip. I pull a hair elastic out of my pocket and tie my hair in a tight bun atop my head, realizing I'm not dressed for crew meetings yet. This will be the last meeting before Sivan and I are named captains.

My thoughts are quickly interrupted by a crisp crack on the ass from Matteo. "What the hell are you standing out here all alone for, Vincent? For heaven's sake, you're not even in your meeting attire. Where is your phone? Your dad's been screaming for you for twenty minutes! He's really pissed off this time. You better move your ass and see what he wants!"

I nod my head, placing a hand on Matteo's shoulder. He's always worrying about me, probably a little too much, if I'm being honest. "Thanks. Where is the old blubberfish?"

"He was down in the office when I saw him, but that was a while ago. Probably slicing his way through your bedroom door with Gwendolyn at this point."

Gwendolyn is my father's favorite sword, named after my late mother. When he found a sword he loved after her passing, one that he said spoke to his soul—whatever the hell that means—he named it after her. He said he wanted to have a piece of her with him.

I give Matteo a smile and head toward the lower deck. "I wonder what this could be about," I say facetiously. My father's ship, *More Booty Than You* is the finest pirate ship that sails the seas, and also the largest. The only comparable ship around is *It's All Mine* owned by Captain Ray Crawford, Sivan's father.

Captain Crawford and my father have been friends since they were kids. Both were raised alongside one another aboard another pirate ship, *The Drunken Dog*. Our mothers both worked in the kitchen of the ship and our fathers were faithful crew members who served the most horrible pirate known to man, Captain Stanley Slicer. But that was a long time ago. There was a mutiny led by my father and Captain Crawford twenty-one years ago, and no one has heard from Slicer since then. These days, the seas are controlled by both Captain Crawford and my father. The two captains meet twice a year to trade and share supplies. They each have their own territory on opposite sides of the sea, and as a result of their arrangement, each has their own set of specialty goods available based on their region.

Today, our crews will meet for the first trade of the new year. I could be asked to participate in some of the more important decisions while we're there. It's doubtful that my father would actually ask me to do anything, though.

The door to my father's office is open and he's sitting at his desk. "You wanted me for something?" I ask.

His gaze shifts to me. "Sit," he says, pointing toward the chair on the opposite side of the desk.

Gwendolyn lies flat across his desk, his eyes flit down to the long slender blade. He shakes his head softly, as he lightly traces the gold embroidered "G" on the hilt. He looks disappointed in something, but it's more likely that he's just sad that my mom isn't here. He so badly wants to make her happy, even though she passed away years ago. I understand that he's sad, but that feeling of wanting someone to be proud of you that isn't here anymore; I can't really understand that. I'm not sure if I believe in the afterlife, but I definitely don't see my mother when I look at his sword. Yet for him, that's all he sees when he looks at it.

"Why aren't you dressed, Vincent? We're almost there. You should have been ready an hour ago."

"I didn't wanna mess my hair up with a stupid hat," I say, leaning back casually in my chair. "Besides, it takes me five minutes to get dressed. Kind of a dumb reason for you to call me in here."

I know that's not why he called me in here. He wants to remind me of all the responsibilities he's planning to entrust to me. He wants to drill them further into my brain. I've known two things my entire life, one is that my name is Vincent, and second, is that I will get a ship of my own under my father's command once I turn twenty-one. My twenty-first birthday is at the end of the year, so I guess he feels the need to go over the same things for the millionth time.

He removes his large crimson captain's hat from his head and looks at it. "Whose hat is stupid? What don't you like about it?"

"I don't like anything about it. I was talking about mine, but yours is worse. Especially that big black feather sticking off it. It's ridiculous. When you give me my ship, can I have a different kind of captain's hat?"

"A different hat? You'll be lucky if I name you captain at

this point. You have bigger problems than a hat. How are things going with Harlow? Are you thinking of proposing?"

"Whoa, what? No. You already know how I feel about Harlow. I'm not marrying her."

He looks down at Gwendolyn and talks to the sword. "You hear that? He says he's not marrying Harlow. You told me this would happen. He doesn't know what's best, though."

I am not marrying Harlow. There is nothing that could make me do that. Not duty, not my father, not money, nothing. She is not the one for me. I don't mind the thought of marriage, especially since my parents had such a good relationship, but when I marry, it will be for love. Not for duty. Why should I be expected to marry someone after I'm named captain? I want to run the seas one day, but I'd prefer to do that with my best friend. I want Sivan standing beside me, not Harlow.

My father is staring at my forearms. It's funny, because when I was younger, I saw my father's tattoos—*Captain* on the left arm, *Crew* on the right—and thought they were really awesome. Now that the time for my tattoos draws closer, I don't really agree with the meaning behind them. My father says the tattoos will remind me of my obligations. He believes once I'm tattooed, I'll become more responsible, and seeing those words will remind me where my honor should lie—with captain and crew. But what about to myself? Don't I have the right to want things for myself? As far as he's concerned, it's fine if I screw around, as long as I put nothing before him or the crew.

"I don't think you understand how rare someone like Harlow is," my father says. "You and Sivan, you two run through girls, and that's fine, but sooner or later you'll have to settle down. The sooner you do that, the easier it's going to be for you. If you want a woman who's not going to complain and nag you, that would be Harlow. She's used to life on the ship, and she's known you your whole life. What's not to like about that? She seems to really love you, too. Love is rare, Vincent…"

I scoff. "Two things: First, she doesn't love me. She only wants to be married to me because of my status. Second: Why should it matter to me if someone is in love with me if I'm not in love with them? Mom wouldn't have tried to force me to marry someone that I didn't love."

"You may be right about that. But she wouldn't want you to miss out on something good, just because you haven't considered it, either."

"What do you want me to consider? Marrying someone because it's convenient? Or marrying someone because you think they're a good match for me? Because I won't consider either of those."

My father groans, leaning his head back. "Vincent. How the hell am I supposed to entrust a ship and crew to you, if won't listen to reason?" He rolls his sleeves up and points at the tattoo on the inside of his right forearm, *Crew*. "Once you become a captain, you have a duty to the crew, a duty as captain to do what's best. A duty to make the smartest possible decisions." He exhales, then pokes the tattoo for emphasis. "For. The. Crew."

"Yeah, okay, fine, for the crew. I get it. But why do I need the captain tattoo on the other arm? I'll already know I'm captain. It doesn't make sense, if I'm being honest. If I can't make decisions for myself, then why do I need the tattoo that says captain?"

My father's mouth is wide open. "What?! First you say my hat is stupid, now you're saying the tattoos are stupid?" He looks down at the sword, speaking to it, "This is what you've left me with. Our son is an imbecile."

"Um, no. I am not. Whoever convinced you and Captain Crawford to get those tattoos was an imbecile. I'm just pointing out the obvious. You've taught me my whole life that the only things that matter are captain and crew, right?" I hold my palms out.

"Yes, so what? That hasn't changed." He's staring at the tattoo on his arm, his eyebrows are drawn tightly together. His forehead looks like it may explode.

I've really done it, now. "What do you mean, 'so'? If my decisions are based on those two things, and I'm the captain, then some of those decisions can be for me and not based on the crew, right?"

My father rubs the stubble on his cheek. He looks like he's really thinking about what I've said.

"No."

"What do you mean, 'no'? That's what you said. So, if I don't want to get married because that's what's best for the captain, then, I'm good. I honestly have no idea why that would be better for the crew anyway, or what difference it would make. But that's not the point I'm making right now. The point right now, is that the tattoo on your left forearm makes no sense. I either serve myself, or I serve the crew. It doesn't have to be both and sometimes those things may oppose one another."

"You need the tattoo to remind you of where your duty lies. Your duty lies with the captain and the crew."

"Dad, listen. You are the captain. Do you need the tattoo to remind you of that?"

"Of course not. That's not the point of it."

"Well then what *is* the point of it?"

"The point is that I'm the captain, and you will get the

tattoos, or you won't be named captain. That's the point. End of discussion. Just go get dressed."

I drop an eyebrow at him and lean forward. "I'm not getting that captain tattoo, until you can tell me why I need it. Was it Captain Crawford's idea, or yours? Maybe he can answer when he gets here. I'll ask him."

"Don't embarrass me in front of Ray. Please?" He holds his forehead, eyes closed. "I'll never hear the end of it. He'll make fun of me until I die."

"He should. You have tattoos that you don't even understand. I'd make fun of my friends if they had tattoos they didn't understand." I stand up from my chair, and shrug at him.

"Okay, enough," he says rolling his sleeves down. He stands up and puts his coat on. "You have annoyed me even more than normal. I had no idea that you could be so annoying. Is this a new skill, or have you always been this way?"

I laugh and head toward the door. "You need anything else, Captain?"

"The tattoos make sense. You just—don't bring them up in front of Ray, or no rum. I'll make sure you and Sivan don't have access to the good stuff for the entire trip.

I turn on my heel. "You're threatening me with rum? Oh my God, you really don't know why you have the tattoos, and you're terrified I'll embarrass you. There's rum at the bar; you can't threaten me with that."

"Then I'll take away something else. What do you like?"

I tilt my head at him in the doorway. "Are you serious? Do you think I'm stupid enough to answer that?"

"Ah, just go," he says. "Life was simpler when you were younger. Get dressed and don't be late."

I give him a playful salute and head toward my room. I

nearly walk straight into Matteo as I round the corner. "How'd that go?" he asks me.

I hang an arm around his neck. "How do you think it went? He was nagging me, same as always. Got pissed because I said I didn't want to wear a hat, or something."

Matteo smiles at me and we continue toward my room together. "Why would he be upset about that? You never wear a hat until meeting time. That can't be what set him off. What else happened?"

I shrug. "How the hell should I know? He was going on about Harlow, and my tattoos, well, future tattoos, and threatened to keep the rum away from me and Sivan if I made him look bad in front of Captain Crawford."

"Hmm. Well, you are going to be named captain this year. It makes sense that he'd want you to behave. Although, between you and Sivan, that's a pretty tall order. You should really try to read him better, though."

"That's easy for you to suggest. He isn't all that easy for me to read. Besides, he treats you differently than he treats me. Some days I wonder if you really are his son, and I'm the one he adopted."

He tilts his head at me. "Oh, be serious, he doesn't treat you badly. You're not exactly making things easy on him. He probably just feels the need to overcompensate because your mom is gone. Don't worry too much about it. What did he want to be sure you didn't embarrass him by doing? Just general stupidity?"

I laugh loudly. "No. He was worried I'd ask about his tattoos and embarrass him in front of Captain Crawford. Speaking of tattoos, do you understand them?"

Matteo stops walking and looks at me. "Do I understand

tattoos? What do you mean? The concept? The ink? What are you asking me?"

"No, *his* tattoos. The tattoos I'll be getting soon. Captain and crew, those. Do you understand them?"

He shakes his head at me and raises his eyebrows. "No wonder he was worried you were going to embarrass him. Of course I understand them. What's not to understand?"

I wave him off as we continue down the hallway. "Just forget about it. It's not important. I won't embarrass the old man."

I'll just ask Sivan. I'm really not afraid of embarrassing my father in front of Sivan's dad. Captain Crawford is my dad's best friend and Sivan is mine. I'm pretty sure we'll embarrass our fathers either way. I'm really looking forward to seeing Sivan, today—well, not *seeing* him, but rather hanging out with him. This is our last meeting together before we're named captains. Normally we're causing chaos during meetings or just missing from them entirely. On any given night together, you can find us taking sips from the rum in the storage cabins and chasing girls in port or taking sips from the rum and annoying our fathers in the trade meetings.

In contrast to us, Matteo, who is the same age, is the model of a perfect future captain. Although, for Matteo to become captain of a ship, a lot would have to work out in his favor. Matteo was left without parents as a baby, and was raised alongside me, being given similar privileges as I have. People treat him as though he is my father's son, because that's how my father has always treated him. Of course, if you ask Matteo about becoming captain, he'd only laugh at such a notion. Matteo has no aspirations of becoming captain, his only dream is to see me become captain one day and to stand beside me as my first mate. Both of those things will happen later this year.

I place my hand on my doorknob. "Are you coming in?" I ask.

Matteo raises his eyebrows at me and gives a light chuckle. "No, I think you're gonna have your hands full in there and you need to get dressed." He looks at his watch. "You have maybe thirty, forty minutes before we're there." He pats me on my shoulder. "See you in a bit." He smiles and heads down the hallway.

"Hey! Why will my hands be full in there?" I shout after him.

Matteo doesn't turn around; he just shrugs his shoulders and continues walking.

Oh, what sort of hell awaits me in my room? I open the door, and the familiar scent of perfume overwhelms me.

Harlow. Now, I'm no genius, but I'm well aware of Harlow's intentions. She wants me for status and nothing more. Truthfully, I'm sure that she's into Matteo, but since I'm the captain's son, she chooses to continually pursue me. I've been more than upfront in stating that I have no desire to be in a relationship with her. She's not interested in listening to reason, though. Doesn't matter, because right now, I need to get her out of here. Especially since I'll be hanging out with Sivan tonight, that means one thing—girls, lots of girls.

"Harlow! What are you doing in my room?" I shout before I even see her.

Harlow is lying in my bed; she's dressed, but barely. What the hell is she thinking? I have to get ready. I'm not even dressed for the meeting, and we'll be pulling into port soon.

"Come now, you aren't really mad, are you?" she asks me with a pout, as she sits up and flips her slender legs over my bed.

Her dress is very short and low cut, there's very little left to the imagination. Of course, I've seen it all anyway, so it's nothing new for me. She's a beautiful girl; any other guy would be happy to have her. There's just something missing. I'm not sure what it is. But if she were the girl for me, I would enjoy being with her, doing the little things like talking or hanging out—but I don't enjoy those things with her. I find myself continually counting down the months until we pull into port, until we pull into *this* port, and I get to see Sivan. It's the most fun I get to have all year.

I've tried to end these hook-ups with Harlow, but somehow, we still end up doing it. She is by far the prettiest girl on the ship, and since we were raised together, I'm quite accustomed to having her around. She is sneaky, though. I've seen her coming out of my room a few times, and even now—why was she in my room? She seemed to be reaching for something behind my bed just a moment ago.

"Yes, I am mad," I answer. "Why are you in my room? I didn't give you permission to come in here. You know how I feel about you being in my personal space. You need to leave. I have to get ready." I walk past her toward my closet.

She stands from my bed and approaches me. Her perfume is quite attractive, it's a scent that draws me in, despite my best efforts to push her away in times like these. There must be some sort of chemical in it that makes me feel this way.

As I thumb through the coats in my closet, she stands behind me, while wrapping her arms around my waist and softly kissing the back of my neck.

"You don't want me? Not even a little?" she whispers close to my ear, as her hands clasp around my waist.

I guess there's no harm in doing this with her quickly. I take her hands in mine and allow her to unbuckle my belt while she kisses the back of my neck and lets out a slight giggle.

"That's better," she says. "We'll be quick, I promise."

She's unbuttoning my pants at a slow, agonizing pace. I really don't have time for games. I turn quickly and grab her by the waist. I press our mouths together forcefully and guide her to my bed. Something feels off here. I'm not… What is happening right now? Something is not working for me… My dick is not working for me. This has never happened before. What's wrong with me? Harlow's eyes are closed and she's kissing me, while rubbing my back the way she does when we're wrapped up like this. It feels strange, my body is not into this at all. My thoughts are elsewhere, but where are they? And why can't I concentrate?

Sivan…soon I'll see Sivan and he'll tell me all the things that I want to hear. The stories of captaincy classes, his friends, and stories of the girls he's slept with since we've been apart. We'll have rum and chase girls. I can hardly wait. A slight moan escapes my lips. I'm ready now. What changed? I was only thinking of Sivan. Harlow did nothing else, nothing out of the ordinary. And yet, somehow, everything is finally working as it should be.

SIVAN

"Sivan! Hurry up, you'll be late," my father calls. I look in my mirror and check my outfit once more. My meeting attire is quite striking if I do say so myself. The cobalt blue jacket, lined with gold buttons, perfectly shows off the muscles I've gained in the past year. I can't wait for the girls in port to see me. I wonder how many girls Vincent and I will run through this time. I check my hair once more and call out to my father. "Yeah, I'm ready. I'll meet you on deck!"

I spray myself with my new cologne; my father got it for me in trade with a new vendor in town. He's been hounding me recently to find a steady girlfriend. He believes in true love, I don't. What even is love? How would one know if they were in it? I can't imagine. It makes no sense to me, this notion that one could find someone and then just be happy by being with this person. Such horseshit if you ask me. Besides, I'm a pirate. I'll always be a pirate. The last thing I need is some girl getting all clingy and expecting me to spend time with her. I'm not interested in that. No thanks. My father can keep his notion of love. My dad is right about one thing, this new cologne will likely double our chances of meeting girls this week, not that we need help there. The ladies line up when they know we're coming into port, and Vincent and I have our pick of them. It's quite easy for the two of us. Aside from being good-looking, since our fathers run the seas, girls want to sleep with us anyway, just for status. It's just sex. That's usually where it ends, at least for Vincent and I. Otherwise, for some reason, they start thinking that we're going to be in a relationship with them. I know that's what my dad wants for me, but I don't. Relationships are definitely not my thing.

This year I'll have my own ship, and Vincent will too. We have the best time together. I can't wait to see him. I want to join crews someday, but we haven't really discussed it. If he weren't going to be a captain, I would make him my first mate, but that's not possible, because we're both of equal ranking, as far as pirate hierarchy is concerned.

I place my hat on my head and leave my bedroom. As I walk up the stairs, the salty breeze brushes past my face. My father looks even more regal than I do as he stands near the bow of the ship.

"Ah, there you are. Dashing as always, just like your dad!" he says, as he grabs my shoulder.

"Yeah, just like my old man," I say with an eyeroll.

"How's Jenny?" my father asks.

"I have no idea. I'm not interested in her, Dad."

"Not interested? What's not to be interested in? She's gorgeous and her parents are wealthy, add to that the fact that she doesn't mind that you're a pirate and it's a match made in heaven," he says proudly.

"Hardly," I say. "I'm not interested. How many times do I have to say it?"

A familiar voice calls in the distance, "Ahoy! You sack of garbage!" It's Vincent's father, Captain Rodrigo.

My eyes scan the deck quickly. Ah, there he is, Vincent is standing on the bow of the ship. His face is quite flushed. I wonder if his trip was rough. I straighten my coat and my father walks toward the loud obnoxious man that is Vincent's father, while I head for Vincent. Our eyes meet for a moment, and I feel happy. I've been waiting to see him for almost a year, so we could run the town, and the moment is finally here. Vincent looks happy to see me, but almost, like, I don't know, seems like something is bothering him.

"Hey, the old man is just as loud as ever," I say while I hang an arm around Vincent's neck. Vincent wriggles a bit from my hold. That's strange. Why would he do that? Isn't he happy to see me? "What's wrong? Seas give you guys a bit of trouble? You don't look well," I say cautiously.

"Well, the old man was in a mood earlier, and I just went for a round with…actually, never mind," he says while looking away.

"Hello, Sivan," Matteo says as he walks over to join us.

"Matteo, how was the trip? Vincent doesn't look so great."

"Ah, well he just rolled around with Harlow a few minutes ago, so I'd say he should be feeling pretty good," Matteo says with a laugh.

Vincent shoots him an uncomfortable scowl. "Thank you for sharing that, Matteo."

"What? Why do you seem upset?" I ask. "That's nothing new unless she's finally pinned you down—she hasn't, has she? God, I hope not, we have the whole port to ourselves. Can't have some ship trash wrapping you around her finger."

"Nah, she hasn't brought up marriage in a while. She knows it's not going to happen. I mean, what do you care for anyway?" he asks, shoving me to the side. "Come on let's go find the rum, Sivan. Rum, then girls!"

Vincent's touch feels foreign to me. He's acting really strange. I wonder what's truly bothering him. There must be something.

"Matteo, are you joining us or hanging out with the old crawdaddies?" I ask.

"No, I won't be joining you right now, maybe later," he says. "I have to chat with someone before meetings convene later. Keep Vincent out of trouble, will you? The last time you two were here, we had to pay for way too many bottles and a few chairs, too. Try to at least act civil, would the two of you?" he says as he places his crimson red hat on his head.

Vincent scoffs. "Thanks, I didn't know you were my effing babysitter."

Okay, now I know something is wrong. He would never treat Matteo that way. As Matteo leaves, Vincent walks beside me. "What's got you upset?" I ask.

"Nothing, same old shit. I tire of him always up my ass. You know how it is. I had a chat with the old man earlier, and he plotted with Harlow, trapping me in my room. Had a lecture from my dad about marriage, then boom, guess what was waiting for me in my room? Harlow in my bed, practically naked. She throws herself at me and one thing leads to another, then you know, here we are."

I laugh heartily and reply, "Well, what's wrong with that? Certainly, you can't be upset because you had sex before pulling into port? Just means you'll last longer for the next round, right?" I say with a smile.

"Boys!" Captain Rodrigo calls out.

"Just keep walking," Vincent says, grabbing my forearm.

"I can't do that. Your dad is the captain. I'm on his ship."

Vincent's head drops forward and we both turn toward our fathers.

"Hello, Captain, how are you?" I extend my hand in greeting and Captain Rodrigo grips it, pulling me in for a hug.

"Whoa, what have you been lifting? Kegs?" He pats my biceps and looks at my father. "He's bigger than you, Ray."

My father nods. "That he is. If only he had half a brain to go with those muscles."

"Oh, I wouldn't be talking about my best friend that way," Vincent says. My father gives him a hug and pats his back. "Not when your best friend can't even explain the meaning of his tattoos," he adds.

Captain Rodrigo's mouth is wide open. He's looking around at the crew on deck. No one can hear us over here. It's far too noisy in the port.

I look at Vincent in confusion. What the hell did he mean?

My father crosses his arms. "What are you talking about, Vincent?"

"Don't say another word," Captain Rodrigo warns Vincent. "Head to my office. We can talk when we get there."

My father cocks his head to the side. "Your office? Don't you want to go get a drink, Rodri? What do we want to hang out with the boys for?"

Vincent smirks. "He's too embarrassed to tell you that what I said was right. He wants us to go to his office, so no one will hear him."

Captain Rodrigo whispers impatiently, "I am taking *all* the rum. Now, move your asses! Where is Matteo?" He looks around. "Matteo!" he shouts.

Most of the crew stops what they're doing and each looks left to right.

"Captain," I say. "Matteo said he—"

"Here, Captain," Matteo says walking up behind us.

Vincent drops an eyebrow at Matteo. "I thought you had to go do something? Ah, whatever, let's go, Sivan." Vincent starts walking toward the lower deck, and I follow him. Technically, I could get my ass handed to me for walking away from the captain without permission, but if Vincent is going to get in trouble, I'll go down with him.

"Are we going to your dad's office?" I ask.

"Yep. He wants to make me look stupid, but it's not gonna work. I made a point earlier about tattoos, a good point I might add, and he got all pissy about it."

I have no idea what kind of a point he could be talking about, but it's probably something to do with our captain's tattoos we'll be getting this year. I'm really more interested in why he's so mad at Matteo. I glance over my shoulder and see our fathers and Matteo following close behind. Why would he be mad that Matteo set Harlow up in his room? Maybe he'll explain more later. He's not usually one to stay quiet if he's upset.

We step onto the lower decks and walk toward Captain Rodrigo's office. Matteo hurries past us and opens the door.

"You know you don't need to do that," Vincent says. "No one expects you to hold doors open for them. That doesn't need to change just because Captain Crawford and his crew are here."

"Well, when you're captain, I'll keep that in mind," Matteo says.

We all file into Captain Rodrigo's office. Vincent and I take a seat on the large, navy-blue couch, while the others join Captain Rodrigo at his desk, sitting across from him in oversized black leather chairs. Vincent and I know better than to sit over there. We only sit there when we're ready to be yelled at for something we've done. Since I just got here, we haven't done anything to warrant that, yet.

My father holds his palms out. "What is it, Rodri? The last thing I want to do is be stuck in your office for hours before meetings."

Captain Rodrigo removes his coat and rolls up his long white sleeves.

"This is so stupid," Vincent mumbles.

"Ray, why do we have these tattoos?" Captain Rodrigo asks, examining his own arms. "Vincent says he doesn't understand them. Can you tell him what they mean? Or why we got them?"

I look at Vincent and whisper. "Is that why we're here?"

Vincent nods. "My dad has no idea what the tattoos mean. Let's just see how this plays out."

My father glances at the two of us. "Sivan, tell Vincent what the tattoos mean."

"Captain and crew. Those are the two things we base all decisions on. We need the tattoos to remind us that our duty as captain is to our crew."

"Not exactly," my father says.

"What?" I ask. "How is that wrong? That doesn't make sense."

"We have the captain tattoo because we are captains. You need to remember that you are a captain once you get that tattoo. Every decision matters, every action or inaction has a consequence. You live for the crew. You live for your captain. And when you're captain you expect that others will do the same."

Vincent laughs and I suck my lips in, stifling a laugh of my own.

"Captain Crawford," Vincent says through laughter. "Why would I need the tattoo to remind myself that I'm captain? Am I expected to forget? Have you ever forgotten that you were the captain?"

Matteo cuts into the conversation. "What's the point of this debate? Vincent, you don't want the tattoos? You've been looking forward to getting them since we were younger. What changed?"

Vincent removes his hat, placing it on his lap. He shakes his dark brown hair free, smoothing it. "First and foremost, I don't think that I will ever forget that I'm captain. Second, if I'm expected to look at both my arms to remind me of where my duty lies, would it matter which arm I looked at first? Because if I look at the captain one first, then the decision is based on whatever I want. So, screw the crew. If I look at the crew first, then screw me, right?"

"I got it!" I say. "The point of the captain tattoo is so that when you're drunk and passed out, someone could easily identify you as captain. That makes the most sense," I say facetiously.

Vincent nods at me in agreement. "Yeah, and if I pass out alone somewhere, someone will know I'm a captain and return me to my ship. It's kind of like a lost and found safeguard. I've been thinking about this all wrong. Thanks, Sivan. You cleared it up."

We laugh loudly together. I elbow him in the side, and he smiles, but shifts ever so slightly to the right. Almost moving away from my touch.

"So, your son is an imbecile, too," Captain Rodrigo says to my father.

"It would appear so." My father shakes his head. "Any chance we can clone you, Matteo?"

"No. I'm not interested in being captain. Vincent can do it; he just doesn't want to be forced to marry. That's what this is all about." He stands from his chair. "Am I right?" he asks Vincent.

Vincent salutes him, sarcastically. "Right on."

Matteo smiles. "May I be excused, Captains? I have an appointment. I'm gonna be late, and I'd rather not be any later."

"Oooh, you got a date?" Vincent asks.

It's too fun of a topic for me not to chime in on. "Yeah, Matteo. Do you have a sexy side piece in the port of Darshley?" I pump my eyebrows at him.

Matteo tilts his head at us, then looks back to Captain Rodrigo, seeking permission to leave.

"Go, go, all of you can go," Captain Rodrigo says. He lifts his chin toward us. "Boys, the meetings start at six. Don't be late. You guys can have fun with girls after."

Matteo smiles and walks toward the door. "Don't be late, Vincent," he says as he reaches the doorway.

"Don't have to tell me twice," Vincent says.

We both stand from the couch quickly. "We won't be late," I add before we leave.

"Let's hit up Pudgy's, Vincent. We can grab a few drinks before the meeting."

Vincent doesn't respond, he's just walking down the hall beside me, as if I'd said nothing at all. "Hey," I elbow him. "What's up?"

"Ah, my head is a fucking mess. This whole thing with Harlow today really annoyed me. But, yeah, let's just go to Pudgy's. We should make sure we're back in time for the meetings, though. So, girls after, I guess."

"What are you so upset about? Harlow or the tattoos? Was the sex bad?"

Vincent stops walking and looks at me like I just asked him something totally out of line. He says nothing and continues walking.

"Well? Was it?"

"I don't want to talk about it. Just leave it. The tattoo is stupid, right? Or am I being stupid?" he asks.

"I see your point, but I think there could be a time you'd need to be reminded you were captain, not because you'd forget, but just as a reminder if you're ever conflicted or looking for the right answer, maybe? I don't know. I want a tattoo that says captain, if for nothing else, just the lost and found thing—I could get lost and who would know I was captain if I don't have the tattoo?"

Vincent laughs. "Yeah, who would help you? Then again, if a girl finds you, who knows what could happen? She'd see the captain tattoo and just go wild on you."

"Oooh is this girl hot? The one that finds me passed out, because if she is…" I air grind my hips and smack an invisible ass, drawing a laugh from Vincent.

"No, maybe it's Ersin, or Jenny that finds you!" Vincent says.

"Oh God, why would you say either of those things? I was grinding, man. Ersin is like a sister to me. Disgusting."

CHAPTER 2
THE TASTE OF HIM

We make our way inside Pudgy's bar, which is located right near the dock. It's a cool crisp afternoon, so the doors are wide open, allowing the salty air to mingle with the smells of booze and smoke inside the bar. The music is loud, and the place is packed. We're in full meeting attire, pompous hats, long gold trimmed coats, and shiny black boots, but we've left our swords on our ships. Honestly, sitting at the bar with my sword at my side is kind of difficult. There's no reason for us to be armed in this port anyway, which I'm glad for. Sivan always carries his pistol with him, but I don't. I've never really taken to them the way he does. My father really doesn't like when pirates use pistols. He's always felt that if someone wanted to kill someone else, they needed to do it with a sword. I'm pretty sure that Captain Crawford uses both a pistol and a sword. Honestly, we really don't have a use for weapons most days. Back when my father and Sivan's staged the mutiny against Captain Slicer, my father vowed that it would be a new age for pirates. Leaving behind the thieving, the pillaging, and everything else that they considered to give pirates a bad name. Most pirates follow the same line of thinking.

As we step inside the bar, all heads turn toward us. I'm

accustomed to this kind of reaction when we walk into a room, it doesn't make me uncomfortable when people stare at me...*usually*. But today, I'm a little shaken by what happened earlier. I mean, I thought of Sivan and got hard, that's the truth. But is it? Maybe it was just a coincidence. I was so distracted, maybe Harlow did something else and that's what triggered it. I'm probably remembering it wrong. I'm not gonna think about it anymore. Sivan is even more comfortable here than me, since this is the bar he comes to the most.

I see Sivan's friend, Ersin, smiling from behind the bar. Ersin is cute, but she's not my type, she's not Sivan's type either, and since she's never flirted with me, I'm going to assume the disinterest is mutual.

Sivan is still surveying the small room. I'm not sure if he's looking for someone in particular. I know a lot of these people, but not by name.

"Hey." I nudge him with my elbow. "Are you looking for someone, avoiding someone, or giving people a chance to stare at you?"

Sivan laughs. "All of the above. Gotta give the people what they want. We look good, they want to check us out, and I want to see what's available."

Ersin waves at us. She points at two empty seats in the middle of the bar. "Vincent!" she calls out with a smile.

"Come on, let's sit. We don't have much time," I tell Sivan.

We take our places at the bar. I remove my hat, placing it on the shiny counter. Beside me, a petite brunette smiles brightly. "I like your hat. Are you a captain?"

I smile and shake my head.

Sivan, overhearing her, leans forward and looks over. "He's not a captain, do you want to know how you can tell?"

She smiles even brighter, and her eyes take on a far more flirtatious look. "How can I tell the difference?"

Ersin drops an eyebrow at the conversation, as she fills a large glass with beer at the tap.

"Well," he says. "There's no stupid feather plume. Which this guy hates."

"I don't know," she says to Sivan. "I like the tall feathers; they add a certain sort of sexiness. But his long hair is sexy enough all on its own."

I shake my head, unsure of how to respond to her false flattery. For one thing, I don't like being talked about as though I'm not here. Also, she was asking if we're captains, which means she came here looking for the captains. I try to avoid women like her. They're usually looking for money, or they're just after bragging rights. I'm gonna shut this one down quickly.

"You know, since you came here looking for the captains, AKA our fathers, you may want to leave and come back later. We have meetings in just a few hours, and they likely won't make an appearance just yet. I'm not interested in the superficial compliments on my hat or my hair." I point to Sivan. "Now, he likes to be flattered, but he's far more interested in the chase. You've already lost in both categories, since you flattered me first and insinuated you were looking for the captains. So, if I were you, I'd pack up and come back later."

Sivan laughs. "Oh, I guess we're being direct today. I didn't know." He points toward the corner of the bar where two men are huddled together at a table. "I see your two friends over there. I noticed them as soon as we walked in. See, the trouble for you, and them, is that I know everyone in this town. So, you three are here looking for money, some way to extort one or both of us, well, our fathers, I should say. If your friends hadn't given it away as soon as I walked in, you complimenting Vincent first would have done that. I'm obviously the better looking of the two, so starting with him was your second problem. Your third problem is that Vincent here is kind of in a mood today, so that puts me on edge as his best friend. We don't have time to screw around, literally. So, you can sit there if you want or go tell those two that you failed. Makes no difference to me."

Well, he just laid it all out on the line. I actually didn't notice those two guys. Sivan has always been more observant than me. The woman stands and heads for the exit. While her two friends in the corner appear very interested in what's going on.

Ersin laughs and places a tall glass of beer in front of Sivan. "Well, hello, ugly."

Sivan takes the glass and sips from it. "Don't call me ugly. Why did you let her sit here. You knew she was here for trouble. Why didn't you throw her out?"

Ersin rolls her eyes at him. "How should I know if she's here for trouble or a threesome? She asked when the captains would be here. I'm not obligated to try and figure out why she wants to see your fathers. Also, you are not the better looking one." She pours rum into a small glass and places it in front of me. "Vincent is much cuter; he's actually kind of beautiful." She gives me a wink.

I shake my head, mildly embarrassed. "Thanks for the drink."

Sivan drops an eyebrow at her. "Why do you think he's better looking? What about him makes him cuter?"

"Do you want me to break it down for you, Sivan? You won't feel good when I'm done," she says.

"Please don't," I say, sipping my drink.

Sivan takes a large swig of beer and looks around me, then

back to Ersin. "Those two guys just left. If they're here later, make sure you warn our fathers. Now, go ahead, what makes Vincent cuter than me?"

"Dimples so deep you could swim in them, big brown eyes, he's got a gorgeous complexion, his hair is smooth and wavy, never frizzy, full eyebrows, strong jawline, his smile is fucking blindingly white. Plus, he just seems nicer, sweeter, and he is, while you're kind of a dick. I've also seen him shirtless; his abs are no joke."

"When were you shirtless?" Sivan asks.

"No idea," I say.

"He was shirtless the last time you were here, you guys were screwing around by the docks that one night. You both fell in the water, and when you got out, you took your shirts off."

Sivan laughs at the memory. "Oh yeah! We were trying to decide who was going to pay the bill and decided whoever pushed the other off the dock first would pay. Ha!"

"Yeah, both of you wanted to pay for the other, and neither of you ended up paying. My father was kind of pissed, until Captain Crawford came in and paid for everything. You two really do make a mess when you're together."

My phone buzzes inside of my pocket. I pull it out and see a text from Matteo.

Move your ass. Everyone is starting to gather.

I stand up from the bar, taking my wallet out. I pass Ersin my card. "Here, charge me for whatever that was from last time, too. I don't want Captain Crawford paying for our mess. Your dad has always treated me well, Ersin. I don't want him to get the wrong idea about me."

She takes the card and smiles at me. "Well, at least one if

you is taking the fact that you'll be named captain this year seriously. My dad will appreciate that, Vincent."

Sivan's mouth is hanging open as he stands from his stool. "I just found out about this! How does that make me less serious? Here, take my card, too. Charge me the same. Vincent isn't supposed to be paying for drinks while he's here, my father will kill me if he thinks I'm not being a good host."

Ersin charges our cards and hands them back to us.

"We gotta go," Sivan says. "We'll probably be back later tonight after meetings."

"Good, I'm sure Jenny will be looking for you, Sivan. Her and what's-her-face from your ship, Vincent? The girl that's always hanging around?"

I shrug, pretending not to know who she's talking about.

Sivan tilts his head at me. "She's talking about Harlow, come on, you know who she meant."

Hearing him say Harlow's name is making me nauseous. I don't want to think about what happened with her earlier. I don't want to try and make sense of it.

Sivan hangs his arm around my neck and places my hat on his head. I take his from the bar and wear it.

"Seriously?" Ersin says. "You two had one drink each, you're not drunk enough to mix up your hats."

We swap hats back and laugh, quickly heading for the door. The air feels better outside, I didn't realize how stuffy it was in there. The sun has yet to set, and we still have a few minutes before meetings start. Matteo really does try to keep me in line when Sivan is here, but sometimes I just get so frustrated with his presence. The awkward sex with Harlow wouldn't have happened if he hadn't set her up in my room earlier. I think that's why I'm so mad at him.

Rum-Soaked Awakenings   29

We step aboard my father's ship, which is full of crew members drinking and laughing. Not all crew members attend the meetings, so this is a good time for them to kick back and relax. Besides, our fathers won't be on deck until after meetings tonight. So, the crew can let loose a bit, hence the number of women aboard that don't belong here.

"Hey," Sivan says placing his body in front of mine. "I've been talking to you for five minutes and you haven't responded. What's going on with you? Your mood has been all over the place since I got here."

"Oh, really? I didn't hear you say anything. Nothing is going on with me. I'm fine." I try to step around him, and he moves in front of me blocking my path. He places his hands on my shoulders, and although I want to pull away from him, I stand completely still.

My phone vibrates in my pocket, and I tilt my head back in annoyance before I even check the message. "Fuck, I'm coming. I swear if this is Matteo telling me to hurry up, I'm gonna lose it. We're not even late, yet."

Sivan drops an eyebrow at me, but keeps his hands on my shoulders.

I pull my phone out and see a text from Matteo, but a welcome one.

Meetings moved to 9 AM tomorrow. Try not to destroy the port.
I turn the phone toward Sivan and half smile.

Sivan reads the text and nods, while giving my shoulders a squeeze. "Alright, that's a good thing, because I'm gonna give you two choices. Something is bothering you, and I want to know what it is. So, I propose we either go and steal some of the good rum, then we head back to Pudgy's and find us a couple of girls, or we drink the good rum, and we talk like a couple of girls ourselves, in the back of the storeroom where no one can find us. Your choice, but there is no third option."

Why does he keep prodding me like this? What am I supposed to say? Am I supposed to say that I was having trouble getting hard with Harlow until I pictured him? Until I thought of him? I can't fucking say that. I absolutely cannot. How could I? Saying something like that would just be ridiculous. It would make me sound like I was… "Rum, then we'll find girls," I say, and shove him back a bit.

The two of us race toward the storage room on the lower deck. Our fathers have probably already left for the night after cancelling meetings, or they're in the office, either way, we shouldn't run into them. Heading toward the storeroom, I feel happy with Sivan next to me, but at the same time I'm nervous. I don't want to say the wrong thing. Oh shit…

"Hello, Sivan," Harlow says with a smile, rounding the corner. She's walking toward us quickly, coming from the direction of my room. Maybe she was looking for me.

"Ah yes, Harlow, how are you?" Sivan asks. "Sorry, don't want to be rude, but it's my turn with this one, and I understand that you two just spent some quality time together earlier, so cheerio, dear," Sivan says, while pulling me by the hand past her.

"Oh, Vincent, it's not like you to kiss and tell. Am I to expect a marriage proposal soon?" she calls out.

Sivan stops in his tracks and turns toward Harlow. He is looking quite sodden at me, as he turns to face her. "Why would he propose to you? He's not even going out with you." He pulls my hand again and we continue toward the rum.

"Thanks," I say.

"No problem," he mutters. He looks quite agitated, though. "The rum is…this door, right?"

"No not that—" I say, but it's too late.

Sivan's face is aghast, as the two of us are faced with the sight of Sam, the cook, asleep naked in his bed. He is a large hairy man whose body overwhelms the mattress. "Shut the door," I mouth silently. Sivan shuts the door and we back away slowly. Once the door closes, I playfully smack him. "Not this door, it's the next one. Didn't you hear me?" I ask.

"Well, yes, I heard you, but the damn door was already open by then. God, my eyes, Vincent. I'll never be clean again," he says with a laugh.

"Well, yes your eyes, but the smell was worse than anything," I say.

"How can you say that?" he asks as he opens the correct door.

I point to the door plate. "See? *Storage*, it says so right there. It does not say it on any other door. Remember for next time, would you?" I say with a laugh.

The two of us walk in and have a seat on the floor. We toss our coats and hats aside, and lean against a large stack of crates. I grab a bottle of rum and open it. "You first," I say passing him the bottle. He takes the bottle and a quick sip, then passes it back to me.

"That's good rum," he says with a smile, as he wipes his mouth.

I pause before bringing the bottle to my lips. His mouth has just touched this, is it okay that I drink from it, too? Why am I questioning this? We've always shared bottles before. This is no different. I bring the bottle to my lips and a strange feeling comes over me as I sip from it. I can't explain it. It's a happy feeling, but what exactly am I happy about? What is it that makes me feel good just by sitting here?

I pass Sivan the bottle again and watch his mouth as he takes a drink. I can't peel my eyes away from his lips. He sighs loudly wiping his mouth with the back of his hand. "My father is bugging the hell out of me these days. Wants me to get married next year. Even brought up old Jenny. Can you believe that?" he asks while passing the bottle back.

He looks completely exhausted, now that I get a good look at him. "Jenny? Why would he bring up Jenny? She wasn't even serious, was she?"

"No more serious than Harlow."

"Well, Harlow is different. I mean, her mom is basically a mother to the entire crew. I can't just toss her overboard or leave her in port. She knows we aren't going to get married, though," I say, somewhat doubting my own words. He takes the bottle from my lips as I barely finish a drink.

"Does she?" he asks, while his right eyebrow drops at me.

"That girl definitely thinks you're getting married. And I'm sure you will. Not me, though. I'm never getting married. Some stupid girl cackling and whining all day in my ear, nagging me, taking fifty percent of everything I own, forget it. Besides, can you imagine being with just one person for your entire life? Oh, come on Vincent, that's not for me. It never will be," he says in absolute confidence.

Never getting married… He's never getting married. Why did him saying that make me feel weird? That's nothing new, he's always said he'd never get married.

"Hello…Vincent?" he says while waving his hand in front of my face.

"Oh, right, sorry. Yeah. You, getting married? No. I can't imagine that either."

"Where did you go? You were quiet there for about three minutes, just staring off," he says with a laugh.

"Three minutes? You do this all the time. Come on. It was probably ten seconds. You're so dramatic," I say, and lean my head back against the hard crates.

Sivan exhales loudly and leans his head back, letting out a large yawn.

"Sivan, have you ever not been able to, you know…" I say, before I can stop the words from coming out.

Sivan's eyes are closed. I think he's asleep. That's good. I can't believe I was actually going to ask him that. What the hell was I going to say? Hey, have you ever not been able to get hard until you thought of me? Shit, who would say that? Damn rum must be getting to me. It's screwing with my thoughts already. It's so hot in here, too. The light shining through the small porthole is hitting the side of Sivan's neck. His light brown hair is pulled tight in a knot atop his head. His skin looks so smooth, the marks of stubble are nowhere to be seen as I look him over. What is wrong with me? Why am I feeling this way? What am I thinking? Should I wake him? I feel the strangest urge right now. I move closer to him, as I look him over. It's fine if he wakes up, I'll just flick him or something, but what am I doing? He smells amazing. This smell is drawing me in, maybe it's a new cologne? I can barely breathe. His lips are pressed tightly together and he's sleeping so soundly. Something is definitely wrong with me. I lean back against the crates and lift the bottle from his hands. He doesn't move as I slide the bottle from his loose grip.

    I look at the bottle as I bring it to my lips. I wonder what he tastes like. I have the strangest urge. I inhale deeply before drinking, but I allow my tongue to trace the rim of the bottle first. Is that what Sivan tastes like? Oh, my God. I have to stop this. I tip the rest of the rum into my throat and swallow. The rum drips from my lips and my gaze remains locked on Sivan. I close my eyes and lean my head back. Shit. This isn't me. There must be something in the rum. What did I just do? I licked the damn bottle, so I could taste my best friend? What the hell is wrong with me? I can't do this. I can't think this way. I have to stop. I close my eyes tight and try to picture a girl…any girl. Maybe I can force these thoughts from my head. Yeah, I can just push them away. It should be easy. I've never thought this way before, so it can't be that hard to stop. After all, this just started today. So, leaving these thoughts behind should be easy. Especially when I don't even know what these thoughts are.

SIVAN

What happened? It's dark as I open my eyes. Vincent is asleep next to me leaning against the crates. Oh, right, we were drinking rum. I must have passed out, and I guess he did too. Well, I need to wake him up. Who knows what time it is. I pat my pockets in search of my phone. Shit. I left my phone on the ship this afternoon. I didn't even realize that I didn't have it all day. Our fathers are probably going berserk by now. I laugh at my own thoughts. No. They wouldn't be. I'm sure they assume we're out with girls, both are probably surrounded by women at Pudgy's.

I should wake him, so we can go find them. We should find out why the meetings were postponed. I lean my head in to wake Vincent and poke his shoulder. "Hey, wake up," I say. He's moving a bit. "Come on now," I say.

"Unnh…Sivan. Stop. I'm tired. Fuck off."

"What? Did you tell me to fuck off?" I ask with a laugh. I move in closer and whisper in his ear, "That's not very nice, you little bastard. You're completely passed out and you say this to me."

The back of Vincent's hand is rubbing my face slowly.

"What are you doing, you drunkard? Don't touch my face." I take his hand from my face and move it toward his lap.

He squeezes my hand. "Let's go. Find girls…" he mutters while his eyes remain closed. I stand and try to rouse him once more. "Vincent, come on." He's not moving, he's still asleep.

Shit. Do I just sit here with him until he wakes up? No, my damn ass hurts from sitting on this hard wooden floor. I'll have to try and at least get him on his feet.

"Vincent, come on. Let's go," I say, while I shake his shoulder lightly.

"Take me to my bunk. I'm tired. I don't feel like fucking," Vincent says while his eyes remain closed.

"Pfffttt! Hahaha! You don't feel like fucking? Who's offering?" Listen to him, refusing to bed someone. "Alright, on your feet," I say as I pull both his hands up. He stands, but barely. "Ah damn it. Do I have to pick you up now? This is ridiculous. You know that? You are a ridiculous person. Look at you, the captain's son, completely passed out." I swing his left arm around my neck and try to stand him fully upright. He nearly falls and grabs ahold of my neck. "Alright fine. I'll carry you. God, no one better see this. My reputation, Vincent."

I lift Vincent princess style, then grab our hats and coats off the crates. He's still completely passed out. "Hey," I say as I slide the door open with my hand and foot. "Hey, you little bastard, do you want to wake up? I don't want anyone to see me carrying you into your room like this."

Vincent hasn't moved at all.

"Alright," I say as we head down the narrow walkway toward his room. I think it's this room. I grab the handle and twist while wincing. Vincent's head bumps the door lightly. "Whoops, sorry." I say with a laugh.

"Shit, what'd you hit me for?" he asks with his eyes closed.

"Shhh. I didn't hit you."

Thankfully, this is the right room. Ugh, it smells like disgusting perfume in here. I drop our hats and coats on the floor and carry him to his bed, gently placing him down. His arms are locked around my neck, and my face is close to his, as his head reaches the pillow. His eyes are closed, but mine are wide open. "Hey," I whisper. "Let go of my neck." He's sleeping so soundly and yet his grip is so tight, he's pulling me closer. How is this possible? The air feels strange in between us. His lips are wet and slightly parted. I suddenly feel like I want to taste him…to kiss him…I want to feel my body pressed against his. What is happening to me? Why am I thinking these things?

If I just unlatch his hands from my neck, I can escape this strange feeling. Vincent's grip tightens, and he pulls my face closer. "Vincent, what? What are you…?" Before I can say another word, our lips are overlapping. My tongue is moving inside of his mouth and his is in mine. What the hell am I doing? This is Vincent! This isn't a girl. I can't do this. He's drunk and I'm not gay. Wait—he's not gay either. His hands remain locked around my neck, and he pulls me in even tighter, grasping my hair. Shit, this is the hottest kiss I've ever had. I can't stop it. I climb atop him and his eyes open.

Our mouths meet again, as our hands begin to undress the other. No words are spoken, only hot warm breaths, and the sound of our clothes leaving our bodies.

I lean down and kiss him again, his tongue is sweet, his body is hard and warm beneath me. I've never felt this before. I've never even thought of these things before. But I don't want to stop. I don't need to think about what's happening. In this moment, it just feels right. I must be drunk. No…I didn't drink that much. Maybe Vincent is, though. Wait, I can't do this. I pull my mouth back and stop the kiss.

Vincent immediately pulls my face toward him and our lips touch. He traces my lips with his tongue and teases my tongue with his for just a moment. "Sivan. I'm not drunk," he whispers, while our mouths remain close.

I'm trying desperately to read him inside the dimly lit room. "I'm not drunk, either," I reply. I take his lips back into mine. He reaches down and a breathy moan escapes his mouth when he touches my cock. I've never allowed another man to touch me there. Until this moment, I'm sure I would have likely thrown someone overboard for trying such a thing. But, right now, I'm trying very hard not to grunt at the overwhelming pleasure that's coursing through my body as his hands rub me. Our mouths remain locked, and our kiss is hot, deep, and wet. I can barely breathe, and at this point, I don't want to. If breathing makes me leave this moment, then I never want to breathe again. I reach my hand down and unbutton his pants and he slides out of them. "I…I'm not sure if this is okay…" I say. God, I sound like such a coward right now.

"Sivan. I want you…this *is* okay because we both want it."

Something about the way he said that, makes me fully submit to this feeling. I can't fight it; whatever this is. I lift his chin as I sit up on my knees.

"I want you," he says again, his voice filled with lust and desperation. I place my finger in his mouth, and he begins to lick it. God, how can this feel so good? Holding his chin and looking into his eyes, I want nothing more than to be inside of him. Our bodies are pressed together, both hard and hot, naked and sweaty. I'm kissing and licking my way around his chest while he sucks on my finger. I want to devour him. I want to make him mine. What is this passion? Why have I never felt it before?

Vincent takes my hand from his mouth and brings it down

between his legs. "Touch me here," he says, pressing my finger against his hole.

I hesitate for just a moment, then press my finger against his warm flesh. This feels hot, but it also feels tight, like there is no way my dick is gonna fit in there. I press against the center, testing to see if there is any sort of give to it. I've had anal sex with girls before, but I definitely made sure there was lube on hand. I continue lightly massaging him and begin to kiss his neck. He reaches toward the side of the bed, and I lift up. "Are you okay? Do you want me to stop?" I ask.

He shakes his head no, and opens his side drawer with his right hand while placing his other hand on my chest. "Here," he says, shyly as he passes me the small bottle of lube.

I feel like we should talk about what we're doing, but I also really want to fuck my best friend right now. Rising to my knees I squeeze the lube on my cock. My hands are shaking a bit, which I can't say feels comfortable at all.

Vincent grabs my dick and begins to stroke it. "I want this—will—will you give it to me?" he asks.

Fuck, he looks so sexy. Why have I never noticed until this moment? I nod at him and place my hand atop his, while he strokes me. "Mmmm—your hand. It feels so good." I lean my head back, and remove my hand, allowing him to take over. Vincent's cock is beginning to leak, and I suddenly have the urge to do something. I lean down and lick the crown. The salty taste makes my dick harden even more. I can't believe I just did that. But the taste, it was delicious.

"Fuck—Sivan," he moans.

I grab the lube and rub some on his hole. It's so tight. I press on it and slide my finger around the rim. "Do you think you can take it?"

Vincent moves his hand from my cock and sticks his finger inside of himself. He's giving me the most intense eye contact that I've ever had with another person. I rub my hand down his chest. Vincent is all muscle. I can't help but to watch him as he fingers himself. I begin jerking myself because the sight of him doing this is making me really want to come.

"I can take it. Put it in," he says.

I shake my head no at him. My dick is so hard right now, I don't know if he really understands how much this is gonna hurt. I take his hand and pull it away from his ass. I quickly replace it with my own finger. I swirl it around inside. It's so warm and so tight. I add a second finger in and Vincent's breath hitches. He lets out a soft whimper of pleasure. I spread my fingers inside, stretching him, pressing in and out. I can't take it anymore. I've never taken this much care with any girl—but with him, I feel the need to be sure he's ready. I line my cock up with his ass and part his legs wider. I look up at him, his eyes are watching me so intently. "Are you ready?"

"Fuck me, please, Sivan."

I press my dick against his entrance, then trace his rim with it. I press the head in slowly and Vincent turns his face to the side, while closing his eyes.

I keep pushing inside, inch by inch. His hole is squeezing my cock so tightly. He raises his ass slightly, until I am fully inside. "Fuuuck," I growl. I've never felt any space so warm and comforting. I lean down and place a kiss on his lips.

He grabs my face and kisses me softly. "Keep kissing me, please?" he asks.

I would do whatever he wanted right now; I've never felt such an emotional connection to anyone in my life. I kiss him again and our tongues touch, softly.

I begin moving slowly and Vincent whimpers a bit. Fuck… I don't want to stop, but I also don't want to hurt him.

Vincent pleads through broken breaths, "Go…you can go faster…I want you to."

I grip the sides of his ass and look him over, my cock fully buried inside of him. I shake my head no, at him. I do want to go faster. Why am I concerned with hurting him?

He places a hand on my chest. "You wouldn't do this if I were a girl. Don't treat me differently. Fuck me, Sivan."

He's right. I wouldn't. I nod at him and begin thrusting in and out, his tight ass clinging to my cock. With each thrust, Vincent's head hits the headboard, and I can't help but feel even more turned on as I move. It feels so good fucking him. Have I always wanted this? Why does it feel so damn good? I lean down and lick across his open mouth. He still tastes a bit like rum, which is my favorite thing to taste. I kiss him softly, caressing his tongue with mine.

He pulls back slightly, while holding my face.

"Shit, your tongue, Sivan. You kiss so good…" He presses his lips against mine again, freely exploring the inside of my mouth.

I chuckle a bit through the kiss. It makes me feel kind of proud hearing him say that. He seems so lost in lust, like he's a different person entirely. But as much as I'm flattered by that, I realize that my pace has slowed again. It's almost as though I just want to be kissing him. The closeness between us, I want to capture it, I want to swallow it up.

"I like kissing you," I say.

"Do it again."

I crush my lips against his and savor the taste of his mouth. His strong muscular legs lock around my waist and I grind deep into him, drawing my hips back and forth rapidly. Fuck, he's wrapped tightly around me, clinging to my cock, clinging to *me*, it's unbelievable. His body shudders, and his breath hitches, while he lets out a soft moan. I don't know what I just did, but he liked it.

"Oh, fuck—Sivan. I think that was—do that again."

I grab his hands pinning them over his head. Whatever I did that made him shiver like that, I want to do it again, too. The curve of his muscles and the sight of the two of us connected is the hottest thing I've ever seen. I swirl my hips searching for the spot I hit, that made him shake.

"Yes—ffffuck—yes—Sivan..."

Hearing my name from his lips, in between those breathy fucking moans, makes me drive in further, harder and faster. My balls are slapping against him, and the sound alone is enough to bring me close to coming.

"I love that fucking sound," he says.

"Mmm—me too. I'm really close."

He nods at me, eyes closed. Then turns his face toward mine. "When you hit that spot, I almost came."

I release his hands and look down in between us. "I can make you come. Is that what you want?"

"Do it. Make me come. Then I—I want—"

"What?" I ask lifting his chin. I grind slowly inside him, searching for that spot, again.

"I want to feel—fuck." His eyes close, and he pulls me in tighter with his legs. His hands rake through my hair, from the bottom up, he grabs a fistful. "There, right there," he pleads.

His sticky cock jumps against me, and I soon feel hot wet spurts pelting my abs, accompanied by breathless gasps of pleasure and Vincent's asshole squeezing my cock.

"I'm coming—"

Holy shit—before I can process what's happening, my cum is shooting deep inside of him. "Mmm—fuck—" I grunt at the overwhelming pleasure and release. I've never felt an orgasm so powerful, so strong, so mind-blowingly amazing. I drop my head on his shoulder. The sweat drips from my forehead, and his hot, damp skin is pressed against my lips. I kiss the side of his neck, tasting the sweetness of his skin.

Neither of us has said a word, and neither of us has moved. My cock is softening, and I let it slip from his ass, then reposition myself beside him on the bed.

CHAPTER 3
THE BEGINNING OF THE END

The sun is shining brightly through my window. My body aches and my head hurts. Sivan is asleep next to me in bed. What the…? Holy shit, that was real? The pain in my lower half, combined with the fact that Sivan is asleep next to me in bed, while in his underwear, tells me it's real. What does this mean for us? What if he wakes up and he's disgusted? There was no conversation after we had sex. We cleaned off in the bathroom without saying a word. We exchanged smiles, a few soft kisses, and laid down in bed, falling asleep shortly after. I can still taste him on my lips. I've never tasted anything so delicious. I can still feel him moving inside of me. The sweat dripping from his body, as he ravaged me. I'd never felt so free, and so vulnerable. My body was his, and I felt at peace for the first time in my life. My head was so clear. The scent of sex lingers on my sheets. Should I wake him? I hope he isn't upset when he wakes up. No, that's ridiculous. Why would he be upset? That wouldn't even make sense. I pull the sheet up a little higher.

Sivan shuffles a bit in bed and scoots a bit closer to me. "Mmmm…the sun is so bright…Tilly. Close the drapes. I don't want to get up," he says.

I laugh loudly. "Tilly? You think you're in your own bed?

Your maid isn't here." There is only silence after I speak. That was incredibly stupid of me. Why would I think that was funny? Why was that the thing I chose to say the morning after having sex with my best friend? The first words I spoke were that? God help me.

Sivan lets out a light laugh. "I definitely know I'm not in my own bed. But I could almost feel your overthinking and thought it would be funny to tease you a bit." He turns toward me. There's a softness in his eyes I've never seen before.

He starts again while staring into my eyes. "I'm in the bed of my best friend…and we…" He looks so handsome with the light illuminating his face. The scattered sunrays make his gorgeous blue eyes sparkle.

I feel sort of giddy just looking at him, and yet I feel incredibly uneasy. We both stare silently at one another. It's as if we've both realized there is much more at stake here than just a simple lay. It feels like there's so much riding on this, that neither of us wants to make a move. But I need to know how he feels. I have to ask him, even though I'm afraid of what he'll say. "Sivan, I…yesterday."

He rubs my cheek with the back of his hand softly. Why is he being so tender with me? I've never seen him treat any girl this way…let alone me. What is this? Am I dreaming? Is that what's happening?

"We don't have to talk about it," he says softly, cupping my face in his hand.

"Okay, but what does this mean? Are we going to be a couple? We can't do that."

Sivan pulls his head back as if that was the craziest thing he's ever heard.

I don't blame him. What would make me even think that?

Sivan's never even been in a relationship. But still, there's a part of me that wishes he hadn't made that face.

Quickly I try to rebound. I say with a laugh, "No, no that's ridiculous. I was just kidding. Of course, we can't be a couple. Let's just forget all about it. We can pretend it didn't happen." Those words…how could I say them? That's the last thing I want right now, but what was I supposed to say? That look he gave me, I'm sure this is what he wants.

"Forget all about it?" he asks. "Why would you say that to me? Is that what you want? You want to forget about it?" He removes his hand from my face and lies on his back, his arm draped across his forehead. "How can you even suggest that? You're my best friend… Why would you? I'm so fucking confused right now, Vincent." He sits up in bed and pulls his knees to his chest. He looks angry or hurt, maybe both. I can't tell if he's sad, or if he's just pissed off.

"I'm confused, too. I don't know, Sivan. I've never done that before. Have you?"

He looks at me again with his eyebrow bent half down his face. "What do you think, Vincent?" He asks me in a mocking sort of tone, one that I'm much more familiar with. "Have I ever told you that I did? No, because I haven't. Fuck. This is…" He lies back down and exhales. "How do you feel?" he asks in a softer tone.

I let out a laugh. Half in sarcasm and half at my own mockery. "Well, I don't feel great. I'm just really confused, and yeah, my ass has definitely seen better days."

"Sorry about that," he says, while he rubs his thumbs together avoiding eye contact.

"No, don't be sorry about it, I wanted it. I just don't really know what comes next. What do *you* want? Do you want to—I don't know what I'm even asking you."

He turns to face me. "What? Do I want to what? Finish your question. You just basically said it would be ridiculous for us to be together, which was something I was thinking about for quite some time last night, while you were asleep. Now, you're sitting here looking at me like you're the one whose feelings are hurt. What do you want me to say right now?"

I have to try and reply rationally, even though every muscle in my body wants to grab him and hold him. "Well, I guess we probably just need some time to think things over. I mean we should just go on about our days like we normally would and see what happens." Saying those words was painful, it feels like my father sliced through my stomach with Gwendolyn and the sword is twisting deep within me.

"So, you want me to just spend the next four days with you, and not talk about what we just did? I can't do that. How the hell could I, Vincent? Could you go on as if nothing happened?"

"I—"

Our conversation is interrupted by two loud knocks on the door. "Vincent, I'm coming in!"

"NO! Sheena don't! I'm not dressed!" I shout.

The door opens and Harlow's mother, Sheena, comes in with her eyes closed. "Calm down, it's nothing I haven't seen before. I'll keep my eyes closed; you need to get up. Everyone's in a tizzy, thought you'd gone missing like Sivan."

I silently mouth to Sivan to hide, although I have no idea where he could go. His arms are crossed, and he isn't moving, I can't tell if he's being an asshole, or if he just has no idea where to go. He's just lying in my bed looking at me. He doesn't even look nervous.

Sheena has made her way inside my bathroom; she's looking for something. I hope she doesn't see Sivan's clothes. I have no idea where they ended up.

"I need your coat from last night," she says. "Wait. What is that smell? That doesn't smell like your cologne."

I cover Sivan quickly with my comforter just in the nick of time. She makes eye contact with me, coming out of my bathroom. I yell, "Get out! I didn't even say that you could come in! I'm not dressed, and it's making me uncomfortable having you in here!"

She's always taken liberties coming in and out of my room. She's responsible for making sure my meeting attire is ready, amongst other things, but in reality, I'm sure she's just here to snoop. She tilts her head at me and silently studies the human sized lump on my bed. "Unbelievable that you would bring a girl here and let her stay the night with you. Your father will hear of this, and I hope that little slut in there with you knows her place. "Whatever she's after, it ends today, just like every other girl. You're lucky Harlow is so forgiving of all this behavior. Once you're married, things will change."

"Get out! Who do you think you're talking to? I will never marry Harlow, and you are not my fucking mother!"

"What?!" Harlow's voice screams through the closed door.

Sivan is so still, and I have no idea what he's feeling right now. Damn it, I can't have Harlow coming in here, too. I'm already trying to get rid of her mother.

Sheena is still studying the bed from a distance. Harlow's voice didn't shock her, so Harlow must have been out there the whole time.

Harlow yells through the door, "I'm not coming in! I just stopped by to see if you were here. Do you know who Sivan went home with? His father said he didn't come back last night. Everyone assumed you two probably passed out somewhere."

Sivan's hand has made its way to my thigh under the covers, and he's gently squeezing it. I laugh loudly once; I am incredibly ticklish.

I can't answer Harlow, I've known her too long. She'll know I'm lying right away.

Sheena points at me. "You need to get dressed and get that girl out of here, whoever she is." She turns toward the door and reaches for the handle. "Meetings start within the hour. By the way, that cologne, if that's what you wore last night, it smells terrible, so surely that thing in your bed is of lower class if she liked that."

"What?!" Sivan shrieks from under the covers as the door opens.

Harlow nearly falls in while her mother turns on her heel and looks at my bed.

"Please go," I say.

Both Harlow and her mother leave without any more words spoken between us.

Sivan pulls the covers off his head and looks up at me. His face is all red and agitated. "Why would she say that about my cologne? I'm no common whore," Sivan says with a laugh.

I lean down and press my mouth to his. I have no idea what I'm doing, but all I know is that I want to kiss him, and his hand on my thigh did a lot more than tickle me a few minutes ago. The feeling of his hand reminded my lower half of the pleasure he gave me. He's holding my face gently as I kiss him.

Our kiss is loud and quickly turns ravenous. "I want to do it again," Sivan whispers as he holds the back of my head. I begin kissing his chest and slowly kiss down, reaching the perfect line of hair beneath his navel. This is new for me, but I want to do it. This urge is more than sexual—I can't stand the fact that he heard Sheena spouting all that bullshit about me marrying Harlow. Well, that and her insulting his cologne, I'm not sure which one he hated more. He holds the back of my head and massages my hair softly, while I slide his briefs down. He's so big. No more than twenty-four hours ago, I wouldn't have thought this was something I'd be doing—but here I am sucking my best friend off.

"Mmmm—fuck, Vincent." He places his hands under my arms and lifts me gently, then pushes my body onto the bed. "Lay down."

He climbs atop me, and we kiss even more intensely than before. "I don't want to hurt you, Vincent," he says as he pulls the only layer of clothing off that separates us from my lower half.

Three loud bangs on my door stop Sivan from going any further.

"Vincent! I'm coming in!" Matteo yells as he enters.

Well, there's nothing I can do about this. Sivan is on top of me naked; we're only covered by a thin white sheet.

My view of Matteo is blocked by Sivan's body. Sivan drops his face onto my pillow beside my head and lets out a sigh. "Make him leave, I can't move right now," he whispers.

"We have bigger problems than your position. You realize that, right?" I whisper.

"What the hell am I looking at?" Matteo asks.

I raise my right hand up and wave. "Well, no one told you to come in, but I'm assuming you're surprised that I'm not dressed yet. Is that right?" I ask facetiously.

Sivan laughs into the pillow and whispers, "You just said we had big problems and you're joking around."

"Well, he can clearly see what's happening. What the hell am I supposed to do?"

My room is quite large, so Matteo can't hear our whispers, and with Sivan's broad shoulders blocking my view, I have no idea how Matteo is reacting to this.

"Tell him to leave. I like him, I don't want to be rude," Sivan whispers.

"Matteo, just tell my dad I'll be there in a few minutes and tell Sivan's dad that he'll be there too. We don't really need to talk about this."

I can hear Matteo's footsteps heading back toward my door. "Uh, yeah. You got it," he says, as he leaves my room.

Sivan raises his eyebrows at me. "Do you want to get back to it, or do we have to actually go to the meeting?"

I place my hands on his chest and press him back a bit. "Sivan, do you understand what just happened? Matteo just saw us naked on top of one another. He's probably freaking out. I have no idea what he's gonna do."

"So, what you're saying is, no sex before the meeting that we're both not going to?"

"I think not," I say with a chuckle. "And we better get to that meeting. Matteo is good at covering for me, but I have no idea what he's going to be like after seeing that."

Sivan kisses me softly and stares into my eyes. My face feels incredibly flushed. "Are you worried that he's going to tell someone, or are you embarrassed that he saw us?"

I close my eyes and kiss him without a reply. The truth is, I think I feel both of those things, but I also feel happy that Sivan didn't seem to care at all that Matteo saw us. For some reason,

I'm kind of flattered that he wasn't embarrassed. I think if I would have let him, he would have gladly thrown Sheena out while yelling in his underwear. Just the thought of her seeing him in his underwear makes me mad, and it didn't even happen. God, what are these emotions? Where did they come from? Sivan kisses my forehead and sits up. He looks down at his dick and raises his eyebrows at me.

I cover my eyes with my hand. "Stop, we have to get dressed. And you're gonna have to wear my clothes. Yours are probably all wrinkled."

His eyes look me over and he stands up from my bed. Damn, he's hot. "I'm gonna wear your clothes? I mean this in the nicest possible way, I had sex with you last night; we are not the same size. Your clothes are not going to fit me."

I stand up from my bed and look down at my own body then look at his. "Well, some areas are close in size, but yeah your shoulders are broader than mine."

"My shoulders? You think I'm talking about my shoulders?" he asks me while tilting his head toward the back side of my body. "I'm talking about that ass you got back there," he says with a smirk.

I turn and look at my own ass in the mirror. "Wow. Just wow. I can't believe you just said that. What size pants do you wear?"

Sivan lifts his pants from the pile in the corner and jumps into them, wrinkled as they are. "Not wearing your pants, and we're not talking about the sizes of our pants, either." He lifts his white dress shirt from the floor. "Now this…this is too wrinkled. I may need to borrow a shirt."

I walk toward my closet in my underwear. "Nope, wear your

own damn shirt. Talking about my ass and wearing wrinkled pants. Forget it, you're not wearing one of mine."

Sivan walks toward me with a mischievous smile. "Why would me talking about your ass be a bad thing? I really like your ass. And who cares about my pants?"

"Who cares about your pants? You're kidding, right?" I ask him, as I thumb through the jackets in my closet. "You care about your pants! You're always obsessed with your clothes. Did you hit your head or something? Is that what happened? Last night before we came in here, and, you know…did that." I gesture toward his pants. "Did you fall and hit your head?"

Sivan pulls his mouth to the side and looks down at his pants. "Come on, they're not that bad. Also, no, I didn't hit my head. If you don't loan me a shirt, I'll have to wear the wrinkled one, and I think that we both know that out of the two of us, you will be the one most embarrassed by that. You care much more about your clothes than I do."

"Really?" I ask while tilting my head at him. "You think I care if you show up wearing wrinkled clothes? Hardly. Why should I care about that? Your dad will probably be pretty pissed though, and my dad will definitely make fun of you."

"I don't know…you seemed pretty embarrassed when Matteo came in here," he says.

"Of course, I was embarrassed! You were halfway—and then the—and he just—and you. Shut up. That and this are two different things." I'm fully dressed now and buttoning my jacket while Sivan stares at me. This makes me feel so strange. The stuff he's saying and the way he's acting. What am I supposed to think? I don't even know what the hell is happening. I'm so confused.

Sivan begins buttoning his wrinkled shirt. "You're very hot, you know that? I wonder why I didn't notice until last night?"

"I don't know, this just started for me yesterday, too." I watch as he finishes buttoning the most wrinkled shirt I've ever seen. His jacket should cover his shirt anyway, and besides, it's none of my business if it doesn't.

"Come here," I say, while waving my brush at him. "I'm leaving my hair down today, but you want yours up, right?"

"Uh…yeah. Why? Are you gonna put it up for me?"

"I was going to, but is that weird?" This was a stupid idea, why would I think he wanted me to brush his hair?

He sits on the chair by my desk. "I hate brushing my hair and since I didn't dry it after the shower last night, it feels all tangled. If you want to brush it, I'm not gonna turn that down."

I begin brushing his hair and instantly hit a knot. "Oh wow, this is a big ass knot."

He nods in agreement. "Told you. I knew it would be tangled. I never go to bed with it wet."

"Lots of firsts last night, then," I say awkwardly. I work my way through the knot and pull his hair tightly atop his head in a bun. "There, perfect," I say.

He stands and looks in the mirror on my wall. "That feels great. It's so tight. I'm usually the only one that can get my hair this tight. Thanks."

"Anytime."

I catch a glimpse of us in the mirror on the way toward the door. My crimson red jacket with Sivan's cobalt blue jacket behind me is extremely eye catching. We look really good. As I grab the doorknob, Sivan hugs me from behind. "Hey, I…" he says.

I turn to face him, and we squeeze each other tightly.

"Sivan…I don't know what to say. It feels like we're saying goodbye forever or something, but we're just going to a meeting. Why do I suddenly feel sad?"

He holds my face in his hands and looks at me. "Goodbye? I will never say goodbye to you. You're my best friend, no matter what happens. No one could ever make me say goodbye to you."

I swallow hard. I want to say something equally as sweet, or kiss him, but as I open my door, I hear footsteps hurrying down the hall. I smell the scent of Harlow's perfume. She was most certainly eavesdropping the entire time. Well, that's fine. I'm not really too worried about that. She's not going to say anything to anyone and honestly after last night, I really don't want to sleep with her anymore. What I shared with Sivan was perfect. I had no idea sex could feel so good. The two of our bodies pressed together, joined as one, that was what nature intended for the both of us.

"Ugh, that's a terrible smell," Sivan says as he leaves my bedroom.

I laugh. "I would expect that you would think so, that's Harlow's perfume."

"Oh, well, no wonder I hate it then."

"Funny thing is that just yesterday I actually rather liked it. But now, I—"

"It's fine, you don't need to say anything. It's not worth talking about. You hate her perfume, you like her perfume. It's nothing I can control. I can only control…well, I guess, nothing. I guess there's not much I *can* control," Sivan says.

Why do I have this urge to comfort him? "Hey, we'll figure everything out. Why do you sound so upset?" I ask while pausing to look at him.

"Nah, I'm not upset. Just confused. What do you think she

was doing? Why was her perfume lingering outside of your room like that?"

I shake my head and raise an eyebrow at him. "I think that she was probably outside the door snooping."

"So, you think she heard everything?"

"Yeah, I think so. I'm sure her mother was out here with her, too. The two of them would do something like that. Whenever I bring girls home, they—"

I stop speaking as I see Sivan's facial expression change. He looks hurt or sick. I don't know what it is, honestly. But I don't like seeing him like this. I place a hand on his shoulder and squeeze it lightly. His jacket fits him so nicely and his shoulders are so strong. "Hey, I—"

Before I can finish my thought, Sivan's eyes raise and meet mine. I want to kiss him, and I don't think I can stop myself, as my face moves closer to his. I look at the ground contemplating whether I should do this or not. Using two fingers he lifts my chin lightly and tilts his head.

"Ah, boys! There you are!" my father's voice calls from down the hall.

Sivan's father's voice follows behind as he enters the hallway, "Boys? Sivan is here?"

Holy shit that was close. One second longer and our fathers would have seen us kissing. I don't even know what that would have looked like. Would they have yelled, fainted, or pulled us off one another? I feel like either way, it would have been pretty bad. But admittedly I'm disappointed that I didn't get to kiss him again.

"Where have you two been?" Sivan's father asks as he looks over our shoulders. "Where are the girls?"

"What girls?" Sivan replies. "I spent the night with Vincent, there were no girls."

I quickly cover Sivan's mouth, rather stupid of me, I might add. But I was afraid of what he was going to say.

Our fathers look confused staring the two of us down. They would never suspect that we've slept together, though.

"What the hell are you covering his mouth for?" my father asks.

"I um…we…well this morning Sheena came in being all kinds of nosy and rude, and I was afraid that Sivan was going to say something mean about her and get on your bad side."

My father's eyebrow drops and he gives Sivan a sort of discerning look. Sivan is rolling his eyes while my hand remains covering his mouth. I should probably move it, but I don't want to. The feeling of his soft lips against my hand is strangely comforting.

"Sivan wouldn't speak ill of your future mother-in-law," his father says.

I feel Sivan's mouth open in protest and I apply a bit of pressure against his lips with my palm.

My father says, "Yes, well, I would doubt that she'd do anything to purposely get on Sivan's bad side."

Sivan looks mad, probably at the fact that his father just referred to Harlow's mother as my future mother-in-law. I feel like I should say something, but would that just make this situation worse? No, I should say something. Looking at his desperate eyes tells me that I should.

"I apologize Captain Crawford," I say. "But has my father given you the impression that I would be marrying Harlow? Because, if so, that is never going to happen." I can feel Sivan's smile against my hand. Oh God, he's lightly licking the inside of my hand. I'm trying hard not to react, but I can't fight the smile that's forming on my face.

"Take your hand off his mouth already!" my father yells at me.

"Oh, right," I say and pull my hand off.

As soon as I remove my hand the words fly from Sivan's mouth. "Dad, why would you think that Vincent was going to marry Harlow? He's never once said that to me."

"Indeed, Ray," my father says. "Vincent has no interest in Harlow, anyone with eyes knows that. Now, Matteo and Harlow, that may be a thing. I've seen those two looking at each other when Vincent isn't around. That might be something."

I know my father is trying to bait me. He knows that I have a jealous side, but not over Harlow, so he's mistaken here. I laugh and nod. "That's great. You should tell Matteo to go for it. He's always trying to get your approval anyway, so maybe if you tell him that you approve, he'll go for it. Then she can leave me the hell alone," I say.

Sivan scoffs and shakes his head as our fathers start to laugh. "What are you two old booze papas laughing about?" Sivan asks. "We both know Captain Rodrigo was trying to bait him into acting jealous and it didn't work, so what's funny?"

"Now, now," Sivan's father says. "Calm down, it's not a big deal. We're just poking fun here. What are you acting so sensitive about? You looked moody since I laid eyes on you, when I rounded the corner. You're mad about Sheena, Harlow, or whatever the hell, and now you got your damn pants in a twist because we're teasing Vincent?"

"Ah, give him a break, Ray, they're obviously tired from all the trouble they must have gotten into last night. I can imagine it must have been a wild time for them to end up here with no girls, and Sivan here with a wrinkled shirt under his jacket.

I elbow Sivan. "Told you your shirt was too wrinkled."

"Well, I was told I could not borrow one of yours. Do you remember that?" Sivan asks me with a grin.

I can feel my smile growing as I look at him. It's almost as if for a moment our fathers aren't here as I look into his eyes. God, I want to kiss him.

"You told him he couldn't borrow a shirt?" my father asks me.

"Oooh, ruthless, just like your old man!" Sivan's father says.

"When did I ever tell you that you couldn't borrow one of my shirts, Ray?"

"You never let me wear your clothes. I've asked multiple times to borrow a jacket and you've never once let me. You're stubborn."

"Come on now, I let you borrow underwear before, you think I wouldn't let you wear my jacket?"

"No, I don't think you would," Sivan's father says.

"Horseshit!" my father yells. "Do you remember that night down at Pudgy's with Miriam, when the old lady was nowhere around? What happened? You lost your clothes in a round of cards, and who gave you his jacket to wear? That was me!" my father yells.

"Bullshit! Are you losing your mind, Rodri? You lost your clothes in a card game, not me! And I gave *you my* jacket. What the hell is wrong with you? You're remembering this wrong."

"Am I? No, wasn't that the night you had to borrow my underwear?"

"No, see that was not at Pudgy's, that was at Muffy's. That was with that one ship hugger, whatever her face was with the lipstick, remember? That was when I came back to your ship and then she—"

My father finishes his sentence "She stole your clothes and left you naked in my quarters!"

"Yes! That's what you're thinking of!" Sivan's father says.

"Oh, well, why did I think it was my jacket?"

"How the hell should I know why you thought that? So, yes, you let me borrow your underwear, pants and shirt, but then I asked for a jacket, and you refused."

"Oh, now I remember! You smelled terrible and we had no time for a shower. Ooh, Sheena never complained so much as when she had to wash that shirt," my father says.

"I smelled bad? I've never been told once in my life that I smell bad."

"That makes sense," Sivan adds. "Sheena complained about the smell of my cologne in Vincent's room this morning."

"Yeah, well, she was probably just angry that you were in there. Probably blamed you for Vincent being late. Who knows?" my father says.

"Oh, uh, Dad, the thing is, that she didn't know Sivan was in my room. She just smelled the cologne and complained."

Oh God...I hear the sound of heels clacking against the wood, and before I even look behind me, I already know that its Sheena.

"Hello, Captains," she says.

"Yes, hello," our fathers reply in unison, as she walks in between the four of us, staring at Sivan and me.

"Now this is interesting, where did you come from?" Sheena asks, looking at Sivan. She turns her attention toward me. "Where did that piece of trash go that was in your room this morning?"

"There was no trash in my room."

"Right," my father says. "Sivan was the only one in Vincent's room, he spent the night it seems. Too drunk to get to his own ship."

Sheena's eyebrows raise and she looks the two of us over. It's almost like she suspects that something happened, but she isn't going to say anything. But how could she even suspect that? Oh right, she saw someone hiding in the bed, and I was shirtless. But still, that proves nothing.

"Captain, you say there was no one there aside from Sivan and Vincent…this morning?"

"Yes, the boys just ran into us out here, and that's it. Girls were already gone, it seems."

She cracks a crooked smile and raises an eyebrow at us. "Well, I find that interesting, because when I came into the room this morning—"

"Unannounced," Sivan interrupts. "She entered his room without his permission, and I was changing clothes. I got so damn nervous that I hid under the covers, so she wouldn't see me in my underwear."

That was a really nice cover. I can't believe he thought of that so quickly. I'm more than impressed. She's not buying it, but my father looks kind of pissed at her.

"Yeah, Dad, I asked her not to come in, and she just barged in anyway. You know, I'm an adult, it's a bit weird for her to still be able to barge into my room whenever she wants. I was so afraid she was going to see me naked, too. Even after I asked her to leave, she wouldn't."

Sivan has that look he gets, right before he's about to really dig into someone. "She even insulted my cologne, and said I smelled like a cheap slut. And her daughter was eavesdropping outside the door, too."

My father crosses his arms. "Now Sheena, Sivan is like a son to me, and I have to draw the line at you calling him a slut."

"Yes, Captain. I understand. Forgive my impertinence. I had no idea that Sivan was the one hiding under the covers. How should I have known there would be a man in your son's bed?"

"You say that like there's something wrong with it," I say loudly. "Is there something wrong with two friends sharing a bed after a night of drinking?"

"Right, right," my father says. "Nothing wrong with that. I mean, if they were naked in bed that would be a different story, but surely you can't see anything wrong with the two of them sleeping in the same room."

"If I may add," Sivan's father cuts in. "It seems you have insulted my cologne on two instances now. What is it that you find disagreeable about this scent? It's the same one I bought for Sivan. It smells great." He sniffs his own sleeves. "This is expensive cologne."

The rest of us give a chuckle, but he's quite serious and really isn't joking. This is good, though. It's a diversion from the fact that Sivan was naked in my bed.

"Oh, I don't believe I've ever insulted your cologne. I find it most agreeable," Harlow's mother says. "I truly apologize if I have offended you in any way."

"I'd understand if you were talking about his cologne, smells like low tide!" Captain Crawford says as he pushes my father. "Let's go, Rodri."

"Time for the meeting, lets head out boys," my father says.

Phew, we made it through without further interrogation.

Our fathers turn away from us and Sivan and I exchange a glance, one that says that we both realize how close that was.

"Just a moment," Harlow's mother says.

Our fathers stop and turn toward her. "What is it? We're gonna be late for our own meeting."

"Well, I would feel ashamed of myself if I didn't mention something to you captains."

Oh no, she's gonna tell him about Sivan. What the hell? She's actually looking at Sivan and I, as if she's telling us that she knows everything.

"Vincent and I are going on ahead," Sivan says, walking away. I quickly follow behind.

"Yes, it's just as well, I've forgotten what I was going to say anyway," she says with a chuckle.

Sivan and I both know…she heard everything. That was definitely meant as a warning to us. It was a silent threat.

We enter the meeting room, and sit beside one another at the long back table. It smells like freshly painted lacquer; this table is constantly being replaced. Crew members can't help but to start fights in this room, which nearly always leads to a sword in the table, or a good table flipping. Sivan scoots his chair a bit closer to mine, as he takes his seat. We're the only two in here so far, our fathers must have gotten held up in the hallway by something. Sivan's warm hand squeezes my thigh.

"Don't do that, I'm so ticklish!"

"You're ticklish? If you hold my hand under the table during the meeting, I'll let go of your thigh."

"I can't hold your hand! Are you crazy?" I ask through laughter. "Come on stop!" He squeezes my thigh again and I wiggle away.

"Hold my hand, and I'll stop," he says, pumping his eyebrows at me.

"No, stop, come on." I can't stop laughing and continue squirming in my seat. Both his hands are on my thighs and he's still tickling me. The door opens wide, and I jump backwards into my seat.

Thank goodness, it's just Matteo. He scans the room quickly. "Oh, where is everyone else?"

"Hello to you, too," I say. He looks at Sivan and I, up and down. It's a look I've never seen from him before. It's almost contemptuous.

"Where is everyone else? Where are the captains?"

Sivan and I look at one another. I guess I should be understanding of what he's feeling; he did walk in on the two of us naked on top of each other, so it's probably not easy for him to be in here with us right now. But, honestly, why should it really matter? Male, female, what difference does it make to him?

"Matteo, are we to understand that you are uncomfortable around us?" Sivan asks.

Matteo rolls his eyes in reply, as he approaches the table. "Well, Sivan, yes, you are to understand that. Are you not the same? Do you not feel uncomfortable after doing that?"

"Do I feel uncomfortable after having sex with Vincent? Is that what you're asking me?"

"Wow!" I say. "Don't go saying it out loud like that!" My face feels incredibly hot, probably due to a mixture of embarrassment and overstimulation.

"What? I'm not embarrassed! Are you?" he asks me.

"Well, you should both be embarrassed. What would you do if Harlow or your father had come in instead of me? What does this mean? Have you two been doing this the whole time? Sleeping together? You're both going to be named captains this year, and you're sleeping together? No wonder you don't want to marry Harlow. When did this start?"

Before I can answer, the door opens, and our fathers enter. "Boys, where the hell is everyone else?" my father asks.

Matteo answers him, "I can send for them, perhaps they confused the time after last night's round at the bar." He leaves the room quickly, to presumably notify everyone else.

Our fathers sit at opposite ends of the long table. "So, boys, how do you feel about the latest news of Captain Slicer coming back around? What do you make of it? Rumors? Or do you expect they are true?" my father asks.

"Well, I hadn't heard that, to be honest," I say.

Sivan shakes his head no. "We didn't talk about that. No one mentioned it to us."

"Didn't talk about it?" Sivan's father asks me. "What did you two spend the night talking about then?"

"We didn't spend the night talking. We spent half the night passed out," Sivan says.

"Oh, well that solves it," Sivan's father says.

"Yeah, we hit the rum early and passed out pretty quickly after," I add on.

My father taps the table. "Oh, well, the rum was delicious this trip. Don't blame you at all for that."

The door opens and several crew members barge in loudly. The table is quickly filled with boisterous pirates.

"First order of business," my father says. "Why the hell were all of you late?"

"Easy, we were late because we got held up in the hallway.

Sheena was out there consoling Harlow and we just offered some friendly advice."

"Oh, Harlow was upset about something?" my father asks.

"Upset about him," he says pointing at me. "She says Vincent keeps breaking her heart."

"Oh, come on," Sivan says. "That girl is ridiculous; he doesn't even like her."

"Okay, calm down, he does like her, he's just not going to marry her," my father says to Sivan.

"He doesn't like her as anything more than a friend, and she can't seem to understand that," Sivan says resolutely

"Yes, that may be true. But why would you need to make that distinction?" my father asks.

My stomach is in knots, thinking of the thousand ways this conversation could go wrong. Honestly, Sivan is usually pretty vocal in the meetings we show up to, so I don't know why my dad is poking at him. Doesn't really matter. I can't take a chance that Sivan says something about us sleeping together. "Captain," I say. "He's making the distinction because I don't like her, and everyone thinks I do. Sivan knows the way that I feel." I have to call my dad Captain in front of Captain Crawford's crew, if it were just our guys, it would be fine, but it's considered an insult not to address him as captain with the others here.

My father drops an eyebrow at me and leans back in his chair. "Oh, is that right?" he motions for a drink toward the cook in the back of the room.

"Yes, that's right," I say.

Captain Crawford is carefully studying the two of us. He'd normally have interjected at this point. It's making me nervous that he hasn't. But maybe I'm just afraid that somehow he knows. I'm afraid of everything right now. Suddenly I feel like all eyes are on me, like everyone knows our secret.

"Well, you're not yet twenty-one, once you see what's out there, maybe you'll realize what's in front of you," my father says.

I purposefully turn my gaze toward Sivan. Our eyes meet and the words I want to say are caught in my throat. They're strangling me from the inside out. This secret, these feelings…I don't understand them. I can't make sense of anything. It feels like I'm suffocating.

"He sees what in front of him," Sivan says.

I can't move and I can't react. I feel frozen in this moment. I have no idea what anyone else is doing, I just know that I feel strange. I feel kind of lightheaded and dizzy. Everything is suddenly spinning around me. I'm falling toward Sivan, and I can't stop myself. I feel my head land on Sivan's lap. I hear my father shouting my name, and other people too, but I can't react.

CHAPTER 4
GET OUT OF MY BED

I look at my phone and decide to text him. *Where r u? I miss u. It's my birthday.*

I delete those words before I send the text. I close my eyes and lay the phone on the bed beside me. I've already sent him so many messages since that night. It's been nine months since we last saw each other and he hasn't returned a single text or phone call. I haven't talked to him since that morning before he passed out during the meeting. I still don't understand what happened. I question it constantly. Was it the stress? Was he disgusted with me? Was he disgusted with himself? His father was digging into him about Harlow, and he just stared at me and then passed out right onto my lap in front of everyone. Well, I caught him on my lap would be more accurate to say.

Why is he ignoring me? We felt the same that night, and the morning after. I know we did. You can't fake that kind of connection. I can't imagine why he wouldn't respond. It's been nine whole months, there is no logical reason for him to ignore me. Well, at least we'll be together soon. Then he can finally give me some answers. Maybe his phone just hasn't had reception? Yeah, right, what a stupid thought. His phone hasn't received a single text of mine? Oh my God, what if he's gotten engaged to

Harlow? What if his father has convinced him to get married? No, no, he wouldn't. I'm absolutely certain of it. Okay, I'm going to text him one more time. No, you know what? I should just try to call him again. Ah, but that would be embarrassing if he does answer and he has actually been purposely ignoring me. I could just pretend I dialed him by accident, then when he answers, I'll just say that I didn't mean to call him. Yeah, that's what I'll do. At least I'll get to hear his voice. What's wrong with me?

Why would I even think of something like this? What have I become? I've resorted to pretending to call him on accident? I stand up from my bed and slide my phone into my pocket.

As I walk down the hall, I hear my father screaming. "Enough, I've had enough! Tell Sivan to get his ass in here now!"

Now, I should just go back to my room, but I know that's not going to work, so I head straight inside my father's quarters. "What are you screaming about?" I ask him.

"I'm screaming because you have been holed up in your room sulking for the past, I don't know, nine months or so. It's your birthday. We need to celebrate. We leave to meet with Rodri tomorrow. You'll be named captain soon."

I look down at the floor, finding it hard to meet my father's eyes. "Dad, I, uh…how has, um…I was wondering…"

"Lift your head. What are you muttering about? I'm telling you we're gonna hit the bar together before we leave for your birthday and you're, what, upset?" my father asks, as he leans back in his chair.

"I'm not upset about that." Why *should* I be upset like this? My father is right.

"Son, listen, whatever some girl has done to you, whichever one it was, I'm sure it will work out. And listen, any girl that doesn't want you, is not worth your time. You're destined to run the seas; any woman would be lucky to have you. If your mother were still alive, she'd tell you the same. Now you're freshly twenty-one, let's go and hit the pub, huh?"

He *is* right, well not about the girls, but if I can just imagine this in a different way, then maybe I can actually have fun today. What's wrong with me having fun? It's my birthday, and if Vincent wants to act like a coward, then, well, let him. I'm not gonna sit around and cry about it anymore. I've wasted nearly an entire year obsessing over this. I'm not even interested in what's been going on with him. I'm completely over it. "Dad, how is Vincent?" I blurt out. What the hell is wrong with me? Why did I ask that? I can't even look at my father. I'm terrified of what he might say.

"Vincent? Well, I'm sure he's fine. I haven't talked to Rodri in a few months, left me a message a few months back about—I don't know, something or other, but I assume all is well. You can ask him soon yourself."

No, I can't, I think to myself, because I know that when I see him, I won't know what to say. I won't know why he's chosen to ignore me. I feel so stupid. The memory of sex with him is all-consuming. I can't get it out of my head. I can't get *him* out of my head. Have I been the only one thinking about what happened between us? I don't even know how I'll react when I see him. "Yeah, Dad, I'll just ask him myself."

"Good. Now, go get dressed and let's head out, we've got the whole day ahead of us!"

The day really got away from us. With all the pre-trip preparations, we're just now reaching the bar at eight. As we walk inside Pudgy's, the room is crowded with people, all staring over, of course. I feel like they all know, they can all see that I'm not the same guy I was the last time I was here. I haven't been to this pub in so long, and the last time I was here, I was happy because I was with Vincent. I haven't been happy since I left him. I've avoided coming here, blaming it on being too busy with captaincy lessons. But the truth is, nothing has been fun since we parted. Even rum has lost its flavor.

"Happy birthday Sivan!" I hear Jenny say.

Oh, I am not in the mood for her today. Please not now. Luckily, Ersin pulls me to the left before Jenny reaches me. "Happy birthday, ugly," she says with a crooked sort of smile.

"Thank you, you smelly old fish."

"Smelly old fish? Is that how you talk to the girl that you love?" she asks me.

"Love? Who loves you?" I ask, dropping an eyebrow at her.

She playfully pushes my face to the side. "You look bad, what's wrong?"

"No, I'm good." I stick my hands in my pockets and give her a shrug. Ersin has known me all my life, I'm not about to fool her. I avoid eye contact and look around the room.

"Quick, play dead," she says, pushing on my chest. "Jenny is coming right behind you."

I shift to the left hoping to avoid any physical contact from Jenny. Unfortunately, she was coming from the left and my shoulder bumps right into her large chest.

"Oh, you're ready to play already?" she cackles. "Well, it is your birthday, I certainly won't say no." She tugs her already low-cut shirt down and shakes her boobs at me.

I close my eyes and wince to avoid looking at them. "No, I'm not interested in that," I say. "Not tonight. Definitely not."

I haven't been interested in girls since having sex with Vincent. Even when jerking off, my mind is flooded with visions of Vincent writhing underneath me. The only thing that takes me over the edge is him, and the memory of his hot, hard body against mine.

"Who are you kidding? We both know you're going to end up with me tonight. I've already packed a bag for your place. Don't play hard to get with me. I want it, you want it. There's no need for emotional intimacy, which I know that you loathe," she says, placing her hand on my shoulder.

"I do not!" I shout, while pulling my shoulder back from her hand. I suppose I was a bit too loud, since everyone in the bar is looking at me. Their faces appear confused even though no one knows what we were talking about. They're likely just in shock because I shouted.

"Since when don't you mind intimacy?" Ersin whispers.

I immediately picture Vincent lying beside me. I remember what it was like when we held each other. I could have laid with him in bed all day. That was the first time I'd ever not wanted to leave after sex. All I wanted to do was kiss him. But I'm not going to say that. "I do mind it. I just don't loathe it, and I do not appreciate everyone in this bar staring at me," I say loudly. Most of the people are turning their attention away from me, and going back to their own conversations.

"You don't mind intimacy?" Jenny scoffs. She presses her body closer to mine "Well, then why don't we go be intimate together?" Just the thought of sleeping with her makes me feel queasy, now. I hate it. My thoughts are full of all sorts of horrible memories. The way she felt, the feeling of her being wrapped around me. All of it makes me feel sick to my stomach. I feel like I owe my dick an apology. How does just the thought of sex with her make me feel sick now? With all the preparations for me to become captain this year, I've barely talked to or been around any girls.

"Jenny, please. I don't want to, not tonight. I want to be alone," I step to the side, trying to avoid any further contact. She scoffs loudly, placing her body in front of mine.

My father, who I noticed was staring over for the past few minutes, finally intervenes. "Jenny!" he yells from across the room. "Come here for a moment. Let Sivan mingle with his guests, don't try to take him away just yet."

"Coming," she says, as she purposely brushes her body past mine.

Ersin smacks me three times with the back of her hand. "What the hell was that? What are you getting her all riled up for? We both know you're gonna sleep with her, anyway. Why bother teasing her?"

I want to tell someone about what happened with Vincent. I want to talk about the ways I've changed and the things I'm feeling, but I'm afraid. I can still remember the way Matteo looked at us the morning after with those judgmental eyes, dark and ominous. It was like he wanted to kill us both right then and there, he had such a contemptuous tone, too.

When he helped whisk Vincent away after he fainted, he looked back at me in a way that I'll never forget. It was like he was telling me with his eyes that what happened was my fault. It wasn't, of course. Well, I don't think it was. I actually have no idea what it was, because no one has explained a damn thing to me. For the four days afterward, no one could explain what happened, just that he was sick and needed time to recover. They wouldn't even let me see him. I didn't ask our fathers to intervene, because I was so damn afraid that my anxiousness would give something away. I had to keep reminding myself that regardless of what happened, we're both expected to be named Captains of our own ships this year.

If what we did got out, there could be many pirates who wouldn't know how to react to it. I've thought about my feelings for Vincent constantly since we slept together. I don't think another man could make me feel this way. I think the sex was only so incredible because of our deep emotional connection. I've looked at other men since then and can't imagine myself doing the same things with them. The desire isn't there, but neither is the desire for a woman. I only want him. I want to talk to him; I want to know how he's feeling. But I can't, since he's decided not to answer my texts for some reason.

I could talk to Ersin, I know she wouldn't judge me, and I trust her. But, still, the thought that someone else would know what happened is somewhat terrifying. I'm also not sure if that would be fair to Vincent. What am I supposed to do?

"Sivan," Ersin says, as she pushes me back, dragging me from my trance.

"Yeah, what?" I ask.

"What do you mean what?"

"Why did you push me? I was thinking something over, don't shove me like the damn bar is on fire, Ersin."

"Uh-oh. I know that look. Don't go falling in love with me, okay? I recognize that look in your eyes, you've fallen for someone, and since you're standing in front of me looking as stupid as ever, you must have fallen for me. Well, listen, Sivan, I'm not feeling it. Just shut that shit right down. Whatever crazy notion you have running around in your head, just let it go," she says straight-faced.

I scoff loudly, shaking my head. "Hardly, I'm definitely not in love with you."

She's staring deep into my eyes; she knows something is wrong. What the hell am I supposed to do? I'm too afraid to tell her the truth, but I don't want to lie to her. Damn it. I'm so frustrated. She tilts her head, looking quite concerned. "Hey, really, what's going on? I thought you would be alright, because it's your party, but whatever has been bothering you, is obviously still a problem. We haven't hung out in almost a year; I assumed that was because you were getting prepped to take on your own crew. Now, I think…there's something much more than that happening."

"Can we maybe go outside and talk?" I ask her.

She looks around the room, toward each of the exits, then motions with her chin toward the side door. "I'll go out first."

I wait a few seconds, smiling at a few other friends gathered at the bar. If we walk out together, Jenny will be sure to follow us. I have to try and sneak outside unnoticed. The last thing I need is her or my father following me. This is my chance; my father is laughing loudly in conversation with Jenny. I quickly slip outside into the cold autumn air.

Ersin throws her hands up at me. "Well, what the hell is it? I don't want to be out here, it's freezing. Say whatever you need to say."

"If you're cold, then just go back inside. We don't need to talk about this."

Her head tilts to the side. "Spit it out. Who has you upset? You're leaving for Vincent tomorrow, aren't you happy about that? Your father told mine that you'd been pouting non-stop lately. Rather stupid, if I say so myself. You're of legal age now, why would you be pouting or upset about anything? I thought it was just pre-stress of the captaincy; this is not stress, this is more. What is it?"

"Ersin, I have something I want to tell you, but…" I can't finish my sentence, I swallow the words down, they're fighting to come out. Why can't I say it? Am I truly embarrassed to admit that I feel this way for another guy? Am I afraid of what she'll think? Or afraid that she'll tell? All I can do is tell her how I feel. If she doesn't accept it, then that's that. I can't go on pretending. We've been friends our whole life. Shit, but what about Matteo? He's Vincent's best friend and look how he reacted.

"Spit it out," she says, rubbing her exposed arms. "Damn air is so cold out here. I wanna go back inside if you're just gonna stand there with a scowl on your face."

I'm too much of a coward. I can't do it. I can't tell her. I can't tell anyone. Maybe I'd feel different if I had spoken to Vincent, but since he's decided to ignore me, I can't take the risk of alienating the only other person that I can count on. What if I tell her and she freaks out? No. I need to keep this to myself. Bury it deep inside. Never speak of it again. Maybe I should just go inside and find some girl to distract myself with. I have to take my mind off him. Ugh. No. Just the thought of it repulses me. What the hell am I supposed to do? I'm so confused.

"Alright," she says. "If you're going to just stare at me, I'm going back inside. You're starting to creep me the hell out." She sighs loudly and heads toward the door.

"Ersin, listen, wait."

She stops just a few feet away from the door. "I am in love with you," she says, without turning around.

"What?" I ask.

"Is that what you were going to say?" she asks me, still facing away from me.

"No, I most certainly was not."

"Okay good. Me neither. I'm going inside to see if Jenny wants to go home with me. Whatever is bothering you, I'm ready to listen when you want to talk. You need to figure your shit out, though. You snapped at Jenny in there, and now you're out here staring at me like a lost puppy or something."

I have no idea why she said that. I mean, it's Ersin, she's not in love with me. So why would that be the thing she chose to say? Especially now when my head is already such a mess. I walk toward her, with my hands in my coat pockets. "Why did you say that?"

She reaches for the door and turns to face me. "Say what?"

"Ersin, come on. Why did you say you were in love with me?"

"Did I?"

I tilt my head at her, raising my eyebrows. "You did."

"I said it, because you are definitely in love with someone. I thought if I said that, you may make a grand declaration of who you were in love with. There was no other reason besides that. Usually, I can push you into giving me info that way. Just didn't work this time. I am genuinely curious who you are in love with. Had to have been someone you met during trades earlier in the year. Oh, by the way, does Vincent have a new number? I think he changed it," she says.

"Vincent?" I ask. Why would she want Vincent's phone number, and wait—why did she say she thinks he changed his number?

"Yeah, Vincent, you know your other best friend, hot guy about ye high," she says, holding her hand up to Vincent's height.

I roll my eyes. "I know who Vincent is, don't be stupid. What I want to know is why you're saying that you think he changed his number. And while we're on the subject, since when do you talk to Vincent outside of trade weeks?"

"I texted him a few times and he never responded. He didn't even read the texts. That was a few months ago."

My heart instantly warms. I am so incredibly relieved. That's what happened. He probably got a new number. I almost want to cry. I have to avoid looking at Ersin, or she'll see the tears forming in the corners of my eyes. I can't help it, though. He hasn't been ignoring me. This explains everything.

A faint sniffle escapes my nose and pierces the silence between us. I try to clear my throat in an effort to mask the sound.

Ersin's eyes are wide. "Are you crying?" she asks, as she begins to walk toward me.

"No, I'm not crying. Why would you even ask me that?" Damn it. I have to hold in these feelings.

"Holy shit, you are crying. I haven't seen you cry since we were kids. What the hell?"

"I was just thinking about something, it's nothing. But I'm not crying. I'm just cold. Come on let's go back inside."

I take a few steps toward the door and Ersin stops me, placing her body in front of mine.

"What happened? Did you guys have a fight? That would make sense. He's like a brother to you. Did you two argue the last time you were together?"

I shake my head no. "Definitely not."

"Then what is it?" she asks, placing her hand on my forearm.

"I, um. I'm—" Before I can finish my sentence the door swings open wide and out comes Jenny.

"Sivan, I've been looking everywhere for you," she says, clutching the sleeve of my coat.

"Well, *I* was just going to come looking for you," Ersin says to Jenny.

"Oh? Why? What's wrong? Is Sivan ready to go? The captain will be upset, but I can certainly take care of him if he's ready to leave."

"I'm standing right here!" I shout. "Why are you acting like I need your help taking care of myself? I don't want to leave with you. You are not coming home with me. Go home with Ersin, or someone else," I say.

Ersin raises her hand along with the corners of her mouth. "I volunteer to take you home. Sivan wants to go have a chat with his dad about something, but we could have a good time together," she says with a wink.

Jenny pulls her mouth to the side. "Hmm…Sivan, I've never thought about this before, but for your birthday I may be willing to share you for the night. Do you want that? All three of us could have a roll around tonight. Bit of a free for all in the bedroom. How about that? You wouldn't mind sharing me with Ersin, would you?"

"What the fuck did you just say?" I ask while shaking my head. "No. I don't want that, and I don't care who you sleep with. We've been over this so many times.

Ersin raises her hand, again. "Not for nothing, but that idea is out for me, too. I'm not interested in sex with Sivan, definitely not."

Jenny rolls her eyes at me. "Oh, God. I wasn't serious, Sivan. I mean I am interested in what that would be like, but more from an experimental perspective. I thought I'd try to get a rise out of you, see if I could make you jealous by saying that," she says, then cackles loudly.

"Damn it! You two!" I shout. "Screw the both of you. I was

sad, then I was happy, now I'm fucking aggravated." I point at Ersin and step around Jenny. "First you tell me you love me, to try and get me to react—"

"You what?" Jenny interrupts.

"And you"—I point to Jenny—"come out here asking for a threesome. What the fuck is wrong with you both?"

"Excuse me!" Jenny screams at Ersin. "Why would you tell him that you loved him? You know that Sivan belongs to me! How could you do that? I thought you two were just friends all these years."

"Calm down, everyone knows you're obsessed with him," Ersin says. "I was just goading him, like he said. I was trying to get him to tell me who he's in love with, and before you interrupt me, I can tell you, sweetheart, it's not you."

"Now I'm even more confused," Jenny says. "What do you mean? Who are you in love with, Sivan? Is it Tasha? Is that who it is?"

"No, it's not Tasha, what the hell? Enough, both of you. I've never been more annoyed in all my life. My right coat pocket begins to vibrate, and my heart skips a beat. It's Vincent. I can feel it. I reach into my coat and pull out my phone. *Unknown caller*

I press the accept button and answer while Ersin and Jenny are both screaming at me, "Hello?"

There is only silence on the other end of the line. "Hello?" I say it, again, but no one answers. "Vincent?" I ask and close my eyes as tears fall. I have no idea why I'm crying. Damn it, what the hell am I crying for? There's no background noise or voices. Nothing is coming through, but the call hasn't disconnected. I hear a giggle and a voice that repeats me and says "Vincent?" through laughter. The phone call ends before I can say anything else. I've heard that giggle before. Who the hell was that? Why did they mock me? Fuck this. I'm done with this. I can't take it. I'm out here crying like a baby and Vincent is off doing whatever he pleases. You know, I felt better earlier and now I'm mad again. Vincent is one of the only people that even has my phone number and everyone else that has it is here tonight. The call couldn't have come from inside the bar. It's so loud in there. This was someone that knew me and they mocked me calling Vincent's name. Why would he let someone do that? No, maybe he didn't have anything to do with it. I don't know what to think. Wait, that laugh…it was Harlow. I'm sure of it. Maybe Vincent fell asleep, and she grabbed his phone? It doesn't even matter. I can't stand out here agonizing over this anymore. I just need a drink. I walk past Jenny and Ersin and reach for the door handle. They're both staring at me in confusion on opposite sides.

"What are you doing?" Ersin screams.

Jenny throws her arm up at me. "Yeah, what the hell, Sivan?"

"I've had enough of this." I turn to the right and point at Jenny. "You're not going home with me ever again."

I turn to the left and look at Ersin whose arms are crossed tightly across her chest, "Ersin, I thought I had feelings for someone, and, unfortunately, I don't think those feelings were reciprocated. I'm not in love with anyone and I never will be. I felt something for someone, but all I feel now is the opposite. I feel pure loathing, loathing for myself, loathing of my body, and loathing of all people. So don't push me tonight."

I walk inside and head straight for my father who is seated at the bar. "Dad, let's drink," I say and place a hand on his shoulder.

My father lifts his beer high in the air. "Cheers! My son is here, the birthday man is finally ready to drink!"

The crowd at the bar all raise their glasses in salute.

Ersin's father, the bartender, passes me a shot glass full of green liquid.

I sniff it. It smells quite sweet. "Thank you. But what is this?"

"Poison apple," he says.

"Down the hatch," I say and drink it. Oooh, what a tangy little shot. "More," I say as I slide the glass back. He passes another shot to me. I tip it back quickly. "Whooo!" I shout. "Another!"

As I open my eyes, I turn to my left and see blonde hair on the pillowcase beside me.

Oh no…nononono. What did I do? I didn't come back here with Jenny. I wouldn't have. I look under the covers and I am still fully dressed. The only thing missing is my jacket and shoes. Oh, thank God. We mustn't have done anything. But why the hell is she in my bed, and how the hell did I get here? Shit, my head hurts. We leave at sunrise, which is probably any minute now, considering the clock says its 5:45 AM. "Jenny, get the hell out of my bed."

She turns toward me, wiping her eyes awake. "Oh, you're welcome."

I have no idea what she's talking about, especially because I told her she was not coming home with me. "I'm welcome? For what?"

"You're welcome that I came here with you and made sure that you got home safe. Your father and Ersin's father passed out drunk, doing God knows what with God knows who, and there you were leaning on the bar, blubbering about Vincent."

"Vincent?" There's no way I was talking about Vincent.

"Yes, Vincent. You were nearly in tears. Tell me something," she says, looking over at me.

I flip my legs out of bed and stand up. "Don't ask me anything about Vincent."

"Why shouldn't I? I know what I heard and what I heard was you basically professing your love for him. Now tell me, is that who you are in love with? Is it Vincent? You might as well tell me everything. You owe me for saving your ass last night, Sivan."

"I owe you nothing, no one asked you to help me. When I was sober, I told you I didn't want you coming home with me."

"Hey, I know that you feel something, just tell me. I'll listen. I won't tell anyone."

"Jenny, I'm sorry. I just can't. We're not going to talk about this. Please leave."

"Alright, well, I know you're leaving soon, but I want to say something to you. Even after all of the times you cheated on me and screwed around behind my back. I still find myself drawn to you. So, if you are in love with someone who doesn't love you back, then that person is—"

"What the hell are you talking about? We were never even together. How could I cheat on you?"

"We have been together for a year, on and off, even when we're not together, we're together."

"No, that's not how it works. If I'm in a relationship with someone, they're gonna know, and I'm sure I would know! I was never going out with you. Don't go telling people we were together when you know that we never were."

"We could be together, if you would just share your feelings with me!" she shouts.

"I'm going to speak plainly, because what you're saying makes no sense. I feel nothing for you. I have never been in a relationship with you— if you thought that, that's on you. Please just go, I need to get ready to leave. Don't be going around telling people that I cheated on you, either. I would never cheat on anyone."

"Fine. You are truly such an ass, Sivan." She shuffles her feet into her shoes and heads for the door. "Goodbye. Don't worry about your little secret getting out. I won't tell anyone." She opens the door and leaves.

"Jenny, good thing you're leaving, we're about to ship out," I hear my father say.

"Yes, goodbye, Captain. Have a safe trip. He's still pouting."

I hear my father sigh, just before he enters my room. "What was that about?" he asks me.

"Oh, nothing, just Jenny being Jenny. She said she owed me for bringing me home, she's insane. I would've rather slept on the floor of the damn pub than have her come home with me. I wish you would've stopped it."

"Now, come on. I don't even remember you two leaving together." He sits down on the edge of my bed. "This has gone on long enough. What are you so damn upset about? You can tell me anything. Are you worried about being named captain? Missing your mom? Just talk to me."

Technically I *could* tell him, in the sense that I can tell anyone anything. Much like I could tell someone that my name is Sivan and that I love shrimp. Not so much in the sense that I can say, hey, Dad, I'm gay, and I have feelings for my best friend who has ignored me since we had the most mind-blowing sex ever. No, definitely can't tell him that.

The horn outside signaling that we have thirty minutes before we leave sounds loudly. I'm still in my clothes from last night, and I need to shower, but my stomach is in knots. "I'm fine, Dad. I'm looking forward to seeing Vincent soon. I have a lot to catch up with him about."

My father's face twists a bit. "I wish I was half as excited to see Rodri, which I'm not," he jokes. "This Slicer business is getting out of hand. I'm sorry that you two will be dragged into it. We've planned for so long that you two would be named captains at twenty-one. No amount of rumors are going to change that."

The rumors of Captain Slicer's return have continued to swirl since earlier in the year. We have a close eye on all the ports under our control, so I'm sure they're just rumors, but my father feels they're substantiated. I know my dad is getting nervous about giving me some of the crew, and my own ship during a time like this. I'm not nervous about it at all. I'm more nervous about Vincent.

I lie down in my bed. "Dad, I'm not feeling well. I'm gonna close my eyes for a bit."

"Well, you did drink quite a fair share last night. Get some rest then take a shower. Long trip ahead of us, so no need to rush."

"Yeah, I think all of the alcohol and the stress just hit me. I'll be fine later on."

"Good. I hope so. I'm glad you're looking forward to meeting up with Vincent, hopefully you can get whatever it is that you want to say to him off your chest."

What does he mean by that? Damn it, I have no idea what I said at the bar last night.

My father turns the door handle and looks back at me. "Don't wanna talk, right?"

"No thanks, Dad."

I hear a scuffle outside the door and my father steps out to deal with whatever is happening. I'll just sleep for a while. Closing my eyes feels so nice right now. What did I say last night? What did everyone hear? Why did Harlow call me last night? I know that was her. Vincent wouldn't have let her do that. We've been best friends our whole lives, I know him. He wouldn't just cut me out of his life. That connection we shared during sex; it was more than just physical. I don't know what that means for me. I just know that I want him.

After four days of travel and constantly agonizing over what I'm gonna do when I see him, the day is finally here. I only meant to relax a bit this afternoon; and ended up sleeping for far too long. Looking at my phone it's already 5:30. Shit. I need a shower, and I have to hurry up and get dressed. I jump out of bed and quickly get into the shower. As the warm water washes over me, I'm completely lost in thought. So many things are swirling around inside my head.

After I shower, I dress quickly, putting on my meeting coat. I wonder what will happen when I see him. I want to kiss him, take him in my arms and tell him to never do that to me again. But the other part of me wants to yell at him a bit.

I hear the loud horn signaling that we are pulling into port, and I quickly place my hat on my head. As I leave my room, I walk faster than I ever have. I'm nearly running toward the stairs leading to the deck. As I step onto the deck, our two ships are already docked closely together.

CHAPTER 5
FLAMINGOES, PIGEONS, AND SHIP TRASH

VINCENT

Sivan is finally here; I see him walking towards me. It's been so long since we've seen each other. I still have no idea why he hasn't been replying to my texts. I wonder if he's missed me or even thought of me. I've been going crazy thinking of him. Standing on the deck beside my father, I smell Harlow approaching. She's been pretty distant, thankfully, but she hasn't left me completely alone either. We haven't slept together since before I slept with Sivan, but that doesn't mean she hasn't tried. I know that she knows something about Sivan and me, but she hasn't come straight out and said anything. "Here comes your boyfriend," she says behind me as Sivan approaches.

My eyes meet his as he steps across the ship. I want to run to him, but that would be way too dramatic. I must maintain a sense of dignity, at least a little.

Sivan looks hotter than ever. His blue jacket and tan skin are so eye catching. I don't know why Harlow called him my boyfriend. I mean, I would love for him to be my boyfriend, but we haven't discussed that. Technically, we haven't discussed anything about us. Regardless, Sivan isn't a relationship guy, despite what it seemed like after we slept together. As he gets even closer, my heart feels like it may explode.

"Vincent," he says. His eyes are piercing right through me. He doesn't look happy to see me.

My cheeks feel warm, and my palms are sweaty. "Hi, Sivan. Have you been well?" God, that sounded so stupid. I practiced what I was going to say to him for the past four days, that was not it.

"Have I been well?" He laughs. "No, I have not been well," he says tilting his head. His face is near my ear, and he inhales deeply, then whispers, "How can I be well, when the man that I fucked has ignored me for nine months. My best friend, who I was quite certain felt the same way, has ignored me. And why?" he asks, still whispering. "Why would he ignore me? What did I do wrong? Because I have been asking myself for nine months. So, tell me. What did I do wrong, Vincent?" He pulls his head back and looks me in the eyes. My mouth is open and my cheeks are now burning hot.

I place a hand on his chest—holy shit, it's hard. "How dare you speak to me that way? What did I do to you? I didn't ignore you. You ignored me. For months I texted you and called you, and I got no reply. Now, you come here, and you whisper in my ear, your damn breath smelling sweet like rum, and dare to have the audacity to ask me why I've been ignoring you?"

"What the hell are you talking about?" Sivan asks, looking confused. "You ignored me. Then that little piece of ship trash called my phone yesterday and mocked me."

I have no idea what the hell he's talking about. He only calls Harlow ship trash, why would Harlow have called him, and how?

"What the fuck are you talking about, Sivan?!" I yell.

Our fathers appear to have heard the commotion, judging

by the concerned looks on their faces. "What are you two yelling about?" my father calls over.

"Nothing!" we both shout back.

"Get over here," I say, pulling him by the hand to the side of the ship, out of earshot of our fathers. I can't hold his hand though, so I just latch on to a few fingers.

Standing by the side of the ship. I can feel everyone's eyes on us. At least that's how it feels. Sivan is flittering with his jacket, avoiding eye contact. "Hey, look at me. What the hell are you talking about?" His eyes are slightly wet. "Are you crying? What the hell is going on?"

Sivan leans over the side of the railing on his elbows. He wipes the corners of his eyes. "I thought something happened to you. I don't understand. How can you be standing here right now perfectly fine? I texted you so many times. I thought that we were going to be together. Before you say that's ridiculous, that's what I thought. I can't explain it, but after we had sex, something changed in me. Then you passed out in the meeting, and for the next four days, I wasn't allowed to see you. No one would say anything except for that you were sick and needed rest. I heard nothing from you after that. Not a word, not an update. Nothing. Didn't you care? What happened? Why did you pass out? Why didn't you text me when you were better? Why didn't you reply? I just want to—" He sniffles, his voice cracking.

I look around, feeling the eyes of Harlow and her mother staring holes through the two of us. "I don't understand what you're saying. I passed out, they said it was from stress. I have no idea what Matteo told the doctor at that time; I just know I slept for the next four days. As soon as I was able to, I texted you. You didn't answer. My father said that your father had been worried about you. You know who else was worried about you? Me. I was worried about you. Worried that you'd regretted everything. Worried that you'd regretted me. I haven't been sleeping well. I've been so nervous about seeing you. Now you're here and you smell—"

"I smell?" he says turning toward me.

I laugh. "Not like that. You smell good, you just don't understand how long I've wanted to smell you again. Your scent has taken ahold of me. It is the only thing I've ever yearned to smell. When my sheets were cleaned after you'd left, I was so upset because I couldn't smell you anymore. Then you didn't reply, and I thought I'd never get to smell you on my sheets, again. I'm so confused—you weren't ignoring me on purpose?"

"Boys!" my father shouts from across the deck.

We both look toward him. He has the worst timing of all. Is it possible that parents were put here to just annoy the shit out of their kids, even as adults? I need to talk to Sivan; I can't be bothered by whatever he needs.

"What? We're in the middle of something!" I shout back, rather loudly, too.

Sivan's father is looking the two of us over. He can't know anything, though. Unless Sivan told him. No, he wouldn't have. Would he? I hadn't even considered that he might do that.

Sivan appears to possibly be questioning the same thing as I am. I look at him, then his father and raise my eyebrows. Somehow, he knows exactly what I'm asking, without me saying a word.

He tilts his head at me. "No," he says.

"How do you know what I asked you, Sivan?"

"Simple, you were questioning whether my father knows about us, because he has that stupid look on his face."

"Yep. That's exactly what I was thinking. He's looking at us like he knows something. But I've been feeling that way with my own father since you left."

"Boys!" my father shouts again.

"Yes, yes, we're coming!" I whisper to Sivan, "We're not finished talking. Let's just try to ditch them quickly."

"You both look miserable," Sivan's father says as we reach them. "Sivan couldn't wait to get here, but now he looks rather sullen. What's the situation?"

"Yeah," my father says pressing his shoulder against Captain Crawford's. "You both look like you're mad about something. What is it? A girl? Did you fight over someone the last time you were together? Harlow has been walking around pretty miserable," my father offers.

This draws a small smile from Sivan. "She should be miserable," he mutters. "The rest of us are."

"Ohhh…I see," my father says, looking at Captain Crawford.

"You see what?" his father asks mine.

"It's easy to see that your son is in love with Harlow, and Harlow is in love with Vincent. Vincent doesn't want her, but Sivan wants Harlow, who in turn doesn't want Sivan, so Sivan is miserable. Now it all makes sense."

"Ha!" I say. That's the most ridiculous thing I've ever heard. Sivan looks more than infuriated. He looks absolutely livid at my father's suggestion.

Captain Crawford looks quite shocked. "No? Is that true? Sivan doesn't normally go after girls like that. He prefers them, bigger," he says holding his hands to the front of his chest.

Sivan shakes his head no, but he is at least smiling a bit now. "You are so far off that you're not even in the realm of possibility at this point, Captain Rodrigo. If there were a prize for the worst guess made in the history of guesses, then you would win. That was terrible. Awful. I hate Harlow. Despise her—her smell, her face, her voice. I hate that she lives on this ship. I hate her mother. I hate her, wholly and completely, but what I hate even more, is that for the past nine months she has not had to suffer the same cruel reality that I did, because she has been here happy, on this ship with Vincent."

His breathing is so rapid that he looks like he may faint.

"Wow. Said all that in one breath," his father says. "There is a thin line between love and hate, son."

"True words," my father says. "True words. We hate them, we love them. Although, I would say one thing. She has not been happy on this ship. Although I try hard not to pay attention to these things, the news that Vincent had ripped her heart out traveled very quickly throughout the crew. If you look close enough you can see she's been crying. So, whatever you want from her Sivan, I'm sure she'd be willing to give it to you, because Vincent has made her quite miserable."

My father is an absolute idiot. "Dad, sorry, I mean, Captain, he wants nothing from Harlow. Didn't you just hear what he said? He said he hates her."

My father crosses his arms and nods along. "Yes, I know, but it's all in the eyes. Sivan says he hates her, but what do his eyes tell you?"

Looking into Sivan's big blue eyes, I see only frustration and sadness.

"You're wrong," I say. "He doesn't feel that way for her. Did you two need something, because we were in the middle of an important conversation."

"Yes, as a matter of fact, we did, but we saw your miserable faces and thought we'd intervene. Tonight's meeting has been cancelled, so we've decided to take you boys out with us."

"No, no thank you," I say.

Sivan shakes his head resolutely. "Nope. We don't want to do that."

I hold my hand on my forehead. We absolutely can't get stuck at the bar with these two tonight. "Captains, we've been waiting to talk to each other. Why would we want to go out with you two?"

"Girls, Vincent. Lots of girls. Both crews are invited to Muffy's pub. We were told there would be a whole flock of pigeons coming in tonight. Some kind of a conference."

"Flock of pigeons?" Sivan asks.

"Yes, women, girls, birds." My father turns to Captain Crawford. "He doesn't know what birds are?"

"Flamingoes sounds better," Captain Crawford offers.

"No, it definitely does not," Sivan says. "Either way, I can't speak for Vincent, but I'm not going. I want to stay in tonight. I feel"—he looks at me—"sick," he says.

I have no idea if he feels sick, or if he's using that as a way to get us out of this. It's hard to tell because he was pretty pissed about Harlow a few seconds ago.

"You feel sick?" My concern is obvious in the rising pitch of my voice, which came out somewhere between concerned and almost hopeful. I clear my throat and deepen my voice. "I didn't know you felt sick." My change in tone brings curious looks from our fathers.

"Yes, I feel sick. And this whole conversation has made me only feel worse. I'm gonna head back to our ship," he says taking a step in the ship's direction.

"Wait, you just got here, Sivan. We haven't even talked yet," I say.

He turns back toward me. "Is there a rule that prohibits you from following me?"

That sounded pretty jerky, but still, I think that was more of an invitation than a rejection. At least that's how it seems.

"Well, go ahead then, Sivan," his father says. "You weren't feeling well when we set off a few days ago, either. Remember when Jenny left the other morning? You probably just need to rest. We'll take Vincent with us, and we'll see you when we get back."

I'm going to throw up. For real. He was with Jenny before they left? They leave at the crack of dawn, which can only mean that she spent the night with him. I'm so confused and pissed off. What the hell am I supposed to think right now? We aren't together, I remind myself. He's allowed to do whatever he wants. I cover my mouth, truly feeling nauseous at this point. "No, no, I don't want to go either. I'm feeling rather sick, too."

My father shakes his head at me. "No. He doesn't have to go because they've been traveling, but you have to go. There's no getting out of it for you."

I give Sivan a silent pleading look.

He shakes his head at me. and shrugs. "Have fun with the girls. If you want to check on me, I'll be in my room," he says, as he starts walking toward his father's ship.

What the fuck was that? What am I supposed to even do right now? We haven't talked; I have no idea how he's feeling. I don't know where he stands, and now, he's leaving. Damn it, I'm going to have to go drinking with our dads. This is the worst.

"Wait, Sivan. I need you to wait," I say.

"Oh?" he says lifting his chin and looking over his shoulder at me.

He looks hot, like actually hot. Not hot like I want to kiss him hot, even though I do. It's more like he really looks like he could be sick. I jog quickly toward him. "I'll come check on you in a bit, okay?"

Sivan gives me a sort of pensive look as he turns away. I'm standing here dumbfounded, completely fucking confused. I don't even know which point to focus on.

Harlow is scampering over from the right side of the deck. She was clearly waiting to see how things played out between Sivan and me.

"Harlow!" my father says loudly.

I see Sivan shaking his head. I assume he can hear what's happening.

"Do you want to join us?" my father asks.

"Yes, of course I do!" she says excitedly. "Wouldn't miss it. If I have the chance to get Vincent for the night. I'll take it."

Well, I'm certain Sivan heard that, seeing as he's stopped in his tracks. I want to run to him to tell him not to worry. I want to tell him I won't spend the night with her, but I don't need to. Besides, does he even care? He was with Jenny before they left. I still feel the need to tell him, though. Do I go after him, or should I stay? The words won't come out, as much as I want them to. If he turns and looks at me, I'll do it. I'll go to him. I'll tell him all the things I want to. I'll tell him that I've thought of nothing else, and that I only want to be with him.

I give Harlow a glare of warning, knowing full well that she knows what she just did. Sivan is walking toward his ship, again, he's not looking back. Damn it. I told myself I would run after him if he turned around, but he didn't. Just forget it. He doesn't care, he must not care the way that I do. He couldn't. How could he? He doesn't even believe in love. All that tenderness during sex and after…maybe I imagined it. I feel Harlow's lips on my cheek, and I jump back.

"Harlow, back the hell up. Why did you kiss me?"

She gives me a giggle. "More where that came from later," she says loudly. I know that she's really trying to egg Sivan on, but he's walked away already. It's not possible that he would hear her.

"Let's meet back here in just a bit," my father says, while Harlow smiles brightly as though she's done nothing wrong at all.

"Come on, Harlow, back up. We aren't together," I say.

My father and Sivan's are looking me over carefully. "What are you so grumpy for?" Captain Crawford asks me. "Are you really not feeling well, Vincent?"

This is it. This is my chance; I can feign sickness. Which, at this point, isn't too far off from the truth. "Yeah, I'm feeling sick. I don't know what brought it on. I think I just need to lie down for a bit."

"Oh! I'll stay behind and care for you." Harlow offers.

"No, definitely not. I don't want that. I'll go out. If it's between going out and being with you, I'll go out."

Harlow scoffs, then pulls out the fakest puppy dog eyes I've ever seen. "You see, Captain Rodrigo? Look how he treats me. Any man would be happy to have me. Why is he the only one that doesn't want me?"

"I can take care of him," Matteo says, placing a hand on my shoulder.

"Why is everyone touching me?!" I shout, jumping backward. I feel like everyone is in my space right now and the one person whose space I want to be in isn't around me at all. He's gone. It sucks and I hate it. I want Sivan. If I stay behind with Matteo…then I can't get to Sivan.

"You want to take care of me?" I ask, tilting my head.

"Of course, I do. It's my job, isn't it?"

"Ha! Since when?" I lift my chin at him.

"Oh, look, Captain, he is sick," Matteo says, with a stupid grin. He is giving Harlow quite the stare down. It's the strangest look. If I didn't know any better, I'd think there was actually something going on with the two of them.

"Fine, shit…I'll go. I don't want to stay here. I'm going to my quarters; I'll be out in a bit." I turn quickly before anyone can stop me.

Harlow shouts after me, "I'm going to wear red tonight, I'll stop by in a bit, so we can coordinate our outfits."

Okay that's enough. I turn back around. "Harlow. I am not going to be with you tonight in any sense of the word. Wherever you are, I will not be. Where you aren't, I will be. Do you understand? I can't be any clearer," I say with my hands on my hips.

Everyone on the deck is staring at me.

"Um, say, Vincent, what, uh…what are you saying? You said you can't be any clearer, but that was not clear, you will be wherever she is, or isn't, or you is, or she isn't… What the hell did you say?" Matteo asks.

"I suppose that was a bit of a stupid way for me to phrase that," I say. I cross my arms across my chest. "Hmmph—well, what I said was, I will not be with Harlow tonight. The end."

I turn and resume walking toward my room. Stepping below the deck I feel alone again, and confused. It's the same feeling as before. I walk inside my room and flop onto my bed.

I can't take this. I don't want to feel like this anymore. Oh, wait, now that I know he wasn't ignoring me, I should text Sivan.

A loud banging on my door interrupts my thoughts. I stand up quickly. "What the hell? Who is it?"

Matteo opens the door. "Hey, you've gotten everyone all flustered. Why do you push her buttons like that? You know how she feels, and you insist on treating her like shit. I li—"

"Bullshit. I didn't push anyone's buttons. She knows we aren't together, and she kissed me on the cheek. Before you got there, she was purposely trying to get Sivan to react. She was trying to make him uncomfortable when he was walking away."

As soon as I said Sivan's name, Matteo's demeanor stiffened. He really doesn't trust him, or like him, since he caught us earlier in the year. He was pretty convinced that Sivan was trying to use me. His reasoning for thinking that was that Sivan was too smart to have been caught in bed with me. So, according to Matteo, Sivan wanted that to happen, as some sort of elaborate plot to ruin me. Obviously, I didn't believe that. You don't fuck your best friend to try and screw him over. Besides, I was there, I know what we shared. Still, that hasn't stopped him from filling my mind with his delusions for the past nine months.

"I like her, is what I came here to say. I didn't come here to talk about *him*. I saw him leave. Where was he off in such a rush to? Maybe meeting with someone?"

I can't deal with his damn conspiracy theories right now. "Wait, you like Harlow? Since when? You've never once said this to me. Anyway, it's all the same. Take her, don't take her. I don't care. We both know I only want Sivan."

Truthfully, I am bothered. Not because I want Harlow, but because I feel somewhat like I have to apologize now, for sleeping with her. When did this start for him? Have they secretly been together, too? I'm afraid to ask because if I do, he's gonna think I care, and I don't. At least not in that way.

"Wow. That's pretty cold. I mean she's liked you her whole life. Are you really saying you truly feel nothing for her?"

"Of course I don't. This isn't new information, Matteo. If you want her, then have her. I need to get ready; can you leave now? I want to get this over with, so that I can be with Sivan. I don't want to deal with this anymore, honestly. It's all too damn frustrating. I just want to be alone, or with Sivan…neither involves you. So just leave."

Matteo is approaching quickly. "Hey, I've had enough of your smug attitude. Okay? You're my brother, but you cannot treat a person like this. Just because you've decided that you like men now, does not give you the right to go around being an asshole to every woman that you meet."

"Fuck you," I mutter.

He raises his eyebrows. "Fuck me?"

"Yes, fuck you. Get out of my room. Go find Harlow, go jump off the ship, just go away. I need time to think."

Matteo steps back, like he's considering whether he may hit me. I know this look because I've seen it many times.

"You gonna hit me?" I ask.

"No. I'm not gonna hit you. Last thing I need is for your boyfriend to come over here and get his dad in on this. Besides, I respect the captain too much for that," he says, as he leaves, slamming the door behind him.

"Hey!" I shout. "Get back in here! You can't say that shit and walk away!"

I'm left with only silence. Silence and the smell of Harlow's perfume for some reason.

"Vincent?" she says meekly outside the door accompanied by two light knocks.

"Damn it, now it's you. Yeah, just come in, Harlow."

She's been crying. Her face is red and puffy.

"I want to talk. Really talk," she says.

I sigh loudly, hands on my waist. "Sit," I say pointing toward the sofa in my room.

"I want to know why," she says.

"You want to know why what?"

"Why can't it be me? Why is it Sivan? What's wrong with me? Men love me, but you, you just don't. You don't care. You couldn't care less what I do. It's like you decided a long time ago, that I wasn't good enough, probably when you and Sivan did…whatever you did together. I have no idea how far you went."

The thought of Sivan's body and mine intertwined, quickly takes over my thoughts, it's beautiful and exciting, but the memory is also painful, and it hurts. I don't know what to do with these feelings, but I know that I can't discuss them with Harlow. That much I know. I can't trust her, and I wouldn't want to. This is not the first time she's tried to get the full story out of me. I'm still not sure how much she really knows. One thing about Harlow is that she's a very good liar. I've caught her in more lies than I can count. For all I know, she already knows we had sex and is secretly in a relationship with Matteo. I don't even think that would surprise me, if I'm being honest.

"How did you get this way? How did it come to this?" she asks me. "I've been here for you since we were kids, and you just hate me." She sniffles.

"I don't hate you. I just don't like you the way that you like me."

"Why not? What is it?"

"I'm sorry. It's just not the same." I really want her to leave. She's getting me close to confessing my feelings for Sivan, and I really don't want to do that. Especially when I have no idea how he truly feels about me.

"So, you do love him?" she asks me.

I knew this was coming. "Harlow. I'm not going to discuss this with you. You need to leave. I have said all that I'm going to say about it. That's all that's to it. Please just go."

"Did you—you know, do it all the way?" she asks, still not moving from my couch.

"Harlow, enough. Leave." I place my hand on my doorknob.

"You know what I think?" she says, her tone changing a bit. She sounds almost challenging, now.

I release the door handle and hold my palms out. "What? What do you think?"

"I think I've had enough of this. I think I'm ready to tell everyone all about the two of you. Yeah, that's what I think." A nasty sort of smile forms on her face.

Shit. I didn't think she would threaten me with that. No, I have to get a grip here. I haven't admitted to anything. She has no proof of anything. There's nothing that she can do to hurt me. No one would believe her anyway. I have to double down.

"Get out, Harlow. There's nothing to tell anyone. Whatever you say, no one would believe because everyone already knows that I'm straight. Just go. Also, rather stupid of you to try and force me to give you affection under threat. Don't you think?"

I open my door and gesture for her to leave.

"Close it," she says. "I have all the proof I need right here." She shakes her phone at me.

"What? What do you have on your phone? There's nothing,

so how could you have anything? What are you even talking about?"

"Eh, I think I'll go pay your boyfriend a visit. He may be willing to listen. Especially after last night." She presses a button on her phone.

"Hello? Hello…? Vincent?" I hear Sivan's voice through the phone.

"Aww, your widdle Sivan was so worried when I called him. What did you do, Vincent? Did you ignore him, the same way that you ignored me after every time we slept together? Is that what happened?" She presses the button again, replaying Sivan's voice. "Listen to that desperation, that thirst. He's definitely had you." She laughs. "Tell me I'm wrong."

I feel sick. I'm going to throw up or pass out. Why did she call him? How did she have his phone number? "Enough, get the fuck out. That proves nothing because there is nothing to prove."

"Whoa, whoa. What are you yelling at her for?" Matteo asks, walking inside my room.

She holds her phone toward him. "Matteo, I think you should know something."

I have to play this game, if I don't want everyone to know. Matteo won't be able to keep what happened between me and Sivan a secret from my father if he knows that Harlow is aware of what happened.

We'd agreed that he wouldn't tell my father unless he felt that my captaincy was in jeopardy, and this would definitely push him into action. He'd tell him straight away. Shit.

"What have you got on your phone, Harlow?"

She looks at him then at me. "Oh, just a little conversation between my future husband here, and me. I was just bragging. Isn't that right Vincent?"

"What the hell are you saying?" I ask her.

"What are you talking about?" Matteo asks looking at me, then shifting his gaze to Harlow. You called him your future husband. Since when? I just left ten minutes ago. What the hell is going on. One of you explain quickly."

"I don't know what she's talking about. She's lost her mind."

"Is that so?" he asks me.

Harlow smiles, then points to the door. "I think it's best if you give us a minute, Matteo."

He scoffs looking at me. "You're fucking unbelievable, you know that?" He walks outside of the room and closes the door behind himself.

"Harlow, enough! You know nothing because nothing happened! What the fuck was that about?"

The sounds of broken moans and grunts are heard as she presses a button on her phone, again. There's my voice: "Sivan more, please…I want this…more." Then Sivan's: "Fuck, Vincent…this feels so…"

Oh no…that's us…having sex. How did she? How?

"How did you get that?"

She laughs loudly. "This? Oh, this audio of you getting railed by another man? This audio of two future captains of the greatest fleets pleasuring each other in ways that women can only dream about?" She cackles. "Quite easily. You see, I had a recording device in your room. Usually do. I'm not ashamed of it. After all, I deserve to know who my future husband is sleeping with, don't I? This ship will be half mine one day. Now, are you ready to listen? Because I'm willing to play nice, if you are. And I don't mean that in the sexual sense. Since obviously I lack the necessary tool to please you. That much is obvious from the audio."

I don't even know what to think or what to say. I'm so confused. What do I do?

"What? Why? If you knew this, why did you toy with me? What do you want Harlow?"

"I want you. Well, rather…I want the appearance of you. I'm fine with you doing whatever you need to do with him, so long as no one finds out and you two are discreet, but what I want is your hand. I want to be the one to stand beside you. I want to be the one to be near you. I want to be the one to marry you. I've been by your side my whole life and now I'm gonna get shut out, why? Because you decided to like boys? No. That's not gonna happen."

I can't even process what she's proposing to me right now. I can't focus on anything. I'm so confused. I'm sweating and my neck feels all clammy. I want Sivan. What am I supposed to do?

CHAPTER 6
WE'RE PIRATES, VINCENT

Lying in my bed and looking at the clock feels almost painful. What was Vincent talking about? What did he mean that he'd been texting me? He still hasn't come by yet. I thought he would. What do I expect from him? What do I want from him? I can't even focus on this. I'm so upset. He looked good, too. So good. That little harlot was just running her mouth. I really hate that girl. Always getting in the way. I wonder if he's having fun at the bar? He must be, or else why isn't he here with me? I can picture it now…her arms draped around him, laughing at the bar. The thought sickens me. I need to get up, I need to go out. I can't let our first night together be spent apart. Not when I've waited to feel him for so long. I want to hold him. His scent was so soothing, and his skin was so soft. When my cheek brushed his during that brief whisper, I wanted so badly to kiss him. It was torturous. I need him. What can I do, though? If I go out, it won't be as if I can actually be with him. I'll have to pretend that we aren't together. I'll have to pretend that everything is fine. That I'm just another straight guy who's looking for girls. I really don't want to do that. There would be no way around it, though. But isn't it worth it? If I can pretend just a little, then I can maybe at least have Vincent all to myself later. I need to force myself up. Maybe if I shower again, I'll feel better.

Before I make it to the bathroom, my phone is vibrating in my hand. *Unknown caller.*

"Hello?"

"I wanted you to know that Vincent is not feeling well, so he's staying in with me tonight," Harlow says.

"What? Who is this?" I won't give her the satisfaction of knowing that I know it's her.

"This is Vincent's fiancée. I know that you know who I am, don't try to play dumb with me."

I end the call. The phone vibrates again in my hand. Same number. "What do you want?" I ask.

"Sivan? It's Vincent."

"What is happening?" I ask him.

"I wanted to tell you that Harlow and I got engaged. I… she…we…please don't go to the pub tonight," his voice is cracking with every word.

"Congratulations," I say. I toss my phone onto my bed and lie back down.

No. Why? Why would he do this? He doesn't want her. I know he doesn't. Something must have happened. Something to force him into this. I can't accept it.

I'm hurting, choking on words left unsaid, feelings unshared, but still, I want him. I'm chasing the feeling, that rush that I felt when we were together, that indescribable feeling, to feel it just once more is worth it.

I have to push through, because at the end of all this pain, there will be us. The two of us together, side by side. I know it.

He asked me not to go to the pub tonight, which means he doesn't want me to see them together.

I'm going to that pub. I'm taking what's mine.

I remove my day attire and quickly switch into my nighttime suit. I spritz my cologne on and head off the ship. I know which pub they've gone to. In fact, I can hear them now, rowdy bunch that they are. I hear my father and Captain Rodrigo laughing loudly, before I even see them. Where is Vincent? I don't see him. What I do see are a bunch of women, though. Hardly any men here, which is really saying something since both crews are dispersed inside and outside of the place.

There they are. Our fathers are sitting toward the back of the pub at a table. I see him. I see Vincent. I want him. I should be the one holding his hand, not her. Look at her over there. Pretending, knowing that he doesn't love her. But why then? Why is he doing this?

I push through the crowd and sit beside my father, across from Vincent and Harlow.

"Oh, Sivan! Glad you made it," my father says. He pats my leg and gives me a big smile.

I don't even look at Harlow once I sit down. My eyes are drawn to the only thing that matters to me right now—him.

A server walks over and puts two beers in front of my father and Captain Rodrigo. I don't remember her name, and they don't wear nametags here. "Can I get you something, Sivan? Rum?"

"Nah. I'm not really in the mood for anything. Rum seems to have lost its flavor."

My father looks at me in confusion for a moment, then smiles. "Oh! He had some kind of apple shots at his birthday party. Can you make something like that?" he asks the server.

She giggles. "I can make anything Sivan wants."

Rum-Soaked Awakenings

Vincent's head drops and I can see him squeezing his eyes shut.

"Rum has lost its flavor?" Captain Rodrigo asks me.

I'm staring at Vincent, my eyes haven't left him once, but he hasn't even looked up at me. I decide to answer his father. "Yeah, I tasted something even sweeter than rum, the last time I was with Vincent. I haven't been able to find anything comparable. I've been desperate to taste it again. I'm almost afraid of how much I want it."

"What the hell did you drink that tasted that good?" Captain Rodrigo asks me.

My father slides his beer over to me. "Take a sip. Was it this beer?"

I pick the bottle up, as the server comes behind me and whispers in my ear. "I get off at midnight, if you're interested." Now, Vincent is looking at me. I take a swig from the bottle, while we stare at one another. "Sorry. You're not my type," I tell the server.

"Don't take it personally," my father says to her. "He's like that with everyone."

Vincent is staring at me. His gaze is piercing, angry, or maybe full of anguish? I can't quite make it out. It's like he's angry, but certainly not at me.

My father looks in between the two of us, pointing. "What's going on, did you two have a fight? Or are you still feeling ill?"

My gaze is locked on Vincent as I reply, "I'm fine. I just need to use the restroom quickly."

There's a window inside the restroom that we've used to escape women more than a few times before. In the past, whenever one of us needed to get out of a situation, we'd share a look, then meet up in the bathroom, and slip outside unnoticed.

I stand and walk toward the restroom and hear Harlow's voice shouting something. I refuse to turn around. I know he'll follow me. I turn the doorknob and step inside. So many things still don't add up for me, but I know my best friend, he'll come.

"Harlow, back up!" I hear Vincent shout outside of the door. The door barely opens, but does just enough that I can see him, before a hand pulls it closed.

Harlow shouts, "Back up?! Why? So you can go in there with him? No. I don't think so."

He followed me. I knew he would. This little game she's playing with him ends now. I open the door and quickly pull him by the arm inside with 0me, then I lock the door.

Just thirty minutes ago, I had so much to say, and now with him standing so close, my hand on his forearm, I'm speechless. I only want one thing with him this close to me.

Vincent is moving in closer, his hand is sliding up my chest, while the other, cups my cheek. His lips are so close, I can practically taste him. The two of us are staring at one another, our bodies now pressed together while Vincent grabs a fistful of my shirt. I can't wait any longer. I press my mouth to his and kiss him. Vincent lets out the slightest whimper and it's only furthering this urgency I feel right now. My tongue brushes his softly, while his massages mine at a much stronger pace. I don't want to stop kissing him, I want more. I want to savor the taste of him.

Two loud bangs force us to separate. "Open this door!" Harlow shouts.

"You have to get out of here. I can explain later," Vincent says, pushing me toward the window.

I don't have time to think about the kiss we just shared when he's pushing me away. The two of us eye the window in the bathroom. "You want me to go out the window by myself? You just want to go back out there with her?"

He places his hands on my shoulders. "No. I want to be with you, Sivan."

He wants to be with me.

"You go first, she's not gonna wait much longer," he says. "She'll get Muffy to open the door."

I hop onto the counter and push the window open, squeezing out first. Then I jump down to the ground, while Vincent follows behind. We're on the opposite side of the pub, so we'll have to go around the back side to avoid running into anyone.

"Alright, we need to walk fast. We can't stay here. Where should we go?" Vincent asks, wiping his hands on his pants and straightening his bright red coat.

"Let's head back to my father's ship," I say.

"That's smart, it's the one place she really can't follow us," Vincent says.

We start walking quickly toward my father's ship, which is pretty close by. His hand is only a few inches from mine, as we walk side by side. We're not even talking, but Vincent seems really nervous. I want to protect him and make whatever is bothering him better. But I'm also mad and I want answers, but he's here with me, and in this moment, I only want to comfort him. "I want to hold your hand, but we can't chance someone seeing us. If anyone else were to find out…"

He takes my hand in his for just a moment and squeezes it, looking over his shoulders. "Well, I have news on that," he says.

"What news?"

"You're not gonna be happy, so brace yourself. But we're almost to the ship, maybe we should wait until we get in your room."

"Just tell me."

"Harlow has an audio recording of us—"

I have no idea what he's talking about. "Us? Us as in what?"

"Us as in—sex. She has audio of it."

"I don't remember having sex with you," I say snarkishly.

"Oh, right. Well, I suppose you wouldn't. Probably didn't mean anything to you. You always were the one that never caught feelings for anyone. Why should I be any different?" he asks me.

I sigh loudly. I normally enjoy our banter, but not right now. Not when I can tell there is real pain and real feelings buried in there.

I look left and right to be sure no one is around. There's a large beam holding up the empty vendor stand that's beside us. It's quite empty in the port right now. I press him quickly against the beam and bring my mouth in front of his, stopping before our lips touch. I suck his scent in through my mouth. I want to kiss him, but we haven't talked yet and there's still so much I don't understand. Our lips are less than a paper's width apart.

"Are you just going to stand there and not kiss me?" Vincent asks, his breath tickling me, while the sweet scent of him flutters across my lips.

Hovering my mouth even closer, I say, "I will not kiss you." My lip brushes against his, but it's enough to make him squirm. "I want to talk to you. I don't care about kissing you right now. Not when I need answers, and you just spouted all that bullshit."

He raises his eyebrows at me, almost challenging me. Our

bodies are pressed tightly together, with him up against the beam like this. He can feel that what I've said isn't true. I'm so hard right now. I most certainly do want to kiss him. I want much more than that. I crave him, desperately. My body is begging to feel him again. But I refuse to do this until I have some answers. I need to understand if what I'm feeling is one-sided. I step back. "I'm going home. If you want to join me, you can, but I'm interested in talking— despite what other areas of me seem to be doing."

He grabs my hand and quickly kisses it, before letting it go.

"What are you doing? Someone could see you," I whisper.

"There's no one around. Besides, did you hear what I said earlier? Harlow knows, she knows everything."

"I heard you, but before we talk about that, we're talking about us first."

He gives me a nod and looks down at the ground.

We walk silently toward my father's ship. Hands bumping into each other ever so slightly, with each step. I have no idea how Harlow could know everything. There's so much I need him to explain. I don't understand what happened with the texts while we were apart, and why did he call me with her to tell me they're engaged? My brain is struggling to try and piece things together, but it's best if he just explains it.

Stepping onto the ship, it's pretty empty. Vincent hasn't been in my room in a long time. Every year our fathers alternate whose ship the meetings will be held on. So, this year it's Captain Rodrigo's ship, for both meet-ups. Which means that Vincent hasn't been in my room in over a year. Good thing my cabin is always clean, but that's mostly thanks to Tilly. I walk down the corridor with Vincent behind me. I just want to talk, I remind myself. Just talk, nothing else. I need answers. I have to control myself. I open the door and gesture for Vincent to go inside, then I lock the door behind us.

Vincent's hands are on his hips. He glances at the bed, then back to me. He's unbelievable, but also damn sexy. I have to talk to him first, but for some reason, I can't recall any of the things I want to talk about, because he's currently taking his coat off, while maintaining intense eye contact. He's moving slowly, like beast in the woods, staring me over before he pounces, it's thrilling. He wants to give himself to me, and I want him to. I can't fight this feeling, especially when I can't even remember why I want to talk, or what I want to talk about. I only know that I want him, *now*.

He's moving closer to me, and my back is suddenly pressed against my door, while Vincent's body is closing in.

He places his hand on my chest and bites his lower lip. "Sivan…"

I swallow hard, momentarily unable to speak. I'm more turned on than I've ever been in my entire life. "I want to…talk," I say unconvincingly.

He is slightly smaller than me, but he's really coming on strong right now. I can't fight how turned on I am by it. My hands find his waist, and I squeeze, pulling him in tighter. We're both so hard, and there's no hiding that, when our bodies are crushed together like this. He slides his palm down the outside of my pants, feeling me. His breath hitches, as he grazes me gently with the back side of his hand. He whispers, "I'll ask you one more time. I promise to do whatever you say. Do you want to talk, or do you want me?"

"I want…you. I want all of you."

I grab his face and press our mouths together kissing him hard, sealing our lips together, our tongues quickly entwined.

The kiss is sloppy, wet, and delicious. I really missed the taste of him. He's rapidly unbuttoning my coat as I walk him backward toward my bed, our mouths never separating, our hands unable to stop undressing the other, clothes dropping to the floor. I need him. I pull his shirt open and lick along his neck. "I'm so fucking mad at you," I say.

He looks at me with eyes that seem to feel the same. "I'm mad at you, too, but I need you. I've been craving this for almost a year, give it to me."

He's fully unbuttoned my shirt and he's rubbing my chest. The back of his legs hit my bed, and he lies down, pulling me by my belt, urging me to climb atop him. Looking at him lying on my bed, his naked chest exposed; I'm completely entranced. He unbuckles my belt, his fingertips grazing the exposed skin just above it, sending chills up my spine. I slide my pants down, and grab the bottle of lube from my nightstand, while he takes his pants off, kicking them to the foot of the bed. Every piece of this man is perfect, how is it that I never noticed all these years? He's beautiful. My dick is rock hard, and sticky with precum. I squeeze the lube on my fingers, massaging it around his tight little rim. This ass is perfect, it was made for me. I gently tease him, pressing my finger in and out, slowly stretching him, until he's panting and moaning, riding my finger, a beautiful sexy mess, ready for me to devour. I need to be inside of him. I slowly drive my cock inside. "You're so tight, it feels—so good."

He winces a bit as my cock fully slips inside. I press our mouths together, again, and hold his face with one hand. Fuck. I really like kissing him.

Vincent parts his legs wider and moans, pulling back from the kiss. "Yes—fuck—ohhhh, fuck."

The way he makes me feel… I was desperate, lost, and

thirsty before him. He is my water, he is my life, he is, fuck—he is all of it. He is mine.

I thrust harder, working my hips back and forth. His eyes are closed, and I'm ready to come. Watching his mouth hang open and hearing his dirty little moans makes my balls tighten. I lean down and kiss him again, this time it's softer, sweeter. Does he know how much he means to me? I feel the pressure building, ready to release. "Fuck—Vincent, do you want me to pull out?"

He pulls my face closer, wrapping his legs around me, "No, but kiss me."

I bring my mouth to his and kiss him, while he moans, and squeezes my face. His pelvis jerks upward, and I feel his cum shooting onto my abs, while his cock is trapped in between us. The feeling pushes me over the edge, and I come deep inside him. "Holy fuck—Vincent." I drop my head onto the pillow next to his face, kissing his cheek, panting, just trying to catch my breath.

I slide out and lie beside him. The room is still and quiet for a few minutes, but our breaths are rapid. I feel like I can finally exhale, now that he's beside me again.

"Sivan," he says softly, turning toward me, while placing a hand on my cheek.

"Yeah?"

"I need to tell you this…I can't find the words, though. You need to know what happened."

"I do want to know what happened, but first tell me something. Did you really text me while we were apart, and did you really not get any of my texts?"

"Of course, I texted you. I called, too. A few times I asked my dad if he knew what was going on, he said your father told him you were upset, so I figured it was because of me, and you were ignoring me on purpose. I never got any texts from you."

I kiss his lips softly. "I was not ignoring you. I didn't get any texts, or calls. I was texting and doing the same things. I was terrified that my dad would pick up on something happening between us, so I was really careful in asking if he knew anything. He was useless every time. He didn't even know what happened when you passed out. I don't understand why I wasn't allowed to see you after that."

He shakes his head side to side. "I don't know, I don't remember much. I just slept for like four days and when I woke up, meetings were over, and you were gone. Matteo stayed with me pretty much 24/7 to make sure Harlow stayed away."

Something about that isn't sitting right with me. Matteo had never tried to keep her away from him before. It probably had more to do with him keeping us apart.

"Did the doctor say everything was fine after? Has it happened again?"

"All good, I think. I do get dizzy every now and then, but it's usually only if I'm really stressed out. Earlier today with Harlow, I felt really lightheaded, and dizzy, but I'd just had a fight with Matteo, then she came in and just—"

"Somehow convinced you to propose?"

"I didn't propose. I would never."

"Then what happened? Why did I get a call from you telling me you were engaged? Do you know how much that hurt? Fuck, it felt like my heart was being ripped apart from the inside. I know you won't go through with it, but how did this happen?"

He's not saying anything, but there are tears forming in the corners of his eyes.

"I can't," he squeaks out. "I can't stop it. You'll be ruined if she tells anyone, Sivan. If anyone hears that audio; your future, our fathers, our ships, everything will be ruined."

I can't believe this. Is he really trying to tell me he's going to marry her? "No, no. You can't be serious? You just... How can you think this is a good idea? How can you be willing to go through with this? No, Vincent."

"I have to do this for you. For us. She said that we can still be together, she said she won't interfere."

I sit up against my headboard. "What does that mean? How can we be together if you're married to her? I can't do it. No. You can't marry her, Vincent. We have to stop this. Please? Don't do this. You're agreeing to marry her?! Do you even understand what that means?"

He takes my hand softly. He doesn't seem as angry as I am, but his hands are shaking. "She knows everything, Sivan, and she'll tell. Please, please understand that there is no other recourse. There is no other way out. She said she won't care what we do as long as I keep the appearance of being her husband in public."

"Oh my God, Vincent. Listen to what you're saying. You're not keeping up an appearance if you are legally married! You would be legally married, it's not just for show. She's manipulated you. Do you even understand what you're asking me? You're asking me to just be a side piece for the rest of my life? While you two have babies and get married? No. I can't do it. I won't let you."

"You don't have a choice. I will not let her ruin your life. She will destroy you. She is cold and calculating. I know this better than anyone else. She has the audio of us having sex on her phone, Sivan. For shit's sake, listen to me. Be rational about this. I'm doing this for you, I won't let her hurt you."

I stand from my bed and put my underwear on. I need a shower, and I can't even do that right now. "Who asked you to worry about me? Who asked you to do this? Did I ever ask you to protect me? Damn it. I don't need your protection, Vincent. I need—I need you. Do you think I could honestly handle seeing her as your wife? You say you'll marry her for appearances, but what does that mean for your body, for your mind? You're not thinking this through. What will she do? Just allow you to sleep there without any emotional or physical connection? She'll just let you basically be numb? No, she's not going to stop at that. What about kids Vincent? Will you have kids? Will she be the mother to your children? While I'm treated like some common side-whore? No. This isn't right."

"I...I hadn't thought of that before. We didn't get that deep into details. She let me hear the audio, threatened to ruin the both of us, and I agreed to do what she wanted. What would you have done? What would you do if someone was threatening to ruin me? If they had the same evidence that Harlow had?"

"I for damn sure wouldn't give into her. We don't give into people that threaten us, we stand up to them. We're pirates, Vincent. You know this from captaincy lessons, it's the same principle. You're suggesting that you marry her and I become someone on the side. You're suggesting that the first person that I've ever lo—" I cover my mouth with my hand. What is wrong with me? What was I about to say? What would even make me think such a thing? Do I love him?

"Sivan," he says softly. "What are you saying to me? You realize how this sounds? You haven't expressed any of these fears or these feelings to me until now. I had no idea you would feel this way. Wait…were you about to say that you love me?"

I think I may be sick. Is this really what love feels like? "I don't know how I feel, I really don't. I just know that I've been miserable. While we were apart, I thought of nothing else but you. I didn't want to eat, I didn't want to sleep, I only wanted you. There were friends who tried to comfort me, despite not knowing what was wrong. They assumed it was because of the captaincy lessons; it wasn't. I'm prepared to be a captain, I've been ready for it for years, but you and me, I was not prepared for us. I just—I don't want to be with anyone else, ever again."

"What do you mean 'with anyone else'?"

"The things that we're doing with each other. Sex, our friendship, all of it. I won't ever want to be with another person. My body only wants you. My soul only wants you. There are no other feelings left. What else can I do but to be honest with you?"

He reaches toward the bottom of the bed and grabs his briefs, sliding into them. He stands up, and now he's walking toward me. What did I just say to him?

He takes my hands in his. "Sivan, ever since we kissed, I have wanted no one other than you. You have been the only one, the only one that I need. I had no idea I could feel this way for you, but after we slept together, everything felt right. I saw you differently, I felt differently. I want to take you and keep you for myself. I had no idea what you were feeling while we were apart. I want you the same way that you want me. I want us, but I can't do this to you. It will ruin you. *She* will ruin you. She will ruin *us.*" He's cupping my face with both hands. "Please, please listen to me. This is the only way."

He turns me into a version of myself that I don't even

recognize. I'm so soft for him. I kiss the inside of both his hands. I only want to make things better. I'm running through ideas so rapidly in my mind, each one is a worse idea than the last. "Wait, what if we get her phone from her? Wouldn't that solve everything?"

He tilts his head at me, placing his hands on his hips. "Well, I hadn't thought of that, but, I mean, she still knows, and that's not going to solve anything if she's sent it to someone already. I also have no idea what device she used to record it on. Could have been anything." He shrugs his shoulders, like what he just said was totally fine.

"What do you mean you don't know? You don't know what she recorded you on? What if it's still in your room, Vincent?"

"Oh, yeah, I didn't think of that."

See, in these moments, though, the softness goes away, and it has to, because at the end of the day, he's still my best friend. "Well, what the hell have you thought of? The girl proposes that you get married, then tries to blackmail you, and you just agree without any thought? Come on, Vincent, you're smarter than this."

He looks at the floor, then back up to me. "I'm not, though; you've always been the smart one. My head is a mess right now. I can't think. Since we've been apart, I've been a fucking mess, snapping at people, crying like a child. It's been awful. I can barely process what's happening."

I'm kind of glad that I wasn't the only one. I've never felt so battered and bruised because of another person. I still don't know how this happened. "I was so sad and mad at you, but those feelings, the months apart, they mean nothing, because you're here now, and we have to find a way to fix this."

"So, what do we do now? Do we try and get the phone?"

"Haven't figured that out yet. But she's always around you, I'm sure you could easily grab the phone, but that doesn't solve the problem of the recording device, whatever it may be. It could just be the phone she recorded with, but I doubt that. She wouldn't just leave her phone in your room. At least I don't think so."

"Yeah, well, what if I just ask her?"

I shake my head side to side in absolute awe of how dense he is sometimes. "Vincent, why would she just willingly tell you? She's not stupid."

"I don't know, isn't there a way I could ask it that sounds…not stupid?"

"No, there most definitely is not. I think the phone has to come first. You could get that easily. Just snatch it from her miserable hands. After that, we can figure out where the recording came from."

"Isn't that even more unrealistic than me trying to ask her about the device? I think I need to find out where the device is, because like you said, she could just continue recording me, and she probably has been this whole time."

"Yeah, okay. Maybe that is smarter. Plus, since she's had the recording for this long, then she's likely not going to share it with anyone since you already agreed to do whatever she wanted."

"I think you're right; the trouble is I have agreed to go along with her plan. She made sure everyone knew about it tonight. How do I fix this? I don't want to marry her." He flops onto the bed, clearly exhausted.

A year ago, if he had agreed to marry someone for reasons he felt were noble, I probably would have laughed at him. He really doesn't think things through sometimes. "I…I don't know.

I'm trying to figure it out. You're not going through with it. That much I can promise."

"Well, if you say you can fix it, then let's not talk about it anymore. All this talk about her has exhausted me, well, that and the sex. I don't want to keep going over it."

I scoff at him and drop an eyebrow down. "Who's in charge here? You or me? I thought in a relationship one person is in charge, like the captain?" I ask, standing beside the bed.

"No one is in charge, and what even is our relationship? You haven't told me. What are we calling this? Will we ever be able to have a real relationship? I'm afraid that we'll always have to hide this. But keeping it hidden means that you won't suffer, it means that you'll be protected. It means that our father's lives won't be ruined, the trade alliance will remain strong…it means all of those things, but I—"

I cut him off quickly. "Then what am I to you? You expected to come here and have me agree to be your secret—whatever, then you don't want to talk about it, and now you're asking me what our relationship is. What the hell am I supposed to do with all of this, Vincent?" Damn it, I'm crying. I didn't want to cry. Why does this keep happening to me? I squeeze my eyes shut, trying to hold the tears back, but I can't.

"No. You can't be crying. Why are you so upset?" He flips his legs out of bed, and walks toward me, quickly. "I don't think I've ever seen you cry. How did I make you so upset?"

"Why am I so upset? I want to be with you. You're making me pour my feelings out, feelings that I don't understand and have never felt before, that's why I'm crying. I'm so frustrated. I want to be the one standing by your side. She does not deserve that." I swallow hard, trying to compose myself. "She can't have you."

He's wiping the corners of my eyes. "She could never."

Vincent's pants are at the foot of the bed, his phone rings loudly from within the pocket. He closes his eyes and doesn't bother trying to look at it, ignoring the incessant ringing.

"Probably her," I say. "I'm gonna get in the shower and cool off. You wanna join me?"

"You and me, naked and wet, yes."

I grab two towels out from beneath the vanity, hanging them on both hooks outside of the shower. I've never put a second towel out for anyone before. There were times I'd look at that hook and wonder what the hell its purpose was. It always felt so silly having an extra hook there. It was empty and just looked out of place. It's weird because the bathroom has always felt like it was missing something, but now, looking at the two navy blue towels side by side, there's something strangely comforting about it. I can see its purpose. It's like a puzzle piece just fell into place. Has he always been the missing piece for me? As I try to understand my feelings, old memories rapidly resurface, I'm flooded with remembrances of the fun we've always had, but the memories look different now; they've changed. Before, I just saw Vincent, my best friend, and now I see *him*. I see his dimples, his gorgeous white smile, I hear his infectious laugh, and I'm starting to realize that I've only ever been truly happy when he's around. I thought I only wanted to protect him because we'd slept together, that the sex had changed me, but no, it didn't, I've always felt this way. I just couldn't see it. I was so programmed to like girls, that if I had just taken a step back and thought for myself, I would have realized sooner.

I feel Vincent's hands on my waist and his forehead pressed in between my shoulders. He kisses my back softly. "You, okay?"

I turn around and wrap him in my arms. He nuzzles his face against my chest, inhaling deep.

Holding him is so comforting. All of the uncertainty I feel melts away when I hold him like this, chest to chest, skin to skin. I can feel his heart beating against me, and for some reason, it soothes me. "I thought you were the weak one," I say rubbing his back.

"What?" He laughs. "I mean, I am weak, but it's more like I'm weak for you. I don't think you understand what you've done to me. If I'm weak it's your fault." He kisses my chest. "I'm feeling the same things as you. I tried to think of anything else when you were gone, but everything came back to you. Nothing felt right without you." He lifts his head from my chest and holds my waist. He's looking at me with the same look he gets before he has a really bad idea. "Can't we just pretend nothing is happening and just be together in secret? Can't we do that? Just—who cares about Harlow and the engagement? She doesn't want my love or the attention, she just wants the appearance. I want to be with you."

"That's a terrible idea. Why should she get to stand beside you? That's not the answer."

He sighs. "I know, I know. Let's just shower, maybe after we're clean we'll think better."

I turn the water on hot and we both step inside, sliding the glass door closed. I pass him a washcloth from the shower caddy. "Thanks," he says.

I grab the shampoo and clean my hair, then pass it to Vincent, whose naked body is very close to mine. I laugh and Vincent peeks an eye open while lathering up his hair.

"What? What happened?" he asks, wiping the suds from his eye with the back of his hand.

"Nothing, I can't believe that you're in the shower with me, and just—everything. I think I laughed because I'm just so happy with you near me." I scrub myself with the soapy cloth, washing every piece, under Vincent's gaze.

We're eyeing each other's bodies, silently. The dark hair on Vincent's legs is even sexier when he's wet, how is that possible? How can leg hair look sexy?

"I'm happy, too," he says, "but you know, I realized why I don't know how to fix this situation. I think I figured out what's missing."

I finish scrubbing my body down and stand under the shower head, getting all the soap off. "What's missing?"

He shows me his forearms. "The tattoos. If only I had the tattoos, I'd know how to fix this."

"You're a genius, I hadn't even thought of that."

We both laugh as I try to swap places with him, so he can rinse under the shower head. Brushing past each other is a bit tight, because whoever made this shower did not do so with the intention that two men would be using it at the same time. I don't know how I'm expected to keep my hands to myself when his naked body is this close to mine. He turns to the side with his ass facing me, shimmying past me sideways. My dick brushes over his ass, while the water rains over our bodies. He pauses for a moment, and I hold him gently in place. The water suddenly turns cold, and Vincent is still covered in soap.

"Cold, cold, cold, holy shit! Why is the water cold?!" he shouts.

I press the handle all the way to hot, as far as it will go, and it helps to warm the water, but barely. "Ah, sorry! I have no idea. Just rinse off, and I'll let you borrow some clothes when you're finished."

I open the shower door and grab my towel. I see his towel there, alone on the hook, and I instantly feel cold. What do I do? Would it really be so bad if everyone found out about us? I don't want him to leave tonight. I don't even know if he's planning on sleeping over.

VINCENT

"I'm freezing, Sivan!" I slide the shower door open, wrap the towel around my waist and walk quickly into his room.

Sivan is standing in a comfy looking pair of black sweatpants, and he's shirtless. His body is incredible. I really wanted to have sex in the shower, but there wasn't that much room, aside from that, the water dropping to freezing, definitely put any thoughts of shower fun to rest.

I haven't asked him if I could stay the night. I assume it's fine, but do I ask? Or do I just stay? I don't even have any extra clothes with me. If we weren't sleeping together, and this were last year, I'd just stay, so why do I feel the need to ask now? We've both said we don't want to be without each other, so maybe asking is stupid. Still, we haven't defined what we are to one another, and that's okay, because I don't know what to call it. Whatever I suggest will probably be wrong, anyway. I really thought giving into Harlow was the smartest decision, and now I'm questioning why I thought that.

Sivan slides open a drawer in his dresser and smiles at me.

"Are you staying the night with me? Or do you want to go back to your ship?"

Thank God I didn't have to ask. "I want to stay with you. I don't want to go back there. If the ceremony wasn't at the end of the week, I'd be tempted to just go back home with you, and tell my father I need a break, call off the thing with Harlow, and see how things play out. But then I'd still have to pretend that we were just friends. Plus, all the shit with the Captain Slicer rumors would still have to be dealt with. There's so much going on right now, and I just want to focus on us."

Sivan's eyes are wide. He's digging around in his drawers. "I thought you were gonna say that you wanted to leave. I was fully prepared to beg." He pumps his eyebrows at me. "I have to dry my hair real fast, before we get into bed." He hands me a pair of sweatpants similar to his, but gray. "Do you want underwear, too, or just go without tonight?"

I don't even know what the right thing to say is. On one hand I'm free-balling in his sweats, and on the other I'm wearing his underwear. "Hmm…I don't usually sleep with underwear on, unless I pass out or something." He nods at me with a smile that I can't quite read. Sometimes I hate not being better at reading people. Why does it come so naturally to others?

"If you change your mind or decide you want a shirt, the top drawer has underwear, and shirts are in the middle drawer."

"Thanks. Sorry I didn't bring any extra clothes with me."

Sivan laughs. "Why would you apologize for that? You didn't know you'd be spending the night with me. It's not a big deal. You can borrow whatever you want." He smiles at me softly then points to the bathroom door. "I gotta dry my hair now, or it's gonna look like shit tomorrow."

"Do you want my help?" Why did I ask him that? I really am an idiot.

"Your help?" He raises an eyebrow at me. "You're still in your towel, so what are you offering to help me with?"

"I don't know. I thought maybe you might want me to dry your hair for you. I was thinking about the last time we were together when you let me put your hair up. Just forget I even asked. I'll get dressed and wait for you in your bed."

His eyes have a sparkle in them that warms me from the inside out. "You can dry my hair if you want. Doesn't take long. You don't dry yours, right? Just let it air dry?"

"Oh, no hair dryer for me. My hair wouldn't like that." I follow him toward his bathroom, but stop before going in, so that I can get dressed. I hop into the sweatpants and carry the wet towel into the bathroom. I see his towel hanging on the hook on the wall. I hang mine on the hook beside his. He's watching me intently, almost studying me. Maybe I shouldn't have put the towel on the hook. Shit, why am I getting so nervous with him all of a sudden? I grab the center of the towel and make eye contact with him. "Does this not belong here? I saw yours there, so I assumed that's where mine would go."

"You're absolutely right." He chuckles a bit and grabs the hair dryer from under the sink.

Damn, he's hot. I don't know what he's laughing about, but his laugh makes me tingle in places that I never thought a laugh could. For years I've watched girls throw themselves at him, I've seen their eyes light up when he talked to them, and now I finally understand what they were seeing. When he smiles at me, it's like the entire world around me disappears. It's captivating in a way that I don't fully understand. All I know is I would go to the ends of the earth for him. I'd give up everything I have to be the one that makes him smile. I shake my head at myself, but I came to terms with my feelings for him pretty quickly after we slept together. There was no one else I wanted, nothing else that could compare to the way that I felt with him. Seemed kind of inevitable once I was honest with myself.

He shakes the dryer at me. "You still wanna help me?"

"Of course, let's do it." I follow him out of the bathroom, watching as he plugs the dryer in and sits in the center of his bed. This is gonna be a problem for me. I was already thinking about sex when we were in the shower, before the shock of the damn water, but now he's shirtless and on the bed. But, no, I have to dry his hair, that's what I said I was gonna do, despite the feelings I'm having. People talk about butterflies in their stomach, but what's it called when you feel tingly in other places? I don't have butterflies in my stomach, I have something else—butterflies in my balls, maybe? Pftt. He gives me butterfly balls. That's something I'll never say aloud. Thank God for internal thoughts. I climb onto the bed and sit behind him. He scoots back against me in between my legs, and I back up a little. I turn the dryer on and start drying his thick brown hair. "How is your hair so healthy? It's so soft," I say, as I run my fingers through it.

He looks over his shoulder at me. "Your hair is healthy, too. Why wouldn't mine be?"

"Because I take care of mine. I just took a shower with you, you don't even use any conditioner. The shampoo cleans it, but the conditioner is what nourishes it."

He shrugs and the muscles in his back are on full display. "I didn't know that. Do you think I need it?"

I laugh. "Well, you should use it, but I'm not a hair expert.

Your hair is pretty healthy, so maybe you don't need it." I'm finding it really hard to focus on drying his hair when his broad shoulders are on full display. I wonder if my back looks as good as his. I push my shoulders back and try and look behind at myself. I can't see anything, though.

"Ouch, what are you doing? You just dropped the dryer on my head."

Whoops. "I didn't drop it; I was just looking at something and it hit you. Sorry." I run my fingers through his hair, continuing to dry it.

"It's okay. You know, we haven't talked about the ceremony. It's only a few days away. Are you nervous?" he asks me.

The ceremony—what the hell is that going to look like? I really hope I can fix this before then. "Nah, I'm not really nervous. I just wish we could put it on hold for a little while. I want to be captain, but I just don't wanna deal with the other stuff. The tattoos, Harlow, the fact that I have to hide my feelings for you. I don't want to do any of that."

"Why do we have to hide the way we feel? My whole life everyone's been trying to sell the idea of relationships to me, now that I feel…*something*, I have to hide it. Why should I have to do that? Why does anyone care? Do we even know that anyone would care?"

I want to point out to him that we still haven't defined our relationship, but I'm not sure if I should. I run my hands through his already-dry hair, then kiss his back, in between his shoulders.

"Well…as for our dads, they probably wouldn't care. Sometimes I think they've had a few rounds between the two of them."

He turns around to face me. "What? Are you serious? I never got that impression."

I pass him the hair dryer and fall back onto his pillows. "I don't know. They shared underwear, seems kind of strange for two friends that haven't ever slept together to do that."

He pulls his mouth to the side and walks into the bathroom with the hair dryer. "I was gonna let you borrow my underwear."

"Exactly, and would you even have offered that to me before we slept together?"

"No. Definitely not," he says, walking back toward the bed.

I scoot from the middle of the bed to the side, making room for him.

Sivan lies beside me on his back, and I instinctively scoot closer to him. The last time we spent the night in the same bed I can't remember how we fell asleep, or what our positioning was. I don't know if we held each other, but I need to be closer to him. He lifts his arm up like it's the most natural thing in the world. I tuck myself beside him and lay my head on his thick, hard chest. I've never laid on anyone else like this, and I can't remember letting any girl do it to me either, but I like it.

"Have you always thought they slept together? Or did you just start thinking that after we did it?" he asks me.

"I don't know…something about them has always seemed like they did. But after we did it, I started to really wonder if they could have, too. Either way, I don't think our dads would be mad if we wanted to be together."

Sivan rubs the back of my head. "So, if our dads wouldn't be mad, then who are we worrying about finding out?"

I hate this question, because I've thought about it every day since we slept together. Thinking that there are people that would judge us just for being together is so fucking stupid. Our dads are responsible for changing history, they're known for turning piracy on its head, why should Sivan and I be any different? "Well, I think that tradesman, other pirates, and people who expect us to marry women would care."

"Fuck them. Who cares?"

"Yeah, there's always a chance that no one cares about us, and everything stays the same. I could be wrong about our dads, though. Matteo sure as hell thinks my dad would have a problem with it."

Sivan is silent, but I feel a bit of a change in his breathing, it's subtle, but it feels like he's almost holding in a breath. I lift my head from his chest. "What is it?"

"I don't want to talk bad about him because he's like a brother to you."

My eyes widen. "Certainly doesn't stop him from talking bad about you."

He looks down at me. "He talks bad about me?"

"Not exactly bad, but kind of, yeah. He has this crazy theory that he's been spewing. It's not important." I rub my hand on his abs, gently exploring the ridges. I shouldn't have said that. I lift my head from his chest. "Don't worry about it. Who cares what Matteo thinks?"

"What kind of stuff does he say?"

I stand up from the bed and grab my phone out of my pants pocket. It's easier if I just show him. Plus, my phone has been going off non-stop, and although Sivan thinks it's Harlow, it's more likely Matteo. I lay back down in bed beside Sivan, scooting in close again, while holding my phone up so we can both look at it. The notifications bar shows a bunch of missed texts and even a few calls from Matteo. But none from Harlow, which is surprising. I unlock it and open the long stream of texts from Matteo.

"You don't have to show me your texts with him," Sivan says.

"I kind of do, though, because it will be easier to explain this way. I don't mind. Here, let's go back to right around the time you left." I scroll up, finding the first text that he sent after Sivan left. We'd had an argument before he sent it.

He used you. Stop getting so upset.

Sivan's eyes widen. "He's talking about me?"

"Mmhmm." I nod and continue scrolling.

Vincent, you're being ridiculous.

Do you think he's stupid? You know how smart he is.

I try to make a joke because Sivan's body temperature has risen at least a few degrees since we started looking at these, and his jaw is clenched so tight that I'm afraid he might crack a tooth. I can literally feel the heat coming off him. "At least he called you smart in this one," I say with a smile. Sivan isn't laughing, though.

"Can I see that?" he asks.

"Sure." I pass the phone to him, as he sits up against the headboard. He's just scrolling silently. He looks angrier than I think I've ever seen him look before. Even angrier than earlier when we were talking about the engagement.

"Tch. So, what, he thinks that I slept with you to manipulate you? Did he forget that we're best friends? I can't understand why he'd come up with something that makes no sense. What would I have to gain by sleeping with you if not just personal enjoyment?"

"I have no idea, but the whole time we were apart, it was pretty constant. Well, as you can see from the texts."

His brows are drawn tightly together, while he continues scrolling through the messages.

"That sucks. I wasn't expecting anything like this from him. I'm just not sure what he stands to gain by telling you this shit. He really doesn't want us together, I guess. I mean, that much is obvious. You know, when you passed out, he looked at me like it was my fault. He wouldn't let me go with you, which drew our fathers into it. They were urging me to sit down, then Harlow's mother came in, and I was forced to stay behind. The whole thing still doesn't sit well with me."

"I didn't know that happened. I'm sorry for that." Of course, I didn't do anything wrong, but Sivan's face is a mixture of sadness, confusion, and a little bit of anger. I don't want him to feel any of those things. My phone vibrates in his hand. Oh shit. Another text from Matteo.

If he brings up combining crews, you need to leave. You have to trust me.

"Why wouldn't I bring up combining crews? Of course I want to combine crews. We can't do it, but why wouldn't I ask that? What the hell is he playing at?" He passes my phone back to me. "I'm done looking at them."

I put the phone on the small nightstand beside the bed and sit up beside him. He looks so pissed off right now. "Hey," I say, turning his face gently toward mine. "I don't care what Matteo says. Don't worry about it." I climb atop him straddling him and he pulls me in close. I kiss his lips softly, as our eyes meet in a desperate stare. He holds my face in his hands and presses our lips together, gently touching my tongue with his. I close my eyes and melt completely into the kiss, as our tongues caress each other. I love kissing Sivan, he tastes like rum, and I have no idea how that's possible because he hasn't had any rum tonight. He teases my bottom lip with his teeth, gently tugging it, sending shockwaves through my body, making me harden faster than I ever thought possible.

He pulls back from the kiss. "Vincent, I want to be inside of you again. Will you let me?" He kisses my forehead softly, with my face cradled in his hands. He's treating me so delicately. I wouldn't have expected this from him.

"I want you, too," I say, gently rocking back and forth on him. I don't know if I'd be good at riding him, honestly, but it feels so good rubbing our dicks together in this position, even through our sweatpants. Sivan's hands grip my ass, squeezing tight. "Fuck—Vincent, I hadn't imagined taking you like this. You want to try it?"

"We can try, but I don't know if I can do it."

He lifts my chin with his thumb. "Something tells me you can take it."

I don't know what it was about him saying that, but his tone changed, there was a shift, it felt almost dominant. Fuck, thoughts of him talking dirty to me are running rampant in my mind, my dick is almost leaking at the notion that Sivan could talk dirty to me. I stand up from the bed and take my sweats off, while Sivan pulls his down, and grabs the lube from the top of the nightstand. "Come here and let me play with you, Vincent." My balls are fucking tight, and he hasn't even touched me yet. How can I crave him this badly? His cock is so thick and hard, I'm practically drooling over it. when he makes a "come here" motion with his finger. The first time we had sex, he sucked me a bit and it was absolutely mind-blowing. I don't know if it's that he was really good at it, or just that his mouth was on my dick, but either way, I really liked it. I climb into bed and position myself in between his legs, running my hand quickly up his hard shaft.

His hand runs slowly through my hair, he lightly grips a handful. "Oh, you want to taste me before we fuck?"

I nod slowly, looking up at him, with his dick in my hand.

He grips my hair tighter, tilting my head back. "Open your pretty little mouth and show me your tongue."

Holy shit, I never thought being on the receiving end of dirty talk would get me so fucking turned on. I lick the tip of his head, swirling my tongue around. There's not much taste, probably because we just showered, but it's warm and so fucking hard. I grip the base and lick slowly up the side of his shaft, massaging his balls, while his grip tightens in my hair. I'm just doing the things I like done to me, I have no idea if I'm doing them right. As I take him into my mouth, he lets out a moan that makes my dick weep.

"Mmm—Vincent—your mouth feels fucking incredible. You have no idea how many times I jerked off imagining you sucking my cock, while we were apart."

Damn, the thought of him touching himself only furthers my want to satisfy him. I slide my mouth up and down working up a slow, but consistent, rhythm. His dick is so thick that I feel like I may gag on it if I go too fast. Sivan's fingers alternate between gripping and rubbing my hair while I suck him as deep as I can. I do want to taste him, though, and to do that, I'm gonna have to make him come. I just realized there may be a downside of having been best friends before doing these things, and that's because at this moment I remember Sivan telling me that he'd never come from a blowjob before. He described them as feeling good, but not as good as sex. He said something like a blowjob was more just a prelude for him. Now, I'm determined to make him come. I can't think about anyone else's mouth ever having been on this perfect dick. I pop his cock out momentarily and jerk it, while flicking my tongue on the head.

"Mnnnggg" sound escapes from his lips, it's somewhere between a grunt and a moan. "Fuck, your mouth was made for my cock." He grips my hair tight. "Don't stop."

He's breathing heavier than before; I think he may be close to coming. I look up at him and lick his balls slowly, so he can see my tongue. When we kiss, he seems to really like my tongue, he's almost fixated on it. My cock is so hard, and I'm aching to be touched, too, but I want him to come. I jerk him harder and faster, then slide all of him back into my mouth, taking his cock deep, again. "Mmmm," I moan. He clearly loves the sensation, because I finally get a taste of something slightly salty, and delicious. It's precum and it's unbelievably hot. I'm sucking harder, chasing that fucking taste. I want more.

He squeezes my hair tight, and his thighs tighten against me. I can feel him fighting, but I don't know why. I pull his dick out, and lock eyes with him. "Do it, come for me. Let me taste you." I wrap my lips around him again, moaning, and slurping on his cock, and I finally feel his pelvis jerk upward, his cock nearly chokes me, while he pulls a fistful of my hair. "Fuck—I'm coming—hah—I'm fucking coming."

My mouth is flooded with spurts of hot wet cum, as Sivan fucks my face until he finishes. I pull his dick out, kissing the tip one more time, then lick my lips, which are still coated with the taste of him. He grabs me under my arms, hauling me on top of him, and crushes my mouth together with his, sticking his tongue inside, swirling it around wildly. "Mmm," I moan, as he manhandles my mouth with his, and holds my face in place. With one hand he grips the back of my hair gently, while the other grabs the small bottle of lube on the bed. He releases my hair, but he's still kissing me, while I feel him fumbling with the bottle and hear the sound of the liquid being squeezed out. He grips my waist with one hand and soon I feel him reaching underneath me, and a slippery finger massaging my asshole. His dick is still hard in between us, while mine is sticky with precum, ready to fucking blow as soon as he slides his finger halfway inside. Being fingered like this feels even more exciting than when I'm on my back. He works his finger in and out, then slides another beside it, circling my rim, gently teasing me until he slides both inside. He hits that spot that he hit before, and I shiver, the pleasure is almost too intense. I push on his chest separating from the kiss, breathless. "Hahhh—that—"

"That's your spot. If I do this"—he glides his fingertips over it, fingers deep inside of me—"how does that feel?" He raises his eyebrows at me. "You like that?"

I nod and bury my face in the crook of his neck, lightly sucking on it. How the hell does this feel so good? I'm riding his fingers, panting, licking, sucking, desperate for more, while he pumps them in and out. "Fuck me," I whisper.

He grabs the lube once more, coating his cock with it. He jerks it a few times, and I do the same to mine. I want to come so bad.

Sivan positions his dick, pressing it against my entrance, and I wince at the initial stretch, when his head enters me. If I could skip this part and get straight to the part where it feels good, I'd really like that, because when his fat cock head fully slips inside, I can't help but to grip his chest, scratching it.

He kisses my lips softly. "I'll go slow. Don't try to rush it."

"Okay, just kiss me."

He presses our lips together, while slowly lowering me onto

his cock. He's guiding me gently by my waist, lifting me up and down, while my ass clings to him.

"How is that?" he asks me.

"Getting better, just feels—deep."

"We don't have to keep going if you're uncomfortable."

"Sivan, it's uncomfortable now, but in a few minutes, it won't be uncomfortable anymore. Just fuck me."

He grips my waist tighter and starts working me at a faster pace, and I'm finally able to move with him, finding a comfortable rhythm.

"Look at you," he says, brushing the sweaty strands of hair from my face. "You're so sexy when you're riding my cock." His hand trails down my chest finding my dick. He tugs it a few times, while I bounce on him. "You know what I noticed?" he says, bouncing me harder, driving in deeper.

I'm panting, out of breath, not really able to have a conversation, while he's pounding relentlessly into me. "What? Haah—what did you—notice?"

"Any time I start fucking you harder, your dick responds, it's begging me to wreck you."

I feel my dick jump. He isn't wrong.

Sivan's eyebrows raise. "See? You like it rough."

I bring my mouth near his earlobe and whisper, "Then fuck me. Fuck me harder than you've ever fucked anyone. I made you come with my mouth. Give me my reward. Make me come."

Sivan slaps both sides of my ass and lifts me off him. "Bend over."

I shuffle over, leaning on my knees and elbows, feeling immediately empty as soon as he pulls out. I feel slightly embarrassed in this position, but before I can decide whether to protest, I feel his warm hand in the middle of my back.

He forcefully grips one of my ass cheeks, and slides his dick back inside of me. "Damn. Look how good you take my cock." He squeezes my ass, letting out a moan that's low and deep. "Mmm—fuck you harder than I've ever fucked anyone—that's what you said."

"Yes. I want you to."

Sivan's hips draw back slowly, his dick gliding in and out, while my ass clings to it. "You really want that?" he asks.

"Yyy—yes." I'm quickly rewarded with hard, fierce thrusting. My body is being jerked back and forth as Sivan pounds into me. "Fuck, Sivan—yes—holy shit." The sound of his balls smacking into me while I'm being absolutely torn apart is the filthiest symphony I've ever heard, and I fucking love it. My balls tighten, as this animalistic fucking brings me closer to orgasm.

"Tell me, Vincent," he says as his pace slows. "Is this what you wanted to happen? Did you want to be fucked by your best friend today?"

I nod my head, pushing back against his cock.

He smacks my ass. "Yeah? Did you wake up this morning dreaming about this big cock inside of you?"

I didn't know I would like to be spanked but fuck that was hot. "I did." I press back against him, and he stops me, pulling back, not allowing me to take all of him.

"Greedy boy," he says, sliding deeper inside, before his hips draw back, again. "You want all of it? Tell me. Tell me you want me to make you come and I'll give it to you."

"I do. I want it."

"Beg."

"Oh, fuck. I—please. Please make me come, Sivan. I want all of it. I want all of you."

He grinds in deep against my spot, and then it happens, Sivan hits my prostate from just the right angle, and I come, I fucking come harder than I've ever come before. My fingers claw at the sheets as my cum shoots all over his bed. "Haah—haah—I'm coming—"

"There you go…mmm… Come for me, Vincent."

I drop my face into the pillow. My voice is muffled against the cotton. "Holy shit, holy shit…Sivan…that was so much cum."

Sivan is still ramming into me; each thrust is deeper than the last. I'm basically choking on my own spit at this point, because I can't catch my breath, or find a second to even swallow with the way he's driving into me.

"Do you want me to come in you?" he asks, clenching the sides of my ass.

I mumble into the pillow, "Yes—do it, I want it."

"I can't hear you with your face in the pillow. Say you want it. Say you want me to come in your ass."

My dick—which couldn't begin to come again, after the absolute drenching of Sivan's sheets— jumps. I can barely breathe, but I lift my head and get the words out. "Come—inside of me—I want you to come in my ass. Give it—to me—"

Sivan's pelvis thrusts forward, he grips the sides of my ass tighter, and I feel his hot cum shooting inside of me. "Take it—take my cum."

SIVAN

It's been a few hours since Vincent fell asleep. His phone hasn't stopped vibrating on my nightstand, but with his head on my chest and my arm locked around him, I don't want to move to turn it off.

Someone sure is persistent. I have no idea if it's Matteo or Harlow, it wouldn't be anyone else. I run my fingers through his hair. He's sleeping so soundly; I don't think anything would wake him right now. He needs to sleep; it's been such a long day. I still can't fully understand how it's possible that this person sleeping on my chest is the same person I've known my whole life. How did one moment change everything? I mean, I've always wanted to care for him in the way that a best friend cares for the other, and we've always stood beside each other, but now I see him differently. I don't want to stand beside him; I want to stand in front of him and protect him, even if he doesn't need my protection.

I haven't been able to sleep, because thoughts of what could happen this week are driving me crazy. I want to take him away from all this. I don't know what I'm going to do when we have to leave in a few days. I don't want to be apart again. This is one of the reasons why I wish we could combine crews. We've been looking forward to being captains our whole lives—I couldn't have ever imagined that the week of our captaincy promotions, we'd be lying in bed together, completely exhausted after mind-blowing sex with each other. I also wouldn't have expected that he would get fake engaged to someone, to try and protect me. Damn it, what's gonna happen tomorrow? Captain Rodrigo has to know that Vincent really doesn't want to marry her. I have to come up with a strategy for all of this before the morning, but I'm so tired and I'm not thinking clearly. I gotta try and get some sleep. I kiss the top of his head and close my eyes.

CHAPTER 7
BLUE LOOKS GOOD ON YOU

"Hey, we gotta get up," Vincent says, rubbing his hand on my chest.

The sun is assaulting my eyes. Shit, it must be after eight.

"Good morning," I say, giving him a kiss on the top of his head.

"Good morning. Time to deal with everything that we don't want to deal with," he says, while running his fingers lightly across my chest.

His touch is so soothing. For a moment, I'd forgotten everything that we're up against. I rub his back. "We can deal with it together. We just need to decide which part we're dealing with first."

"I'll do whatever you think is best. We both know I'm not the tactical one in this"—he pauses and looks up at me—"relationship."

Somehow, when he said the word relationship, it didn't make me want to run away like it always has before. "You're definitely not the tactical one, but you are better with a sword than I am."

"Tch. Swords aren't going to help either of us today. What's the plan?"

I can't help but tease him a little bit. "Now, last night, I asked if one of us would be in charge in this *relationship*, and you said no one was in charge, but it sounds to me like I'm in charge. Is that right?" Honestly, I would gladly take orders from him for the rest of my life, but he doesn't need to know that.

"What if we're both in charge of different things. You can be in charge of making plans and decisions, and I'll be in charge of everything else."

"No." I laugh. "You're not gonna be in charge of everything else. Let's just figure it out later. The first plan we need to talk about is whether we tell our dads or not."

"Hmm…what do you think?"

Our eyes shift to my door at the sound of two knocks and Tilly's voice. "Sivan, you awake?"

Shit, it's Tilly with my breakfast. "Just a minute, Tilly. I'm not dressed yet."

"Never stopped me before," she says.

"Just don't come in. Please leave the tray by the door. I have company and they aren't decent."

Vincent's mouth drops open. "I'm not decent?" he whispers.

I playfully nudge him with my elbow. "Not decent as in *not dressed*. What the hell did you think I meant?"

"Alright, I'm leaving it by the door!" she shouts back.

Vincent pulls his mouth to the side. "You let Tilly see you naked?"

"No. Don't be ridiculous. Sometimes she comes in when I'm in bed and not fully dressed. She's never seen me naked."

Vincent hops out of bed and walks toward my door.

"What are you doing?" I ask.

Shirtless and wearing my sweatpants, he turns around and

looks at me. "I'm grabbing the breakfast tray, so you don't have to get up."

"You don't need to do that," I say.

"It's fine. I want to." Vincent squats down and grabs the tray from the door, but pauses before standing. His eyes are wide.

"What is it?" I ask. I quickly walk over and join him by the door. I place a hand on his shoulder and take the tray from him.

"Whose voice is that?" he asks. "I don't recognize it."

"It's my dad. His voice always sounds kind of gruff in the morning."

"Let's listen. He's talking about Slicer. Oh, wait, that's my dad's voice, too."

The sound of Captain Rodrigo's voice is quite loud. "Yes, well we'll take care of the wedding first, then captaincy. Once we spot his ship, we can pincer him in. They say he only has one ship; we have four, well we will have four, once the boys are promoted."

"Why do you want to move the wedding so fast, Rodri?" my father asks. "We're in the middle of a crisis. The seas are uneasy, and you're worried about your son marrying a girl he obviously isn't interested in? Does he know you want to do it this week?"

"Well, who knows how he really feels? Besides, if I don't force it, he may change his mind. Then what? I'm afraid he won't ever find someone. He's so picky. If he's agreed to marry Harlow, I need to make him move on it. Not only that, but Sheena is adamant that it goes off without a hitch as soon as possible. You should've seen her. She acted like she had a secret, kept pushing me, 'you must promise, you must promise.' All while we're naked. Of course, I'd agree to it then. Who wouldn't? No man that I know wouldn't agree to it. That's for certain. You agree to whatever they want when you're naked. That can't be something unique to me."

"I can't say a woman has ever asked me for something like that before," my father says. "What's the rush though? You said she seemed like she knew something. But what? What could she know? You don't think Harlow is pregnant, do you?"

Vincent laughs loudly, forcing me to shut the door.

"Oh my God! What did you laugh like that for? They probably heard you!"

"I don't care. Who would have knocked her up? Me? The stuff those old men come up with. This is what they talk about when they're together? Come on, it's ridiculous."

Vincent's cheeks are all flushed. "Chill. No one thinks that. Come on, let's share my breakfast. You like all this food, too. I can ask for another tray for you if this isn't enough.

He's eyeing the tray. "Is that how much you normally eat in the morning? That looks like five scrambled eggs, and you have fruit and potatoes, too. That's a lot of food."

I pick one of the pieces of toast up and wave it. "Toast, too." I take a bite then hold the bread toward his mouth and he playfully takes a nibble. We sit down on the edge of my bed with the tray in between us.

"Sivan," my father calls through the door, knocking on it twice.

"Vincent?" Captain Rodrigo says. "Open up."

I whisper, "Come on. We need shirts, Vincent!" I walk quickly over toward my dresser and grab two shirts out. I toss one to Vincent, while I put the other one on. "Just a minute, Dad…and, uh, Vincent isn't here, Captain Rodrigo."

Captain Rodrigo answers, "The hell he isn't. We heard him,

kid sounds like a donkey when he laughs, I couldn't mistake his laugh for anyone else. What are you two hiding? Girls? Open the door already."

"Hiding? Who's hiding something? Only you two sounded like you were hiding something," Vincent says.

I grab his face with both hands and crush our lips together quickly. I have no idea what the rest of this day will hold for us, so before it starts, I need to kiss him just one more time.

"You shouldn't eavesdrop on conversations!" his father shouts.

"You two were loud as a foghorn; we didn't need to eavesdrop. People on the docks probably heard you. Also, don't go deciding that I'm getting married without asking me, either," he says, kissing me quickly with a smile.

"You decided you were getting married! No one else decided that!" his father yells back.

"Open this door!" my father shouts. "What the hell are you two doing?"

"Don't make me use Gwendolyn to pop this thing open!" Captain Rodrigo warns.

"You're not going to use Gwendolyn on my door, Rodri," my father says. "There is no chance in hell. Take your damn hand off the hilt."

"Let's not tell them about us right now," I say. "We have a few more days to get everything straightened out. Don't worry."

I open the door, and our fathers nearly tumble inside my room.

Captain Rodrigo struts inside after regaining his footing. He looks around the room, and at the bed, then glances toward the small empty couch, that obviously shows no sign of anyone sleeping on it. The lube is on the nightstand, the cap is open, and our clothes are strewn around the floor. It's so obvious that we had sex in here. Well, it's obvious that *someone* had sex in here, I guess it's not obvious that we had sex with each other. "You two"—he points at us—"where the hell did you run off to last night? I don't see any girls. You had Harlow hysterical. It was terrible. She was just a sobbing mess. She said the two of you up and left her standing outside of the bathroom. Why did you do that?" He's looking at me for an answer.

"What are you looking at me for? I wasn't feeling well. We went into the bathroom and Vincent thought I should get some fresh air. We walked toward the ship and fell asleep once we got into my room. What's so strange about that?" I ask.

"Well, I think the strangest thing is the fact that you both left without saying a word…and I mean, you left through the window," he says.

I really hate the way he's looking at me right now. It could be that I'm just feeling paranoid, but with the way he's looking at me, I feel like he knows what's going on between us.

"Nah, that's not strange," my father says. "They sneak out of that bathroom window all the time. Almost every time they're here."

Captain Rodrigo shakes his head at my father. "That was before, Ray. Now, Vincent has a fiancée. He has a responsibility to her. He can't just up and leave her whenever he wants to."

"Why not?" I ask. "Is there some sort of law that says he lost his freedom when he became engaged? Because if so, I have to say that's the most ridiculous thing I've heard. He can do whatever he wants. He isn't married to her and even if he was, what would it matter?"

Eyebrows high, Captain Rodrigo looks me over. "You get very upset on his behalf. You're a good friend to him, but surely you understood that Harlow would be devastated when he left last night. It was the night they announced their engagement, and it ended with her alone and crying. Any woman in their right mind wouldn't tolerate that." He finally turns toward Vincent. "You, too. She's your fiancée, what were you thinking leaving her like that? You have to be aware of other people's feelings."

"*You* need to be aware of other people's feelings," Vincent argues. "I don't want to be told how to live my life. I'm doing more than enough right now for everyone else's feelings. So just stop." He's walking over toward me, and I'm so nervous because I have no idea what he's going to say. He could say anything in moments like these. Thinking before speaking is not his strong suit.

"Whose feelings are you worried about if not your fiancée's?" Captain Rodrigo asks.

I gotta bail him out. "We had a long talk about captain and crew and the decisions that we'll be making soon. That's what he's talking about."

Vincent is just shaking his head. Seems like he's getting ready to spill it, and I don't want to stop him if he wants to.

"I'm not doing it. I will not be forced to marry her," Vincent says.

"Who is forcing you? If you don't want to marry her then why did you propose?" my father asks him.

Vincent locks eyes with me. I want to just tell our fathers the truth and I know he does, too. Why can't things just be easy for us? If either of us were a woman, this wouldn't even matter.

A loud bang outside breaks the tension. All four of us jump at the sound. "What the hell was that?" Captain Rodrigo asks.

It sounded almost like a gunshot. My father storms out

first, with the rest of us close behind. We're walking quickly toward the bow of the ship, and all I can hear is screaming. Once we get on deck there is nothing but chaos around the pier. People are running and shouting everywhere.

"What the hell is happening?" I ask. I've never seen anything like it. We're not even dressed; we're still in sweatpants and T-shirts. In any other circumstance our fathers would not allow us to walk on the deck in the equivalent of pajamas. Mine would have shoved me right back into my room, and Vincent's would have done the same. I don't even have my pistol or sword, and Vincent is unarmed, too. I have to assess what's happening, but I don't feel comfortable without a weapon. I'm scanning the scene quickly and feel Vincent's hand on my back. "I don't know what's going on," he says. "But we need to get our swords. I don't like feeling like I can't protect—"

"I can protect you without a sword," I say.

He drops an eyebrow at me and looks left to right. "I don't need you to protect me, I was talking about protecting you. I'm in charge of protection," he says.

I pat his shoulder. "You are not in charge of protection."

My father's first mate, Lyndon, makes his way over to us. "Captains, a fight broke out. Captain Slicer sent a few men to destroy the pub. We caught one of them. He said he wants to meet with you two. Apparently, Captain Slicer doesn't like how business has been running, so he's making a comeback."

"A comeback? What the hell is that supposed to mean?" my father asks.

"What's he coming back on? I don't see any ships," Captain Rodrigo says, gesturing to the open water.

Lyndon is all sweaty, he's wiping his brow with the back of his hand. His dark black hair is sticking to his forehead. "Well, all he said was that he's making a comeback, and he wants to speak with you two."

"So, where is he?" my father asks.

"Hey," I whisper, bringing my mouth near Vincent's ear. "Let's go get dressed before they realize that we aren't ready to go. We need to be ready for whatever the hell Slicer has planned."

Vincent nods at me. We can't actually just leave without being dismissed, though. I do need to get permission.

Lyndon shrugs his shoulders and finally takes notice of the two of us standing behind our fathers. "Don't know. I don't think he's here. This was just a messenger. But he seems a bit off. Speaking of a bit off—what are the, uh, two future captains behind you wearing?"

I close my eyes and exhale. Our fathers turn slowly around toward the two of us. "What the hell are you two doing on deck out of uniform?" my father asks.

Vincent speaks up, "We just woke up not that long ago and you two were talking to us in his room, then we came up here. We didn't have time to get dressed."

"We'll go now. Be right back, Captains," I say.

"Move fast. You two are coming with us," my father says.

Captain Rodrigo turns back toward Lyndon. "Where is the messenger now?"

"He's in the holding cell at Muffy's. Really got under the skin of everyone at the bar by bringing Captain Slicer up like that. Flipped a few tables, then ran through the port until a few of our guys tackled him. Couple of shots were fired, but I don't think anyone was hit. There were two others that got away."

Vincent and I head toward my room. I want to hold his

hand, but I know that I can't. Will it always be like this? Will I always have to worry about holding his hand?

"Hey," Vincent says elbowing me. "I don't have my sword with me. I didn't bring it last night."

"You can use mine. Shit, you don't have any extra clothes with you."

"Nope. Should I just go back to my dad's ship? Grab a change of clothes and my sword?"

I tilt my head at him, as we finally walk inside my bedroom. "No. You can just wear one of my meeting suits. Just borrow something."

He raises his eyebrows at me, picking his clothes up off the floor. Maybe that was stupid of me to offer, but we need to get back to our dads and figure out what the hell is happening.

"Oh shit," he says, lifting the bottle of lube from the nightstand. "This was just sitting here open; our father's must have seen it. Don't you think?"

I shrug and walk toward my closet, opening the door. "I saw your dad looking right at it. I don't know what he thought, but he definitely saw it. I wasn't too worried, because you looked like you were getting ready to just tell them anyway." I chuckle. "You are a bit unpredictable sometimes. That was a quality I always had fun with, but now that we're in a relationship, I have to say it's a bit terrifying."

He laughs and closes the cap on the bottle, placing it back inside the drawer. "You said *relationship*, again."

I pull my mouth to the side peeking out of the closet at him. His dimples are undoubtedly the sexiest thing I've ever seen. I can't even remember what it felt like to see him before I realized how attractive he was.

"I did say that." I step back inside the closet and flip quickly through my jackets. My hands are shaking, how am I nervous to talk about this. We've fucked three times now; how can I feel so embarrassed?

"I don't think I've ever heard you say you were in a relationship with anyone," he says, and today, you've said it several times." He steps inside the closet with me. "I thought *my* best friend doesn't do relationships."

I shake my head. "That was before my best friend stuck his tongue in my mouth."

A strong pair of arms reaches around my waist from behind. Vincent rests his chin on my shoulder. "That doesn't sound like a very nice thing to do. Did you like it?"

I smile and tilt my head next to his. "I did." The air between us is heavy with lust, and desire.

"Mmm, me too." His hands are reaching down the front of my sweatpants. I need to stop this, which is the last thing I want to do, but we really have to get dressed and meet up with our dads.

I wiggle out of his grip and smile at him. "You're trouble, and we're both gonna get our asses handed to us if we don't hurry." I pass him one of my blue coats, a shirt and a pair of pants. "Here, you can't wear your clothes. They're so wrinkled. You don't have a choice."

He takes the hangers from me and eyes them. "My dad is probably gonna be pissed. I don't even know what he is gonna look like when he sees me wearing your ship uniform. Wait, am I even allowed to?"

I shrug at him. "We'll be captains in a few days, and someday we might combine crews anyway, what difference does it make whose uniform you're wearing? My dad isn't gonna care."

"Alright. I don't have much of a choice like you said." We step outside of the closet into the room, and I toss him a pair of underwear. "Just wear them."

We both start getting dressed standing across from one another. I make eye contact with him, as he pulls the pants up. His ass is a bit rounder than mine, but height-wise we're basically the same. He pulls his T-shirt over his head, exposing his hard chest. I close my eyes and shake the dirty thoughts from my head. This is not the time for sex, but I really want to tear into him.

"Boys! Hurry up!" my father shouts, banging on the door.

We both jump at the sound and quickly finish dressing. My coat is only a little loose on him in the shoulders, but it really looks like it could have been made for him. I've never seen Vincent in blue before. It's unreal that a color can look so good on someone. I've worn that color every day of my life and yet somehow it looks like a brand-new shade of blue to me. I'm kind of obsessed with the way he looks in my clothes, especially the way my pants fit his ass. It's perfectly round, like a delicious peach that I want to bite into.

He holds his hands out looking in the mirror, then turns toward me. "I look ridiculous in this color, right?"

I shake my head at him and walk over, taking his hands in mine, and pulling him in close. "No. You don't look ridiculous. You look like—"

"What? What do I look like?"

I bring my mouth next to his ear. "Mine." I take a playful nibble of his earlobe, flicking his earrings with my tongue, then gently tug the lobe between my teeth.

He pushes me back a bit and points to the door, with a smile on his face, his dimples are on full display. "Our dads are out there; we have to hurry. You can't be doing that." He wipes his ear with his hand and moves toward my weapon rack. "Which sword can I use?"

"Whichever you want. The third one from the left is lighter. You could also use my pistol, if you want."

He tilts an eyebrow at me. "No pistols for me. We don't want my dad having a full heart attack; first I'm wearing your clothes, then I show up with just a pistol—he'd probably call off the captaincy promotion."

He picks up a slender sword and moves it around. He's so graceful with a sword, he just handles it much better than I do. That's one of the reasons I hate them. Sword fighting is like an elaborate dance, whereas pistols just get the job done faster. There's no fancy footwork, just taking care of business. Still, I do love to watch him fight with one. He slides the sword back into its scabbard and hooks the holder onto his belt. "Hair tie?" he asks me.

I toss him an elastic from the top of my dresser, and he quickly flips his hair upside down, tying it in a top knot. Damn. That is what a future captain looks like. In this moment I want to drop to my knees and swear fealty to him. I would die for this man.

"Now, can I use Gwendolyn?" Captain Rodrigo asks, outside of the door.

I grab my pistol and stick it inside its holster. "We're coming!" I shout.

Vincent walks toward me with a big smile on his face. "Wearing your clothes really does make me feel like I belong to you. Almost makes me feel like a piece of property. I don't know why, but I like it."

I grip him by the waist, jerking his body toward me. "You

are my property, now. Seeing you like this is making me realize just how far I'd be willing to go for you. It's almost frightening."

"Don't die today," he says and kisses me quickly.

I smile and let go of him. As I open the door, our fathers' jaws drop open at the sight of us. Well, more like they are shocked at the sight of Vincent, more than me.

"What the hell are you wearing? Where are your clothes?" his father asks him.

"I didn't bring any extra clothes with me," he says shrugging.

My father is studying the two of us. As much as I hate to admit it, he's extremely smart, but, really, Vincent wearing my uniform proves nothing, his clothes really are too wrinkled to be worn. He didn't have a choice. "Let it go Rodri, he wasn't planning on staying the night. You saw his clothes on the floor earlier; you want him to wear something wrinkled? Besides, he looks good in blue."

"No, he looks good in red," Captain Rodrigo says, looking the two of us over again. "Ah, damn it. Let's go, we don't have time for this."

We walk behind our fathers, who are having two completely different conversations, yet still keeping up with one another.

Captain Rodrigo is stuck on Vincent's clothes, while my father is going over the plan for when they come face to face with Slicer's messenger.

"Vincent," Captain Rodrigo says. "You need to tell Matteo to meet us there. He's going to be your First Mate. You shouldn't be leaving him behind in these situations. He's always cleaning up after you. Just like last night. Don't know what Harlow would have done if Matteo wasn't there."

I don't know if he's just trying to goad him again or not, but Vincent doesn't seem bothered by it.

"I have Sivan with me. I don't need Matteo with me, Captain."

Captain Rodrigo shakes his head, but continues walking beside my father. "Well, with the way you're dressed you look like Sivan's first mate."

My father looks over his shoulder at us. "Actually, I think they look more like co-captains, Rodri. Except for the fact that they don't have cool hats like ours."

"Co-captains." Captain Rodrigo scoffs. "What an asinine idea that would be."

My father stops in his tracks. "How is being co-captains asinine?"

"A captain already shares his wealth with his wife, is he to further share it with his co-captain? Four people sharing wealth before it even hits the crew… Asinine."

"How did you come up with four people?" Vincent asks as we step inside Muffy's pub.

"He's saying both of us would be married to other people. You married to Harlow, and me married to—"

He drops his eyebrow down at me. "Don't finish that sentence."

CHAPTER 8
THE MESSENGER AND THE CRESCENT MOONS

SIVAN

The pub is a complete disaster. Patrons are flipping tables back over. The floors are a mess, completely full of food. It looks like some bottles behind the bar are broken.

Vincent is quickly swarmed by two women.

"Oooh, Vincent! I haven't seen you in blue before," one of the women says. "This looks good on you." She's touching his sleeve and it's driving me crazy. I don't want anyone to touch him. I've never felt this way before, I don't even know if it's normal.

The other woman is pulling on his other sleeve. I sort of recognize that one. I can't remember if he slept with her, but she's definitely been around us a few times I was here. "Vincent, it was so scary. These guys came in and they were just screaming and throwing bottles. We hid under the table, and, luckily, they didn't bother us."

Vincent nods. "Oh. That's good. Well, the part about everyone being okay is good."

She smiles brightly at him. "But I've been meaning to ask you if you are going to have room on your new ship for me. So…will you?"

Oh, hell no. "I don't think so," I say, grabbing his forearm.

I pull him toward our fathers, who are talking to the bar owner. "Oh! Vincent, you're wearing blue, are you joining Captain Crawford's crew?" Muffy, the bar owner, asks.

Captain Rodrigo shakes his head. He holds up a hand to Vincent. "Don't try to explain. We don't have time."

The four of us walk behind the bar, stepping behind a large black curtain. The staircase in the back of the room leads to the downstairs bunker and holding cells. We head down as a group, and I can't help but to feel a little uneasy. I normally have a plan for everything, but right now I have no plan.

"Hey," Vincent says, hooking his pinky with mine. "I wouldn't let someone you slept with join my crew. I don't even like her."

His pinky is interlocked with mine, it's the closest we can get to holding hands, and for now it's enough. It has to be. "What are you talking about? Who did I sleep with?"

"You slept with Mariah, that woman we were just talking to. Who do you think I'm talking about?"

"I didn't sleep with her. You slept with her." At least I think he did, but I definitely didn't.

"No, I didn't. You did, because she told everyone about it. But, now that I think about it, since I've slept with you, the stuff she said doesn't sound like you. Maybe she was making it up."

"What kind of stuff did she say?"

He shakes his head. "It's not important."

I nod and notice his father looking over his shoulder.

We release our hold on each other's pinkies. Hiding this is already getting annoying, but, truthfully, I need to think like a captain, and worrying about holding hands, or pinkies, or having sex, all of those things are not important for captain or crew right now.

We reach the row of three holding cells. It's dark and depressing down here, the light has no way to get inside since we're underground, which only adds to the somber atmosphere.

"Hello, hello, Captains!" the man behind the iron bars says. He's beaten up pretty badly, although, I wouldn't expect anything else to happen to someone who had just come into port and spouted nonsense about Slicer coming back. He's wearing standard black and green clothes of a crew member, which means he's likely working for Slicer, but he has no ranking on his ship—if Slicer even has a ship.

Wasting no time at all, our fathers approach the cell. "Who are you?" Captain Rodrigo asks.

The man backs up from the bars and holds his hands wide. "Who am I? I'm the messenger. The messenger sent to find you two, and, look, I've found you. Captain Slicer will be so glad when I tell him."

"That doesn't answer our question," my father says. "You're a messenger, but why are you here?"

"Well, he did answer the question," Captain Rodrigo says to my father.

"What the hell are you saying, Rodri? No, he didn't."

"Yes, he did," Captain Rodrigo says. "I asked him who he was, he said he was the messenger."

"That's right," the man says. He's giving my father the cockiest of smiles.

My father pulls his sword from his scabbard quickly and points it at the bars, coming within inches of the man's dirty grime-ridden face. "Shut. Your. Mouth," my father says. He turns toward Vincent's father. "Now, Rodri, don't correct me in front of people. You just took his side, what the hell kind of a friend are you?"

Vincent and I are trying not to laugh, we're both covering our mouths. Only these two would be arguing in front of a holding cell. My father sounds like such a baby. Captain Rodrigo is shaking his head with his hands on his hips.

"Why are you pointing your damn sword at me?" the man asks my father.

Captain Rodrigo quickly unsheathes his sword, pointing it at the man. "Shut it, messenger."

The man backs up from the bars, with both swords pointing at him. "You both are not very nice. I thought you were supposed to be peaceful pirates, that's what everyone says. That's why I volunteered to come here. I just wanted to meet you both," the man says, as he leans forward against the bars. Both swords are poking through the bars on opposite sides of his face.

"We're not nice," Captain Rodrigo says. "Not even a little. We already don't like you. And if you came here to make friends, you picked the wrong pirate to align yourself with. Why are you here?"

The messenger backs up from the bars again. He's smiling in a way that makes me uncomfortable. He points at Captain Rodrigo. "Captain Slicer says you've got something that belongs to him. Says he wants it back."

"Well, what the hell have I got that's his?" Captain Rodrigo asks. "I think I would know if I had something of his."

"I don't know what you have of his," the messenger says. "He said you'd know as soon as I said that. Wouldn't tell me any other information."

My father puts his sword back into his scabbard. "Well, now I'm upset. What the hell is he talking about, Rodri? I thought I was your only friend. Now you're going behind my back and borrowing stuff from Slicer? I can't even look at you." my father says and turns to the side.

I couldn't be any more embarrassed than I am right now.

"Are you serious, Ray?" Captain Rodrigo asks, re-sheathing his sword. "I haven't talked to him at all. Not even once since we took everything from him. You know better than anyone, how I feel about him. We feel the same."

My father turns around and lifts his gaze to Captain Rodrigo. "I didn't think you would betray my trust. But he made it sound like you'd been in touch with him. I'm your only friend, right?"

"Ha!" I say loudly, causing my father to turn around.

"What are you laughing about?" he asks me.

"I'm laughing at you. You're acting like a child. Pouting about your friend. You know he hates Captain Slicer. What are you getting so worked up about?"

"Shut up. I don't know. I just thought for a moment that maybe—"

Captain Rodrigo pats my father's shoulder. "No, no, there is no moment. You're my only friend."

"Now, messenger," Captain Rodrigo says. "What was your entire purpose in coming here? Just to tell me that I have something of Captain Slicer's that he wants back, or were you and the others that got away supposed to stir up trouble and scare everyone half to death in the pub?"

"Oh, a little of both I suppose. Captain said to create some mayhem, but he also said not to get carried away. I was trying to take it easy, but, you see, as soon as I said Captain Slicer's name, people got jumpy and started to scatter. It was the craziest thing."

"So, you came here for this, most likely knowing you were

gonna get taken into custody, and still, you did this for your captain. But why? You don't even know what he wants from me. Neither do I, for that matter."

"Yeah, well, I owe Captain my life, I'd do anything for him. I suppose I had wanted to meet you both a bit as well." He smiles at our fathers.

"That's really nice. I don't care," Captain Rodrigo says.

"Yeah, he doesn't care because he's *my* friend. So why should he care that you wanted to meet him?" my father asks, folding his arms. He looks like he's in high school right now. Maybe Vincent was onto something with the two of them.

"I don't think I've ever seen a pirate jealous of another's attention," the man says to Captain Rodrigo. "You're not together, right? You like women…you both have children." He lifts his chin toward my father. "But he acts as though you're together in *that* way."

"That's none of your business," my father snaps.

Well, I was expecting a no, but instead he just denied him the answer.

"Right, it's none of your business, but, yes, we like women, how else would we have these two men here with us if we didn't?" Captain Rodrigo asks.

The messenger looks like he's in disbelief. "Well, you both had them when you were younger, lost your wives, then maybe—"

"We're done talking," my father says. "This conversation has gone on too long. He turns on his heel toward the staircase.

Captain Rodrigo is following close behind my father, neither man looking back. "Where can we find Slicer?" he asks the messenger, over his shoulder.

"You can find him under the double crescent moons. He said you'd know what that meant."

Captain Rodrigo stops walking and throws his hands up. He turns toward the cell. "I have no idea what that means! How the hell should I know? We haven't spoken to him in twenty-one years? Why the hell are you here talking to us in code?"

"I should shoot you," my father says, stepping onto the staircase. "This has got to be the most frustrating conversation of my life!" He continues walking up the stairs; he's just muttering to himself at this point. He must be really pissed off to threaten shooting someone, though. This guy really struck a nerve.

"Shoot me? I did nothing wrong. What would you shoot me for?"

Captain Rodrigo is standing just to the side of the staircase, looking quite confused. "Where is his ship docked? Just speak plainly."

The man smiles with a grin wider than a crocodile. "Says he'll find you in three days if you don't find him first."

The ceremony. He's planning to attack on the day of the captaincy ceremony. That's what happens in three days. I guess our fathers haven't realized that. I'm sure Vincent has, because he's nodding at me like he's figured it out. Which is surprising given the fact that not even our fathers appear to have realized it.

"How does he know where we'll be in three days?" Captain Rodrigo asks.

"Rodri!" my father shouts from the top of the stairs. "Let's go. He knows because he has someone here working for him. Let's go figure out who it is. Just stop talking to him."

Vincent and I are following behind our fathers. I wonder

how this interrogation would have gone if it were just Vincent and I here?

The messenger gives a whistle. "Vincent," he calls out.

Vincent and I both turn to look at the man. "What is it?" he asks.

I place a hand on Vincent's shoulder and the man's eyebrows raise.

"Ah, would you look at that. You put your hand on his shoulder." The messenger flutters his eyelashes exaggeratively. "So, little Captain Crawford is jealous, too. Is this a personality trait amongst your whole crew, or is it just you and your father that act this way?"

Vincent reaches for his sword, and I place my hand atop his and shake my head. "He's not worth it," I say, lifting my chin toward the staircase.

Our fathers are already out of sight, basically at the top of the stairs. We shouldn't stay down here with him. Nothing good will come from this. Vincent nods at me, but he looks really angry. Thankfully, he starts walking beside me toward the stairs, again.

"I wanted to congratulate you on your engagement," the messenger says. "Best take care of that girl."

Vincent laughs. "How do you know I'm engaged? Just happened last night."

"Saw the lot of you at the pub and I watched for a bit. Strange thing was you two leaving in the middle of the celebration to do whatever it was that you did. I waited a while for you to come back. Your fiancée looked nice and cozy with that other fellow from your crew. The one they say will be your first mate."

Vincent exhales, but we're still walking toward the stairs. I really don't want to stay down here any longer. Kind of strange for the messenger to bring Matteo up— but I shouldn't dive too deep into what he's saying. Pirates like him just thrive on chaos, he's trying to get Vincent worked up, hoping to sow discord between him and Matteo. It would be a juicy story if Vincent actually cared about Harlow, so it's not a bad angle, it just won't work here since the engagement means nothing to him.

The messenger, not getting the reaction he so clearly hoped for, starts in again. "Yep, he swooped right in and wiped her tears. Definitely a bit more going on there if you know what I mean. Of course, for us pirates, nothing is really ours, is it? All property of the crew. So, you must not mind sharing, is that it?"

Vincent is shaking his head as we reach the stairs. I give him a gentle push, urging him not to listen. "Just keep walking. Ignore him," I say.

"I don't know…something tells me you won't be worrying about one of them for too much longer," the messenger shouts.

CHAPTER 9
THROWING THE TRASH OUT

What the hell was that fool going on about? He smelled like piss, and he looked even worse than he smelled. I was taught pretty early on that pirates that don't agree with our ways will try to cause problems; it comes with the territory. Pirates will resort to anything to get what they want. It makes sense that he was trying to piss me off. He did annoy me, but not in the way that he was probably hoping to. Sivan looked so upset listening to him. How did I ever think this plan to marry Harlow would work? And damn it, why is Slicer coming around now?

Sivan's hand lightly squeezes mine, as we stand behind our fathers inside of Muffy's pub. He releases it quickly, only squeezing it enough to let me know he's here. This is so fucking stupid. I haven't even had a second to process all the stuff that's happening with us, and now all this shit with Slicer is going down. I know that I want to be with Sivan, but every once in a while, I just can't believe that it's real. How can I be good enough for him? The sex is amazing, and we've always had so much fun together, but what scares me is that he's never really been in a relationship before. I just feel like everyone needs to go through a few bad relationships before they find the right one. I don't want to be the wrong one. I want to be the one for him, *the only one*. He said so many sweet things to me last night, and this morning, too. I really like that he isn't worried about what other people might think of our relationship, because I feel worried enough for the both of us. My whole life I've been programmed to marry a woman, and now I don't think that's something I could ever do. Why exactly is that so strange to some people? Isn't it stranger to be told that you must love someone of a certain gender? Same as Captain and Crew, I don't care what anyone says, it doesn't make sense. Because right now, if I was captain, the best decision for me would be to be with Sivan. The best decision for the crew wouldn't matter at all to me.

"Vincent," Sivan says, placing his hand on my shoulder. His face is so close to mine, and I'm suddenly feeling a bit overheated. "Everything okay? Did you figure something out?"

"No. I'm as confused as ever. I have no idea what that guy was going on about." I shake my head and exhale, walking beside Sivan. Something doesn't feel right, my vision is fine, but my head feels light. I have so many questions and I need to do so many things. Everything I have to do is urgent right now, and I don't know which thing to focus on, but it feels like all my problems are swirling around me. I just want to hold Sivan's hand, or a piece of his jacket…something to keep me grounded, but I can't.

"Well, let's go see what kind of a plan our father's come up with," Sivan says.

The sun is blinding as we step outside. I normally love the feeling of the sun, but not right now. I squint at Sivan, as my eyes try to adjust. Seems like it's taking things longer to come into focus, but that's probably because we were underground in the basement for so long.

"What did that man say a minute ago about Matteo and

Harlow, and not worrying about them? Everything is a bit hazy, Sivan. Nothing feels real to me right now. I think I'm having one of those out of body—what do you call those? Out of body experiences? I feel like I'm watching myself with you right now. Like this is some sort of a movie."

Sivan tilts his head at me and feels my head with the back of his hand. "You feel a little warm, Vincent. Hey, wait, when you passed out last time, you said it was just stress, right? Does this feel the same?"

"What do you mean?"

"Did you feel like everything was fuzzy before you passed out last time? Or was everything out of body like?" He places the inside of his wrist on my forehead, again. "Yeah, you really are pretty warm. Let's get you back to your room. We can tell our fathers that you aren't feeling well."

He takes my hand briefly and locks eyes with me. Our fingers interlock for just a moment, before he lets go. Up ahead, our fathers have put quite a bit of distance between us. I can't hear their conversation. They look like they're arguing, though.

"Hey, Captain!" Sivan shouts. Our fathers stop walking, and Captain Crawford turns to face us.

"I'm gonna take Vincent back to his room. I think he's running a fever."

"Oh? What's wrong? You don't feel well all of a sudden?" my father asks.

"I just feel a bit dizzy," I say.

"Well, we're headed back to the ship, anyway. We need to gather the crews and hold a meeting."

I need to tell my dad what the messenger said to me as we were leaving, even though I can't imagine it will make any difference to him. He'll probably say the guy was just trying to get under my skin, which I'm sure he was. We're not too far from the ship, now. I look left to right, making sure neither Matteo or Harlow are around. "Captain," I say. "When you guys went on ahead of us, the messenger mentioned Matteo and Harlow. He said he was at the pub last night watching all of us. Then he said something about not having to worry about one of them for much longer. Sounded almost like a threat."

"Well, now that's a bit dramatic," my father says. "How could him saying you won't have to worry about one of them be interpreted as a threat? You made your fiancée cry, and your first mate, well, soon to be first mate, consoled her. I have no idea what the messenger meant by not having to worry about one of them, but it didn't sound like a threat."

Sivan cuts into the conversation. "Is there any chance that Captain Slicer is already here in port?"

My father gestures with his hand toward open water and our ships. "Hmmm," my father says, looking around the empty pier. "No, I don't think so, he wouldn't leave his ship, and I see no ship. I don't even know what the hell he wants. All that nonsense about borrowing something."

"The idea of you borrowing something from him is preposterous," Captain Crawford says.

"Yes, yes, I would never. We both hate him to infinity, does that make you happy, Ray?"

"Well, of course it makes me happy. Much better than thinking that you've borrowed something from him."

Oh no, Harlow is walking toward us as we reach the ship. We've not stepped aboard yet and I would really like to just bolt. But I know that's not going to work, I have to just deal with her.

"The phone," Sivan whispers. "Get the phone or the recording device."

"Oh, right!" I say smiling. "I almost forgot that we have a plan!"

"It seems more like you completely forgot and less like you almost forgot. So, which is it, Dimples?"

I laugh and fan myself. "You can't get mad at me, because I'm sick. You can't yell at a sick person. Wait, did you just call me dimples?"

"I did. I kinda wanna poke them right now, too."

I feel my cheeks warm. I'm sure I'm blushing.

Sivan giggles, until he makes eye contact with Harlow. I've never seen a facial expression flip so fast. The two of them exchange a glance that indicates just how much they hate each other.

Harlow is walking with her arms extended. "There's *my* fiancé. I was worried sick about you!" she says in the most overexaggerated manner. "What are you doing in blue? Where are your clothes?"

"Worried sick, huh?" Sivan asks, looking her up and down.

"Of course, I was worried, since *my* fiancé was gone all night. I had no idea why you'd gone through the window instead of just telling me what you needed. Silly boys."

Wow, she's really putting on a show for our fathers, who are both watching very closely.

She grabs my arm, hooking hers around it. "Now you're here with your dear friend, Sivan, and I feel nothing but relief," she says, looking at Sivan.

Sivan is covering his mouth. He looks like he may snap. I don't want to do this, but she holds all the power right now. If I jerk my arm away, will she just blurt everything out? I can't make a scene in front my father and the crew on deck. Still, I can't do this to Sivan. I can't imagine how frustrated he must be. He doesn't even look hurt; he just looks angry. She knows what she's doing, so maybe if I just reason with her, calmly...

"Harlow," I say quietly. "I don't feel well. I'm going to lie down; so much has happened that I just can't do this right now." I lightly pull my arm back.

Sivan steps closer to me. "I'm going to drop him off in his room, Harlow. He'll probably be ready for company in an hour or so."

She scoffs loudly, so loudly that people are looking over. "Are you serious? I don't think so. You two have had your play time. It's time for my fiancé to be with me. I need his attention now. I've been more than patient."

Our fathers hear Harlow's shrieking and turn toward us. My dad is gonna lose it on me. If there's one thing he can't stand, it's seeing girls upset. He doesn't look angry yet, but Captain Crawford is whispering something to him. He's giving us a discerning look, but seems to be agreeing with whatever Captain Crawford is saying. He's gesturing for one of us to come over. Damn it. "Harlow, darling, let the boys get settled, I need your help with something," he says.

"Yes, of course, Captain," she says, rather obediently, and smiles. She's holding her pointer finger up toward him. "I'll be just a moment." With the way she's smiling, you'd never know how truly horrible she is.

Harlow turns her attention back to Sivan. "As soon as I'm done with whatever the captain assigns me to do, I will be back. I don't want to see you in his room when I get there. I trust that my fiancé has already told you that I'm aware of this thing between the two of you." She gives him one more fake smile and heads toward our fathers. "Coming, Captains!" she says as she hurries over.

Harlow is only about 5'3", and Sivan and I are 6'0" and 5'11" respectively, but man, the way she just talked down to him, you'd think he was small enough to squish with her heel.

Sivan's mouth is wide open, and his cheeks are flushed. I kind of like the way he looks right now after being bullied. It's like his pride looks hurt, but he also looks kind of adorable, like he needs someone to console him. "Who the hell does she think she is? You aren't even engaged for real and look how she's treating you? Shit, look how she's treating me," Sivan says.

I think he's forgetting that Harlow has no idea that I don't intend to marry her. As far as she knows, I'm going to go through with it. I don't even know how to deal with all this, I just want to lay down.

"Come on, let's go," I say. Sivan and I are walking toward my room, and the hall is full of crew members. Each one is smiling, but then giving me the weirdest looks. I have no idea why everyone is staring at the two of us like they know our secret. They couldn't possibly. But, still, we've passed three different groups and each time it's been the same. With the halls being so busy, my father must have already passed the message on about the meeting. He didn't say that either of us needed to go, though. Just as we reach my room, two more crew members approach us.

"Vincent, what are you wearing?" Iggy asks. "The captaincy ceremony is at the end of the week. Did you decide to join Captain Crawford's crew instead?"

"Yeah," Petra says. "You look like a proper member of Captain Crawford's crew in that blue."

Both of them are just standing in front of us waiting for an answer. This explains why everyone was looking so strangely at me. I completely forgot that I was wearing Sivan's clothes. "No,"

I say, turning my door handle. "I had to borrow his clothes, that's all. Carry on, you nosey shits." They both laugh and walk away, while Sivan and I head inside my bedroom.

"I really feel terrible, Sivan." I unbutton the coat I'm wearing and lay it on my dresser, placing Sivan's sword atop it. My head is really hurting. I pull my hair tie out, and scrunch my hair, immediately I feel slightly better. Maybe my bun was too tight? I'm still overwhelmed, but my head doesn't feel as light. Damn, how am I supposed to deal with all these emotions. I can't put them on Sivan. That wouldn't be right.

Sivan is unbuttoning his coat, while walking around the room. He puts his pistol beside the sword on my dresser. He looks really serious, as he pulls his coat off and lies on the floor near the foot of my bed.

"Uh, what the hell are you doing?" I ask. He's on his stomach looking under the bed. His back is so muscular, not that it can be seen right now, but I've seen it enough times to have a pretty good mental image of it.

He looks up at me. "What do you think I'm doing? Showing you how many pushups I can do?"

He's not doing pushups, although I would really like to watch that right now. "I have no idea, honestly. How many pushups *can* you do, by the way?"

He smiles. "I don't know how many pushups I can do. But what I'm actually doing is looking for a recording device, before she comes back. Wait, did you forget again?"

Shit, I did forget, again. "I don't feel good, Sivan. I still feel a bit dizzy." I flop onto my bed and unbutton my pants. I quickly pull them down, and kick them off the side of the bed, then tuck myself underneath the covers.

Sivan stands up from the bottom of the bed and walks

beside me. He pulls the covers up tightly and feels my forehead again.

"You are a bit warm, but you also feel kind of clammy, too. How can you be both?" He kisses my forehead. "The problem is that there's a recording device in this room, and I need to find it. Just close your eyes and rest while I look. I'll leave after I find it."

"I don't want you to leave when I fall asleep. I need to get up and help you look," I say.

"Okay. Don't worry," he says, lightly raking his fingers through my hair. "I've got you. I'll stay here while you sleep. I just won't open the door when she comes."

"Please don't leave me, Sivan. I promise I'll fix everything."

I feel his hand rubbing my hair. "Shh…" His warm lips press against my forehead, again. "You need to rest. You're talking nonsense. I will never leave you. We'll be together, no matter what."

My body jolts and I find myself wrapped in Sivan's arms. It's still light outside, so I probably didn't sleep for too long.

"Lay back down," he says rubbing my arm from behind. "It's just Sam knocking on the door. He said something about your father telling him to bring you something to eat, so he's leaving the tray outside for you."

"Oh. Well, aren't you hungry? I can go grab the tray; I feel better than I did earlier. I think I just needed a nap."

"No. I don't want you to get up. You've felt so warm all afternoon. I was afraid if I moved something would happen. Just relax."

"Alright," I say and lay back down. My body fits so nicely

beside him. He is slightly bigger than me, so tucking up like this with him wrapping me up from behind feels so comforting. Now I understand why people say they want to be the little spoon.

Sivan kisses the top of my head and inhales. It's strange that having his arms wrapped around me gives me all the comfort I need in these moments. I wonder if he feels this way when I hold him?

"By the way, she hasn't come by, and I didn't find the recording device," he says. "I looked for a while before getting into bed with you. I don't believe that she took it out of your room, but I honestly have no idea where it could be at this point."

"Well, I'm happy that she hasn't come by yet. But the recorder thing…where could it be? What are we gonna do?"

"I don't know. I looked everywhere before I finally gave up. Maybe it's not in here anymore. It's really strange that she hasn't come around yet. Especially because as far as she's concerned, you're still going to marry her. Ugh, I almost threw up when I said that."

He's not the only one who got nauseous at the thought. "Yeah, but you know I'm not going to marry her. I completely forgot that my dad is trying to force that to happen this weekend, too. He loves saying stuff is asinine, but what's he thinking? Our ships should be coming in tomorrow, then we have the inspection, the tattoos, the promotion, now Slicer is poking around, and my dad thinks now would be a good time for a wedding?"

"Yeah, but in his defense, he said that before we met the messenger. Also, he's always wanted you to get married, you heard him; he feels like if he doesn't force you to do it now, you'll back out, and be alone forever, since you're so picky."

"I'm not picky, I just didn't know what I needed, until I had it."

"Yep, you just needed my dick."

I laugh loudly and turn to face him. "Well…"

Sivan is holding my face with both hands. "Aww, your cheeks are getting all red. Don't be embarrassed. I am actually picky, and didn't know what I needed until I had your ass. Technically, the kiss did it for me, but the ass sealed the deal." He kisses my lips quickly and presses his forehead to mine. "Your filthy little tongue saved me that night."

I kiss him softly, then realize that my tray is still outside my door. "I have to get that tray, or people are going to start knocking." I roll out of bed and quickly grab the tray. The halls are empty, which is good, and I don't smell Harlow's perfume, which is also good. I place the tray on my dresser and lift the lid. "I'm not in the mood for any of this. Are you hungry? There are some chicken fingers, fries, and a peach."

Sivan is lying on his side with his head propped up on his hand. He's patting the bed. "No, thank you, but I'll take your peach right here."

As I walk over to him, I'm surely smiling like an idiot, not because he just called my ass a peach, but because I just realized that my sheets will smell like him, again. I need to keep him in bed with me for as long as possible.

I get back in bed beside him and lie on my side with my back against his chest. He wraps his arm around me and squeezes. "Vincent, I know we have so much going on, but all I can think about is how happy I am to have you wrapped in my arms like this."

Soft kisses tickle the back of my neck and bare shoulders. "Wait, where is my shirt? How did my shirt end up off?"

"You did that about an hour after you laid down. You mumbled that you were burning up, then fell right back asleep."

Wow. I don't even remember that.

More kisses softly litter my shoulders and neck. "There's something about the warmth of your skin against my lips that is driving me crazy right now," Sivan says.

The kisses that started as soft little pecks have gradually increased to light sucking and licking. "Mmm, I love the way your tongue feels on my neck." My cock is beginning to stir. I scoot in closer, grinding my ass against him.

He responds in kind, placing both hands beneath the covers and jerks my lower half against his.

I reach behind myself and rub downward, feeling the outline of his cock. "I wish you would take these off. I want to feel closer, like this morning."

Did I just say I want to feel closer? What is it about him that makes me want the closeness more than the sex? Why was that what came out of my mouth?

"Mmm," Sivan moans, and begins fumbling with the front of his pants. "Are you sure you're feeling better?"

I take his hand and slide it inside my briefs, and he grips my dick tightly, letting out a low growl that makes my cock harden even more.

"I forgot you were wearing my underwear," he whispers, as he tugs my underwear down and turns me onto my back. I reach my arm toward the nightstand, attempting to get the lube from inside the small drawer. Sivan stands from the bed and grabs the bottle. "There's not much in here," he says. He narrows his eyes at me. "I remember using this bottle the last time I was here. It was a full bottle…why is there so little left?"

Uh, probably because I was using it while thinking about him for the past nine months. "Your absence may have been responsible for that."

He's smirking at me. "Were you jerking off while thinking about me?"

"What if I said I did more than that?"

Sivan gets back into bed with me, he grips one of my thighs, parting my legs, and climbs in between them. My cock is rock hard, and his is too. I am so eager to feel him again, but even more than that, I want him to kiss me.

He flips the cap of the lube open and squeezes some out. I never thought I'd be obsessed with looking at another man's naked body, but, damn, I can't pull my eyes away from him. The ridges of his abs, and the deep V leading to his dick are the last things I want to see before I die.

He's making eye contact with me, while he starts to stroke himself. "If you said you did more than that, I'd be interested in what that means. But while you're lying here naked, I only want to hear about the things that you did while thinking about me. Now, tell me, did you rub your cock, imagining it was me, or did you finger yourself?"

Sivan is jerking his cock at a slow, deliberate pace. I feel like I've learned how to handle his dick pretty well, but I'm still mesmerized watching him. "I did both."

"That's fucking hot, but…" Sivan moves in closer placing his cock next to mine and begins to stroke us both together. "That means you stole from me."

"What? How did I steal from you?"

"That cum was mine. It belonged to me."

I bite my bottom lip and nod. I'm high on the feeling of our dicks being rubbed together. I can't even speak. A meek "Mmhmm" escapes my lips.

"So, you acknowledge that your cum belongs to me. That's good…but what you did was bad." His strokes slow and for some reason it's only bringing me closer to bursting. "Don't do that again. We don't waste cum."

"Yyeemmm." I don't even know what the sound was that just came out of me. "Okay," I whimper.

"Now tell me, did you do it like this?" he asks, rubbing slowly.

"Sometimes, but other times it was faster."

His eyebrows raise and his grip tightens, while he increases the speed, working our cocks together. It sounds sloppy and wet—delicious. "Fast like this, Vincent?"

Holy shit. I'm gonna come. I don't know why this feels so good, but there is something deeply erotic about both of our warm hard dicks rubbing against one another. "Yes…yes like that, but—fuck, Sivan. I'm gonna come."

He nods, jerking us together faster. "How many times did you come thinking about me? How much cum was spilled when you moaned my name?"

My back arches and I scratch my nails down Sivan's chest, and I come—I fucking come all over his hand, while Sivan pumps the two of us together. His cum is spilling out, mixing with mine, it's running down his fingers, dripping onto my abs, while he slowly milks the both of us.

Sivan wipes the cum from my abs with two fingers then brings them to his mouth, licking the cum off them. Damn, he's so fucking hot. Taking another swipe, he shoves his fingers in my mouth and watches while I suck them clean. "Fuck, Vincent.

Your tongue." He presses his lips against mine and kisses me deeply, then drops on the bed beside me.

I am utterly spent, eyes wide, panting, breathless, just staring at this beautiful fucking man…now I know how he felt earlier. No one else can ever have him. He is mine.

I close my eyes while trying to catch my breath and feel Sivan's lips softly touch mine. "Why can't we just do that all day?" he asks.

"I wish. Maybe when we're captains, we can change piracy, again. We'll be the pirates who just have sex all day." I flip my legs out of bed and head for the shower, so I can rinse off, while Sivan follows behind.

"Can I join you if you're taking a shower?"

I smile over my shoulder. "Of course, but I'm just using the hand-held, not taking a full shower. Just a quick rinse." I grab two towels from under the sink inside my bathroom and hang them on the towel bar on the outside of the shower doors.

We step inside my shower, and I turn the water on. I quickly spray my hands down, and then do the same to Sivan's. He's giving me such a devilish sort of grin right now, while I lather up a bath pouf. My shower is a little bigger than his, so there's room in here for other things. I shake my head at him, and we both quickly clean ourselves. As much as I wish we could stay in here all day, or get back in bed and have more sex, we really can't. There's way too much to be done. Sivan is tilting his head to the side and shaking out his ear. Now he's looking around the shower like he lost something.

"What's wrong? I'm sure she doesn't have a camera in here. Is that what you're looking for?"

"No, I thought I heard a door open. Probably just hearing things. Or someone just walked inside your room."

"I really hope that's not the case. I'm gonna be so pissed if we walk out there and see Harlow or Matteo. Oh shit, what if it's our dads?" There is no way in hell I could explain coming out of the shower with Sivan as something that we'd normally do. Our dads would definitely know we were sleeping together. I turn the water off and grab our towels. Once I'm wrapped in my towel, I open the door, wincing.

"What the fuck? Where did that come from?!" I shout, completely shocked at the sight.

"You have a pet monkey? I thought your dad forbade pirates from having monkeys as pets?"

The small monkey on top of my dresser turns to look at us, then quickly makes his way over. Instinctively, I back up. I have no idea what it's going to do, or where the hell it came from. The monkey is climbing up my leg. His fur is scratchy as he reaches my chest. I don't know if I should pet him or...

Whack. The monkey just slapped me in my face. "Whoa, get down!" I pull the monkey off my side and place him back on the floor. The slap didn't really hurt, but I sure as hell wasn't expecting it. "Where did you come from? You can't just smack someone." I turn to Sivan. "He's not my monkey. I don't have any pets. I'm pretty sure you would have known if I had a pet monkey."

The monkey drops its head down, like I hurt its feelings or something. It's making its way over to where Sivan's clothes are. Before the monkey can do anything to them, Sivan walks over toward the pile of clothes and picks his things up. "Thank you. I wasn't sure where I left these," he says, while patting the monkey's head. The monkey makes a loud screeching noise in response.

"I guess it wants me to get dressed," he says with a shrug.

"Just open the door and let it out. I have no idea how it got here. Could it have opened the door by itself?"

"Yeah, hypothetically speaking. But where the hell did it come from?" Sivan asks.

I walk into my closet and take my meeting clothes out. I have no freaking clue how a monkey got in here. I place my clothes on my bed and drop my towel. The monkey hops on the bed and starts making its way over to me. I put my underwear and pants on quickly, before it reaches me. "How did you get in here?" I ask it. The monkey jumps at my chest, and I catch it against myself. It's latched on tight with its feet. "Hey, get down," I say, trying to pry him off my chest.

Whack. The monkey slapped me again. "Oh my God. Why do you keep hitting me?"

Sivan is trying hard not to laugh, but it's not working. "I don't think that monkey likes you. It must have bad taste," he says.

The monkey jumps down and makes its way toward my door. "I can't believe it just slapped me again," I say, rubbing my cheek. "What the hell?"

The monkey looks at me and smiles, it's almost taunting me. "Why hasn't it smacked you, Sivan?"

"No idea. I'm still not sure any of this is really happening. Starting to wonder if this is all a dream."

Someone is knocking on my door. Sivan holds his finger in front of his mouth, telling me to be quiet.

Harlow's voice shouts through the door. "No use in pretending you're not in there. I gave you two plenty of time to sleep and even tolerated whatever that abhorrent act was a few minutes ago. I can't allow this, Vincent, I'm sorry. If you two want to do these kinds of things, it can't be in the bed that we are going to share."

I am instantly full of rage, but remind myself that I have to stay calm. I can't really do that, though. "What the hell are you saying?" I shout back. "You're acting like we're doing something, when we're just lying in my bed."

"Let me in and I'll show you exactly what I'm talking about. Oh, but please do finish dressing first."

"There is still a camera in here," Sivan whispers.

The rage I initially felt is nothing compared to the surge of fury I feel at the thought that she just saw Sivan's naked body. "Shit, we just gave her more of what she wanted."

"Mmm, hardly," Sivan says passing me my shirt off the bed. "I think she's probably rather disappointed to be honest. But there's no way I'm letting her in here. Tell her to go away, Vincent."

"Harlow!" I shout, while buttoning my shirt. "Ahem… Harlow," I say, softening my tone. "I need you to leave. We're not done talking and I need to finish this discussion with Sivan. I can't have you in here."

"No. No, I'm not leaving. Open the door or I'll show everyone what I've got on this phone," she says.

"Do it." Sivan challenges. "Do it, Harlow, just go ahead. Don't just stand out there and threaten him."

"What the hell are you saying to her? Don't tell her to do that."

"She won't fucking do it, because then she's got nothing on you. Right now, she has you by the balls, she's not gonna tell anyone."

"Harlow, please don't tell anyone, okay? I already agreed to do whatever you said. Just give me some time, here."

Her mouth is presumably pressed near the door frame as she whispers loudly. "No, I will not be sent away like some ship trash. I am your fiancée, Vincent. Open the door,"

"Oh, screw you," Sivan says. "You're only his fiancée because you've blackmailed him! You're not his fiancée by choice. Besides, I thought you were going to tell his father?"

"Ugh!" Harlow's foot stomps loudly outside the door. "I hate you, Sivan. You're ruining everything! There are so many girls that like you. Can't you just go away?"

"Never," he says with his mouth right beside the door. The monkey is just sitting by his feet. Honestly, I'm almost afraid to look at it. I don't feel like getting slapped again.

"Your fathers have been storming around all afternoon; they've only not bothered you because you said you were feeling sick, Vincent. They sent me here to check on you, and here you are ignoring me for Sivan. Open the door, or I *will* tell your father about you two, and don't listen to Sivan, because I'll do it. I have more than enough on this phone that you wouldn't want anyone to see. Trust me."

I have to let her in. I'm just going to try and reason with her. I don't know what else to do. I'm going to make a shitty captain. All I can do is think of Sivan. If I was ruined, I would be okay with that, because between the two of us, there is one who deserves to be a captain, and it's not me.

I'm walking toward the door when Sivan stops me. Placing a hand on my chest. "You're gonna open it?" he asks me.

"I don't have a choice. If she goes out there whining and gets her mother involved, I'll be in more trouble than I care to deal with at this point."

Sivan pulls me in close, while the monkey runs past us into my bathroom and pushes the door shut. I need to get that monkey out of here, but I guess it's good that it ran into the bathroom. One problem at a time.

Sivan kisses my forehead and squeezes me tightly. "No matter what happens, I won't let her, or anyone else, have you. I'll never stop fighting for us."

"Who are you going to fight with? I don't want you to fight with anyone."

"Shhh. I just needed you to know. I don't know what's going to happen if she tells everyone, but even if every pirate in the world stands against us, I will stand by your side."

He's being so sweet to me. I never saw him act this way, not with any girl…not with anyone. He hasn't even picked a first mate yet, because he really doesn't trust or let people in. What can I do to keep him here with me? How can I protect what we have? These feelings that we have for one another—how do I keep them safe? "Sivan, I want you to stay with me," I say meekly, looking into his deep blue eyes.

Our lips touch softly, and he taps his tongue against mine, then pulls back slowly. "I will stay until you tell me to leave," he says and kisses my head.

"Oh wow," Harlow says outside the door. "This is priceless. I already told you both that I could see you, and now what? You're just ignoring that I'm outside here? You don't even care?"

"No, neither of us care," Sivan says. "Because here's the thing, I'm in here and you're out there, and his eyes haven't wavered once."

"I want to talk to her," I whisper.

Sivan inhales and nods at me. "Alright, then let's let her in."

I walk toward the door, leaving the warmth of his embrace. "Sivan, go ahead and sit down, you don't need to stand, just try and relax."

I open the door for Harlow, and she shoves her phone into her pocket. "Thank you. Let's have a little talk, my dear fiancé," she says, and pinches my cheek. I pull my face back and step to the side, closing the door once she's inside.

"Don't touch him," Sivan warns. He's refusing to sit down, but at least he's standing on the other side of the room.

Harlow holds her palms out toward him and takes a few steps back from me.

"Harlow, listen, I don't think I can do this. You're still recording me? How am I ever supposed to trust you?" I ask.

"Trust me? Trust *me*? What the hell do you need to worry about trusting me for? You're the one that can't be trusted. In here having se—doing that with him. We were supposed to have an understanding; I didn't mean that you could just do whatever you wanted."

"I don't understand what the hell is happening," Sivan says. "Where is the camera? Just tell us where it is, Harlow. He shouldn't even be having this conversation with you. You know how he feels and yet you manipulated him into this. And now you're here demanding that he respects you, when what amount of respect have you shown him? You think that watching someone without their permission is an okay thing to do?"

"I don't need to be lectured by you. Especially when I'm trying to help you two."

"Oh, don't give me that," Sivan says. "You're not trying to help us. You're trying to help yourself. Otherwise, why would you demand that he marries you? Helping us would be deleting whatever you have recorded and moving on with your life. You don't care about him. You care about yourself."

"Vincent, is that how you feel?" she asks me.

"Well, yeah, I mean I told you I didn't want to do this with you. I don't even know why you want to marry me, other than status. I have never given you anything—aside from sex, which you always initiated. But, emotionally, I have never misled you. You had no reason to be recording me. I don't understand."

"You always were a little slow," she says. "I had every right to do that. Everyone on the ship expected that we would be married when you turned twenty-one. They assumed that because that's what our parents planned for. Don't you think that's what your mom would have wanted? Do you think she'd really want you to be with him? What about your father?"

"She is such a manipulator," Sivan mutters. "Vincent, I'm happy to leave if you need me to, because I can't just sit here and be quiet while she does this to you."

"No, don't leave," I say.

"You should go," Harlow says. "This has nothing to do with you. It's between me and my fiancé."

Sivan rolls his eyes at her and pulls his phone out. He looks like he's texting someone. I want to ask what he's doing, but as long as he's sitting down, which he is now, it's better that I just leave him alone.

I hold a hand on my forehead. "Enough of this. What the hell am I supposed to do here? I don't have the right words for how frustrated I am with you right now, Harlow. I don't think this arrangement is going to work out. You're already getting in the way of the two of us, and we're not even married yet. I think we need to call this off."

"You selfish son of a bitch. I have been on this ship with you our whole lives. My mother has served your father for twenty-one years, and I have tried to do the same for you. Of course, I didn't care that you slept around with other girls, because you weren't mine, as much as I wanted you to be, but now we're engaged—what will everyone think of me knowing that you chose to be with a man. What does that say about me?"

I run my hand down my face. "I have no idea how this affects you at all. If you mean because we would call the engagement off, then I'd say that's your fault. You can't twist this around on me, when I didn't ask for any of this."

"Vincent, I would be the laughingstock of the entire ship, and your father may not even make you a captain when he finds out. It would be a travesty. I'm standing in front of you saying that I'm willing to become your wife, just to save you two from the embarrassment of everything. Please...don't you have any feelings for me after all this time?"

I look to Sivan who is avoiding eye contact with me. "Harlow, I just don't care for you in that way. I'm sorry. The truth is that there's always been a wall in between the two of us, and I never fully understood it until recently. What you have to accept is that this world that you've created is just built on this illusion of us eventually being together. I never once led you to believe that would happen. I know that you realize that."

"But can't you just pretend? I mean, what about Captain and Crew? Being with Sivan is not what's best for the crew. I know *you* realize that."

I can't believe she just tried to throw that in my face. "No outdated motto is going to determine who I marry or how I live my life."

Harlow shakes her head at me. "I tried. I tried to do this the nice way. So, what, you think I'm going to just give up? Leave forever? No. I won't accept this. I refuse," she says crossing her arms and staring me down.

"You refuse what?" Sivan asks.

Ignoring Sivan's question, she steps closer to me. "I am not giving up. I have worked too long for this. You agreed to marry me, and I will tell everyone about what happened if you don't go forward with the marriage. Plain and simple."

"Back to this again," Sivan says, dropping his head forward. "Vincent, do you trust me?"

"Of course," I say.

Sivan stands up from the couch and walks toward the door. "Harlow, go tell everyone on the ship. Tell them that you caught us fucking. Show them the video, tell his father, go to the pub—do whatever you want. Go right ahead."

My mouth drops open, and I quickly cover it, while Sivan opens the door.

"Goodbye, Harlow, let us know how it goes," he says gesturing to the open door.

Harlow crosses her arms across her chest and cocks her head to the side. "I'm not leaving!"

Sivan is not about to back down either. "Oh, you *are* leaving because the way I see it, is you have three choices: One, you leave and go do something that doesn't involve us. Two, you go tell the entire crew what you found out, and how you discovered our relationship, you'll also have to tell them the engagement is off at that time. Three, refuse to leave, and I will tell the captain myself that you have been recording Vincent for years. So, what's it gonna be?"

"I guess we'll find out," she says, walking out the door.

"Well, that was quite dramatic...even for Harlow's standards. She didn't even shut the door," I say laughing.

Sivan pulls me close and kisses me, his tongue is moving softly inside my mouth, while he holds the back of my head. I really love being kissed by him. The way our mouths move together, never separating, is one of my favorite things.

Rum-Soaked Awakenings

As I reach for his waist, Sivan pulls back from the kiss and his eyes are wide. "Oh shit, Vincent, the monkey! It's in your bathroom!"

We quickly walk inside my bathroom and find the monkey sitting on the bathroom counter. I'm looking around to see what it might have gotten into, but everything seems fine in here. Nothing is out of place, and the monkey is just sitting there looking at the two of us. The monkey makes its way across the counter and jumps onto my chest. "I swear if this monkey slaps me, again…"

Whack, the monkey slaps me across my face again, and this time it laughs, it freaking laughs, and jumps down, quickly bolting out of the bathroom and my open bedroom door.

I'm rubbing my cheek, completely stunned that I was slapped three times by a monkey today. But the slap brings back the realization that Harlow could be on her way to tell our fathers about us. I have no idea what she's going to do, and I just don't know what the hell I'm supposed to do right now. I can't believe she even brought my mother into it.

"Well, that takes care of the monkey," I say. "Now what? What should we do? We really need a plan for how to deal with this."

Sivan walks out of the bathroom and closes my bedroom door. "We're lucky no one walked by when I kissed you a few minutes ago. But you asked what we should do, and I have a few ideas." He pulls me in by my waist pressing our bodies together.

I tuck my face into the side of his neck. "What kind of ideas?"

He lifts my chin and kisses me softly. "Let's leave the ship for a while and forget about everything. Come on. I want us to spend the day out. Our fathers aren't bothering us, and we only have a few days of freedom before all the craziness starts."

"Mmmm…I don't know." I place a kiss on the side of his neck.

He squeezes my waist tightly and kisses the top of my head. "Come on, just for a little while. Only a few hours. We need to talk about us somewhere that we aren't worried about everyone around us."

I want to talk about us, but I am kind of afraid, as stupid as that sounds. Still, he's right. We do need to talk. "Okay, but we need to go quick before our fathers call for us."

CHAPTER 10
HE CALLED ME BABY
AND I LIKED IT

SIVAN

I'm glad we decided to leave the ship. The fresh air feels nice. Most days I'm stuck in captaincy lessons, well, more recently I'd been doing lessons from my room, and barely talking to anyone besides my teacher. Walking beside Vincent now is both comforting and terrifying. Terrifying because I truly feel like I would give up everything for him. How can I feel this way? My whole life I've never believed in the idea of true love…am I in love? Is this what it feels like? I wish my mom were here. If there was anyone that I could have talked to about this, it would have been her, well, her or Vincent's mom. They were both so full of love for us, the kind of love that I understood. They were never angry—just always dancing and having a good time. I can't even remember a time that my mother ever yelled at me, now that I think of it. Our moms yelled at our dads sometimes, but never at us. I remember asking my dad when I was a teenager how he was happy with just one person for so many years, to which his answer was that my mother was the most beautiful. At that time, I laughed because there were plenty of beautiful girls, but none was prettier than the other, I also thought it sounded kind of superficial. When I laughed, he explained to me that beauty starts in the soul and radiates outward. Then he said a bunch of other stuff that I don't really remember.

"Sivan," Vincent says. "Let's go over behind the old boat yard. I don't think anyone will be over there this time of day."

I want to hold his hand, but I…shit, this is why we need to talk. I can't just hold his hand. I can't just kiss him whenever I want. And all I want to do is kiss him. "Yeah, that sounds good. The port seems calm now. Part of me was afraid that Captain Slicer sent more men, and we may be caught in the middle of a fight." I flash him my pistol. "I'm ready if it happens, but, still, I hope it doesn't."

"I have my sword for the same reason. It's crazy that this is happening. Here we are stuck in the middle of this fucking threat that has nothing to do with us. What the hell is he pissed about anyway? Our dads asked him to let them leave his crew, it's not their fault that he refused. That was twenty-one years ago anyway, what could my dad have of Captain Slicer's?"

I'm looking all around as we reach the dock behind the boat yard. It's empty, and quiet, which is nice because we have this whole spot to ourselves. "I don't know, I think it has everything to do with us. At the end of the day, there will always be pirates who stand against our way of life, it's up to us to show them why we live the way we do. As for your dad having something that belongs to Captain Slicer, I don't really know. Is there like a weapon or something?"

Vincent shakes his head. "Nope, don't think so. Pretty sure I'd have seen or heard about it."

There's a bench at the end of the boardwalk that we've come to more times than I can count. Sometimes with girls, and sometimes just the two of us. I look over my shoulder to be sure there's no one following us and see that we are completely alone.

I take his hand in mine and interlock our fingers. When our hands connect, I exhale, it's like I was holding in a breath this whole time without knowing. I look over at him and see his lightly reddened cheeks. Oh my God, he's actually blushing. He could not be any cuter. His dimples are going to be the death of me. One of these days I'm gonna be in a fight or something and see his dimples, I'll get distracted and probably get stabbed with a stupid smile on my face.

Vincent giggles under my gaze and bites his bottom lip avoiding eye contact.

I tug on his hand. "What are you laughing about?"

"It's just surreal being here with you. I'm your best friend, so I can ask you this: how did we get here? Not literally here, just here, me and you? You have never wanted a relationship with anyone and you're here with me, holding my hand. You're smiling so much, which really isn't any different than when we're normally together, but your smile—it's changed. It's brighter, it just looks different. Do you know what I mean?"

I lift our clasped hands to my mouth and kiss his hand. We sit on the old sea-battered bench beside each other. Our initials along with countless others are carved into it. "I do know what you mean, because I can't see you the way I saw you before, well, before I realized how I felt. You're the same person, but you feel different to me. Maybe it's not that you feel different, maybe I'm just aware of the way you make me feel now. I can't remember a time when I didn't want to be near you, and that makes me think I've always felt this way and just didn't realize it."

"What are we gonna do? And do you want to actually be together, like in front of people? I feel so stupid asking you that, but I need to know. I don't want to pressure you, but I feel like—"

I crush his lips with mine and kiss him deeply, holding his face. A light whimper escapes his lips in between breaths. I'm trying to kiss him softly, but I can't help myself. Vincent deepens the kiss, caressing my tongue with his. I pull back slowly and press our foreheads together. "I want to be with you. I will do whatever it takes. I told you this earlier, and I meant it. I will do whatever you want me to do, as long as I can do it with you beside me. If you want to tell everyone, then we'll do that, if you want to keep it a secret, then…well, I'll like that less, but I can wait until you're ready. I'm not nervous, Vincent. I'm more worried about the ceremony, and the threat of Captain Slicer, than I'm worried about the crew or our fathers' reactions."

"But doesn't it make you nervous that you've never been in a real relationship before? I'll probably get on your nerves a lot. Then there's the whole distance thing—what are we supposed to do? See each other twice a year?"

I squeeze his thigh. "No. I want to be in a relationship with you *because* it's you. With the distance thing, we'll have our own ships in a few days, remember? We can do whatever we want, provided a war doesn't break out. This is why I want to combine crews. If we join our crews together, then we won't have to separate."

"There is a lot of sense in it, but our fathers won't allow it. Even putting our relationship aside, they'd be pissed that we didn't want to do things their way. I can't see that going well," he says.

"Yeah, then maybe we should tell them about us. Both of our fathers are pushing us to settle down, what's the difference if it's to each other? Right?"

Vincent leans his head on my shoulder. "What am I so afraid of?"

I wrap my arm around him. "I don't know. We're not the first men who have liked other men; besides we'd be telling our fathers that we're happy, what more could they actually want? Isn't that all any parent wants? Is for their kid to be happy? By the way, I'm sorry that Harlow brought your mom up like that earlier. Call me stupid, but I think your mom would have been pretty happy if we ended up together." I rub his cheek with my thumb. "I know my mom would have been happy."

He laughs and lifts his head from my shoulder. "I think your mom would be so confused. She'd be trying to figure out how I ruined her perfect son."

I tilt my head at him. "What the hell are you talking about? How did you ruin me?"

Vincent holds his head in his hands. "Sivan, I—I just feel like you were okay before, then we slept together and now I'm taking up all of your time and energy, we're gonna be named captains in a few days, and instead of getting ready for that, you're out here with me trying to figure out how publicly shunned you're going to be because of me."

I shake my head and lift his chin. "Hey, look at me. What are you talking about? I'm out here with you because I want to spend time with you. I want to tell our fathers about us, I want to tell them how I feel, but I want to make sure you are comfortable enough to do that. I don't give a shit what anyone says. If everyone we know turns their back on us, then I won't care, as long as I have you. Let them leave. I just want you. I feel like I've been pretty clear about that. Relationships are new to me, but am I doing something wrong? I don't want you to feel like this."

"You're not doing anything wrong. It's me. I just—maybe I don't feel good enough for you or something. I don't know.

When you were gone, Matteo kept pointing out all the girls you slept with, oh wait. Your dad said you were with Jenny the morning before you left—what was that about?"

"Yeah, I was so wasted that I apparently was talking about my feelings for you at the bar. She somehow got me home, and when I woke up, she was in my bed."

His eyes are wide and he's covering his mouth.

"No, no. Stop. We were fully dressed when I woke up, and she left two minutes after that. She wanted me to explain my feelings for you, which I refused to do. Also, I told her when I was sober that she was not going home with me, believe me, nothing happened."

He just reminded me of something, but I want to let him process what I said first.

"Why did she sleep in the same bed as you? And what did you say at the bar? Was your dad there?"

"I have no idea why she did that. I also don't know exactly what I said, but she was pretty sure of my feelings for you, even though I told her I wouldn't talk about it. And, yes, my dad was there, but he was too drunk to remember anything."

He lets out a long exhale. "I feel so much better. That was really weighing in the back of my mind. I wonder what you said. Probably would have been better if your dad heard everything."

"Yeah probably. I had the same thought initially."

"Got wasted on your birthday, huh? I did the same." Vincent shakes his head. "I tried to text you. Still don't understand what happened."

"Oh, I have news on that. Well, I think I have it figured out, but if I'm wrong, I'll sound crazy."

"I do like when you get a little crazy. What did you figure out?"

I pull my phone out of my pocket. "Check your phone. Did you miss any calls or texts in the past two hours? From me specifically."

Vincent is checking his phone. He turns the screen toward me. "Nope. Nothing. Why?"

I turn my phone toward his, showing him the four texts I sent when Harlow was in his room earlier.

I think she screwed with your phone.

Maybe she restricted my number.

But that doesn't answer why I wouldn't have gotten your texts.

You look really sexy, and I want her to leave.

"Let me see if your number is restricted. Wait, how would I know?"

He passes me his phone and I search the blocked numbers. "Ahhh. Yep. You blocked me and some other numbers. How could you?" I chuckle, showing him the phone.

His mouth is wide open. "No, how could she have done that? When would she have done that? I really wasn't around her at all while we were apart."

I stand up from the bench and exhale. I'm so pissed off about this. "I don't know, but, wait, don't you have me saved in your phone?"

"Of course I do." He taps the contact and shows me my name, with the favorite star beside it.

"There's one part I don't understand. Try to call me. She couldn't have blocked me from receiving your texts or calls."

Vincent presses the call button, and we listen as the phone rings on speaker. We're both looking at my phone, seeing that no call is coming through.

"How do we explain this?" Vincent asks.

"Wait. I think I know. What's the phone number you have for me?"

Vincent pulls up the phone number and shows it to me. "I assume it's the same one I've always had. I didn't change it."

"Well, you may not have, but someone did. That's not my phone number."

Vincent stands up from the bench and rakes his hand through his hair. "Are you fucking serious, right now?! This is why? This is why you didn't answer me? Because she made sure I couldn't reach you. I am so pissed off right now, Sivan. I fucking cried so much. I was so upset, thinking that you were ignoring me. Damn it. What do I do?"

"I have no idea. That level of deceit is insane, though. She not only blocked my number from reaching you, but she changed my number in your phone to make sure that you couldn't reach me, too. I didn't realize how smart she was. It almost seems too smart for her to have come up with. I knew she was a manipulator, but this is next level."

Vincent is pacing in front of the bench. "And what about Matteo? How come he didn't realize this? He's always five steps ahead of me figuring shit out. He never even considered this. Just said you were ignoring me because you were using me. He's gonna be my first mate—shouldn't he have seen this as a possibility? Shouldn't I have? Damn it, when did I stop thinking for myself? Am I really this stupid?"

I've never seen him like this, he looks like a frightened puppy. I can't tell if he's going to cry or punch something. Luckily, we're on a dock and there isn't anything to punch, aside from me, or the bench. I'm not at all surprised that Matteo didn't figure it out.

"Hey," I say, sitting on the bench. "Sit down with me. It's okay."

Vincent sits beside me, leaning forward on his elbows.

"Give me your phone, I'll fix it." He passes it to me, and I remove the block from my number, and update the number he had saved for me, then pass it back to him. "Look at me, Vincent. You are not stupid." I kiss the side of his head. "You don't give yourself enough credit. You only rely on him because that's what you've been taught to do. This is why I haven't chosen a first mate. Do you realize that? I have two people I trust, well, really one, but I guess two. Neither of those people can be my first mate. You have to trust this person even more than you trust yourself…that's what we've been taught, right?"

He nods. "Yeah, and that's…wait two? Who?"

"You and my dad, but that's not important right now. You don't need Matteo to figure things out. You can do this. Why wouldn't he have considered that Harlow messed with your phone? There are four reasons I can think of right off the bat, probably more. I want you to really think. What is the most obvious reason?"

"I don't know. Probably because he hates you and doesn't want us to be together."

"Yeah, well that's true. Still haven't figured out why he hates me, but I have a few theories. That's exactly right, though. He didn't bother thinking about it, because he already had the answer he wanted. If you're trying to help someone figure something out, and your first possible solution is the one that favors your line of thinking, you're not gonna dive deeper unless you're willing to consider something that could potentially be less favorable for you. You get it?"

"Yeah, he's a little prick. "

"Well, a little bit, but I still really don't want to talk shit about him because he's gonna be around for a long time, and he's part of your family."

He's laughing at me. I think he's finally cracked.

"Sivan, if we're together, you have to back me up. If I say he's a prick, he's a prick. Those are relationship rules."

"He's a prick. The biggest prick I've ever seen."

He kisses me on my cheek and smiles. "That's better. What are the other reasons he wouldn't have figured it out?"

His dimples are so deep when he smiles at me. I can't help but kiss each one before I answer. "Sorry. It's your fault for having such a kissable face. Your dimples are so distracting."

"*Your* face is distracting. I can't even remember what we were talking about."

"I was telling you that you don't need Matteo or anyone else to think for you, and you proved my point. You're more than capable of determining motive. I've seen you do it. Might not be something that comes naturally to you, but you can do it."

"Maybe. I'm starting to not feel really good about having him as my first mate, because of my relationship with you. If he can't accept us, I can't have him as my first mate, Sivan. I really can't have him as anything. What the hell am I supposed to do?"

"It's up to you. No one can force you to do anything that you don't want to do. I'm not selecting a first mate. It's never happened before, but I don't care. My dad doesn't even bring it up anymore. Who even knows what will happen; Slicer says he's gonna come see our dads on that day, so I'm ready for anything."

"Yeah…I guess we need to be." Beside my leg is one of the many spots Vincent carved his initials when we were younger, my initials are just a few inches away from his. The whole bench is covered in carvings. My initials, his initials, even Matteo's initials, it's just one of those things we did when we were younger. I never carved any girls initials into this bench, though. Even at that age, I didn't like the idea of being with just one person forever. I run my finger over the letter V remembering the time that we carved this particular set.

"Something is missing," he says, tapping the S beside his leg.

"What's that?"

He pulls his small pocket blade out and smiles at me. He's carving something. Our initials are spaced pretty close to one another, but they're separate, because, well, it's not like we wrote them with the intention of being together. But still, among the many on the bench these two were carved deeper than the others.

"There," he says. "SC plus VR. Now it shows everyone that we're together." He slides the blade back into his pocket and gives me a cheesy grin. "I don't know why, but doing that felt really liberating."

I giggle and pull him in for a quick kiss. "Now that you've done that, you realize that you officially belong to me. No one else can ever have you, Vincent Rodrigo."

He kisses me quickly, then hovers his lips by mine. "No one else ever will."

He captures my lips with his, and I gladly let him take control. He's such a good kisser, there's something about his tongue that drives me absolutely feral. I want to swallow this man. He gets me hard so fucking fast. His warm slippery tongue is gliding all around mine. Our mouths are twisting and turning, faster than our tongues can even follow. Vincent's hands are all over me, and I may just fuck him right here on his bench if I don't get ahold of myself. Anyone could come by. Anyone could see us. He stands from the bench and removes his sword from his side, placing it on the bench beside me, then reaches inside his coat pocket. He's putting his hair up in a tight knot and giving me the dirtiest look I've ever seen. He can definitely see my dick pressed against my pants. I'm achingly hard right now. I rub my palm down it and make eye contact with him. "I don't know what you're thinking, but I can't be rational here."

He reaches forward and slides my coat off my shoulders. He kisses the side of my neck and whispers in my ear. "Move your pistol. I'm gonna suck your dick."

My dick is leaking already. I can't let him suck me off on this boardwalk, though. What if someone sees him? I look left to right while Vincent reaches beside me and pulls my pistol from its holster.

He takes my earlobe in his mouth, lightly pulling it with his teeth and unbuckles my belt. "Sivan, baby, I can feel how nervous you are. I want to get on my knees for you. I want to make you come right here on this bench. Don't you want that?"

"Oh, fuck, Vincent…"

He called me baby, and I liked it. He's the only person to ever make me come from a blowjob and my cock knows it even better than me. I pull my pants down, and Vincent tugs them down even further. He drops to his knees, he's so eager to please me. He's looking up at me with his big brown eyes. With my cock in his hand, he lightly licks the tip and moans. "Mmm. I want to taste you again."

I grab the bun in his hair and guide his mouth onto my cock.

His warm lips wrap around me and my toes curl inside my boots. Vincent slowly slides nearly all of me inside, and I feel him almost gag. He pulls back and begins playing with the head of my dick, licking the tip, swirling his tongue around, while I grip the knot in his hair tighter. I want to fuck his mouth so bad, it's incredibly hard to hold back when his tongue is right there. He's staring up at me, while he drags his tongue up the length of my cock. "Mmm…you taste so good, Sivan."

"Your mouth feels so fucking good, Vincent."

He seems to like that bit of praise, based on how eagerly he takes me back into his mouth. He's gliding his mouth up and down, bobbing while I thread my fingers through the top of his hair, then grip his bun again.

I can feel my balls tighten, my orgasm drawing closer. I can't believe he's going to make me come with his mouth, again. My breaths are heavy, and I drive further into his mouth, matching my thrusts with his pace. "Fuck—mmm—just like that."

He pulls my cock out and slides his hand up and down it, pumping me at a slow pace, making eye contact. "Are you gonna come for me?" He kisses the tip, then slides all of my dick back inside his mouth and squeezes my balls. I drive harder and faster into his mouth.

I'm so drunk on the feeling of his mouth wrapped around me that I can't even remember where the fuck I am, I just know that I need to come. I'm grinding hard into him, and when his throat tightens, I can't help but try and drive in further. The feeling of him choking on my cock is enough to push me over the edge. "Fuck—I—I'm fucking coming." My cum shoots inside of his mouth and Vincent's head moves up and down, as he eagerly sucks out every drop, jerking my cock until I finish.

He looks up at me and wipes his mouth with the back of his hand. "Twice. I made you come with my mouth twice." He raises his eyebrows at me. "Who would have known I'd be good at sucking dick?"

I hold his chin in my hand and kiss him softly. "You're good at everything. That was incredible. What about you? You want me to…" Before I can finish my offer, I look around and suddenly realize where we are, again. Oh my God, anyone could have seen us doing that. Thankfully, I don't see anyone around, though.

"A bit late to worry about anyone seeing us." He smiles and stands up, patting my thigh. "Don't worry about me. My knees hurt so bad from the wood; I couldn't come even if I tried. Before you offer, that is not a challenge. He laughs and grabs his sword, hooking it back onto his belt and puts his coat on.

"Well, thank you," I say pulling my pants up. "I owe you later, then. You come first next time." I stand up from the bench and admittedly I'm a bit weak in the knees from that blowjob. Not just physically, but, damn—he's doing things to me in ways that I never even thought possible. There is literally nothing that makes me happier than being near him. I adjust my pants, and pistol, then straighten my collar.

"Deal," he says. "You have a thirty second rebound rate after orgasm, though, so I'm fine with you coming first." He smiles and pulls his phone out of his pocket. I don't like the look on his face, it just changed from happy to concerned. "Ah. Shit. Got a text from my dad." He turns the screen toward me.

Both of you…in my office, now.

"Ooh. That doesn't sound good. He didn't even say why."

"It's probably about Slicer," Vincent says. "Although, you really pissed Harlow off, so she may have told our dads about us. I've never seen her as mad as she was today. She could do anything, really."

I pull him in for a hug before we make our way back to the ship. I realize now that we didn't actually decide what we want to do as far as telling our fathers, or anyone else, for that matter. His face is tucked against my neck, and I can feel his heart beating fast against mine. I rub his back. "Hey, you, okay?"

He's nodding his head. "Yeah. I'm good. I just hate not knowing what to do."

"Then do whatever you want to do. Don't worry about everyone else. I told you that you were the most important thing to me, and I meant that. However you want to tell people about us is fine with me. If you want more time to think about how we do it, then that's fine, too."

He presses his lips to mine in a soft sweet kiss and squeezes me tightly. "Thank you. Let's just do what feels right. I don't feel like getting on my dad's bad side before the inspection tomorrow, so it may not be the best time. But if he already knows, then maybe we don't deny it."

"Right. He's also planning a wedding for you, Vincent. It's probably good if we shut that down. It opens us up to Harlow telling everyone, if she hasn't already, so I don't know what that will mean for us. You can't have him planning a wedding, though."

We start walking back toward his father's ship, and there's still no one around. I really hope that no one saw us earlier. Even if they did, it would have been from the back side of the bench.

The port is still pretty calm, you'd never know that there was so much chaos here earlier.

"There actually was a monkey in my room this morning, right?" he asks me with a giggle.

"Mmhmm. It slapped you three times. I saw it with my own eyes."

Our attention shifts toward behind the pub, where two

men are having what looks like an intense conversation. "I don't recognize them," Vincent whispers.

I nod and we continue walking past them, with the ship now in sight. We step aboard and walk quickly toward Captain Rodrigo's office.

Harlow's mother is headed straight for us. She looks even meaner than normal. She's sizing us up, but still walking at a leisurely pace. "Hello," she says through gritted teeth, as she walks past us.

"What do you think that was that about?" Sivan asks.

"I don't know, but her eyes looked angry or maybe worried. Maybe she came from my father's office?"

"Hmm, she could have been coming from almost anywhere on the ship."

"Sivan," he says stopping in the hallway.

I turn and look at him. "What's wrong?" I ask.

"If Harlow told him everything; what do I do? Do you want me to deny it?"

The concern in his heart is palpable. I just want to comfort him. "No, don't deny it for my sake, but if *you* want to deny it, you can. I won't be upset."

"Thank you," he whispers.

CHAPTER 11
DID YOU NOTICE SOMETHING?

"Where the hell is my son?" I hear my father shout.

Once we reach the room, things are more chaotic than I've ever seen them. Crew members are bumping into one another, shuffling in and out of the room past us as we walk in. There are papers strewn all over my father's desk, and Gwendolyn is lying atop the pile. He's pissed. He never takes his sword out inside his office unless he's angry, or lecturing me. Since there are so many people here, he's not gonna lecture me.

"What took you two so long?" my father asks.

"We came as soon as you asked us to. What are you yelling about?"

My father sits on the corner of his desk, while Sivan's father walks over and stands beside him. "You boys left the ship," Captain Crawford says. "Thought you weren't feeling well?"

"We just needed a bit of air," Sivan says.

My father nods his head slowly at us. He's taking in the sight of the two of us right now. "Well, it turns out that Harlow has decided she wants to call off your engagement. Now, why is that?"

I am completely frozen and unsure of what to do, or how

to answer. One part of me wants to celebrate what he said, but I have a bad feeling about this.

Lyndon, Captain Crawford's first mate, hastily makes his way over toward him. He whispers something into his ear, then walks back outside of the room.

"Alright," Captain Crawford says. "Seems like the last time Captain Slicer's ship was spotted was ten days ago off the coast."

"Which coast?" my father asks.

"Your coast, here, what else would I be talking about?" Captain Crawford says.

"Doesn't make any sense," my father says. "How would none of my guys have seen that?"

I just had an ominous feeling wash over me, along with a thought that I definitely won't share with anyone. But in three days this will be my problem, since I'll be a captain then. This also gives me a chance not to answer the question about Harlow.

"Captain," I say to my father. "If he was here ten days ago, and the messenger is still here; what does that mean for us?"

My father points at me. "This doesn't concern you right now. The only thing I want to hear from you is what happened with Harlow. *We* will deal with Captain Slicer."

I pull my head back. Kind of embarrassing to be talked to like that in front of the crew, but it's my father's ship, so there's not much I can do about it. I had no idea she was going to call it off, but I'm still a bit hesitant to be happy about it. "What do you mean what happened? Nothing happened, Captain."

My father is not buying the shit I'm trying to sell him right now. He stands from the side of the desk and walks around it. "Well, that's not what her mother said. I heard that the engagement is off. Now, try again. What happened?" my father asks, sitting down in his captain's chair. He rubs the blade of his sword and looks at Captain Rodrigo.

I turn toward Sivan, who's displaying the most neutral expression ever. He's not giving anything away right now. No one has any clue of what we've been doing, it's strange that hiding this can feel both exciting and awful at the same time. I don't know where Matteo is, he normally bails me out of these situations. I look around the room for him, but he's not here. I just realized he hasn't texted me at all today, which is also really strange. I didn't see him this morning, either.

Sivan leans close to my ear. "Why are you looking for him?"

I turn my face toward his, he's so close to me now. My body, despite the situation we are in, is kind of reacting to the scent of him, and his warm breath on my ear. "How do you know who I'm looking for?"

The tip of his nose touches the top of my ear, brushing my earring. "You're looking for Matteo because you are used to him bailing you out. You don't need him. You belong to me," he says and steps toward my father's desk.

Chills, actual chills, run up my spine from the hotness of what he just did.

"Captain," Sivan says. "Vincent was still not feeling well after he rested. I took him out to get some fresh air. We saw Harlow briefly before we left. She didn't mention that she would be calling off the engagement."

Our fathers exchange a glance. It feels like they know something, but that can't be it. We've been really careful. Well, I did just go down on him on the dock, but no one saw that.

"Is Harlow pregnant?" Sivan's father asks.

"What?!" Sivan and I both shout.

"No, of course not, why are you asking me that, Captain Crawford?"

Sivan holds a hand on his head, rubbing his temples. "Yeah, Captain, why would you ask him that?"

Captain Crawford holds his palms out. He shrugs a bit and glances at my father. "Your dad and I just find this whole thing very strange. You say you don't like the girl, then you announce your engagement. Sheena was absolutely hysterical; she came in here screaming that Harlow wants to call off the engagement."

My father's arms are crossed as he strokes his goatee. "So, if she isn't pregnant…then why did you propose so suddenly? You said multiple times that you wouldn't marry her, you just said it yesterday, in fact. Now just a day later, Sheena is yelling at me because Harlow is crying her eyes out, again. What am I to think about all this?"

I have no idea which way to lead this conversation at this point. "Captains, there's a lot going on. I don't know exactly how to answer your questions. But, no, she isn't pregnant. I haven't slept with her since the beginning of the year, so if she *is* pregnant, it isn't mine."

Sivan lets out a long audible exhale. He's very frustrated and annoyed right now, it's obvious on his face. "Hey," I whisper. "Don't worry about it." Instinctively the back of my hand brushes his cheek to comfort him. Everyone in the room has suddenly come to a standstill. They're all looking at us. What the hell did I just do? A straight man wouldn't rub his friends face like that. Our fathers look more than a little confused. I quickly pull my hand back and give a little laugh, trying to shrug the behavior off. I pat Sivan's shoulder. Sivan is obviously holding in a laugh. He isn't at all bothered by everyone staring over. The door to my father's office swings open wide, bringing a draft that blows a few papers off my father's desk. What the hell? It's Matteo, his clothes are a bit of a mess and his face is flushed. He's coming at me, no wait, he's headed for Sivan. I quickly stand in between the two. "Whoa, whoa, what the hell are you doing?" I ask. "Why are you coming at him like that? You're not gonna hit him. Back up."

Sivan places his hands on my shoulders and moves me to the side. I step back in front of him again. Matteo won't hit me, but he will for sure hit Sivan. "Don't move me like that, he was gonna fucking hit you."

Matteo's gaze is locked on Sivan. He looks like a wild animal right now. I have no idea what happened to him.

My father stands from his desk. "What the hell are you thinking?" he asks Matteo. "Did he say that you were going to punch Sivan?

Captain Crawford lifts his chin toward him. "Yeah, did he say you were going to hit my son?"

"I haven't done anything," Matteo says, eyes still locked on Sivan.

Sivan's head tilts to the side. The two are evenly matched in height and weight. I'm not quite sure which would win in a fight. But I don't want to find out either.

"You two," Matteo says, looking at the two of us. "You made her cry because you two can't just leave well enough alone. Because you two can't just leave one another alone. Why are you doing this? She was happy. I was happy. And you, Sivan…" He takes one step closer toward Sivan, who matches him, taking a step forward himself.

"Hey!" my father shouts, coming around the side of his desk. "What the hell are you talking about, Matteo?"

Captain Crawford looks around the room, realizing that a

large number of both crew members are still inside and paying close attention. "Rodri," he says, gesturing around the room. "Let's clear some of these out, hmm?"

My father nods and points to the door. "Yes, everyone out."

The crew quickly exit at my father's order, leaving only the five of us.

"Now," my father says. "What is going on? One of you start talking. Preferably you, Matteo, because you wouldn't lie."

Matteo laughs with his mouth open. "Ha! Lie? Me? No, never, now your precious little Vincent here, and this…" he says, still extremely close to Sivan.

"Did you just call me *this*? Don't talk to me like that," Sivan says.

My body is half in between the two of them, which is the only reason I think neither has punched the other. Matteo would be in a lot of trouble for hitting Sivan because of Sivan's status; if it were just a normal crew member, they would have already started punching one another.

"Yes, Matteo, he is quite right," my father says. "Don't care what's happened, you still have to show respect. It's the crew's way. You know that."

Sivan and Matteo are still caught in a murderous stare-down.

"That's right," Sivan's father says. "We still respect Captain Slicer even though I'm gonna blast his head off when I see him."

"No, no, I'm gonna take care of Slicer," my father says.

"No." Captain Crawford stops his foot. "That is not what we decided. We decided that whoever saw him first would take care of him.

Our fathers are stuck in this stupid little discussion while

Sivan and Matteo look like they're going to kill each other. There is so much hate in the silence between them.

"Matteo, what are you even pissed off about?" I ask him. "Sivan didn't do anything. You're being ridiculous."

Matteo points at himself. "I'm being ridiculous? No, no. You will not force me to lie anymore. I'm sick of it. Captains, these two…" Sivan and I drop our heads, he's gonna tell them everything. Matteo smirks, obviously enjoying the reaction we just gave him. "These two have been doing all kinds of things that they shouldn't."

"Shut up, Matteo," I say.

"Move, Vincent," Sivan says. "I can't take this anymore."

"Enough," my father says. "Tomorrow is the inspection. The three of you will need to clear the air between you before that. I don't care who did what. Ray and I need to come up with a plan for Captain Slicer. Didn't realize when that messenger was spouting all that nonsense earlier, he implied that Captain Slicer plans to interrupt your captaincy ceremony."

"What messenger? What the hell is going on?" Matteo asks.

Right, he wouldn't know, because he wasn't there. Where the hell was he all day, anyway? He didn't hear about any of the shit that happened in the port?

"Vincent, you need to take some time to explain to your first mate what happened. I told you earlier that you should have called him."

"With all due respect, Captain, I told you I didn't need to, because I had Sivan with me."

Matteo's mouth is wide open. "Oh, fuck this. First, he takes Harlow's place and now mine? Open your fucking eyes, Vincent."

"What the hell is that supposed to mean? There's no difference between our fathers leaving their first mates behind when they're doing things together. I don't have to bring you everywhere."

"Matteo," my father says stepping beside us. "I've never seen you like this. Take a break. Go grab a drink. I'll send for you later and fill you in. Your clothes are a mess, and you weren't here until hours after I called for you. I don't know what's going on, but tomorrow is a big day. I can't have the three of you acting like this. We have bigger problems than whatever this nonsense is."

He pats Matteo's shoulder, then opens the door. My father takes a step back at the sight. The same small monkey from earlier is sitting in the doorway. It dashes inside past my father and climbs up Matteo's side.

"What the hell? Is that Enzo?" Captain Crawford asks.

Matteo is making a confused face at the monkey, but supporting it on his side.

"Captains, that monkey was in my room earlier. Where did it come from?" I ask.

My father walks closer to Matteo and looks closely at the monkey. *Whack*. The monkey just slapped my father in the face.

"It *is* Enzo! What are you doing on my ship?" my father asks the monkey.

Captain Crawford walks beside my father and leans in toward the monkey. The monkey screeches and smacks him in the face, too. "We have a big problem. He doesn't go anywhere without this monkey."

I don't know what the hell is going on, or who Enzo belongs to.

"Captains, whose monkey is this? Who are you talking about?" Sivan asks.

The monkey screeches loudly looking at Sivan, but tucks his face into Matteo's side.

"This is Captain Slicer's beloved pet, Enzo," my father says.

Matteo pulls his face back from the monkey and places him on the floor. The monkey climbs right back up his side, while Matteo tries unsuccessfully to keep him down. "Get off. I don't want a monkey climbing all over me," he says.

Sivan leans close to me and whispers. "Did you notice something?"

I did not notice anything other than the fact that the monkey is a menace, just smacking people left and right, but I don't want to sound stupid. "Mmmhmm. But just to be sure, what did you notice?"

"You haven't noticed anything?" Sivan asks me.

I shake my head at him. "No, honestly, I haven't. But the monkey seems to hate everyone. I feel better knowing that."

"Why is Enzo here?" Captain Crawford asks. "How did he get on the ship? Ten days…they saw his ship ten days ago, but we have not seen his ship anywhere near here. Where did he come from?"

Maybe he had a little monkey rowboat and made his way over because he wanted to warn our fathers of Captain Slicer's plan. I laugh at myself, I really come up with the dumbest shit inside my head.

"No clue, but he wouldn't be here without Captain Slicer," my father says.

Matteo peels the monkey off his side and places him down. "I'm gonna get a drink like you suggested, Captain. Vincent, I'm sorry about earlier. The stuff with Harlow is getting to me. I'll see you later."

Once he leaves, Sivan nudges me. "We should go while we're still allowed to."

The two of us start walking toward the door. "Wait a minute, you two," my father says, as the monkey chases after Matteo.

"Now did you notice it?" Sivan asks me.

I shake my head at him. "Just tell me later."

My father pokes me in the chest. "You two don't need to hang around, right now. Keep your phone on, and I'll let you know when I need you back. But whatever is going on between you and Matteo, fix it. I do not want this spilling over into the inspection tomorrow. He is your brother; if he's upset, you need to listen to him."

"Yes, Captain, even if my brother *is* being a dick."

"Especially when your brother is being a dick," my father says, patting me on the shoulder.

Sivan's father pulls him aside and whispers a few things that clearly aren't meant for me to hear. He's nodding along to whatever his father is saying.

We walk back toward my room in silence. I'm not sure what to do next. Last night, no one suspected that we'd be sleeping in the same bed together, but after everything that just happened, our fathers may figure it out. Not only that, but Matteo might tell our fathers about us. I kind of want to talk to him to see what he was so mad about.

"Wait," Sivan says. "Let's go get something to eat, or we can go back to my ship. We can't go in your room; she'll just be watching us the entire time."

"Ah, I hadn't thought of that. Damn it, what am I supposed

to do? Not sleep in my own room ever again? I can't deal with this, Sivan."

He turns my door handle, and we walk inside my room. "Just grab stuff for tonight, and if you want to come back later, you can, if not, then you can stay the night with me. I am going to respectfully ask that I stay the night with you, either way. I am uncomfortable with her having access to you while you're sleeping. She can just watch you whenever she wants, or sneak in. The thought alone makes me crazy."

"Yeah, well, now she most likely heard you say that, so I doubt she's going to try anything. I don't want to sleep apart from you, anyway. Even if there wasn't a camera, I still would have tried to find a way to sleep in the same bed."

"Same," Sivan says, perching his chin on my shoulder from behind.

I start throwing things into my overnight bag. I toss the meeting suit and underwear he let me borrow into my hamper. "I'll get your clothes back to you after they're cleaned."

"I'm not worried about it," he says.

"Well, thanks for letting me borrow everything. Don't forget to grab your sword, too," I remind him.

"You can always use anything of mine." Sivan grabs the sword I borrowed earlier from my dresser and slots it into the holder on his belt. "But hurry up, because I owe you for this afternoon, and I don't know how much longer I can control myself." He squeezes my ass, then gives it a light smack.

Walking aboard Captain Crawford's ship with Sivan feels strange to me. I can't explain it, but part of me feels more comfortable here, despite this not being my ship. Maybe it's just because I know Harlow isn't watching me. There aren't many crew members on deck, they're probably all at the pub. I take one last bite of my chicken wrap, finishing it off. "I'm glad we stopped at Andy's, aren't the wraps delicious?"

Sivan nods, crumbling the wrapper in his hand. He holds his hand out for my wrapper, then tosses them both in a trash can on the deck. "Yeah, I love a good wrap. Our cook never makes them." He looks around as we walk downstairs. "There's no one around. We can hold hands now," he says, taking my hand in his.

"I like holding your hand," I say. "I want to do it all the time." I shake my head at myself remembering my own stupidity in my dad's office. "Can you believe I touched your face like that earlier in the room with everyone?"

He smiles at me. "Yeah, good thing Matteo came in and made a scene."

We walk inside of his room, which looks completely different than this morning. Different in the sense that it's clean now. I wonder if he's bringing Tilly onto his ship, or if she's staying here. For my ship, Sheena had a few people in mind for housekeepers, I'm not sure who, but I guess I'll find out tomorrow at inspection.

I sit on the edge of his bed and Sivan stands in between my legs. "I feel like I should get a reward for not punching your brother earlier."

I pat the front of his pants near his zipper. "You had a reward on the dock. Did you forget?"

He raises his eyebrows at my question and sits next to me. "Getting blown on the dock by my sexy secret boyfriend? I won't ever forget that."

I feel my cheeks warm at the word boyfriend. "My knees won't forget it either."

Sivan's phone is loudly vibrating in his pocket, but he's ignoring it. "You don't have to ignore your phone because of me. You can deal with whatever you need to."

"Nah, you're here with me, and before we left, my dad said he wouldn't bother us for the rest of the night. Oh, he also told me to be careful leaving you alone with Matteo. He must have been picking up on the same things that I was."

"Why should you be afraid to leave me alone with Matteo?"

"It's nothing," he says, brushing his thumb across my lip. "I do have a feeling that our dads already suspect what's going on between us, though."

"Why would you think that? Did your dad say something about it?"

He shrugs and leans back a bit. "Well..." He pulls his boots off, then stands, quickly taking mine off, too. He rubs the bottom of my foot smiling at me. Even through my sock it tickles. "He didn't say anything other than what I told you, but it was the way he said that he would make sure we could be alone tonight. But, Vincent—the lube was open on the nightstand, and your clothes were on the floor when they came in. You also rubbed my face earlier in front of everyone. I don't think it would take more than an average IQ to figure out that we're sleeping together."

"Well, what should we do? Do we just tell them? If you think they already know, then what's the sense in hiding it, at least from them?"

"At this point, I have no problem telling everyone. I'll call my dad now and tell him if you want." He pulls his phone out for emphasis and tilts his head at the screen. "Hmm. It's a text from my dad, he said that the inspection was moved to one o'clock tomorrow, and your dad just decided with Matteo that the two of you will go out to lunch beforehand. My dad said I'm not invited." He gives me an uncomfortable smile, laying back onto his pillow. "This is ridiculous."

"I'm not a child. Sivan, I don't want to do that. Don't I have any say in this?"

"If your dad doesn't give you the order directly, then you don't have to do it. It sounds like he just wants you two to talk without me around. I don't like it, but you do need to talk to him. You have to either clear the air or tell him he isn't going to be your first mate. I don't know how hard it would be for you to remove him once you promote him. If you go forward with the promotion and he outright rejects us, and then you don't want him, I'm not sure how much of a process that would be."

I lay back on his bed holding my forehead. "Well, if we take on Captain Slicer's ways, I could just throw him overboard."

"True. I doubt you could do that, though. You've known him your whole life, I can't imagine you tossing him off the ship, even with permission."

I scoot beside him in bed and tuck under his arm. He squeezes me once then kisses the top of my head. "I could maybe do it," I say. "Well, if he hurt you, I could definitely do it."

"Don't think about that," he says. "But you will need to meet with him tomorrow at some point, so you should have some kind of a plan for what you want to do."

"I'll decide in the morning, Sivan. Right now, I just want to lay here with you."

CHAPTER 12
FUCK ME NOW. KISS ME LATER.

Vincent's head is tucked under my arm as I wipe my eyes awake. It's dark inside my room. We must have fallen asleep. I grab my phone from my night stand. It's 2:00 AM. We talked for a few hours, and I guess we both just passed out. I need to get out of my meeting clothes and he's still in his, too. What are the rules for undressing your boyfriend while he's asleep? I want him to be comfortable, but I also don't want to wake him up. I lift my arm and try to slide out of my bed, carefully moving to the side.

Vincent lifts his head, blinking his eyes hard. "What time is it? Did we fall asleep?"

I lean in and give him a quick kiss. "We must have. I don't remember when, though. I'm gonna swap into some shorts and brush my teeth. You want to sleep in your meeting clothes or get changed, too?"

He wipes his eyes. "No, I'm getting up. I brought clothes with me this time, remember?" Vincent grabs his bag, and pulls out extra clothes, quickly changing into gray sweatpants and a black tee shirt. The clothes that he left here are hanging on my closet door. "Hey, looks like your outfit from the other night is clean, which is good, because you didn't bring a coat for tomorrow, right? Unless you stuck everything in that bag, which I doubt."

"Oooh, nice. I'll have to thank Tilly for washing everything for me."

I slip into my shorts, and head into the bathroom to brush my teeth. Vincent is sitting on my bed looking at his phone. He looks so cute when he's trying to figure something out. I don't think I'll ever get tired of seeing him in my room. What the hell am I supposed to do about Matteo? I still can't figure out why he'd try and get Vincent to hate me, could it really be that he just hates us together? He said something earlier about me taking his place. Maybe he's just jealous? If so, I can't blame him for that.

Vincent looks upset, his forehead is all scrunched up. "Hey," I say, with my toothbrush in my mouth. "Everything okay?"

He nods at me. "Yeah, just texting Matteo that I'll meet him in my room tomorrow around eleven, so we can go over some things. Also texted my dad to let him know about the change of plans. He shouldn't be pissed as long as I meet with him."

I want to tell him that my father and I picked up on a few strange things, but I also don't want to damage his relationship with that asshole if I'm wrong. He's been a part of Vincent's life for just as long as I have, it wouldn't be right for me to put an idea in his head for no reason. Telling him his adopted brother could have ulterior motives might be the wrong decision. "Yeah, there's really no way for you to avoid meeting with him before the inspection."

"Well, I'm gonna tell him that he either accepts our relationship, or he can't be my first mate."

I blow air from my mouth. Then I continue brushing my

teeth. I hate that this even matters to Matteo. Who gives a shit who anyone loves? If it's not your relationship, it's not your business. Why is he still so pissed off about it? There is an option I hadn't considered, which is that he could *like* Vincent…but I doubt that. Well, at least Harlow will be watching them in his room tomorrow, so if that's the case, I doubt she'd sit by and watch him do anything. If Matteo tried anything, Vincent would push him off anyway. He's pretty scrappy. No, wait, I'm not okay with that. Thinking of another guy trying to kiss him was a mental image I did not need. I spit in the sink. The immediate urge to claim him overcomes me.

I've never been a jealous man, but, fuck—he is mine and no one else can have him. I take his phone out of his hand and slide it onto the nightstand, then lift him under his arms to the middle of the bed, pinning his arms over his head and crushing his lips with mine. My tongue eagerly invades his mouth, and I'm sucking and kissing him harder than I've ever done before. In this moment, I need to feel him, I need to be one with him. Vincent whimpers a bit, and I pull back from the kiss to be sure he wants this just as much as I do. "Do you want me?"

He nods at me. "I want you so fucking bad, baby."

I release his hands and slide his shirt up, and he pulls it off. His chest is hot and hard, but the skin itself is soft. I lick his nipple, while I massage the other, lightly squeezing it. He loves it, his cock is already so hard in his sweatpants against my abs. I'm sucking and licking all over his chest, but I think it's the squeezing that really drives him crazy. Every time I pinch his nipple, his ass lifts off the bed, while he presses against me.

"Ah, fuck, Sivan…" He grips my hair tightly.

"You like that?" I make my way down his stomach, kissing and licking the ridges of his abs, and stop when I reach his waistband. His thick hard cock is beside my face, and I kiss it through the fabric. "Look how hard you are for me… You're so good, Vincent."

"Sssivan—" He brushes his fingers through the top of my hair. "Do you really think I'm good?"

I nod and pull his sweatpants down and he slides them the rest of the way off, kicking them onto the floor.

"I think you're very good, Vincent." I wrap my hand around his warm hard dick and squeeze lightly. I need to grab the lube, but I want to suck him first. I lick him from base to tip, looking up at him as he watches me. I take all of his cock into my mouth, going down slowly, then pulling up, until I find a comfortable rhythm, one that has Vincent grasping the sheet with one hand and my hair with the other. I pull his cock out, but continue jerking it. "Do you want to come for me like this?"

"Yes—yes, Sivan make me come."

"You want to come in my mouth?" I stick my tongue out flat and flick the head of his cock, trying to draw that delicious hot cum from it. I've tasted him before, but I haven't gotten a mouthful of it yet.

He turns his face to the side, and grips my hair tighter, as I take him all the way inside again. "Mmm—mmm," I moan on his cock. My hand is coated with my own spit, as I continue to jerk him harder and faster. "I want you to come for me Vincent. Be a good boy and give me what I want."

"Mmm—nnn—Sivan, sssay it again…" He grips my hair and thrusts his hips forward. "Suck my cock and call me a good boy."

I wrap my lips around his dick, rolling my tongue around the head and taking him deep. I pop off for a moment. "Come for me like a good boy. Show me how much you like this."

He's panting and grasping at my hair. "Suck...it." He holds the back of my head, guiding my face over his cock, and grinds into my mouth. "I'm gonna come, baby."

I pump and suck him at the same time, eagerly awaiting the taste. I'm taking him so fast and so deep, that I nearly gag when the first pulse of cum shoots in the back of my throat.

"I'm coming...I'm coming for you."

"Mmm—mmm," I moan and continue pumping and sucking, as more cum coats the inside of my mouth. I had no idea the absolute satisfaction I would feel from swallowing his cum. Or maybe it's that I feel satisfied knowing that I made him come with my mouth. No, satisfied is not the right word, because I'm not satisfied, it's not enough. I want everyone to know that he belongs to me. I want to fuck the hell out of him, so that he's walking funny tomorrow, then when anyone asks him why, he'll remember this. I shake my head at myself. I've never wanted anything as badly as I want him. I've never craved the feeling of someone else's body wrapped around me...until him.

Vincent is panting, trying to catch his breath, and rubbing the top of my head. I pull his dick out, kissing the tip one more time. I climb atop him, dragging my cock over his. I press my lips against his, kissing him with force, as he grabs the back of my head pulling my face in closer, crushing our lips together. I pull back from the kiss and rub his cheek with my thumb.

He tilts his head at me. "What's wrong? You don't want to kiss me?"

I smile, then kiss is forehead. "The problem is that I want to kiss you."

"How is that a problem?" he asks, lifting his head from the pillow, and touching his lips to mine softly.

"The problem is there are two sides of me at war for what I want to do with you. One side wants to kiss you sweetly, and the other wants to just fuck you so hard that you're walking sideways at the inspection tomorrow. I can't do both, so that's the problem."

He raises his eyebrows and reaches in between us, sticking his hand in my shorts. His mouth hangs open while he squeezes my dick. "Fuck me now. Kiss me later."

I kiss him once more then stand up to get the lube. "I want you to bend over for me, Vincent."

He shakes his head at me. "No. Only if you tell me I'm good."

I nod slowly at him, while dropping my shorts to the ground, then squirt the lube into my hand. "I think my boyfriend has a bit of a praise kink. They say that people who have praise kinks sometimes have the opposite, too." I stroke myself slowly, rubbing the lube all over my dick. "You want to test that theory?"

He nods at me. "Yeah, I might like that, too."

"Bend over now, you filthy fucking boy, and let me come deep in your tight little hole."

"Whoo—yep. I have that, whatever that is, the opposite of praise kink. *Fuck me.*" He giggles flipping over onto all fours, raising his ass in the air for me. "I still feel a little embarrassed in this position, but I love the way it feels."

I don't want him to feel embarrassed. I stand up from the bed and quickly turn the light off. "I don't like that I can't see you as well, but does that feel less embarrassing?"

"That's sweet. Put the lights on. I like watching you fuck me in that mirror over there." He raises his chin toward the mirror on the opposite wall of my room. "I noticed it last night;

it was so hot. Well, you looked sexy, I don't know about me. That was the embarrassing part."

"Wow. You are a filthy little boy." I flip the light back on and walk back toward the bed. I squeeze the lube over his entrance, watching it slide down. "Now, loosen up for me." I slowly roll my finger around his rim, then push one finger inside slowly. "You're so tight. Relax…" I'm pumping my finger in and out gently, while Vincent pushes back against me. He's always so anxious for me to go inside, but I'm afraid that if I don't take my time, I could really hurt him. His ass is clinging to my finger while I swirl it inside of him. "How does that feel?"

"I want more. Don't tease me, fuck me."

I kiss his left ass cheek then give the other a light smack. "You're not ready yet. But I do like how eager you are to take my cock."

He hangs his head down. "Sivan, I know my own ass, I can take more. Give it to me."

I slowly stuff a second finger inside and his body lurches forward. He drops his head on the pillow. I'm stretching him faster than I normally do, but he's aching for it, and I want to please him. Not only that, but it's not exactly easy for me to hold back when he's begging for it. My dick is rock hard and throbbing while I fuck him with my fingers. I graze his prostate, and he moans, "Mmm—Sivan, give me your cock, now."

I pat his ass and line my dick up with his entrance, going in gently. He's so tight, but it feels so good once I'm fully inside. I thrust in and out, slowly at first, but I can't hold back anymore, so I don't. I start pounding him deep, my balls are slapping against him, while he grips the sheets with both hands.

He lifts his head from the pillow. "Sivan, look in the mirror."

I turn my head and admire how beautiful he looks bent over with my dick inside him. "It's hot. You look sexy."

"Baby, fuck me…harder. Please, I want to watch you come inside of me," he begs, pressing against me.

I pick up my pace and begin riding him harder. I'm squeezing the meat of his ass tight while I fuck him. I look over at our reflection and see that he's watching me fuck him in the mirror. "You're such a good boy. Look how pretty you look taking my cock."

"Oh fuck, Sivan. The praise kink is stronger—I—I—feel like I could come again."

"Greedy. I haven't come yet, but maybe we can come together. Rub your cock while I fuck your tight little ass, but don't come until I say."

He nods and starts jerking himself. Watching us in the mirror may be my new favorite thing. I can see every facial expression and how he responds to every inch of my cock, as I feed it to him. I feel his hand graze my balls with every stroke and it's bringing me closer to orgasm. I'm panting and thrusting deep into him, and I feel my balls tighten. "I'm gonna come, Vincent. Are you close?"

"Fuck, yes…come inside of me. Do it…"

"Take it…take my cum."

I feel my cum shoot inside of him, as he moans and releases at the same time, his hole gripping tighter on my cock. "Haahh—mmm—Sivan, I'm coming…I'm coming, too."

The fucking thrill of coming inside of him is something that I'll never take for granted. But at this moment, the connection that I've only shared with him washes over me, it wraps around me like a warm blanket, just like him. I never want to leave the feeling of him. I need this feeling…the feeling of us…forever.

"Vincent…"

"Mmhmm?" he mumbles with his face in the pillow.

"I…I want to tell you something later."

He looks over his shoulder then looks at us in the mirror and nods at me.

The sound of Tilly's voice and a few knocks on my door wakes the two of us. "Sivan, it's well past breakfast time!"

"Leave it, Tilly. Thank you," I say.

Vincent wipes his eyes and smiles at me. "Good morning."

I turn on my side to face him and kiss his forehead. "Morning. We are probably very, very late."

"Let's just stay here all day," he says.

"I wish." I chuckle at our predicament. "You know, we've been waiting to get our own ships since we were kids, who would have ever thought that on this day, we'd be waking up in bed together, after having the greatest sex of our lives with each other."

He looks at his phone and his eyes widen. "Holy shit! It's ten-thirty!"

We both jump out of bed and quickly start dressing, going over the things that we know need to be done today.

"Ahh," he says wincing and jumping into his pants. "Well, you got your wish. I'm definitely gonna be walking funny today."

I laugh a little. "Hmm…well, if it's any consolation I am completely drained right now. I don't know how I'll pay attention during the inspection."

"I'm more worried about what might happen before the inspection."

"Vincent, it's fine. I'll go to the pub and hang out while you meet with him. It's not a big deal."

"Everything is going to be okay, right? If I tell Matteo that he can't be my first mate unless he accepts our relationship, he'll say yes, right?"

Times like these I just want to pat his head. "I don't know if he will. Most people don't like being told they have to do something. But everything will be okay whether he accepts us or not. Are you ready for him to tell our fathers about us if he doesn't accept? That is a likely scenario that we should be prepared for."

He shrugs at me. "I don't have the ability to keep it a secret much longer. If I have you, but lose everything else, then I'll have truly lost nothing. Because without you, nothing means anything."

I have to repeat what he said several times in my head before I realize that it was very sweet. "I don't care what I lose, as long as I have you, too. But, listen, keep your sword on you, and just be aware of your surroundings. I know you don't like using your pistol, but just keep it close-by."

He drops an eyebrow at me. "In my room or at the inspection?"

"Both. You are about to be named captain in two days, and Captain Slicer has already threatened our fathers, promising to show up on the day of our promotions. If he was smart, he'd do something before then."

Vincent's mouth drops open. He obviously hadn't considered that. "That would be so fucked up. He already said Friday. You think he would just change the date?"

"You are cute when you're like this, but I worry about you. We're pirates. Just because our fathers changed piracy, doesn't mean everyone else will fight fair. They took everything from Captain Slicer, now he's coming back on one of the proudest days of our fathers' lives. I have no idea what to expect, but it won't be good." I walk toward him and pull him into an embrace. "We'll win, whatever happens. We just have to be careful. So, don't lose your shit today if Matteo doesn't want to be your first mate."

CHAPTER 13
CAMERAS, MONKEYS, AND SNEAKY PIRATES

VINCENT

I make it to my father's ship a few minutes after eleven. Sivan went to Muffy's to pass the time while I talk to Matteo. He's going to meet me back here before the inspection. He wanted to hide in my bathroom or under my bed, but I wouldn't let him do either. The last thing I need is for him and Matteo to get into a fight today. As I round the corner, I see Matteo leaning against my door. "Hey, sorry I'm late. We woke up late this morning."

He shrugs at me. His eyes look tired, there are dark circles under them like he hasn't been sleeping. "I didn't remind you to be here on time, so of course you'd be late."

His tone is half between joking and serious, so I'm not sure how to respond. "So, it's your fault?" I open the door and toss my bag on my bed. I look around the room, trying to make sure the monkey isn't hiding somewhere, and I'm also looking for anything that resembles a camera. I start to remove my sword from my coat, but pause, remembering what Sivan said. I didn't even have a chance to tell Matteo that Harlow blackmailed me, which was the reason for the fake engagement.

"What are you looking for?" Matteo asks.

"Cameras, monkeys... sneaky pirates...I don't fucking

know anymore." I drop my head backward, already feeling overwhelmed.

"That's a rather odd combo. I wasn't expecting you to say any of those things."

He's standing no different than he normally does, but things feel weird between us. I look him up and down, trying to pinpoint what's changed, but can't find anything. I just know that something is off. We haven't really talked in days, aside from the fight in my father's office, so I really owe him an explanation for the Harlow stuff. He did say he was in love with her.

"I, uh—don't know where to start with everything," he says, ruffling his hair. "I'm just gonna say whatever comes to mind. Your dad isn't here, so let's just lay it all out in the open. Why the fuck did you propose to Harlow?"

I hold a hand up. "Stop. No. I did not. Is that what she told you?"

"Yes. She said you wanted to marry her, that you had a change of heart. Then she said that you and that shitface went out the bathroom window—which you did, leaving me there to try and make her feel better. Then yesterday she said you wanted to call it off. What's your version of what happened?"

"First, don't call him a shitface. He doesn't talk bad about you; it would be cool if you did the same."

"I don't have to respect him right now. He's not here; it's just me and you...*brother*."

I promised Sivan that I would keep calm, but all I want to do right now is punch him. He has the smuggest look on his face. "That's where you're wrong, *brother*. You do have to respect him—pirate hierarchy and all."

"Don't throw that bullshit in my face. I was raised on this

ship by your father. I have the same status as you do. Do *you* have to respect Sivan?"

He is wrong. I mean my father does grant him the same privileges, but that doesn't mean that he's of equal ranking. But there's no real way for me to point that out without sounding like an asshole. "Listen. We can't continue talking if you're going to fixate on Sivan. Damn it, Teo. We have so much shit to go over before inspection."

He tilts his head at me. "Did you just call me Teo? What's really bothering you? You wouldn't say that unless you were feeling really helpless. That's your go-to when you need me to bail you out. What happened, Vincent? Did you promise to join crews? Or is it worse?"

"Stop. I called you Teo because I'm trying not to absolutely lose my shit on you. I have something to say to you, but I want to get the stuff with Harlow over with. I did not propose to her. I have no interest in her. When relaying our engagement news to you, she purposely left out the fact that she blackmailed me."

"It's always something with you. How did she blackmail you?"

We're standing only about three feet apart and I'm starting not to trust myself. Between what happened earlier and everything that he's said the past few months, I think a few good punches between brothers is warranted. But I'm going to be a captain in a few days, so I need to try and handle this with words. "Listen to me, you are being a real asshole right now. She blackmailed me by having a camera in my room. She has a video of Sivan and I having sex. She said if I promised to marry her, Sivan and I could be together in private, as long as I kept up the appearance of being her husband. If I didn't go along with her plan, she said she'd tell our fathers and everyone else about us."

"That wasn't part of the plan…" He holds his hand over his mouth. "Are you lying to me right now?"

"What? No. What plan? Why would I lie?" He's never questioned my integrity before. I'm a bit thrown off by everything he just said.

"You're full of shit. She wouldn't do that." His hands are on his hips and he's pacing in front of me now. Something is really off.

"You've never called me a liar before. I may be a lot of things, but I'm not a fucking liar. Ask her if you want. But do you honestly believe that I would propose to her? Think about everything that's happened. What have I been like for the past year? Was I happy about being separated from Sivan? No. I was miserable. If I wanted to marry her, don't you think you would have been the first to know? Think about it. A proposal wouldn't even make sense."

"Ha! Are you trying to explain something to me?"

I'm gonna punch him.

"Vincent!" Harlow's mother shouts on the other side of the door, while knocking.

"What? I'm busy." I shout back.

Matteo shakes his head at me. He's still nervously pacing around the room.

"You men need to be on the dock by noon," Sheena says. "Your father wanted me to remind you of that."

It's weird that she called us men. Not that we aren't men, because we are, but she's only ever called us boys when we're together.

"Thanks, I got it." I say loud enough for her to hear.

"Before we sign the paperwork for you to be my first mate

today at inspection, I need to know that you can accept the fact that I'm gonna be with Sivan."

"What do you mean *be* with him? I know he's gonna be there. You don't mean that you two are going to be together, like, *together* in front of people, do you?"

"I do. We don't want to hide our relationship. We've been talking a lot about what we want the next generation of piracy to look like, especially with Captain Slicer coming back around."

"Right, and that goes down tomorrow..."

Tomorrow? No, it's supposed to be Friday. I'm sure that's what we figured out. He must be confused. I shouldn't correct him right now, though.

"It's hard for me to deal with all of this," Matteo says, sitting on the couch in my room. He exhales loud and long. His legs are bouncing nervously. "I'm really lost, man. I have so much shit happening right now, and the one thing I always held firm to is just falling apart. Everything is just collapsing around me. I can't be in control of all of this—I don't know what's right anymore, Vincent."

"I'm sorry for whatever you're going through. I don't know what I can do to help. If anything, I'm just gonna make things worse for you with what I have to say."

"Yeah, that is one thing that I guess won't ever change. You've always made things worse for me."

I chuckle until I realize that he's not joking around. "What's that supposed to mean? When have I made anything worse for you?"

"Alright, stop," he says. "The whole time you were sick, he didn't ask about you once. On top of that, he ignored you and didn't answer your texts. You've given up on girls that treated you far better for doing a lot less. What makes him special? Do you even understand how people are going to react to this? The crew won't accept it. You have so many problems coming your way and you're worried about whether *I* can respect the two of you?"

I swallow hard. I don't want my voice to convey the pain that his words just caused me. "You're supposed to be my brother…don't you want me to be happy?"

My eyes meet his and he shakes his head at me. "No. I'm tired of caring about your feelings."

"Vincent," I hear Sivan's voice call outside the door.

Shit, it must be time to go. This is gonna end badly. "Yeah, come in."

Matteo stands up from the couch as Sivan enters. Sivan is walking toward me, but looking quite concerned.

"Time to go?" I ask.

Sivan places his hat on my dresser and stands beside me. He kisses the side of my head, which I'm sure is quite sweaty right now, because I am so fucking nervous and shaken by what Matteo just said.

"Yeah, we should head," Sivan says. "Did you two"—he points at Matteo—"clear things up?"

Matteo shakes his head. "Nah, we're not gonna clear things up. Vincent is a completely different person thanks to you. I don't even recognize him anymore."

Sivan backs up taking a bit more of a defensive stance. "Why is he different? Because he's sleeping with me? Is that what makes him different?"

"Shut up," Matteo says. "Your father isn't here now, and as far as I'm concerned, you're no different than me. I don't have to respect you. You've ruined him."

Sivan takes a step closer toward Matteo and I quickly place my body in between the two feeling their tempers escalate.

"What?" I ask. "How has he ruined me?"

Matteo is staring me straight in the eyes. Now that he's closer, his eyes are a bit bloodshot, and the dark circles underneath are worse than I thought. "How can you ask me that? You know damn well that you were fine before all of this started. And it's got nothing to do with you liking men, it has everything to do with him."

"That doesn't even make sense," I say. "What is your fucking problem with him?"

"My problem?" Matteo asks, pointing at his own chest. "You two are supposed be the next great captains, and this thing with you two, it's ridiculous. All Harlow wants is you. I will never be enough for her because she only wants you. My entire life I've had to watch her cry over you. And for what? So you could choose him? He's never respected anyone. You're gonna throw everything away for a guy with a huge ego and commitment issues?"

I take Sivan's hand in mine and give it a tug, urging him to look at me, his gaze is locked on Matteo though. He's not in the mood for whatever I'm saying. "Hey," I say firmly. "Don't listen to him." I look back at Matteo. "You know that I have never cared about Harlow in that way. Why am I suddenly the worst man in the world? And all the shit you just said about Sivan isn't true."

These two are gonna go at it soon if I don't get them away from each other. I'm still holding Sivan's hand, but his grip is loosening.

"Ha!" Sivan says. "Ego? I don't have a huge ego, and I don't have commitment issues. You've had a problem with me since you caught us together. That's why you wouldn't let me fucking see him when he passed out. Another thing, I asked you to make sure to let me know when he was better, and somehow, conveniently, my phone number was changed in his phone and blocked from calling him. Now, you, one of the greatest tactical minds on this crew, couldn't figure out that something was wrong? Bullshit."

Matteo smirks at him. "I don't remember any of that."

I'm so confused right now, but it's obvious that Matteo is lying.

"Oh, you forgot about all that?" Sivan asks.

Matteo shrugs as he pulls his phone out of his pocket. "Right. Well, I don't care. I only care about Harlow. She is obsessed with you, Vincent, and I don't think that's ever going to change. But you have to make a decision. You either throw it all away for him, or go along with what she wants and you get everything. It's not even a choice. It seems quite easy to me. You choose her. You don't choose him."

"I choose him. It's always going to be him." I squeeze Sivan's hand.

The sounds of shouting and gunshots outside pierce the silence between us. I freeze momentarily, as Sivan pulls my hand toward the door. The three of us quickly dash out of the room toward the deck.

"Shit we're gonna be in so much trouble!" I shout, while we're running through the hall. We should have left twenty minutes ago, so hopefully whatever this is, it doesn't end up being my fault.

Rounding the corner and heading up the stairs, the fighting sounds intense. "Sounds like a lot of them, Sivan."

Matteo bumps into my back and Sivan turns toward him.

"What the fuck?" Sivan asks.

"Sorry, sorry. I wa—I wasn't watching where I was going," Matteo says.

"It's okay," I say, pulling Sivan. That was weird. Pretty big difference in the tone Matteo just used and the way he was acting thirty seconds ago. "Be careful, Matteo," I say. He is definitely distracted. Even though he's been an asshole, I'm kind of worried about him.

The scene is chaos as we reach the deck. There's fighting everywhere, pirates wearing black and green are on the deck, it's an all-out brawl. "Where is my father?" I shout to no one in particular. Sivan looks to the right and a scraggly-looking pirate, wearing black and green, quickly approaches me from the left, with his sword drawn. Before I can even react, Matteo has kicked him out of the way. He follows up with a punch that knocks the pirate off his feet, causing his sword to land on the deck beside him. Matteo picks the sword up and places his boot on the man's face. "Thank you for the sword," he says, and steps on him. Matteo generally uses daggers, so seeing him fight with a sword will be interesting.

"Thanks," I say, while continuing to look for my father.

Sivan steps in front of me. "Stay behind me while we look for our fathers. I didn't even see that asshole."

It's absolute chaos on the deck right now. I've never been in the midst of such madness. Oh shit…

"It's Henry." I say to Sivan.

He's a fucking monster of a pirate, he's probably seven feet tall. I've heard stories of him and seen his picture. We don't have any trouble with the inner police that deal with non-pirate business outside of the port, but there are pirates who are wanted by both captains and police alike for crimes. Henry is one of those pirates.

"Aww, fucking hell," Sivan says, raising his chin toward the ball of pirates battling it out.

Our fathers are both facing off against Henry and someone else I don't recognize.

"My father looks tired, I'm going in," Sivan says.

Without thinking I instinctively pull Sivan back. "We can't interfere in their fight. You know that!"

"I do, but my father looks exhausted. He'll lose at this rate!"

"Then all the more reason for us to stay back. If your father is tired and you ju—"

A sword slices in between us narrowly missing both of our chests.

I pull my head back. "What the hell?"

"I'll kill you both where you stand!" the pirate holding the sword in between us says.

I recognize his dirty grime-ridden face. It's the messenger pirate from the jail earlier. "It's you!" I say. "How the hell did you get out?"

"Got a little surprise for you!" he says. "Found out something interesting. Your—"

Matteo knocks him down from behind, sweeping his feet from under him.

Sivan grabs the sword that the messenger dropped at his feet. "Your whole crew just drops swords? What are you, a gang of clumsy asses? I don't understand," he says. Pointing the sword at the man's face, he asks, "Now, why are you here?"

The messenger holds his hands up. He's giving us the most wicked smile I've ever seen. "You might not want to kill me. In fact, you might want to point that sword at that man right there," he says, pointing at Matteo.

"Oh, I agree," Sivan says. "But maybe I should kill you first."

"Why should he want to point a sword at him?" I ask the messenger.

"Because he's family," he says, pumping his eyebrows at me. Sivan is still pointing the sword at him, the tip only a few inches from his brow.

"Yeah, he is part of my family," I say. "Sometimes I do want to point a sword at him."

Matteo kicks the man in the face. "So what if I'm family? You don't even know me. What are you scum sucking bastards here for? Who do you work for?" Matteo asks.

"Oh right, you weren't there earlier," I say to Matteo. "This is the messenger that works for Slicer."

"*Captain* Slicer," the messenger says, rubbing his face.

"Shit, why does everyone correct me?" I ask. "Yes, okay. Captain Slicer. He said he came here to collect something that my father has of his. We still don't know what it is."

The man on the ground spits to the side and laughs looking up at Matteo. "What, indeed?" he asks. "You should just sit back and watch the show…" the messenger says. "Things are about to get interesting."

I pull Sivan's pistol from his holster and point it at the messenger. This pistol does feel nice in my hand. Why was it my instinct to grab it instead of my sword? I haven't drawn my sword once since we've been out here. Everything is happening so fast.

Sivan's eyes widen, looking at me. He squats down beside the man's face. "What do you know, Messenger? Tell me, or I'm gonna let him shoot you. He doesn't really use pistols, so he may shoot you by accident anyway."

"I'm *gonna* shoot him," I say. "It's like 90/10 at this point."

Sivan chuckles looking up at me. He turns his gaze back toward the messenger. "Well…he's gonna shoot you anyway, and I kinda like him, so I don't think I should get in his way."

This is why I dislike pistols. It's too easy to take a life this way. I don't really want to kill him, but in this moment, I could, and there's nothing he could do about it.

The messenger is staring up at me. He doesn't really look afraid at all. "Well, if he's gonna shoot me, then why should I say anything?" he asks. "What about parley? That's what I want. You two aren't captains, yet. You can't touch me now that I've requested parley." He spits to the side again and smiles at us.

"Oh shit…" I groan.

"Who gives a shit of he's asking for parley?" Matteo asks. "I don't give a shit. Do you? Shoot him. The captain is busy with Henry over there."

Why is Matteo so anxious for me to shoot him? He's never encouraged me to choose violence over peaceful solutions.

Sivan is studying Matteo's face and slowly standing up.

"But if I shoot him and he doesn't die, then what?" I ask Matteo. "I'll be in trouble when the captain finds out he asked for parley and I didn't give it to him."

"Then make sure you kill him," Matteo says.

Sivan stands beside me and holds his hand out for his pistol.

I pass it back to him. "This is why I don't like pistols. I almost shot him," I say.

"Draw your sword, Vincent. But not for him. We need to take him to your father," Sivan says. He turns toward Matteo.

"And, Matteo, if you want him dead, then you kill him. But you'll be the one to explain it to the captain."

As I draw my sword, a high-pitched scream draws my attention. I know that loud obnoxious squeal. It's Harlow; she's on the opposite side of the deck and she looks terrified. Why the hell is she out here?

"Harlow!" Matteo shouts and runs toward her.

Matteo shouts back to me, "Vincent, help me!" Harlow is being slung over another pirate's shoulder, her feet are kicking wildly, as she continues screeching.

"Damn it! We have to help, Sivan!" I look down at the messenger. "You want a fucking parley? Get up and interrupt my father yourself."

Sivan and I quickly push through the pirates who are still scuffling.

Matteo is a few steps ahead of us. He's trying to catch up to the man who has Harlow. It looks like he's going to carry her off the ship.

One of our men is belly up on the deck, and Sivan swings the sword he took from the messenger to stop another pirate from driving his sword into him. Their swords clang together, and Sivan is quickly locked in a swordfight. He looks really good fighting with a sword. He is very sexy… What the hell am I thinking? I can't be drooling over him. I need to help him. I point my sword at the man that Sivan is currently in battle with.

"Help Matteo. I'll be fine," he says, meeting the other pirate strike for strike. I hesitate for a moment. "Hey now, don't look at me like you're worried," he says, as he blocks a strike from the man's sword.

"Don't die!" I shout and head toward the man carrying

Harlow. I'm swiftly pulled back by my collar after only a few steps. "Who the hell is touching me?!"

I turn around and am greeted with a punch right in the jaw. My vision goes hazy, but only for a moment. What a fucking hit. "Son of a bitch!" I say rubbing my jaw. I raise my sword to strike the large pirate that is now standing in front of me, and he backs up a fair bit, slicing the air in front of himself with his sword, daring me to come closer.

My jaw is stinging and I feel a bit dizzy, but I can still take him.

"Back!" Sivan shouts from behind me. He has such a commanding voice. No less than half of the pirates around us stop to see what's happening. He points his sword at the pirate. "You dare to punch the son of the captain of this ship?"

"Course I do," the pirate answers with a laugh. "And I'll punch you, too," he says charging at Sivan, rather stupid of him, since his sword is drawn.

"Great. Make it easy for me," Sivan says, keeping the sword pointed at him.

At this rate the man will impale himself on Sivan's sword.

I'm tempted to intervene, but before I can, a large bang pierces the air and the man's body falls in front of us.

All the fighting on the ship momentarily stops.

Loud footsteps hit the deck following the shot. A tall thin man I don't recognize with a long scraggly beard, wearing a black and green coat approaches the now-lifeless body on the deck. The rest of the pirates are all paying close attention.

"Get the hell off my ship!" my father shouts.

"Yeah, get out of here, Louie," Sivan's father says.

Louie doesn't acknowledge either of them and squats down to examine the body. He pats the man on the head and closes his eyes. I can't hear what he said, but it seems like it was something meaningful, at least it seemed that way based on Louie's posture.

"Who is Louie?" I whisper to Sivan.

"I think I remember hearing stories about someone named Louie," Sivan says. "I think they were friends, maybe?"

"Who was friends?" I ask.

The pirates that don't belong to our ship walk toward us, standing in a line behind Louie. There are about fifteen of them. They just stopped fighting because this pirate was shot. I think it was Louie that shot him, but I can't be certain, because I didn't see where the shot came from. It's strange to me that they've all gathered behind him, even Henry stopped his fight with our fathers.

Louie shakes his head and stands up tall. Stroking his long black beard, he looks at Sivan and me. "You two—" he says to us.

Before he can finish his sentence, he's interrupted by our fathers, who are now standing beside us. Captain Crawford throws a hand up. "Louie, Rodri told you to get the hell off his ship! Did you hear him?"

"Be quiet, Ray," Louie says, making a "shushing" gesture with his hand.

Captain Crawford's mouth is open wide. I don't think he's used to being disrespected. "Did you hear what he said to me, Rodri?"

My father slowly shakes his head at him. "Louie. Why are you here? Where is Captain Slicer? You assholes come on my ship, start a fight over something I'm supposed to have, now you prance up here as if you have any right to do so. I will ask once more; what do you want?"

"Right and he's very mad that you just disrespected me, too," Captain Crawford says.

Louie sighs loudly. "I'm not in the mood for either of you. We came for one thing and we're leaving with two. I'll take him and be on my way." He places two fingers in his mouth and gives a crisp whistle. Quickly, two large pirates come from behind him and grab the lifeless body off the deck, carrying him by the shoulders and feet.

I want so badly to know why he was here to begin with, and I'm really curious what he was going to say to us. I won't ask, though. This is my father's ship and he would be extremely pissed off if I interrupted.

"Hey," Sivan's father says. "What the hell did you come here for anyway, Lou-Ee?"

I'm finding it hard not to laugh at this moment, because Captain Crawford is just ridiculous. "Does your dad always act like this?" I ask Sivan. "I mean, *I've* never seen him act this way. That's for sure."

"He seems to act a bit different these days around your father. I noticed it earlier. It's like he's more openly showing when your father hurts his feelings or something."

"Answer the question, Louie," my father says.

I point at the two of them. "Didn't they just do this bit, Sivan?"

"Yeah, seems like it," he says, with a smile.

As the two men carry the lifeless pirate off the ship, Louie shakes his head.

"I hate the both of you. I can't believe I had to come here for this," he mutters, while heading off the ship.

"Louie! What the fuck did you come here for?" my father shouts.

"We've already taken it." He gives my father a devilish grin, then steps off the ship.

"Captain!" someone yells from behind us. "Should we go after them? See what it was they stole?"

My father turns toward the crew member and waves him off. "No, they can keep whatever it is. It can't be that important. No one went into my chambers and our sons are here."

"Matteo!" my father calls out, looking around the deck.

He looks at Sivan and me. "Where is he?"

I shrug. "Think he went off the ship chasing after Harlow." As soon as the words left my mouth, I realized that I hadn't even thought of Harlow being carried off for the last ten minutes. Shit, that's right, she was being carried off and Matteo was trying to save her.

I look at Sivan and we nod at one another. "Captain, I need to speak with you, but it's a private matter."

He points in the direction of his cabin and motions with his chin for us to go wait for him. His first mate, Rooster, quickly appears in front of us.

"Ugghh," Sivan's father gives the loudest groan ever.

"Guess he doesn't like Rooster," I say to Sivan.

"Not that much. He hates him. Really hates him."

"Let's go wait for my dad in his chambers," I say. I almost grab his hand to hold it, but remember that we haven't told anyone about us yet, so I probably shouldn't.

CHAPTER 14
WHOLEHEARTEDLY
AND UNDENIABLY

SIVAN

I just want to hold his hand. I'm already feeling touch-starved after not being around him for a bit this morning. I didn't know I could miss another person after being separated for only a few hours. We're nearly at a standstill, walking toward his father's office at an agonizingly slow pace. I'm trying to process everything that just happened and I'm having trouble connecting a few things.

Vincent looks over his shoulder. Our fathers aren't far behind us. "Sivan, what do you think they came for?"

"I don't know, but they took Harlow, so maybe she was what they came for? Unless that was just a diversion."

"Hmm…maybe, but something seemed off with Matteo. Besides just the fact that he was being an asshole, the thing that stood out the most was the thing with the messenger. He was encouraging me to kill that guy. He's never been one for violence, but he was practically telling me to do it."

"Yeah, I've never seen you like that, either. I was afraid you were going to shoot him. Wouldn't have mattered, but we can't touch someone asking for parley when it's not our ship. I didn't like that he told you to shoot him. I'd always trusted that he would make a good first mate, until recently. His actions are throwing me off. He even kicked the messenger in the face. It was a fight, so it's a free for all, and kicking isn't so much of a big deal, but I'm used to seeing him much more composed."

"He's always been the calm one, but today he was anything but calm. I don't know what's going to happen with the inspection. And as far as Matteo is concerned, he didn't exactly say he wouldn't be my first mate, but I'm sure that's where our conversation was heading."

We walk inside Captain Rodrigo's office and take a seat on the couch.

Our fathers enter after only a few moments, and shut the door.

"Where is Matteo? What's the private information?" Captain Rodrigo asks Vincent.

"The last time I saw him; he was chasing a man that had Harlow slung over his shoulder. He was carrying her off the ship and Matteo was in pursuit. But Captain, something was off with him, he was really not acting like himself today."

Captain Rodrigo tosses his hat on his desk and sits in his large captain's chair. "Shit. Why didn't you two help him? We gotta find out where those two are. What the hell am I gonna tell Sheena when she asks where Harlow is?"

My father sits in a chair in front of Captain Rodrigo. "Seems strange they would come here for one woman. Captain Slicer wouldn't do that."

"No, he wouldn't," Captain Rodrigo says. "He'd have no interest in Harlow. He was a bastard, but he wasn't a pervert." He turns his attention to Sivan and me. "Rooster is going to check your ships. They arrived about an hour ago, so they were a few hours late getting into port.

"Can I have permission to speak freely, Captain?" Vincent asks.

I pull my head back and try to control my facial expression. I'm not sure what he's going to say, but he's only asked for that maybe once before and it was years ago. I want to scoot closer to him, but I shouldn't.

Captain Rodrigo looks around the room. "We're all alone, go ahead."

"Dad, something was really fucking wrong with Matteo. He was acting like a complete asshole this morning. I tried to talk to him and clear the air, but he wasn't having it. Honestly, if the fight hadn't broken out, I don't know what would have happened between the three of us in my room."

My father looks at me. "What were you doing there? They were supposed to meet alone."

"I had just gotten there to pick Vincent up so we could head over to the inspection. If the fight hadn't broken out, I would have knocked him out for the shit he was saying." I shift my gaze to Vincent's father. "I've respected Matteo this long because he's Vincent's brother, and he's part of your crew, Captain Rodrigo, but he went too far today."

"Speak freely," Captain Rodrigo says to me. "What did he do?"

"There were a number of things he did that were out of line, but without context they won't make sense. The worst thing he did was telling Vincent to shoot a pirate that asked for a parley. When Vincent expressed his concern at shooting him, Matteo simply told him to be sure he killed him."

"When were you in a position to shoot someone? On the deck?" Captain Rodrigo asks Vincent.

"Yeah, the messenger from yesterday came at Sivan and me.

He was saying some stuff about Matteo being family and it really pissed Matteo off. Sivan and I were trying to figure out what the hell he was talking about, but I don't know, Dad, it was weird."

"Where was your sword?" He drops an eyebrow at Vincent. "You pulled your pistol out?"

Vincent shakes his head. "No, I didn't have my pistol on me. I was lucky I had my sword on me since we rushed out of the room. I, uh, pulled Sivan's pistol off his belt and pointed it at the messenger." He shrugs.

"You don't like to use pistols. What made you do that?" Captain Rodrigo asks him.

"Am I on trial here? I pulled the pistol on him, because the pistol was right there. I grabbed it and pointed it at him. I didn't shoot him, despite being encouraged to do so. It's not a big deal."

"Whose idea was it not to shoot him?" Captain Rodrigo asks.

"Vincent decided that on his own," I say. "I also told Matteo that if he wanted to shoot him, he'd need to explain it to you. It's concerning that he told Vincent to do that."

"It is concerning. But for now, we need to figure out where the hell they ran off to. There aren't any ships in port, aside from ours and your two new ships. Which means they're hiding out somewhere. There were probably fifteen men here earlier. Bastard changed the plan, showing up here today."

"Does that mean it's over?" Vincent asks.

Captain Rodrigo shakes his head. "I don't really know. I'd expect something else, but I have no idea what they came for. I'm more concerned about getting you two promoted without any more interruptions. Captain Slicer will negotiate with us directly before doing anything major. Well, he'll negotiate with me, and Ray will be there, but he won't deal with him."

"I don't want to deal with him, either. He's such an arrogant asshole. We should have burned his ship to the ground, Rodri. I told you it would backfire."

Captain Rodrigo tilts his head at him. "How did it backfire? It's been twenty years, Ray. He could have a new ship by now, might not even be the same one."

"Dad," Vincent says. "You said he'd negotiate before he does anything major. Wasn't coming on your ship a major thing?"

Our fathers are both laughing at his question. Vincent throws his hands up. "What's funny?"

"Son, listen. That was nothing. They wanted something so they came for it, no big deal. We still have rules that are followed, shit, even with the mutiny there were steps that had to be followed. Did you learn nothing in school all these years? Why do you think Louie shot the pirate who was coming at you two?"

"I don't know, I wasn't even sure it was Louie that shot him. Sivan almost impaled him."

"It was Louie that shot him, and he did it because that man was going straight for you both," Captain Rodrigo says. "There would have been no chance of any type of negotiation if something happened to either of you. Captain Slicer also sent the messenger yesterday, which means he really doesn't want to fight."

I tilt my head at his father. "This idea that he's a reasonable pirate sounds kind of ridiculous. They did take Harlow off the ship."

"I didn't say he was reasonable, but there are some things that we all abide by. I haven't talked to him in twenty years, and he could have changed, but rules are rules. If he wants to change things, he has to go through us, and he'd do that in negotiations before anything major," Captain Rodrigo says. "We'll send some guys out to see if they can figure out where they've taken Harlow. In the meantime, you two will need to inspect the ships with us tonight. You could still sign off on Matteo being your first mate, but the ceremony would have to wait until he's back and able to sign. Try and get ahold of him, I don't care what happened earlier, just text him."

"Are we still speaking freely?" I ask.

"Depends," Captain Rodrigo says. "If you're gonna say Vincent shouldn't have to text him, then no, we're not still speaking freely. If you want to ask me a question about something else, then yes."

"I was going to say that he probably won't answer, since he and Vincent are pissed at each other right now."

Vincent stands up, so I do, too. "I don't want to text him, Dad. I don't even think I want him to be my first mate anymore. You've always told me I needed to consider captain and crew, and while I still disagree about needing the captain tattoo, if I'm thinking about my future crew, I don't think Matteo can be trusted after today. If I have to decide tonight, then I won't sign off on him."

My father stands up and holds his hand up to Captain Rodrigo, telling him to wait. He walks toward Vincent. "Vincent, you want to deny him the right to be your first mate because of one bad decision?"

"No, it's not based on just one bad decision." He tilts his head back, raking his fingers through his hair. "I need a drink. This day has sucked. What time do we need to meet you to check out the ships? Could we just go now?"

Captain Rodrigo crosses his arms. "No, we can't just go now. We have a lot to prepare for. You two can be excused to go and have a few drinks, but, Vincent, you need to be careful. Regardless of the way I expect things to go with Captain Slicer; you and Sivan are the biggest targets right now. You're both big guys, but if you're both too drunk at the pub to notice someone sneaking up on you, that could be a problem. Don't worry about texting Matteo, I'll try and get in touch with him."

"He'll probably ignore you, too," Vincent says. "I mean he is in love with Harlow. Since she was in danger, I don't expect him to be sitting around texting on his phone."

"I *knew* he was in love with her!" Captain Rodrigo says. "So much makes sense, now. Why didn't you say that earlier? Of course he's been acting like an asshole. Kid is in love with a girl that doesn't love him back. Well, since the engagement between you two is off, maybe he'll have a chance."

"Maybe," Vincent says. "I'd be a little worried about him if his mood swings had all been about Harlow. I think there's a bit more to it."

I give my dad a look and he rubs the tip of his nose, a silent way of telling me that he knows what I'm thinking. I don't like keeping my thoughts from Vincent, and I'm not really sure in a relationship if what I'm doing is even right. It's not that I'm withholding information from him, I just have a few theories. I'm going to talk to him about them when we leave.

Captain Rodrigo pulls his sword from its sheath and places it on his desk, lightly running his finger along the blade. When I used to see him talking to his sword, I used to think it was kind of strange, but now I think it's actually kind of beautiful. He loved Vincent's mom so much that he wants her to be a part of everything he does. "Well, love makes you do stupid things—

the four of us loved you two so much that we staged a mutiny for the future of all pirates. It was the best decision we ever made, but we couldn't have done it for anything but love. We'd talked about it before we married your mothers, but the motives were selfish. Love may be affecting his judgement right now. One thing I do know is that if he's in love with her, he's probably already gotten her back by now. He's nothing if not determined when he sets his mind on something."

"Rodri, we need to make contact with the chief, to let him know that we'll get the boys to sign off tomorrow," my father says. "Unless you want to try and get it done tonight? But Vincent doesn't seem confident in having Matteo as his first mate—so, maybe we wait?"

The signing of the captaincy papers is really important, it's the only thing that gives us immunity from the inner police. Since the port is on the outside of the city, they are only concerned with what happens on the inside, provided we respect their rules and stay outside of their jurisdiction. If pirates start causing problems that spill across the border, the treaty will be void. The chief in our town has only spoken to me once or twice in my whole life, and he's always been friendly, I've never met the chief here.

"Ah, fuck. This is the problem when other pirates come around. The chief leaves us alone because we agree to follow rules, now these assholes just came here and screwed everything up. It's better if we do it tonight, but Vincent is gonna have to make a decision. If we postpone it another day, he's gonna want answers. I don't need to give them a reason to start poking around in our business." He sighs loudly. "We've never had a problem with the inner police before, I don't want to start now, they'll see the boys as a source of trouble. It won't look good that on the same day we're signing their papers, there was an abduction, a shooting, and possibly a rogue monkey running around."

Vincent is heading for the door. "I can't make a decision yet. I need to talk to him one more time. What time were they meeting us to sign off?"

"Supposed to meet us at the dock by the shipyard at six," Captain Rodrigo, says." If you see the chief, remember to stick to the story that the inspection was delayed because the ships were late, everything that happened with Captain Slicer's cronies had nothing to do with the delay, so remember that. The chief usually shows up right on time for official business, so he may not suspect anything is amiss."

"I have a question," I say. "Is it better for him to sign off on Matteo now, then possibly have to revoke the agreement, or is it better for him not to sign off on him at all? He's taking responsibility for him the second he signs off on him as his first mate."

Our fathers look at one another, they appear just as unsure as me. "Well, I don't know, you make a good point. If it were anyone other than Matteo, I'd say he should be worried, but Matteo wouldn't do anything to ruin the treaty, which is all that matters."

Vincent grabs the door handle and opens the door. "Right, because he didn't just tell me to blow the messengers head off," he says facetiously. "We'll meet you there at six, Captains."

As I follow Vincent out of the room, I hear my father say to Captain Rodrigo, "He is so much like Gwendolyn that it's scary. Little smartass."

"Hey," I say tugging on his coat. "Where do you want to go? You want a drink? Or you want to go back to your room, or my dad's ship?" His eyes are watery, this is why I don't think telling him what I suspect about Matteo is the right thing to do. He's upset, and it's definitely because of him.

"I—I don't know, Sivan. I want to go somewhere where we can be alone, and you can just hold me so I can think properly. My head is such a mess."

I take his hand in mine as we walk down the hallway. I'm holding his hand now, and I don't care who sees us. If he doesn't want to do it, he can let go. He pushes me against the wall, quickly crushing my lips with his. My eyes are wide as he kisses me. He's holding my face in his hands and his kiss is quickly losing momentum. He presses his forehead to mine, breaking from the kiss. His body is shaking a little as I lift his chin. "Why are you crying? Look up at me."

He shakes his head softly, and a few tears fall. "I—what is happening? Why does he hate us together? Why is he acting this way?"

I hold the back of his head, tucking him against my neck. "Shhh… He's just going through something." I rub his hair softly. "Don't cry."

We're in the middle of the hallway and anyone could walk by and see us, including our fathers who are literally ten feet away in the office. But I don't care. He's hurting and I need to comfort him. I hate that Matteo is making him feel this way. I squeeze him tight and kiss the side of his head. "Let's get out of here. We can go for a walk and go get a drink, or we can just go take a break in your room. You want to do either of those?"

"I don't feel like walking anywhere, but I don't want to stay here."

"You don't feel like walking? Well, that's an easy fix." I turn to the side and squat down. "Hop on. I'll carry you."

He chuckles and wipes his eyes. "You are not going to give me a piggyback ride off the ship."

I look over my shoulder at him. "Yes, I am. I'm gonna carry you straight to the pub, or we can grab a beer from one of the stands. Your choice, now hop on."

"Sivan. You can't be serious. Someone could see us!"

"So what? Someone could have seen us kissing at least five times already, and I think you're forgetting about what happened on the dock. By the way, I am not going to be able to concentrate when we get over there for inspection. I'm just going to be picturing you on your knees." I shake my head. "Come on, hop on me."

He giggles a bit, which is really quite cute. His laughter does something to me, it's soothing, and the crushing weight I felt from his tears is quickly replaced with a much lighter weight—the weight of his body pressed against mine. I hook under his legs and stand. "You're not heavy at all."

"Sivan, really you should put me down. People are gonna stare and say stuff, they'll definitely tell our fathers."

"So? What are they gonna say? Sivan was giving Vincent a piggyback ride? Sivan was carrying Vincent? Better than saying Vincent was on the dock giving Sivan the best head of his li—"

He covers my mouth with his hand. "Shhh, shhh, okay. Let's go get a drink."

Stepping off the ship, the port is bustling with people. "Where to, boss? You want to go to Muffy's or grab a beer from one of these?" I lift my chin toward the row of vendors.

"Hmm…" he says, leaning down near my ear. "Everyone is staring at us."

Rum-Soaked Awakenings

"Kiss me, that'll really give them something to stare at." I look up at him. He seems like he's considering it.

"You want me to?"

"I always want you to kiss me."

He looks at the crowds walking past us, then leans down and kisses my cheek.

I had no idea that a kiss on the cheek could make me feel so happy, but it does. Something that probably seems so small to other couples, means so much to me. "Thank you for that," I say.

There are two men that were looking over when Vincent just kissed me. I've never seen them before, but I don't know everyone here. I noticed that the taller man placed his hand on the small of the other man's back when they just walked into the pub. Hmm. Maybe they're a couple, too.

"You want me to put you down before we walk into the pub? Or you really want to make a scene?"

"I think I'll get down. I want to relax without everyone staring over."

I release his legs and he hops down. "That was fun. I like carrying you around."

"Thanks for the ride. I've never been carried like that. I do kind of remember you carrying me into my room that one time, but that was different."

I hold the door to the pub open and Vincent steps inside first while I follow behind. I see the two men that walked in a few moments ago. They definitely look out of place here. They're both dressed in casual suits, one is wearing gray, and the other is wearing dark blue, they appear around the same age as us, probably in their twenties. There are only two seats at the bar and, of course, they're right beside those two. Most of the people inside are staring over while we walk toward the empty seats. We both take a seat at the bar. The man on the left of me doesn't bother looking over as we sit down. I angle my body so that I'm half-facing Vincent. "Do you know these two next to me?" I whisper.

Vincent leans his head around me. "Nope. Never seen them before." He waves to Muffy who is currently serving someone at the opposite end of the bar.

Muffy passes the customer their drink and heads over toward us. "Ah, the two future captains! Only a few days left! Two beers, right?" he asks.

The man in the gray suit is craning his neck to look at me and Vincent. Normally I'd offer a smart-ass type of greeting with the way he's staring over, but something about these two is telling me I shouldn't say anything.

"Two beers is good. Thanks," Vincent says. He gives the guy in the gray suit a nod. "You guys aren't from around here. I don't recognize you."

Muffy places two beer bottles in front of Vincent and me. The man in the navy suit swivels his chair toward us, but doesn't say anything. "We are from around here, actually," the man in the gray says. "I'm—"

The man in the blue shakes his head. "Don't. There's no reason to introduce yourself right now."

"Oh, Michael, it's fine," he says. "I'm Brody and this is Michael. We're here for work stuff. You're Vincent and he's Sivan, right?" he says to Vincent.

"Yeah, but it's strange that you're from around here and I've never seen you."

"Anyway," I say, cutting in. "You guys enjoy your afternoon.

We're just here for a drink or two." I lift my beer toward them in salute and turn slightly toward Vincent.

"Sorry about earlier," Vincent says. "I don't know what came over me. I was just really upset over Matteo. Makes me feel stupid that I even cried about it."

I can't talk to him about Matteo with these two over my shoulder like this. "It's okay. You don't need to apologize for having feelings. He's your brother and he's acting really shitty. Are you worried about him? Or are your feelings hurt because of his reaction to everything?"

He takes a long drink of his beer, nearly downing half of it. "Both, plus I'm just confused as to why he lied to me the entire time we were apart. He repeatedly told me that you never asked to see me while I was sick. And what was his whole angle with trying to make me hate the idea of joining crews? The only reason we can't is because of our fathers and stupid tradition, it's all so fucking dumb. The treaty is dumb, Captain Slicer is dumb, this bullshit about the captain tattoo is dumb, getting slapped by that monkey was really dumb. This day is dumb." He takes another drink finishing off his beer.

Brody nearly spits his drink out; I assume he was listening to Vincent.

Before I say what I'm thinking about Matteo, I really need to gauge what these two beside us are doing here, because my gut tells me they aren't just here for drinks.

"Yeah, that monkey was crazy," I say. "Did you notice anything strange about it? Our fathers definitely did."

He waves a hand over to Muffy, flagging him down for another beer. "Why does everyone notice stuff that I don't? I have no idea. It was a slap-happy monkey who ran around smacking everyone, which like I said yesterday, made me feel better. I thought he just hated me."

I can see Brody stifling a laugh in the mirror behind the bar. Yeah, these guys are definitely listening to our conversation, which is probably why they aren't talking to each other at all.

I lean in close toward Vincent and tuck his hair behind his ear. I whisper, "Hey, those guys are listening to us. Look in the mirror and see if they're watching."

The other people behind Vincent are definitely looking over since I'm so close to him. His cheeks turn a light shade of red as he nods his head. "You're blushing, Vincent. I'm finding it very hard not to kiss you right now."

I look to the left in the mirror and see the two men watching us. I pull back from Vincent and swivel my chair to face them. "So, what kind of work are you guys here for? The kind of work that pays you to watch the two of us?"

Michael cups his face in his hands, rubbing his temples. Brody gives me a smile. "No, we're not here for you guys right now. We're just having a drink. But since we're talking, how long have you two been sleeping together?"

Vincent spits his drink out at the question. I pick my beer up before answering and take a quick sip. "Excuse me? What did you just ask us?"

Michael shakes his head and gives Brody a disapproving look.

Brody shrugs at Michael then turns to me. "I asked how long you two have been sleeping together."

I don't know how to respond, because I really feel like I shouldn't engage with these two. At the same time, who in the hell would ask someone they just met that kind of a question? I was leaning in toward him, but it's not like I kissed him. Oh, they saw us outside, that's right.

"Are you gonna answer him? Or should I?" Vincent asks me.

I take another sip of my beer. "Who said we're sleeping together?" I ask, looking at Brody.

"Oh, you're definitely sleeping together. It doesn't take a genius to figure that out. It may take another gay man, but not a genius."

"Holy shit. Brody, be quiet," Michael says. "I told you not to talk to them. We're here for work, not to socialize."

"Excuse me," Brody says. "I *am* working, same as you, but I can talk. I'm just curious how long they've been sleeping together, because I'm pretty sure no one else knows."

Vincent leans forward looking down the bar at Brody. "What did we do that makes you think we're sleeping together? Because we…that's not important. Just tell me why you think that."

Michael shakes his head and takes a sip of his drink, it looks like whiskey, but I'm not sure. "Don't answer him," he says to Brody.

"What? Why not?" Brody asks him. "He's asking me what I noticed. It would be rude not answer." He waves Michael off and leans forward. "Well, we saw Sivan carrying you which, unless you were hurt, drunk, or maybe if he lost a bet, wouldn't happen unless you were sleeping together. Toxic masculinity dictates that you'd be worried girls might get the wrong idea if another guy was carrying you. I also saw you kiss his cheek. A kiss on the cheek is nothing, but that coupled with the piggyback ride, paints a pretty clear picture. I'm pretty sure both of your faces lit up at the kiss, but I was trying not to be obvious when I saw it. Sivan did not sit down until you did, which is pretty cute." He clears his throat and starts again. "Therefore, he's treating you subconsciously like something he treasures, he wanted to make sure you were comfortable before he got comfortable. To top it off, Sivan here tucked your hair behind your ear and whispered to you, but made sure that the bartender was at the other end of the bar when he did so. He also caught on to us watching you two and asked if you noticed it. All of those things, combined with a few others, are enough for me to come to the conclusion that you two are definitely sleeping together."

"You also haven't denied it," Michael adds. "That's not an invitation to talk about it, I just wanted to point that out."

I shrug. "None of that means we're sleeping together."

"As my husband here pointed out, you haven't denied it." Brody says.

I drop an eyebrow and look at their hands for wedding bands, which I don't see.

Michael seems to notice my expression and sticks his hand in his pocket, then slides a black band onto his ring finger. Brody then does the same. "We don't wear them when we're working," Michael says.

"You guys are actually married?" Vincent asks.

"Five years this year," Brody says with a smile. "I'm only asking how long you've been sleeping together because the bond between you is obviously strong, you're very comfortable with each other, but the shifty eyes and the body language toward the outside world, tells me that no one else knows. It's like you've been sleeping together a short time, but have known each other forever. That's what it seems like."

Michael is shaking his head at him. He seems not to approve of anything Brody says or does.

"Yeah, everyone knows we've known each other our whole lives, though. Doesn't really prove anything, but it's cool you guys are married," Vincent says.

Brody rolls his eyes. "It *is* cool. But there was a time that we weren't sure if we'd get married because Michael was a bit afraid of what people would think. More specifically, he was worried about my father—he's kind of a big deal in the community, so coming out as gay might not be a huge deal to some people, but in my family, I was expected to marry a girl, have kids and follow in my dad's footsteps. I didn't really care about what anyone else wanted for me, though, because I knew I wanted this grumpy, well-hung bastard once he put it on me—well, in me." Brody laughs and for once Michael does, too.

"You'll never change," Michael says. "The stuff you say to people."

Brody smiles and kisses him on the cheek. "You love me; besides I said you were well hung before calling you a bastard."

"We're working!" Michael says, leaning away from him.

The love these two have for each other is obvious. It sucks that we're around another gay couple and we have to hide our relationship. If I could just shake the uneasy feeling they give me, I'd feel comfortable enough to talk to them about us, but there's this voice in my head warning me to be careful.

"You've been married five years?" Vincent asks.

"Yep, got married when we were your age, twenty-one. Best decision we ever made," Brody says.

Oh, okay. They know too much. I stand up from my chair and pass my card to Muffy. "Let's go," I say to Vincent. He stands from his chair, looking quite confused, as he waits for me to get my card back. I'll explain it to him when we get outside.

I take my card back from Muffy and give a nod to Brody and Michael who don't look confused at all. They both seem to realize what happened.

"Nice to meet you," Vincent says.

Brody gives him a smile. "You too."

The sun is finally starting to set as we step outside. It's still really busy in the port. "What happened? Why did we leave so fast?" Vincent asks.

"They knew way too much about us. Your dad said to be cautious, which I would have done even if he didn't say that, but since he did warn us, we needed to leave. It was just a little strange that those two knew the things they did about us, especially since you didn't recognize them."

"What do you think they wanted?"

"I'm not sure. They didn't seem like bad people, something about them just made me nervous."

We're walking toward the dock where our new ships should be. It's less than an hour until we have to meet our fathers and the chief anyway, so it's good that we left.

He nods at me in agreement. "Sivan, I've been thinking a lot about the first mate thing."

"Yeah? What have you decided?"

"I want to be your first mate, and I want you to be mine."

I stop walking and tilt my head at him, while people walk around us. "How would that work?"

"Well, a better way to say it would be to say that I want us to be co-captains. I want to combine crews."

"What made you decide this?" I ask. I'm trying hard to control my facial expression, because as much as I want this, and as unbelievably happy as this makes me, I need to make sure he's thought it all the way through.

He pulls me to the side out of the crowd of people, behind a building. We're out of the way now, so we can talk without the worry of people overhearing us. "Sivan. I only trust you. I don't even trust myself as much as I trust you. I know that no matter what happens, you will always be with me. There is only one thing I want in this world, and it's you. I used to think I wanted my own crew, and my own ship, but the more I thought about it, the more I realized, I've always wanted you beside me. I want *our* crew; I want *our* ship. I don't want anything, unless I can share it with you."

I've wanted to say the same things for a while now, those are the words I've been hoping to hear. My heart is beating so fast, it's begging me to hold him close. I just want to pick him up and carry him back to the ship. "Can I kiss you?"

"You can kiss me anytime you want," he says, grabbing my shirt in the center and pulling me toward him.

I press my lips against his and kiss him gently, holding him by the waist. Kissing Vincent is always exhilarating, but right now, it feels almost dangerous knowing that anyone could walk over and see us. We are off to the side, so it would be unlikely, but still our fathers will be passing by at any moment. They're never late for anything.

I separate from the kiss, and look side to side, trying to see if anyone is watching us, but Vincent keeps his grip on my shirt. "You're worried about our fathers seeing us?" he asks.

"Anyone could see us. We should probably talk to them about us before someone else does. Especially if we want to join crews. I have a feeling it's not going to go so well with your father. Mine will likely be okay with it. What are we going to propose to them? We have a lot of logistics we need to go over. We also have two ships, but will we just use one?"

"Hmm. I'd say we need both, but we just use one for when we're doing separate patrols or jobs. One can be our home ship, and the other will be for travel. I don't know. I think that makes sense. My dad will be worried that the north won't get enough attention if I stay with you in the south."

"Maybe we propose to stay in the middle? Your dad will want to know that you've considered everything. And what about the tattoos? We need to get those tomorrow, too. I know you've been wanting to skip the captain one, but we'll both be captains, and those are the rules. Captains have to get the tattoos. *Captain and Crew* tattoos, it can't be helped. Unless you want to really piss him off, in which case, I'll back you up."

"I have an idea. Remember how on the bench I added the plus sign, so it made sense for us?"

I nod. "Yep, I remember."

He takes my arm in his hand and slides my coat and shirt sleeve up. "This one is supposed to say *Captain*. So, let's just add *My* to it. You're my captain, and I'll be yours. If we add that, it will be a tattoo for us, *My Captain*." He traces his finger drawing the words.

I take his arm and slide his sleeve up. "This one can say *Our Crew*, because we will build a crew together and share everything. *My Captain, Our Crew*. Those will be our tattoos. You like that?"

He kisses me quickly, then smiles. "Yes, that's what I want. Can we get them now? Or do we have to wait until tomorrow?"

"You really are cute, but we definitely have to wait. Our fathers will have to agree to all of this. Not really the tattoos, because we can just do what we want, but the rest of it, they'll have to agree to. We should propose a fifty-fifty split for the crew. They were both planning on giving us fifty crew members each, so what if we tell them we just want twenty-five from each?"

"Fifty crew members is good for one ship, but what about when we need to use both ships? Also, I keep thinking about Matteo, as much as I don't want to. He basically said he didn't want to be my first mate if we were going to be together, what if there are other crew members that feel the same?"

I shake my head at him. "Not that many people care who someone else is sleeping with. The crew will be concerned about what they'll get from our arrangement. They'll want to know that they will be fed, paid, and that they'll be treated fairly. I don't think anyone is going to care about us being together. But if it will make you feel better, we can ask our fathers if they think we need to disclose it to the crew, first."

"Alright. I like this plan," he says bouncing on his toes. "Let's go tell our dads that we're gay and we want to combine crews," he says with a giggle.

I chuckle a bit. "Maybe we tell them about the co-captaincy thing first, then we tell them about us. One shock at a time. But if you feel like blurting it out, I won't stop you. I would say that we shouldn't do anything in front of the chief that might embarrass our dads. We want the inner police to know that we're not going to cause problems."

He's pouting at me. "That means we still can't hold hands outside until we tell them."

"Just a few hours hopefully. But I'll hold your hand while we sleep tonight to make up for it."

"Deal," he says.

We start walking toward the docks and the ships are finally

in view. They're both amazing. Mine has blue sails, while Vincent's, of course, has red. There's a part of me that wishes we would have been born in a time when cannons still existed on ships. Ship battles now mostly consist of boarding and burning or trying to just ram the other in a weak spot, forcing the other ship to sink. I've not seen anyone try that yet, and honestly it sounds pretty stupid. My father's ship has been boarded a few times by rogue pirates who run on smaller, faster boats, but none have been successful at doing any real damage.

I have no idea what kind of a ship Captain Slicer has, but when I was a kid, I used to imagine that it had spikes coming off it. All this shit about him respecting the treaty sounds really stupid. The stories we've been told don't paint him as someone willing to negotiate, and regardless of whether I like Harlow or not, his men still took her off the ship…even though part of me doesn't think she looked like she was putting up that much of a fight.

Vincent tugs on my coat. "Those are our ships! I'm so excited, come on, walk faster!" We're speeding toward the dock, like two kids running below deck on Christmas morning. "I can't wait to see what's inside! Do you think they stocked them already? With food and liquor?" he asks.

"I don't know, probably!"

"Come on, baby, you're walking so slow," he teases me, pulling my hand.

He couldn't be smiling any bigger. He's so happy right now, and in this moment, looking at those dimples and the amber sunrays reflecting in his gorgeous brown eyes, I know two things: the first is that I will follow him anywhere, and do anything to make him smile, and the second is that I am wholeheartedly, undeniably in love with my best friend.

CHAPTER 15
SO MANY GAY PIRATES

I step aboard my new ship with Sivan following close behind me. It's a surreal feeling to finally be standing here on a ship that was built specifically for me. Sivan is smiling brightly as I pull him around. "Let's go find my room!" I stop in my tracks and turn toward him. "Wait, which ship do we want to use as our home ship? This one or the other? Do we need two rooms? Or will we share one?"

"So many good questions," he says. "We better figure out the answers before our dads get here. If it seems like we haven't thought this through they won't—"

"Hello, guys," Rooster says, stepping onto the deck.

I forgot my dad said he came here to check out the ships earlier.

"Hey, Rooster, what do you think about the ship? Everything look alright?" I ask.

Lyndon, Captain Rodrigo's first mate, appears from below, stepping onto the deck. "Everything looks good," he says. "Rooster was concerned with the storage room being located in the wrong spot. You can have your crew members move things around if you need to."

"Thanks," I say. I notice that both of their uniforms seem to be a bit wrinkled. Maybe from the fight on deck earlier.

I see our fathers approaching on the dock and I walk toward the side of the ship to greet them. My father is clapping at the sight. He holds his hands up. "Hey, look at this, Vincent, your own ship! She's a beauty!" he shouts to me. Captain Rodrigo is smiling beside him.

Sivan whispers to me. "I'm sorry for whatever happens, because he's obviously really excited and I'm thinking he might have a hard time accepting what we're going to tell him."

"About us being gay?" I ask. Oops. I definitely forgot that Rooster and Lyndon were standing behind us. I'm not gonna turn around to see if they heard, just gonna blow past it.

Sivan's eyes are wide at my slip up. But he doesn't turn around either.

Both captains make their way onto the deck and over toward us. My father pats my shoulder. "You looked like your mother leaning over the side of the ship. Where is your hat?"

I pull my head back. "We left our hats in my room this morning. Didn't know we'd be getting into a fight on the deck, then a bunch of other stuff happened."

My father turns toward Rooster and Lyndon. I slowly turn, too. I'm almost wincing, just hoping they didn't hear what I said. They appear to be in their own little world, discussing something, so it's possible they didn't even hear me. It's also possible that they're discussing what I said.

"Rooster, Lyndon, how are the ships? Everything in order?" my father asks.

Captain Crawford points at the two men. "You two look like hell. What happened to your uniforms?"

Lyndon and Rooster shrug it off. "Nothing Captain," Lyndon says. "We gave the ships a good inspection."

"Inspections, my ass," Captain Crawford says.

Rooster steps forward. "Everything is in order, Captains. The storage room on Vincent's ship is not in the traditional place, that's the only thing of note."

We need to pull our fathers aside and talk to them before the chief gets here. I don't want to have this talk in front of Rooster and Lyndon, either.

"Captain," I say, looking at my father.

Before he can answer I hear footsteps approaching behind us.

Sivan and I turn toward the sound and see Brody and Michael standing just a few feet away, and walking closer toward us. What the hell are they doing here?

"I knew they weren't there just for drinks," Sivan whispers to me.

"Is that you, Brody?" my father asks. He shakes his hand. "You're all grown up. Haven't seen you since you were a teenager! How have you been?" He looks toward the dock. "Where is your father?"

Michael is avoiding eye contact with us, while Brody is smiling, and shaking my father's hand. "Hi, Captain Rodrigo, it's good to see you. My father isn't going to attend today. I've been taking on more of the responsibilities at the department. I have my partner, Michael, here with me to sign off on these two."

Michael extends his hand toward our fathers and greets them. My father is looking the two of them over, while he shakes Michael's hand. "Nice to meet you, Michael." My father gestures toward me and Sivan. "These are our sons, Vincent and Sivan."

What do I do? Do I pretend I've never met them? No. I can't do that.

Sivan gives the two of them a wave. "Yes, we had a drink with them at the bar earlier. They told us they were here for work. I suspected it had something to do with us."

Brody flashes him a smile. "You are sharp. Knowing your ages is what finally gave it away, huh?"

"He knew as soon as he saw you both," I say.

My father steps to the side stroking his goatee. "What was discussed during this meetup?"

I look at Sivan. He's better in situations like this. "Nothing, really. I was suspicious of them, based on the way they were dressed, and the way they were acting. They didn't ask us much before we left."

"Excuse me," Michael says. He points at Rooster and Lyndon. "I recognize these two from your paperwork, Mr. Rodrigo and Mr. Crawford, where are the two that are expected to be Vincent and Sivan's first mates? We can't sign any papers without them."

This is not a great time for any of this, but I have to speak up. "Captains, Sivan and I have made a decision—"

Before I can get the rest of my sentence out, I see Matteo stepping on the deck. What in the actual fuck is happening right now? Why is he here? He knows what he said to me. What the fuck is happening?

I see Sivan inhale sharply and back up a step. He's covering his mouth with his hand.

"I made it," Matteo says.

My father walks over to greet him, while Sivan and I stand frozen. "Oh, I'm so glad you made it, Matteo. Did you drop Harlow back off at the ship?"

"Well, when I got your text, I did what needed to be done, Captain. We can talk about the specifics of it later." He extends a hand toward Michael. "I'm Matteo, and you are?"

While they exchange their fake pleasantries, I whisper to Sivan. "What the hell am I supposed to do? Why is he here?"

Sivan whispers in my ear. "I assume your father told him beforehand not to discuss the abduction, so Matteo is just pretending nothing happened. But why is he acting like he belongs here? He couldn't have forgotten what he said to you, or me. I can tell everyone our plan, or you can. Which would you rather?"

The truth is that I don't know what to do. My father doesn't know that Sivan and I are together, so he probably thinks Matteo's behavior has just been because of Harlow. If he knew the whole story, would he even understand? What's going to happen? I don't know what's come over me, but suddenly I'm terrified of the way this is going to play out. I cup my hand around Sivan's ear and whisper. "Baby, I'm kind of scared right now. I think I need you to do it."

Sivan looks at me softly and gives me the slightest nod.

"Alright," Captain Crawford says. "We'll start with Sivan and his first mate, which will be easy, because he doesn't have one." Our fathers laugh, while Michael and Brody look confused.

"Actually, Captains, that's not true. Vincent and I have decided that we will be combining crews. Vincent will be my first mate, and I will be his, we'll be co-captains."

Everyone on the deck is staring at us in shock, except for

Brody and Michael. "Sounds like a good plan," Brody says. "Let's head down to the office and get everything signed."

Matteo closes the distance between us. "What?!" he shouts. "Are you fucking kidding me? You're naming him your first mate, Vincent? You're combining crews? What the hell are you thinking?"

Sivan takes a step forward. Coming within inches of Matteo's face. "Don't talk to him that way. I have had enough of your shit. You ran your fucking mouth earlier and you got away with it. I'm warning you that I won't let you do it again. Back up."

"Hey!" my father shouts. "Stand down, both of you. We have company. This is not the time for this. Matteo, you have to respect whatever decisions these two make, because they will be the captains of these ships. I wasn't aware of this until just now, the same as you. I don't know what's going on either, but we can figure it out calmly."

Sivan steps back at my father's command, which I'm grateful for. I thought he was gonna beat the hell out of Matteo.

"Do you all need a moment to sort things out? We can't interfere, but we can act as mediators if you need us to," Michael says.

"No, no. We have it under control," Captain Crawford says. He walks toward Sivan and me. "When was this decided? Have you thought it through?"

"We have," I say, looking at Matteo.

Matteo scoffs and shakes his head. "What a bunch of bullshit this is."

"Matteo, who are you kidding right now? Earlier, you pretty much said you wouldn't do it, do you remember?" I ask.

He smiles wickedly at Sivan and me. "All I remember is

that since you two started sleeping together everything has changed."

"Whoo, there it is," Brody says.

I lean my head back in frustration. "I can't believe you just said that."

Our fathers appear to be in shock, staring at the two of us. Lyndon and Rooster are whispering between themselves, seemingly unaffected by what's happening.

My father grips the hilt of his sword. "What did you just say, Matteo?"

"Oh, I forgot that was supposed to be a secret." He smirks. "These two have been sleeping together since the last meeting of the crews."

"I knew it," Brody says, earning a look of disapproval from Michael.

My father blinks hard looking at the two of us. He seems to be seeking confirmation, although he isn't saying anything.

Captain Crawford blows air from his mouth. "I have to speak honestly. Whether they're sleeping together or not, what does that have to do with you, Matteo?"

"That's a good dad," Brody says. His commentary is surely being heard by everyone, but it doesn't seem like anyone is reacting to it.

Matteo is just staring at the two of us silently.

"I asked you a question, Matteo," Captain Crawford says. "I have watched you disrespect my son on two occasions, and I have held back because you are Rodri's boy, but I want an answer from you."

"I don't have to answer you. Vincent has made his decision, and I've made mine." He turns and starts walking away.

"Matteo, I want to speak with you," my father says.

Matteo shakes his head and steps off the ship, ignoring my father.

"He can't do that, right? That was against pirate rules, wasn't it?" Brody asks Michael.

My father steps in front of the two of us, looking quite solemn.

Sivan takes my hand in his, interlocking our fingers.

My father looks down at our hands, then back up to us. "Have you two considered everything that goes along with combining crews? And are you sure this is what you want?"

He's asking us about crews? He's not even asking about us sleeping together. I'm so confused.

"We have," I say. "We propose to patrol the seas in between the north and the south. We would like twenty-five crew members from each crew, along with an additional twenty-five from each, on reserve for special circumstances."

"One more thing," Sivan says. "We would also like to disclose our relationship to the crew members that are joining us, so they have a choice to refuse before agreeing."

"Why would that be necessary?" Captain Crawford asks.

"With the way that Matteo responded to our relationship, we don't want to chance other crew members sharing the same view as his," Sivan explains. "We only want people to join us if they aren't bothered by our relationship."

"I'm surprised you would worry about that," my father says. "The crew wouldn't care who is sleeping with who. Do you two think you're the only pirates sleeping together?"

"Told you there were probably a ton of gay pirates," Brody says to Michael.

"Brody," my father says turning toward him. "Do you

always think out loud? We're having a serious discussion here and you can't be quiet for five minutes."

Michael laughs. "Why do you think his father sent me here with him, instead of coming himself?"

Brody's mouth drops open. "Excuse me. Is it such a punishment to be here with your husband? This is why no one else wants to work with *you*. You're so judgy all the time."

"You two are married?" Lyndon asks, pointing at the two.

"Been married for five years," Brody says. "But Michael is gonna be sleeping on the couch tonight if you're interested."

Michael shakes his head at him. "I'll sleep with the cats. Don't threaten me with a night free of your snoring."

"Captains," Rooster says. "May I have permission to speak freely?"

I have no idea what Rooster is going to say, but I hope it's not anything shitty. Lyndon squeezes his hand and gives him a smile. Oh, wait, are they together?

My father nods. "Everyone else here is speaking freely, go ahead."

"Being in a long-distance relationship is extremely hard, and we don't want to watch Vincent and Sivan suffer the way that we have. We would like to offer our assistance with getting them acclimated to captaincy. Of course, we will need to see where things go with, you know, the other situation, but when things are settled, we'd like to help them."

"More gay pirates," Brody says with a smile.

I had no idea they were sleeping together, but it makes sense. Their clothes were all wrinkled, and I'm pretty sure Captain Crawford made a comment about it earlier.

Sivan squeezes my hand and kisses the side of my head. His father raises his eyebrows and smiles, nodding slowly.

"I can't speak for Ray, but you have my permission to assist as needed, Rooster. Also, we can discuss a different arrangement if you two are in need of more time together. Let's save that for later."

"I agree, Lyndon," Captain Crawford says. "Nothing is more important than being with the person you love. Neither of us would stand in the way of that."

"These are good dads. They're even good to their crew," Brody says.

Michael nods. "As nice as this all is, we do need to sign the official paperwork, so we can be on our way. I have a date with my cats tonight, and I haven't even told them about it. They may be too busy to watch tv with me."

Brody gives him a shrug. "Guess we'll see when we get home."

The eight of us head down toward the office, to sign our papers and I'm feeling extremely relieved. I can't believe I was so afraid to tell our fathers, and afraid of what other people would think. I've been such a coward, because of the way Matteo responded to our relationship. I let one person's views make me afraid, how very stupid of me. We're holding hands, following behind Lyndon and Rooster. The ship is freshly painted, so the smell is a bit strong down here. The smell lets me know that this is real, though. We turn the corner and walk into the office. It's big, just as big as my father's office. The room has a large wooden table in the center, and there are papers stacked neatly on it.

Lyndon separates the papers into two piles.

"Are you two sure this is what you want? You'll be the first co-captains that I've ever heard of. Are you sure you can make it work?" Captain Crawford asks.

"I'm sure, Captain," I say.

Sivan nods. "Me too."

"I don't know, Ray," my father says in a playful voice. "I want to give them what they want, but we haven't even discussed it."

Captain Crawford laughs. "Yeah, right. We've only been discussing it non-stop for the past two days. I wonder if they think they hid their relationship from us over the past week, too?"

My father smirks. "Yeah, the lube on Sivan's nightstand and the clothes on the floor, definitely went unnoticed."

"Oh, or when Vincent causally rubbed Sivan's cheek." Captain Crawford grazes my father's cheek with the back of his hand. The two laugh uproariously. "Yeah, you guys were really fooling us," Captain Crawford says.

"This is the best thing I've ever been a part of," Brody says. "I'm so happy my dad assigned this to me."

I'm happy his dad assigned it to him, too. Having another couple here made me feel less afraid somehow. Now I see that I had nothing to worry about, but at the end of the day, I'm grateful they were here. I wish things had gone different with Matteo, though. Whether my dad adopted him or not, he's still my brother.

Our fathers sign the papers that are required, and Sivan and I do the same. Michael stamps a seal from inside his pocket on them and gathers the papers in his hand. "Now you've agreed to be responsible for each other, and you've agreed to honor the treaty, so all that's left is for you to have your official ceremony. Which happens on Friday, correct?"

"Yes," I say. "You two can come if you want."

"Thank you for the invitation, but we can't do that. It's not personal, because we like you, but we have a job to do, and we can't mix friendship with business. As a detective, my judgement begins to get clouded if I start to get involved in people's personal lives."

Brody smiles at us, and adds, "But, if you ever decide to get married, send us an invitation and we'll definitely come to that."

Michael shakes his head at him. "You're going to get us in a lot of trouble one of these days. We might not be allowed to do that. Before we go, I won't stick my nose where it doesn't belong, but I will say, I would be very careful with Matteo. I won't say any more about it, but given how nice you all are, I just wanted to offer that."

Sivan and I decided to spend the night on his father's ship tonight after we finished inspecting our ships. We thought after everything that happened, we'd want to spend the night on one of our new ships, but without any of our stuff moved in yet, it felt kind of strange. Also, as my father pointed out, without a crew there, anyone from Captain Slicer's crew could easily board us in the middle of the night while we're asleep. We just finished brushing our teeth, and I'm waiting in bed for Sivan to finish up a phone call with his dad. Sivan told me earlier that he and his dad have a feeling that Matteo is planning to defect. I can't see that happening after everything my dad has done for him. Besides, where would he go? I agree that he's been a real asshole, but I can't see him defecting. Sivan's sheets are so warm, it feels almost like they just came out of the dryer, it's so comfortable, I could just fall asleep.

"Alright. We'll meet you guys there at eleven," Sivan says on the phone, before he ends the call.

"Tattoos at eleven. I'm excited for them. Are you?" he asks me.

"I am! I wasn't looking forward to them until we decided on a way to make them work for us. Now, I can't wait."

Sivan flips the lights off and lies in bed next to me. I tuck beside him, laying my head on his bare chest. "Today was such a crazy day," I say, lightly tracing the muscles on his chest. "I can't believe our dads knew we were together. I wish my dad hadn't texted Matteo to meet us at the ship. I would have liked to try to talk to him one more time."

"It's actually better that your dad texted him. I think he did that for you. He needed you to make the decision with Matteo there, so you wouldn't regret it later on. It makes sense." He kisses the top of my head, and rubs his fingers along my shoulder.

"Yeah, he almost miscalculated, though, because I was pretty sure you were gonna punch him."

"Well, he was acting like a little prick to you. Besides, he got a little too close to what's mine. I didn't like it," he says.

My phone starts to vibrate on the nightstand, and I instinctively lift my head from his chest and grab it. It's a number I don't recognize, so I just ignore it and send it to voicemail. No one that I know would ever call me, especially not at this time. It's already 1:00 AM.

I flop back on the pillow and Sivan climbs on top of me. He's so damn gorgeous and his hot hard body is pressed against mine. He kisses my forehead, then each cheek, and finally kisses my lips. "Hey," he says softly, rubbing my cheek with his thumb.

"Hey," I say, lifting my head to give him a quick kiss.

"Vincent, I am so happy with you. I am so lucky that you want to be with me." He presses his forehead against mine. "And I…am so in love with you."

I swallow hard, trying to find the right words to say.

Hearing my best friend who's never believed in love, say those words to me, is the best feeling I've ever felt. "I am crazy in love with you, too." Sivan kisses me deeper than before, and the connection I feel when his tongue touches mine, is more than physical, I need him on a spiritual level. I feel the love I have for him in every part of my soul. There is nothing I won't do for him.

"I don't know if you really understand what you've done to me. Love has made me crazy, possessive, and desperate. I crave your touch; I thirst only for the taste of you." He runs his finger down my chest. "The things I want to do to you…"

"Show me."

CHAPTER 16
QUISLING'S QUARTERS

I think this is the first time I've ever been exhausted after a round with Vincent. Well, several rounds would be more accurate. The way his body bends to my will gives me some sort of a power complex that quickly shifts into something softer every time I kiss him. Love is such a complicated emotion. Loving him makes me incredibly weak and insanely strong at the same time. My heart, which was impenetrable, has been thoroughly claimed by the two dimples that reside on my best friend's face. I will do anything to see those dimples every day, for the rest of my life.

Vincent's arm is draped across my chest as he sleeps. I run my fingers through his soft hair. He smiles and snuggles in closer. What am I going to do about Matteo? I hear a loud buzzing and realize that my phone is vibrating on the nightstand beside me. Who would be calling me right now? It's 4:00 AM. I send it to voicemail and receive a text.

This is Michael, I need you to meet me outside of your dad's ship.

I rub my eyes and gently move Vincent's arm off me, which somehow doesn't wake him. Sitting up in my bed, I read the text again. Why is he texting me? I'm not sure if going out there is the right thing to do. It's four in the morning, what could be so important? Do I wake Vincent? Or go by myself? Maybe I should just ignore it.

Don't ignore me. I am breaking at least fifty rules to help you. I'll give you five minutes. I wouldn't bring Vincent, unless you have to.

Oh shit. This is either something about our dads, Harlow, or that asshole… Or it's a set-up. I'm not sure why he wouldn't want me to bring Vincent with me, but the safest place for him is beside me.

We'll be down in a few minutes. Vincent is asleep. I won't leave him here.

I kiss Vincent on the forehead and rub his chest. "Hey, I need you to wake up. Michael is outside."

His eyes open and he jolts up. "What? Michael? Why is he outside? What time is it?"

"It's four, I don't know what he wants, but he warned me not to ignore him. He also told me to leave you behind if I could help it, but I'm not leaving you anywhere. On the off chance this is a set-up, the smartest thing to do would be to separate us. Let's just go see what he wants."

We get out of bed and quickly dress.

"I am sore everywhere and tired," Vincent says while yawning. "I'm kind of surprised Michael texted you instead of Brody. Michael seemed like kind of a jerk."

I shake my head at him. "Nah, Michael just seemed like he was following rules, while Brody seemed like he kind of does whatever he wants. Probably gets away with more since his dad is the chief."

I take Vincent by the hand and lead him off the ship. It's dark and quiet outside. The deck is empty, and so is the port. I see one man standing alone. He's dressed in a black tactical uniform, that I've only seen certain members of the inner police wear before.

Vincent squeezes my hand tightly. "Is this okay that we're doing this? With the way he's dressed he looks like he's on a mission."

"I don't know what the right thing to do is, but let's just see what he wants."

He's walking toward us, but constantly scanning the area around us. "Hey, guys, I'm gonna talk fast because we can't stand out here. If someone sees me, I'll get fired. I warned you two before I left to be careful of Matteo. I did a little more digging and see the thing is that we—" He holds his hand over his mouth. "I can't believe I'm doing this. I see myself and Brody when I look at the two of you, and the thing is that we had a friend who followed the same path as Matteo, and he's no longer with us. I don't want to see that happen to you guys, too."

"What are you saying right now? I'm so confused," I say.

"We started investigating Matteo about a week ago. He's been crossing over into the city several times a day. That's more than enough for me to take him into custody. He's already broken the treaty by not declaring his business when entering. I'll just cut to it; he's been at a hideout with several other pirates that we've been keeping an eye on. Brody's father really doesn't want another huge pirate war breaking out, and neither do I, but your brother, he appears to be the one who is inciting this whole group of pirates. I know that this is probably hard for you to accept, but if you don't find a way to stop him, I'm going to have to arrest him before this blows up, and if he resists, I won't hesitate in taking his life."

"I don't understand what you're saying," Vincent says. "You're telling me that my brother is not only planning to defect from our crew, but that you think he's actually orchestrating some kind of a mutiny? What about Captain Slicer? Are you guys watching him? He's the one that's doing all of this. I don't think Matteo has anything to do with it. Matteo is probably just trying to keep things under control so that nothing happens." He turns to me. "Right, Sivan? He wouldn't do anything like this."

What am I supposed to say to him when he's looking at me like this? I exhale and squeeze his hand. "I don't know. I—I don't think Michael would be here if he wasn't sure."

Michael looks over his shoulder then points toward the path leading to the city entrance. "Let's go. I'll show you. Brody is there now, keeping watch. I didn't think you'd believe me, and I don't blame you. I'll take you there, but you cannot interfere. No matter what you see or hear, you have to give me your word that you will not make your presence known, and you cannot tell your fathers about this. If you can't promise those things, I can't bring you."

"If we cross into the city at night, we'll be breaking the treaty. And what are you going to show us anyway?" I ask.

"Matteo is there right now." He points to his earpiece. "Brody can see everything that's happening inside the room."

"I want to see," Vincent says. "I refuse to believe he's in the city. You have the wrong guy."

I have no idea what's going to happen, but against my better judgement, we follow behind Michael carefully through back alleys, until we reach a large hotel. Michael leads us into a room with a bunch of security cameras. Brody gives us a nod. "Sorry about this, guys. We only haven't moved on him, because we're waiting on the big fish, but he's making plans here to ruin your whole ceremony on Friday."

Vincent's eyes are wide scanning all of the small monitors. "It's this one," Brody says, quickly changing the largest monitor to another feed.

Matteo is sitting on a couch and Harlow is beside him. He's drinking a bottle of beer. Harlow says something that is inaudible. "I don't care," Matteo says. "I don't care about any of that. He's not my father and I never should have been on that ship to begin with."

Vincent looks to be in shock, and now that he's seen this, I need to get him out of here.

"Why?" Vincent asks Brody. "Why would he do this? Aside from Harlow, who are the other people there with him?"

Brody shakes his head. "Bottom feeder pirates from Captain Slicer's crew mostly. I think a few are from your father's crew, though. We mostly know the big guys. These little fish with him aren't important enough for us to track. Now, if Henry steps on the stage or Captain Slicer, himself. We'll have to move on them."

I want to take care of this right now. Just settle this myself, but I know that's not the answer, because despite what I think, he's still family to Vincent.

"No, I don't care," Matteo says. "The plan is to do it on Friday. He'll be here then."

"We gotta get you guys out of here, now," Brody says. "I can't let you stay any longer. If anyone catches you in here, we'll be in more trouble than I'm capable of talking us out of."

Vincent is still in shock, his eyes are glued to the screen, as I pull on his hand.

"We gotta go, Vincent," I say softly. "Come on. We need to come up with our own plan."

"One more thing," Brody says. "He doesn't care that you

two are gay, that wasn't his problem. I can't share anything else, but it's important to me that you both know that."

It's been a few hours since we got back to my room. Vincent doesn't seem to be in denial anymore, then again, he just fell asleep. I don't know how to make this better for him, because even I was shocked seeing Matteo sitting there. I knew Harlow didn't look like she was struggling when they carried her off the ship. She looked pretty comfy tucked under Matteo's arm. This whole fucking thing has been orchestrated by this selfish bastard. How dare he say he didn't belong on Captain Rodrigo's ship. Twenty-one years ago, during the mutiny when all the women and children were hiding underground at Muffy's, baby Matteo was left all alone. Vincent's parents took him in and raised them as their own. So, hearing those words from Matteo's mouth about Captain Rodrigo and the kindness he showed him, makes me sick to my stomach. He would be just another crew member with no privileges, or maybe even worse, if Vincent's parents hadn't cared for him. I'm glad that we left before we heard anything else. I just don't know what would make him want to join up with Captain Slicer to begin with. The pirates in the room were treating him very respectfully, too. It looked just as Michael explained, somehow Matteo seemed to be the one in charge.

Knock, knock. "Sivan, I was told you had a special visitor," Tilly says outside of my door. Holy shit, it's already time to get up. "I'm leaving two trays," she says. "Also, I wanted to say, that I had a talk with your father last night, and if you and Vincent would have me, I'd be honored to join your crew."

Vincent wipes his eyes awake. "Who needs glue?" he asks in a raspy morning voice.

I laugh and ruffle his hair. "Tilly said she put glue in your food."

He shakes his head and wipes his eyes again. "What?"

"It's Tilly, she said she wants to join our crew, she didn't say anything about glue." I stand from my bed and walk toward the door to grab our trays.

"Hey! You're in your underwear, don't open the door for Tilly!"

I laugh and grab a pair of comfortable shorts out of my dresser and quickly put them on. It's cute that he's worried about Tilly seeing me in my underwear. I would be the same about him, though. I open the door and see Tilly's smiling face. "Thank you for the food," I say, taking the two trays from her. "Vincent and I will talk it over, but thank you for wanting to join us. It means a lot to me."

"You men let me know what you think," she says as she moves to the next room.

I walk back inside toward Vincent who is staring at his phone. I put the trays on the bed and sit beside him. "You, okay?" I ask.

He rubs my face with one hand and smiles. "I'm okay. I just—I don't know what to tell my dad and I don't want to deal with any of this. Today is our day, it's the day we get our tattoos. I don't want to think about Matteo today. It all feels like some kind of a bad dream. As stupid as it sounds, there's a part of me that still feels like it wasn't him there."

"I understand. I feel bad not telling my dad about any of this. But Michael asked us not to, so I really don't think we should. My father already suspected he was going to defect, and he's definitely talked to your dad about it. They probably know more than us at this point. They may just not be able to say anything." I smile at him while passing him his bagel sandwich. "You need to eat, we're getting our tattoos in a few hours, I don't want you to pass out."

"I'm not gonna pass out. I don't think it's gonna hurt at all. But I need your help today, because whatever is going to happen with Matteo, is going to happen, and I can't control any of it. So, if you see me acting differently, I need you to snap me out of it. Just kiss me or something. That will work."

"You want to just pretend nothing is happening?"

"I do, because I'm sure there was a good reason for him being there, and even if that's not true, I'm going to pretend it is. We talked enough about it last night. Until he looks me in my face and says he's leaving, I won't believe it. So, until that happens, I'm not going to think about it."

Walking outside while holding hands is so liberating. The sun seems to be shining brighter today, and for the first time, I'm not at all worried about someone seeing us together, or someone judging us. I can just hold Vincent's hand now wherever we go, and the best part of it all is that I can kiss him whenever I want.

I kiss him on the cheek, while our hands sway between us. We're headed to Captain Rodrigo's ship, before we go to get our tattoos.

"It's nice not having to hide being together, isn't it?" Vincent asks me.

"I like it. I get to show you off now. It will be even better when we can leave and head for the central port. Then it will be just you, me, and our crew."

We step aboard Captain Rodrigo's ship and everyone is moving fast around us. Crew members are carrying things off for our ships. I wonder why they don't just move this ship over by ours? It would take a lot less effort to move things from one ship to the other if they did that.

Several crew members smile at the two of us holding hands while some don't even appear to notice. Rooster is the first one to greet us. "It's branding day," he jokes. "Your fathers are waiting for you in the office. We've got a lot of work ahead of us today."

"Rooster," I say. "Why don't you pull the ship around by ours? What's the point in making everyone carry things all the way down to the shipyard?"

"Good question. If we move Captain Rodrigo's ship and Captain Crawford's ships beside your two ships, what would happen if there was an attack? We could lose all four ships in one go."

"I hadn't considered that," I say.

"The easiest way is not always the right way. It's important to remember that," Rooster says with a smile.

We head toward Captain Rodrigo's office hand in hand. "I wonder how much of my stuff they've moved out of my room." Vincent says.

"We can check it out after we talk to our dads. Maybe we can finally find the camera."

"Boys, come in," Captain Rodrigo says, as we approach the open door.

Our fathers look tired. I don't know what it is about their faces, but they look absolutely exhausted. I meant what I said to Vincent, our fathers are very smart, you don't keep peace among pirates for twenty years by being a couple of idiots. They look like they've been working all night.

"Take a seat," Captain Rodrigo says. "We are supposed to wait until tomorrow to give you your promotion gifts, but just in case things go down the way we expect, we decided to give them to you today. Besides, we're breaking all the traditions now, anyway."

My father nods in agreement. "And, we're the ones in charge, so we make the rules."

"Promotion gift? Oh, no thank you. I don't want the captain hat until tomorrow, that's okay. I can wait," Vincent says.

Captain Rodrigo walks toward the weapon cabinet. "It's not the captain's hat, *that* you actually have to wait for. But I hope you're ready tomorrow for the largest red plume you've ever seen."

He walks back toward us and passes Vincent a sword tucked inside a black scabbard. The handle is braided red and black leather. Vincent is smiling so big as he unsheathes it. The blade is black, and it looks amazing. He stands and moves to the side of the room, slicing the sword through the air. "It's beautiful. Wow, and it's so light. This is folded steel. I've always wanted a black blade. I love it. Thanks, Dad."

His father hugs him and pats him on his back. "I'm glad you like it. Took Manny forever to find folded steel. Had to get it imported, it took months."

My father hands me a black and gold pistol. "This is the pistol that I used twenty years ago, when we staged the mutiny. I want you to have it because you may soon find yourself in a situation that requires you to do something very brave, that may feel very stupid. When you hold this pistol, I want you to remember that there was a time that we were afraid, too, but we did what needed to be done to protect those around us."

I stand and hug my father. He doesn't separate from material things easily. This pistol has been in a glass case in his office for years, the fact that he gave it to me means everything to me.

"Why are you talking to them like we're going to die or something? Do you know something I don't?" Captain Rodrigo jokes with my father.

"Well," my father says, "they have to get their tattoos in just a bit; they're gonna need to be brave then."

"I think most of your stuff has been moved onto your ships," Captain Rodrigo says. "We spoke with the crew members last night that originally expressed interest in joining your crews. Not a single one said they didn't want to join after learning of your relationship. We were missing two crew members, but they will likely be back today, so we can ask them when we get back from the studio," he says.

I bet those are the bastards that were with Matteo last night.

"Oh, and I didn't see Sheena around this morning, which is odd, but Tilly expressed an interest in taking on the lead position of housekeeper for your ships," he adds.

"I am telling you; I remember Sheena having a thing for Captain Slicer," my father says to Captain Rodrigo.

"Not now, Ray." He holds his hand up. "Many women had a thing for him, doesn't mean she would run off and join him. She's probably out doing something."

Wow. How deep does this go? Is Harlow's mom involved, too? My head is spinning a bit, and I suddenly notice Vincent zoning out. I lean over and give him a quick kiss. "You okay?"

He nods. "Yep. And you just kissed me in front of our dads."

I shrug. "I told you I wanted to kiss you all the time. I don't care if the old men are here."

"Hey!" my father shouts. "You can't call us old men; you're not captains yet! And now that you've kissed him in front of us, we have a question about this relationship."

"Oh, Ray, don't. Just leave them alone," Captain Rodrigo says.

"Just one question, boys. Rodri and I have different guesses here. Which one of you made the first move?"

Vincent and I smile at one another. I point at Vincent with my thumb. "Technically, it was Vincent."

"I knew it!" my father says.

Captain Rodrigo shoves him to the side. "Yes, you are the smartest. Well, let's go get you two inked up." He walks toward the door and the rest of us follow behind him.

"I want to stop off in my room and see what's left," Vincent says. "Besides, I can't go to the studio with two swords on me. I need to leave one behind."

Captain Rodrigo gestures toward the door. "When we get on deck, hand the sword over to Rooster. He'll make sure it gets transferred over with everything else, same goes for your pistol, Sivan."

We walk inside Vincent's room, which is now mostly empty. The bed is still here, but the closet is open, and it looks like a good portion of his clothes have been moved over. He slides open a drawer, that has very few pieces of clothing in it. "Hmm," he says. "I guess they wanted to leave a few things behind in case I stayed the night here. He slides the drawer closed. "I wonder if they cleaned out my nightstand." He pulls the drawer out, and there's nothing left inside. "That's awkward, I wonder who cleaned this drawer out. That bottle of lube was basically empty." He shakes his head and walks around the room. "This is weird being in here, knowing it won't be my home anymore."

"Are you sad?" I ask him.

"Oh, no, definitely not. I said it was weird, not that I was sad. I just have a ton of memories here, but I'm really excited to make new ones with you."

I pull him in for a quick kiss and he squeezes me tight. "I love you, Sivan."

"I loved you first," I say.

"Oh, come on, you don't know that. Also, you told our dads that I made the first move on you, but I seem to remember you being on top of me," he jokes.

I tilt my head at him. "After you stuck your tongue in my mouth."

"Ha! So, you admit that I loved you first."

"Vincent, Sivan, let's go," Captain Rodrigo says. "What are you two gonna be known for? Kissing all day?"

CHAPTER 17
YOUR DIMPLES ARE GONNA RUIN ME

"Vincent, let's do yours first," Thalia, the tattoo artist says. "Better to get the crying out of the way now."

"I'm not gonna cry," I say, sitting in the chair in front of her. I've known Thalia my whole life, she's always done the tattoos for our crew. We have a good relationship. She was close friends with my mother, and her personality reminds me a bit of her, too. She's putting a pair of black latex gloves on, they hide the large tattoos on her hands, while the tattoos on her arms cover nearly all of her skin. Her partner, Rui, has done all of her tattoos, but Rui never does any of the ones for our crew, despite being obsessed with pirates.

Rui and Sivan are standing over us watching as Thalia places the stencil paper of my first tattoo on my forearm. *Captain.*

She had already made the stencil before I got here, so I need to let her know that we are changing things a little bit. My father and Sivan's are on the other side of the studio whispering about something. We may have forgotten to mention the tattoo change to them, but honestly, we're adults, so, I'm gonna do it no matter what they say.

I look down at my arm, admiring the cursive writing.

"Looks great, Thalia, but we want to change the tattoos a bit." I don't think my father heard me, because he and Captain Rodrigo haven't reacted.

"Change the tattoos?!" Rui says loudly.

I drop my head knowing that her exaggerated reaction is likely going to draw our fathers into this now.

Sivan rubs my cheek with his thumb. "It was cute you said that quietly. They're coming over now."

"What?" My father asks. "Who is changing the tattoos?"

"It's not a big deal. We want them to make sense for us," I say.

Thalia tilts her head to the side. "You couldn't have told me this before?"

"We're just adding one word to each tattoo. That's it," I say.

"The tattoos *are* one word each, so don't say '*that's it*' like it's not a big deal," Thalia says.

"If you don't want to do it, maybe Rui will do it for me." I look at Rui who shakes her head in disagreement. "Nope. I only paint on one canvas, and it's the most perfect canvas around." She pats Thalia's shoulder and smiles.

"I'm doing your tattoos, Vincent. Don't flash your dimples at my wife. You know she has a thing for pirates."

Thalia giggles, while Rui pumps her eyebrows at me.

"Just tell me what the word is, you insufferable little shit."

"That's not very nice. I'm pretty much a captain now, Thalia. I mean, the paperwork was signed yesterday, so tomorrow is really just for show. Seems like you should be more respectful," I joke.

"If you keep mouthing off, I might write something truly horrible on your arm. What's the word that you want added?"

"Yeah, what's the word?" my father asks.

"I told you that I didn't like the captain tattoo, and I thought it was kind of stupid. I still do, but now that Sivan is my captain, I want to have the word *my* added to this one. Everything I do will be for *my* captain."

Sivan leans in and kisses my cheek. "Right, and I want the same. For the crew tattoo we want to add the word *our* because we will build a crew together. And we will always do what's best for *our* crew."

"Oh, *fuck me*, that's cute," Thalia says.

"Well, it is kind of cute," Captain Crawford says. "Don't you agree Rodri?"

My father nods. "Their mothers would've loved this idea."

It's been several hours since we got our tattoos and my arms don't feel sore, but they feel weird with these clear coverings on them. I really like the way the tattoos look, though. I'll be happy when everything is healed. We're standing on the deck of my father's ship with a few crew members that had some concerns about how a co-captaincy would work. Our fathers, along with Sivan, are talking things out better than I could.

"What about Matteo?" Sam, the cook, asks my father.

What about Matteo? What the hell is gonna happen tomorrow? I've been trying so hard all day not to think about it, but how can I ignore what's happening? Michael mentioned having a friend that went down a similar path, and was kind of urging me to help Matteo, but at the same time he was warning us to be cautious. I don't know what the right thing to do is.

"Can you give me a sec, Captains?" Sivan asks our fathers.

He's pulling me by the hand away from the group. "Hey, what's going on?" he asks softly.

I shake my head and look at the deck, avoiding eye contact. "Nothing. I'm fine."

He lifts my chin and kisses me. It's a soft, sweet kiss, that makes me momentarily forget what I was even worried about.

"Better? Or should we go somewhere to talk alone?" he asks.

"No. It's just…Matteo. Sam asked about him, and I realized that I don't know what's going to happen tomorrow. Is he really going to leave the crew? I know what I saw, but it still doesn't make any sense. And if he didn't care about us being gay, then why didn't he want us together? Why join up with pirates who stand against everything we believe in? Is there any way it was all a misunderstanding? Could Michael and Brody have been wrong? Be honest with me."

He pulls me into an embrace and tucks my head against his chest. "Shhh. Slow down. Vincent, listen to me, I don't want to hurt you when I say this, but I just can't see how they could have been wrong. I want to fix this for you, but I don't know how. It's possible he's been planning this for a while, and that's what they meant by it not having anything to do with us. You said you won't believe it unless he tells you himself that he's leaving, but is that really what it's going to take? Is that what you need?"

I can't cry right now. I absolutely can't cry. I have to be strong. "Sadly, I think that is what it's going to take, but how stupid does that make me?"

"It doesn't make you stupid. Do you want to try and text him? I'll do whatever you need me to," Sivan says, rubbing my back.

I keep my face pressed against Sivan's chest. "Do you think we could just go to the hotel he was at? Maybe we could wait outside until he walks by and try to talk to him?"

Sivan exhales. "We'd be breaking the treaty if we do that. I think texting him and asking him to meet you somewhere would be better. Just know that if you're going to meet with him, I'm going, too."

"What do you think I should do?"

Sivan kisses my forehead. "I want you to do whatever you need to do. If talking to him would help, then we can try and do that. I'm not sure if he'll meet up with you, anyway."

"I have to try." I pull my phone out and send Matteo a text. *Hey, can we meet somewhere and talk?*

I stick my phone back inside my coat. "We'll see what happens."

Sivan holds my hand and kisses it softly. "Okay, now let's go get something to eat and head back to our ship."

Our ship…we get to spend the night on our ship, tonight, together. Pretty much all of our stuff has been moved over there, so it doesn't make sense for us to stay on one of our father's ships. Everything is supposed to be ready to go by noon tomorrow, so there can't be many pirates that haven't moved their stuff over yet. Thankfully, Rooster and Lyndon have been handling all of the transfers for us.

"Are you guys headed out?" my father asks. He looks a bit sad, maybe because we're leaving for the night, or it could be because Sam brought up Matteo.

I give him a playful salute. "Yep. We're gonna spend the night on our ship. But first we're gonna get something to eat." Sivan elbows me, reminding me that we talked about inviting our fathers to eat with us tonight.

"Captains," I say. "We're gonna get a few drinks and something to eat at Muffy's. Do you want to come with us?"

Both of our fathers' faces light up. They look at each other then back to us. "That sounds fun!" Captain Crawford says.

"We were just talking about going to Muffy's ourselves," my father says. "Are you ready to go now?"

"Yes, Sivan and I are starving."

It's packed inside Muffy's bar, which is normal for a Thursday night. There's usually karaoke around ten o'clock, so people get here early for that. I can't remember the last time the four of us walked into a bar together. Even if we had done it recently, this is the first time I'm walking into Muffy's while holding Sivan's hand. Everyone in the bar turns to look at us as we walk inside. They're staring even longer than usual. It could be because we're all together, or maybe it's the fact that we're holding hands.

"Look at everyone staring," Sivan says. "People are obsessed with you," he jokes.

I chuckle and push him toward the empty stools. "They're staring at you, probably wondering how you ended up with me."

The four of us make our way to the bar. My phone is vibrating in my pocket. I take a deep breath as I pull it out, knowing it's Matteo. This one text could change our entire lives. What if he refuses to meet me? I almost don't want to look at it, but I have to.

Where do you want to meet?

I show Sivan the text, while we sit down. "What should I say?"

"Hmm. Somewhere with lots of lights in case it gets dark. You could ask him to meet you on the ship. As far as he knows, you have no idea about what he's been doing. So, asking him to meet you on the ship isn't a crazy thing to do. I mean, it's a bit like rubbing salt on a wound, but if you didn't know he was planning to defect, wouldn't you want to show him the ship?"

I scoff. "Maybe before I basically told him to fuck off by saying we were gonna be co-captains. I don't know, Sivan. Am I the asshole here? Did I do something wrong?"

His fingertips graze my face gently, as he brings his lips to mine, giving me a soft quick kiss.

"You are not the asshole. Even before we were together, you were never the asshole."

The bar around us has gone incredibly quiet. My eyes are wide, I'm not sure what happened. Why is everyone suddenly staring over?

"Ahem," my father clears his throat. "Everyone is watching you two lovebirds kiss. Not sure if you're into that kind of thing, but people have noticed." He points around the bar.

I drop my head forward, feeling a bit embarrassed. Sivan lifts my chin with two fingers and kisses me again.

He swivels in his chair to face the room behind us. "Oh, stop staring! You'd kiss him if you could, too!" He turns back toward me and smiles. "Your dimples are going to ruin me." He pokes them with both pointer fingers, then kisses my forehead.

I look down at my phone and shake my head. "Maybe meeting him is a bad idea. I feel kind of nervous now. He's my brother, Sivan. What if he really does say he's going to leave the ship?"

"I can't make the decision for you. But as your co-captain and partner, we made a promise that all decisions would be for each other, or for our crew. If you need a reason to meet him, you can use me. Because when I look at my tattoo, I know the right thing for *my* captain is for you to meet with him. Because you need to accept whatever he decides, and we have to move forward. I can't stand seeing you hurt like this. You meeting with him, is also what's best for our crew because you will remain distracted until this is dealt with."

"For my captain and our crew…you're right. I have to do this."

"It was also your idea," Sivan says. "So, if you want a reason not to, you could say that your captain also hates the little bastard and doesn't trust him. Either works," he jokes.

"Nah, I want our life as co-captains to start off the right way. I can't move forward until I talk to him. He could lie right to my face, but all I can do is try. If there's a chance I can stop this, I have to."

I text him back:

We can meet on our new ship. I want to show you everything.

The message shows as read almost instantly. I put my phone on the bar and look up to see Muffy standing in front of us, arms crossed. He wasn't standing here when we sat down, but he's giving us the craziest look right now. He holds his hands out to our fathers. "What the hell is this? You two are my oldest friends." He gestures to me and Sivan. "No one told me about this! These are your sons! They're like my own kids!"

"They just found out yesterday…or I guess we confirmed it yesterday," I say.

"Well, it's about time," Muffy says to me, slinging his bar towel onto his shoulder. "I've watched you two go through a lot over the years. I always thought you'd be good together. There was a look that you'd both get toward the other when girls were hanging on either of you. I figured that's why you two went out of the bathroom window together so often. Anyway, where is Matteo? And what about Harlow? That poor delusional girl."

Matteo still hasn't texted me back, despite reading my message eight minutes ago.

"Ah. It's best we don't talk about them, now," my father says. "Can we have our usual? Or are you gonna stand there all night being nosy?"

That was an interesting response from my father. Sivan is probably right. They probably know more than we do.

Muffy grabs four glasses from beneath the counter. "I shouldn't serve you anything, especially you, Captain Crawford. No one is a bigger gossip than you. Can't believe you two didn't tell me about this. But Vincent and Sivan can have their usual."

We don't really have a usual, but I'll just take whatever he gives us. I finally see a text from Matteo.

Is Sivan going to be there?

I show Sivan the text. "He wants to know if you're going to be there."

Sivan rolls his eyes. "I *am* going to be there. No way in hell do I trust him alone with you. Do you have any idea what he could be plotting? I won't take that chance."

"Yeah. I know. He probably won't talk as openly if you're there, though. But I—shit, this is so hard. I want to just tell him that I know everything. All this pretending is driving me crazy."

Sivan raises his chin toward our fathers. "They're going to hear you. It will be over soon. You heard him say that whatever is happening will happen tomorrow. All the pretending will be over then. If you want to head over to our ship, we can see if there's a place for me to hide while you talk. I don't like the idea of hiding on our ship, but if that's what you need, I can do it, provided I'm close enough to protect you."

"You don't need to protect me from him."

"That's exactly why I refuse to leave you alone with him. Let's finish our drinks and head for the ship. I won't tell you to lie to him, so tell him whatever you want."

Am I stupid for thinking that he wouldn't hurt me? I don't think I could hurt him, even though he's been such a dick. Punching between brothers is one thing, but actually hurting him? I don't think so.

Sivan will be there, but I want to talk to you alone. I'll meet you on the deck at 9.

"I told him to meet me on the deck at nine. I'll bring him down to the meeting room. I saw two closets in there. You can hide in one while we talk."

I take a sip of my rum and smile at Sivan. He looks really concerned. "It's gonna be okay. There's nothing for you to be worried about."

"You boys want to sing tonight?" Captain Crawford asks us.

I laugh. "Nooo thank you. If I'm not drunk, I'm not singing. We're gonna head out soon, anyway."

Our fathers are both looking us over. "I hope you two aren't planning to meet up with Matteo," my father says.

Oh shit. Was I too loud?

"If so, that is something you need to back away from."

"What the fuck does that mean?" I instantly realize I shouldn't have said that. "Sorry, Captain. I misspoke. But I want to meet with my brother. Do you know something that I don't?"

My father looks at Captain Crawford, then back to me. "He is your brother. So, if you want to meet with him, I can't stop you. But make sure that Sivan is with you."

Captain Crawford is shaking his head, avoiding eye contact. He's just looking straight ahead into the mirror behind the bar.

"I won't leave him alone with Matteo. One of us is very aware of what he's capable of."

CHAPTER 18
HE'S NOT WEARING HIS COAT

The meeting room is basically a replica of the meeting room on my father's ship. I run my hand down the table looking at Sivan who is currently trying to stuff his large body inside the small coat closet behind the table.

He closes the door on himself. "I can fit, but it will be hard for me to react if he tries something. I'm kind of squished in here. Plus, I can't see anything. What if we leave the door open a bit?" He opens the closet a smidge. "Can you see me in here?"

This whole thing is so ridiculous. I move to the other side of the room and look directly at the closet. "No, I can't, but I can smell you. Then again, I'm kind of obsessed with the way you smell, so it may just be me."

He laughs. "Come in here and smell me, then. I think I can do you standing up in here."

"What?! Do me standing up?" I look over my shoulder as if someone could have heard him.

"Yeah, I can do it. You're not heavy. Bring your ass in here."

"I think you're forgetting about our tattoos. How can you lift me like that? Yours were bleeding a tiny bit. I don't think that's a good idea."

The closet door opens, and Sivan has a huge pout on his

face. "I really wanted to do that," he says. "We have to have sex our first night on our new ship."

"We still can. Just not standing up in a closet. But if you promise to behave when Matteo is here, I promise to be a good boy and do whatever you want…as long as it doesn't mess with the tattoo covering."

"I'll take that deal." He walks out of the closet and points toward the wall. "I like the swords hanging here. It's kind of an invitation for our crew to have a free for all if they forget their own weapons and get pissed off during a meeting."

"Kind of is. But I guess if we were boarded and everyone was in here with no weapons, that would come in handy." I look at the clock on the wall, it's almost time for me to meet Matteo.

Sivan looks at the clock, too. "Almost nine o'clock. Come here, let me hold you for a minute before you have to go up there."

I tuck myself inside his arms and for a moment I wonder why I'm doing this. Why should I leave him for even a second?

Our eyes meet and Sivan tucks my hair behind my ear and kisses me. His hands are holding my face, while his tongue gently caresses mine. Our heads turn side to side through the kiss as it intensifies into something far more urgent than it started out as. Sivan lets out a low growl and breaks the kiss.

I'm panting from the intensity of it, while he tucks his face against the side of my neck. "I don't like that there is a bit of time between you meeting him on the deck and the two of you coming down here. Don't walk in front of him. Walk beside him and get him down here as quickly as possible. If you're not down here in ten minutes, I'm coming up there. And, Vincent, if he tries to take you off the ship; say no."

I give the front of his pants a pat. "I'll be back as quick as I can, then we can pick up where we just left off once this is over."

He kisses me on my forehead. "I love you. Please don't die in the five minutes that we're apart."

I give him a kiss on the cheek and look into his gorgeous blue eyes. "Sivan, I—"

A knock on the door makes us separate. "Get in the closet, Sivan."

He quickly shuffles into the closet, leaving the door open just a crack.

Shit. I wasn't prepared for him to come down here yet. I didn't get to give myself a pep talk.

"Come in," I say, straightening my shirt. As the door opens, I realize my sword is on the opposite side of the table. I put it down when we walked in earlier. I'm sure I won't need it, though.

It's Rooster. "Matteo is on the deck. He said you're supposed to be meeting him. After what happened yesterday, I wanted to confirm that with you, before allowing him access to the ship." He's looking around the room, concernedly. "Where is Sivan? Why are you alone?"

Sivan sticks a hand outside of the closet and waves. "In here."

"Alright. I didn't think you would leave him alone with him. Let's go, Vincent. I'll walk with you up there."

Rooster walks with me onto the deck. "You need to be careful, Vincent," he says as he leaves.

Matteo is standing on the opposite side of the deck. He's dressed in casual clothes. I guess that doesn't mean anything on its own, except that he doesn't consider our meeting to be a formal one. I swallow hard before I greet him. My hands are shaking and the chill in the air somehow makes my tattoos hurt.

Matteo is looking at me, but his eyes are vacant. There's no emotion there. Not like before.

I force a smile. "Hey, thanks for coming to meet me."

He shrugs. "You asked to meet me, why wouldn't I come?"

A few crew members on deck are listening in on our conversation. I need to get him to go below deck with me.

"It's nice out," Matteo says. "Maybe we should go for a walk and talk about whatever it is that you need to talk about. You can show me around the ship after."

"Nah. I'm kind of tired from getting my tattoos. I'd rather just talk in the meeting room where we can be comfortable." It's a weak excuse at best, but it's all I could think of.

"Ohhh, tattoos make people tired. I had no idea." He scoffs. "If you're hoping to try and convince me that I should join you and Sivan, you're wasting your time."

"I just want to talk."

I stand beside him, and we start walking toward the lower deck stairs. He looks at me, seemingly waiting for me to go down first. "I see…" he says.

I have no idea what he means, but I'm sure between my nervous expression and the way my forehead is sweating, he's noticed something is off. I've never been a good liar.

He steps downstairs first and I follow behind. Once we reach the lower deck, I walk beside him. It's completely silent and neither of us are saying anything. He looks unarmed since he's dressed casually, but he usually has at least two daggers on him.

"This is nice down here," he says. "You two must be really happy with the way it turned out."

I don't know if he means the ship or if he's talking about how things turned out between us. "The ships are nice. I'm happy to finally have one."

"I didn't mean the ships. Wow. How *will* you survive without me to explain everything to you?" he asks through a laugh laced with malice.

We walk inside the meeting room and he's looking around. I'm so afraid that Sivan is going to do something to draw his attention. I close the door behind us. "Why would I have to survive without you? Are you going somewhere?"

He furrows his brow looking at me, ignoring my question. "Is that your sword?" he asks, pointing toward the end of the table.

Sivan must be so mad that I left it there. "Yeah, my dad gave it to me. It's my present for my promotion. You like it?"

He walks toward the sword and picks it up, removing it from its scabbard. "Ooh a black blade. That's nice. It's light, too." He makes a few slicing motions in the air with it.

It's making me uneasy. Sivan must be ready to fly out of the closet.

He's admiring the blade and looking around the room. "Why did you leave it down here when you came up to get me? Aren't you afraid of someone attacking you? Your first mate should have warned you never to meet anyone unarmed. You learned that in captaincy lessons." He raises his eyebrows at me. "Where is he? Already running away from his responsibilities, probably."

"Why do you hate him? You've always had an issue with us screwing around, but now I just don't—I don't get it. What did he do to make you hate him so much?"

"Is this why you wanted to meet? You wanted to try and

play peacekeeper between me and Sivan?" He slides the sword back into its scabbard and places it on the table.

"Why *wouldn't* I want to meet with you? We hang out every day."

"Ha! I think you mean that we *used to* hang out every day. Everything changed when you two slept together. You just— became different. Everything was about him. Every conversation, every single day, was all about him. Meanwhile I… I was struggling with my own sort of identity crisis, you could say. But you were too busy to notice. Too busy crying and acting like a child over someone who didn't even want you."

"How can you say that? He told me he asked you to let him know when I was feeling better, and he told me you purposely wouldn't let him see me. When we were in my room the other day, you said you didn't remember any of that. Was that true? Did you really forget?"

"Hmm…I did not forget. I went to great lengths to be sure he couldn't get in touch with you. I had to pull Harlow into this whole mess which I was not happy about."

I'm trying to process everything he just said to me. Why would he do all of that?

"You still haven't realized anything yet, have you?" he asks me.

"It depends on what you're asking me. I do know some things, but what I really want to know is why? Why is the idea of us together so terrible for you? You and I are brothers. Brothers take care of each other. Brothers don't watch each other cry and purposely make them suffer more. Why the fuck did you do that?"

"Oh, Vincent. The stuff you say is really quite funny. I am

not your brother. It's so stupid that I allowed myself to believe that lie for so many years."

"What do you mean? Who cares that my parents adopted you? You're still my brother. No one has ever made you feel any different."

"I feel different because I am different. I am not like you. I am not like your father, and I was never meant to be."

I run my hand down my face. I hate that he's hurting, but I am so confused. "What do you mean? You're family."

"I am not. I am an outsider, and I will always be. I needed your help, and you didn't care. You only cared about him. You didn't even notice that I was struggling. What kind of a brother does that?"

"What? When are you talking about? Are you talking about after Sivan left? Yeah, I was a little distracted because I was trying to process the realization that I was gay! And trying to figure out why Sivan, my best friend, wasn't answering my texts, which was your fault! What do you think I should have been doing at that time? Wondering why you were upset? You were so busy forcing lies down my throat about him that I couldn't stand being around you. If you would have told me you were struggling, I would have helped you. Instead, you purposely cut him out of my life and watched me suffer. Who does that to someone?"

He's standing with his back to the closet that Sivan is in, he's just a few feet away from it. I can't help but be afraid that Sivan is going to jump out at any second and just start punching him.

"Someone who didn't want to be replaced," he says. "Someone who was already feeling like they didn't belong. The last thing I needed was for you to cut me out of your life, when you were my only constant. Instead, when I needed you to help me, all you were doing was worrying about him."

"But I wouldn't have been worrying, if you would have let him see me or talk to me."

"When I came in your room that day and saw you two having sex. I came in there to talk to you about my mom."

"Your mom?"

"I wanted to try and find out who my mom was, to see if she was still around somewhere. I just started to feel out of place a few months before that. When I caught you two in bed, it just showed me that I really didn't belong. I had no idea how long you two had been sleeping together and everything just kind of came crashing down on me. Then, in the meeting room, when you passed out, I just figured if I could keep him away from you, everything would be okay."

"Okay for who? You? I didn't know you were trying to find your mom. Why didn't you just tell me that?" I walk toward him. I think I can fix this. "I would have helped you. I can still help you. Sivan would help you, too. If this is all about just trying to find your mom, I mean, I—I'll do whatever I can to help you."

He drops his head and shakes it. I don't know if I should just tell him that I know he's been meeting with Captain Slicer's crew, or just keep trying to reason with him.

"I already found her. I already know everything I need to know. I don't need your help anymore. It's too late for that."

I take another step closer to him and see the closet door move slightly. I also notice that one of the swords is missing from the wall display. Sivan must have grabbed one before we came down. "What do you mean you found her? Where is she?"

"It's not important. She didn't want me anyway." He holds

a hand over his mouth. He looks like he's fighting back tears. "I really gotta go. I shouldn't be here. I don't belong here."

I grab his forearm. "What do you mean you shouldn't be here? Of course, you should. You can still be part of our crew even if you're not my first mate."

"Vincent, you have to think. You haven't figured any of this out yet? Why do I have to spell everything out for you? I'm not going to be a part of your crew."

He looks down at my hand on his arm, then back up to me, with his right hand he pulls a small dagger from inside the back of his pants and palms it flat against my chest.

Before I can react, Sivan has a sword against Matteo's throat. "Drop your fucking blade."

"Now, this is what I was waiting for," Matteo says. "Rather stupid of you to threaten the son of a captain."

Sivan is behind him and the blade is pressed against Matteo's skin; I can see the pressure building around it, as the skin turns bright red.

The office door swings open. "Both of you, drop your weapons," Rooster says.

"No, I will not. This is my ship and he's holding a blade against my captain's chest."

Rooster gestures to Matteo's neck. "Yeah, and you have a blade against his throat. We can talk about whatever is bothering all of you. No blood needs to be spilled here."

"If he drops the sword, I will drop my blade," Matteo says. "It's not even pressed against Vincent. It's flat against his chest. I knew he was in here; I was just trying to draw him out. I would never stab Vincent. No matter how much I hate him."

"Oh, fuck you, Matteo. No. I'm not gonna drop my sword."

Rooster stands beside us; my heart feels like it may explode right now. "Let me take this," he says placing his hand atop Matteo's.

Matteo releases the blade, but Sivan doesn't move.

"Sivan, drop it, for me. He doesn't want to be here. Just let him go."

"Come over here first," Sivan says. "I know how fast he is with a blade." Matteo holds his hands out to the side. I walk around and stand next to Sivan. "Should my blade find your throat again, I won't hesitate." He finally steps back, removing the sword from Matteo's neck.

Matteo turns and looks at the two of us. "I came here wondering if you still trusted me, wondering if you really saw me as your brother, and now, I truly know that you don't, and you probably never did."

Rooster holds the door open. "You men need some time to cool off. Don't say anything else that you might regret."

CHAPTER 19
CAPTAINS AND SONS

I lift my head from Sivan's chest at the sound of my phone alarm. It's a good thing we set it before we fell asleep. We stayed up talking until almost three in the morning. I'm still a bit in shock from everything that happened with Matteo, and it's probably stupid of me, but there is still a part of me that hopes he changes his mind. I feel bad that he doesn't think he belongs with our crew just because he was adopted. He'll always be family to me.

Sivan kisses the top of my head. "Good morning, Captain," he says.

I give him a kiss on the cheek. "Good morning, baby." I pat his chest and sit up. I know myself too well. If I stay in this position with him, it's only a matter of time until we're both naked. The sex last night was more than enough to carry me through the day. I twist my neck, trying to stretch it out.

"Your neck giving you trouble? Did you sleep funny?" He flashes me a smile and sits up.

I stand up from the bed and walk toward the closet. "No. I didn't sleep funny. I'm sore from you twisting my body like a pretzel. So many new positions."

"Mmm, we did get creative last night. It was fun. Today will be even better. I'm excited, even though I'm prepared for everything to be interrupted somehow."

I grab the hangers with our outfits on them and place them on the bed. Sivan stands beside me in his underwear. I can't look at his body right now. "When your dad called last night, he said to meet him on the deck at ten, right?"

He takes his hanger of clothes and carries it into the bathroom. "Yeah, he said they'll be ready at ten and the ceremony starts at eleven. He also said they told a few people at the bar that the ceremony would start at twelve, just in case anyone was there to relay information to Captain Slicer."

"What if some people show up at twelve when the ceremony is already over? They'll be disappointed."

Sivan peeks his head out of the bathroom. "It's okay, what's done is done. I trust they knew what they were doing."

Once I'm dressed, I grab my brush from my dresser and pull my hair into a tight bun. I don't have to wear my hat to the ceremony, because we'll be getting our captain's hats today. I shudder at the thought of the giant red plume that my father threatened me with.

Sivan walks out of the bathroom and his mouth falls open. He closes the distance between us. "I haven't seen your hair up like that in a while. I gotta get out of here, or I'm gonna want a repeat of last night," he says, wrapping me up in his arms.

I give him a quick kiss. "You want me to put your hair up for you, too?"

"Yes, please. All of it up, as tight as you can."

Sivan sits on the edge of our bed, and I gather his hair together into a tight bun like mine. "There, all perfect," I say, rubbing his strong broad shoulders.

"Thank you," he says looking up at me. He stands and looks

at himself in the mirror, then smiles at me. "Are you ready to officially be named co-captains?"

"Definitely ready. Just promise me one thing, okay?"

"Anything."

I reach my hand toward him, and he grabs a hold of it. "Just hold my hand and stay close to me. I can deal with anything that comes our way, as long as you're beside me."

"Nothing will ever separate us. Don't worry about that." He kisses me softly, and presses his forehead to mine. "I love you, my captain."

"I loved you first, baby."

He rubs my dimples. "I don't think so, dimples."

"Don't die today," I say. It's become a habit at this point, but it always makes both of us smile when either of us says it.

Our fathers decided that we would have the ceremony on my father's ship, since the likelihood of Captain Slicer showing up is so high. In the past few days our fathers seem to have gone from thinking he would negotiate with them, to prepping for something a bit more intense, just in case.

Sivan and I are holding hands as we head toward my father's ship. It's kind of dreary looking outside. There is a storm on the horizon, the clouds are dark and ominous. I hope we finish the ceremony before the skies open up. "The port is bustling with crowds of people, some are likely here for our ceremony, since it's not every day two new captains are named." I'm still loving being able to hold Sivan's hand in public. Now that we're not hiding it, I've definitely noticed more men holding hands. "Sivan, do you notice more guys holding hands now? Or is it just me?"

"I think it's just you. Your perception is your reality. Before you were comfortable enough with us, you felt that surely no one else would be able to accept us being gay. Now that you've come to terms with it, so to speak, you can see that it's not so strange. So, it stands to reason that you'd notice more men holding hands. It was kind of like you were blinded by your own fear. Now that your eyes are open, you can see that Brody was right, there are *so* many gay pirates." He laughs.

"There you are!" my father shouts as we step onto the ship. The deck is full of crew members, each appears to be diligently attending to some sort of a task. Captain Crawford is walking toward us with my father. "How are you guys feeling today? Better than last night?"

My father waves him off. "Ahhh they're fine. No bad feelings today. I do need you both to be cautious, though. Most importantly, and I shouldn't need to say this, but I will. Regardless of what happens, if Captain Slicer should come here, that is not your fight. You will stand down unless attacked."

I open my mouth to argue, and he holds a hand up to me. "Technically, you two are captains already, yes, but this is my ship and whatever he wants, he will have to go through all of us to get, but it will start with Ray and I."

Captain Crawford looks at Sivan. "The last thing we need is for either of you to make a situation that could be handled peacefully into an all-out war. There is a difference between bravery and stupidity, remember that."

"I understand," I say.

Much to my surprise Sivan isn't acknowledging what our fathers have said. He gives my hand a squeeze before letting go and crossing his arms.

"You have something to say?" his father asks him.

"I want to clarify something. If a threat is made toward

Vincent, physically or verbally, I will not hesitate to defend him. I don't care who it is."

"As you should," my father says. "We're pirates; not everyone is going to fight fair. Do what you feel is necessary should either of those things happen." He pats Sivan on the shoulder, then looks at me. "Now, enough of this heavy stuff. We're going to start soon. We need to get a few things squared away, then it's time for your hats. Gotta get moving before the storm rolls in."

"If you don't need us for anything, we're just gonna hang out over here," I say, walking toward the opposite side of the deck. We both lean on our elbows on the railing, looking out at the sea. That storm is coming in fast.

Sivan takes my hand in his and kisses it. "Almost time for your new hat."

"I can't wait to see what my father picked out," I say facetiously. "But I have been wondering if we should change our colors. We have red and blue, because our ships are technically under our fathers' fleets, but doesn't that seem weird now?"

"I thought the same thing yesterday. We could talk to our dads about it. I don't know what they'll say. Do you already have a color in mind?"

"Not really. I like you in blue, but you look good in every color. I *am* kind of partial to red because I've always had it."

"You liked green a lot when we were kids. What about that?"

"I think you're forgetting something. When Louie and Captain Slicer's crew came aboard, do you remember what colors they were wearing?"

"Well, well, well...it's been a while, *Captain Rodrigo*," an unfamiliar voice says.

Sivan's eyes widen, as he looks over his shoulder. "Oh shit. Stay close to me."

I turn my head and see a large pirate with a long red beard walking on deck. He's wearing a black and green uniform and a captain's hat. Black and green…those are Captain Slicer's colors. That's him. Behind him are probably thirty pirates, all in the same colors. I swallow hard and put my hand on my hilt.

Captain Slicer is walking slowly toward our fathers. His monkey is perched upon his shoulder.

"What are you doing on my ship, Captain Slicer?" my father asks.

Captain Crawford stands beside my father. "Better state your business fast," he says. "Crew numbers are looking a little thin behind you."

"Ah, look at you, all grown up, Ray. But you're still holding onto Captain Rodrigo's bootstraps. I'm not here to talk to you." He looks around the deck. "Where are the new captains?"

The monkey screeches in our direction and jumps down. He better not come over here and slap me. He's running the opposite way, thankfully. I'm tracking him, but I can barely see him through all the boots.

"Our sons have no business with you," my father says. "I asked you once already, what are you here for?"

"That's where you're wrong. It would seem our sons have some unfinished business."

"What son?" my father asks.

The monkey has made his way in front of a pair of black boots. I see a pair of hands reach down and lift him up. Captain Slicer's crew appear to be moving to the side, but those boots are walking forward.

"Oh no…" Sivan mumbles. "Vincent. Don't do anything crazy. And no matter what happens, I love you."

"I love you too, but why would you—" I follow the boots upward and see *him*. He's dressed in black and green, and he's wearing a Captain's hat the same as Captain Slicer's.

Matteo…

"I believe you know my son," Captain Slicer says.

Vincent and Sivan will return in book two…

About the Author

Cali Kitsu lives in a very sunny state with her amazing husband and daughters, and she enjoys making people smile. She tries to bring a little bit of her Cali sunshine and energy wherever she goes. Cali believes that love is for everyone, and she's found the perfect way to express that in her writing. Cali absolutely loves writing—she's having so much fun telling steamy boy love stories, with a bit of her Cali sense of humor!

Aside from co-hosting the Cali & Craig Talk… podcast with her bestie Craig, Cali is also assistant to Craig Gibb, publisher at Story Perfect Books and its family of imprints (including Deep Desires Press and Deep Hearts YA), and author of the MM romance books, *You Can Call Me Cooper* (2024), *Froderick, Gay Son of Dracula* (2024), and *Cookies, Candles, and Cute Butts For Christmas* (2024).

Cali's other hobbies include watching Anime, reading Manga, baking, going to the beach, and she's an avid gamer in all forms: console, tabletop, strategy card games…Magic the Gathering is probably her favorite strategy card game.

Also by Cali Kitsu

Cookies, Candles, and Cute Butts for Christmas
Froderick, Gay Son of Dracula
You Can Call Me Cooper

More from Deep Desires Press

You Can Call Me Cooper
Cali Kitsu

Eighteen and newly single, baseball all-star Coop Morgan should feel devastated, but instead he feels...ambivalent. That is, until Ethan Prescott, his coach's gorgeous son, joins the team. Coop and Ethan feel an immediate connection, one that Coop has never felt before.

Just when Coop is about to make a move on Ethan, he stumbles on his late mother's journal and learns old secrets—about his family, about the people around him, about his past, and about his present. Secrets that had forever altered the course of his life to bring him to where he is now.

Between these long-buried secrets, forbidden romances, baseball shenanigans, and more, Coop is driven to embrace what he truly wants—Ethan. It takes everything Coop has to free himself from the shackles of the past, but in doing so, he might just be the key to everyone getting their happy-ever-afters.

More from Deep Desires Press

Cookies, Candles, and Cute Butts for Christmas
Cameron D. James & Cali Kitsu

It's gonna be a hot Christmas in Frosty Bottoms, when Braden, the new hunky veterinarian strolls into town, but this gorgeous man is no stranger, and he's no longer a vet. He's coming back to Frosty Bottoms to bake cookies and dip his wick in Kellan, the local candlemaker, who happens to be his childhood best friend.

Kellan knows Braden is coming back to town and taking over BJ's Cookies and he's unsure how to feel about it. They have a past; Kellan felt something but then Braden moved away.

Sparks soon fly when Braden reunites with Kellan, but they want different things. Braden is only interested in a relationship, while Kellan is only looking for hookups. With mishaps galore, including over-excited family, unrecognizable otters, and motorboating a muscle chest, everyone and everything seems to be pushing the two men together.

When the initial ice between them melts, it's not long before more than cookie dough is being rolled out on Braden's counters… and a certain bottom is getting frosted.

www.ingramcontent.com/pod-product-compliance
Ingram Content Group UK Ltd.
Pitfield, Milton Keynes, MK11 3LW, UK
UKHW040610040425
5291UKWH00013B/5